RED DIAMOND

BY MICHALES JOY

Cover Design © 2018 by Carlos Villas

https://www.artstation.com/VILLAS7

ISBN-13: 978-1-947522-07-7

ISBN-10: 1-947522-07-8

READ UNTIL YOU BLEED!

RED DIAMOND

MICHALES JOY

*Dedicated to
Jeff "Redbeard" Morton,
a loyal friend with whom
I would gladly fight monsters.*

CHAPTER ONE

The slender Vietnamese man behind the Sheriff star tried to speak into the phone and his voice wouldn't work. Something snapped in his hand, making him jump. He looked down at the pencil he was holding and it was broken into three parts clutched in his white-knuckled fist. He dropped the fragments to the desk top.

"Sheriff Yan Corban? Are you there?"

He forced himself to swallow. "I understand," he managed to push through his lips. Corban ran a trembling hand through his short, black hair. "I believe you."

"Please repeat it back to me," the man on the phone said with steely efficiency. "For the records, you understand."

"We are Red Diamond. We are—" Corban licked his lips and took a breath. When he spoke again his voice was steady. "Pikeburn has thirty minutes. The walls go up in thirty minutes. The monster starts killing in thirty minutes." He did not have an accent, but he talked with deliberate and careful enunciation.

"Thirty minutes from now." A bell chimed into Corban's ear. "Do you have any questions?"

"No," Corban said.

"Then I wish you luck in the coming days." The voice softened. "I genuinely hope it ends quickly this year. I always root for the humans. I'm not afraid to admit that."

"Thank you," Corban said. He slowly put the phone back on the cradle with a trembling hand. He stared at his hand for ten seconds and it stopped shaking. He looked about his office as if searching for something vital that had been misplaced. The small room held barely more than his desk, a filing cabinet, a glass-fronted gun cabinet, and a bookcase sagging under the weight of too many books. On one wall was a bulletin board covered with assorted reminders, take out menus, photos of himself with a dark-haired woman, photos of a Great Dane looking goofy and lovable, and a two-foot by three-foot city map labeled "Pikeburn". Under that name was the town's information block. Establish in 1891. Named after Dwight Pikeburn. Boyhood home of Simon Farris. Motto: A bright light for the future. Population 11,301.

Corban snatched up the phone and started jabbing the buttons. At the same time, he shouted toward the open door of his office, "Alice! Get in here!"

On the phone, a man picked up on the first ring. "Legacy Oak Center, my name is—"

"Put Mayor Crewler on now. This is an emergency and I don't give a shit what he's doing."

A small woman with tightly curled grey hair and reading glasses on the end of her nose walked into the office, a yellow pad in her hand. She wore a bright blue sweater tossed over her shoulders.

"Where's the fire?" she asked.

"Call everyone, Alice. Get them back here right away, no excuses. Tell them drop everything no matter what."

"Sir?" the man at the Legacy Oak Center was saying into his ear. "Sir? He's in a meeting."

"This is Sheriff Yan Corban from his town, Pikeburn, and it's a God damn emergency so you put a gun in his mouth if you have to and get him on this phone."

Alice raised both eyebrows.

"Go, Alice," Corban said. "I'll explain as soon as I can. Wait a minute. Did you drive to work? Is your car here?"

"Yes."

"Good. Now get everyone rounded up."

She nodded. She clicked her pen closed and marched down to her desk at the front of the station, shoes clacking like little fireworks on the tile floor.

Dragging the phone with him, Corban went to the glass-fronted gun case. He fiddled a key into the lock and pulled it open. The four weapons lined up were also locked in place by a chain. It took a moment more of balancing the phone on his shoulder and shaking out keys before the pump shotgun was in his hands. As he sat down at his desk with the shotgun and a box of shells, someone began calling his name on the phone.

"Shut up, Don," Corban said quickly. "Pikeburn is Red Diamond."

"What? Holy fuck, Corban. Is that for real?"

"Five minutes ago."

"Holy fuck. No, we need to slow down. Any chance, well, could this be...a hoax?"

"I hope it is."

"But it's not, is it? You wouldn't call unless it was real."

"The guy on the phone was pretty convincing. It's real. We can't slow down."

"Corban," the mayor said, "My God, I'm out of town, Corban. I can't get back there— "

"I know, Don. Do you have Mary and the kids with you?"

"Yes. No! Not Eli!"

"I'll get him out before the doors close, I promise."

"You - you planning on staying to fight? No one can blame you for running. It's not like we all haven't seen what these things can do. It's suicide, you know? So, don't - "

"I'm planning on staying to fight."

There was a pause as both men didn't even breath.

"Ok," Don said at last. "I don't pay you enough, Yan."

"True," he said and both man gave a laugh. "Don, I have to go."

"Good luck, Sheriff."

"Thanks," Corban said and hung up.

He jogged from his office down to the front desk. The wide windows spread brilliant afternoon light around the waiting room. Alice was behind her reception desk, talking into a handset in front of a bank of CB radio gear. As he tapped her on the arm, the door swung open and two uniformed deputies came in: a young woman with black hair pulled under her cap and a pale man blinking his eyes as if woken from a nap. Corban waved them both to wait.

"Alice, we don't have much time. This can't wait. Patch me through to everyone."

"One second, Sheriff," Alice said.

"What's going on?" the female deputy asked. She pointed at the shotgun Corban was carrying.

He glanced at the weapon before saying, "You'll hear about it."

"Do I need a shotgun?" the other deputy asked, suddenly looking less bored.

"No."

Alice held up the handset. "Max is in the parking lot out back and the other three are on the way. I think everyone has ears on."

"Pull over," Corban said into the handset. It felt cold him his grip, like it had come from a freezer. "Hit your lights and pull over just a moment." As he waited, he put the shotgun across Alice's desk. She used a pencil to direct the barrel away from her.

Corban sat on the edge of the desk. He pressed the button on the hand set.

"I don't have time to argue or give a speech. I'm giving orders once and you'll do them or people will die. Pikeburn has been selected as this year's Red Diamond event. We have a little more than twenty minutes now to get as many people as possible out of town. Max, get to the Grade School, grab a bus or two, and get all those kids away, go right now."

"Yes, sir!"

"Luke, you take the High school. I know the principal is going to either faint or want a committee meeting. Put him on his ass. Get those kids out of there. And make damn sure Eli Crewler is next to you. I promised his dad."

"Oh fuck! On it!"

"Howard, radio station. Start broadcasting the message. Samuel, I need you at the hospital."

"No," Samuel blurted. "I quit. No way. I'm getting my family out of here."

Alice made a small choking sound. She had tears on her cheeks but she nodded to Corban she was in control.

"Alice," Corban said, "call the hospital. They have an emergency plan. Let them know what's happening. And then get in your car and get to safety."

Her eyes narrowed at him. "I will not abandon this town, Yan Corban, and you better never ask me to again."

Corban smiled and nodded. He looked at the two stunned deputies in front of him. "Ben. Julie. Get on the streets and use the bullhorns. Tell people..." He looked at his watch. "Looks like 3:15 is our deadline. That's when they shut us in. Tell people that and get their asses moving. If you see trouble, take care of it quickly. Be back here at 3:30. Now do you want a shotgun?"

"Um, no," said Ben.

"I do," Julie said. Corban tossed her the one off the desk and she caught it with both hands.

"Get your job done."

They exchanged a stunned look before hustling out the door.

Corban went to the water cooler and got a little wax paper cup full of brisk water. He filled it three times and drained it three times. He came back to the front desk. Alice was on the phone telling someone to get their head out of their ass.

He leaned to the handset and pushed the talk button.

"This is Sheriff Corban again. If any of you deputies feel the need to get out, I don't blame you. Not one bit. Please warn people as you leave. Don't grab just your family. Grab a neighbor, a friend, anyone. Help me do that, please, and then you can say you did everything you were expected to do. However, if you want to fight—"

He paused.

There was a photo of him on the wall and his eyes were drawn to it. A man in his late thirties, looking like a teenager. A man bearing a Vietnamese first name and a decidedly whiter last name. He was grinning too big, looking like a cook despite the uniform and badge and crisp print identifying him as the newly elected Sheriff of Pikeburn. The date under his smiling face was three years ago. Now at forty years old he still looked like he was playing as Sheriff and would soon be back to delivering kimchi and noodles.

"If you want to fight this fucking thing, be back here at 3:30. I'm not running."

Corban released the button and walked away. He pushed the glass door open and went outside. The Sheriff's office was one block off the town square of Pikeburn on a narrow one-way street of shops and businesses common to every small town. In the town square, the pale stone courthouse squatted in the middle of a bright green patch of immaculate lawn, a three-story cube with the architectural hallmarks of an earlier century. At each corner of the wide lawn was a statue of something important to Pikeburn: a deer, a man with a musket, a woman with a child hugging her legs, and a horse. Corban watched the people and cars going about their business, deeply oblivious to what had started.

Sharing a wall with the Sheriff's office was an accounting firm. A pudgy man in a black suit burst from the door, and a middle-aged woman dressed like she was still in High school followed. They beelined for Corban.

"Good God, Sheriff!" the pudgy man said.

Corban tore his gaze from the peaceful vision of the town square. "Get in your car and get out of here, Peter. Right now. Don't talk to me."

"It was on the radio!" the woman said. "How can they do this?"

"They do it every year," he replied.

"But not us!" Her voice cracked as it hit the last word.

"You have twenty minutes to escape."

In the distance, a man in a delivery uniform came running out of the courthouse, shouting and waving at people. A knot of people pulled around him to listen. The first person bolted from the group ten seconds later. Others held out a few moments more before being convinced. Once the panic hit, they dispersed like a dandelion blown by a harsh wind.

"Come on, Annette," the accountant said. He grabbed her arm and pulled her toward his car.

A minivan turned the corner near them and roared by at well over the posted speed limit, the woman driver sobbing, oblivious to the Sheriff watching. The back of the van was decorated with a waving stick figure family of five, plus a cat. Peter's long, silver car squeaked the tires as it tore after the van toward the south of town.

Rising up like audible smoke, the tornado sirens began to howl. Peace was at an end in Pikeburn.

Back in the station Alice was lecturing at the cell phone smashed between her shoulder and ear, sounding as calm as a person giving driving directions. The phone on her desk for police business was ringing, every line flashing red, and she was ignoring it. As Corban reached for the receiver she snacked his hand away.

Alice said, "I gotta go, Denise, Sheriff's back. Call you later." She looked at Corban as she closed her flip phone. "I wouldn't answer those, Sheriff. I've taken more abuse in ten minutes than I have in ten years. You'd think I was somehow responsible for dumping a monster in town." She clucked her tongue at the idea.

"How hard would it be to move all this CB equipment to the courthouse?"

She eyed the array of metal boxes, cords and wires, and lit dials. "My brother-in-law put all this together. He's moved to Texas. I'm sorry, Sheriff, I have no idea."

"Okay. Be ready to move without it if we have to. I'm not sitting here behind glass windows. The courthouse has stone walls and narrow windows. That'll stop it."

"Sometimes it doesn't," she said. Before he could reply, she grabbed up the desk phone and hit a red button. "Sheriff's Office, talk sense or I hang up."

Corban went back to his office. He pulled another pump shotgun, a hunting rifle with scope, and an AR-15 assault rifle from the gun cabinet. He left the hunting rifle across his desk after checking to make sure it was loaded. He came back to the front office and propped the shotgun in the corner next to a bare coat rack. The AR-15 he slung over his shoulder.

Alice hung up the phone. "Shots fired over at Ross Farms."

"Fired at what?"

"Something in the cornfield, I guess."

"Who called that in? Mrs. White?"

"Of course. She said Stanley Ross was blasting away at something in his corn. She's afraid he's going to hit her house."

"Only if he wanted to," Corban said. "She lives a mile away from the old man and he's a lifelong hunter."

"Could it be...it?"

"No. Too soon. Wait for 3:15. That's when bad shit starts." He looked at his watch. It was 3:05.

He stepped outside again. The tornado sirens had been silenced. To his right, the town square was emptied of people. The parking spots around the courthouse were vacant. A small truck was abandoned in the grass before the statue of the horse, the door left wide.

Someone cleared their throat behind Corban. He turned and nodded to a tall and scrawny man with messy white hair. He wore a stained plastic apron smeared with brown clay. The man was leaning against the door to the business attached to the side of the Sheriff office opposite the accountant. Handsome Pottery was painted on the large display window.

"Calm before the storm?" the man asked.

"I guess so, Titus. You leaving town?"

"I was taking a nap until a minute a go. No sense in trying now." Titus paused to light a pipe and blew smoke into the air. "Not sure I would even if I had the chance. Didn't they give that town in Florida two hours to vacate about fifteen years ago?"

"I don't know. I don't follow the Red Diamond."

"Well, the same percentage got out. Turns out, give people thirty minutes or thirty days and you'll still have about fifty percent staying behind."

"I hope we do better than that."

Titus nodded his head up and behind Corban. "Something's burning."

Corban glanced at the black ribbon drifting into the afternoon sky. "That might be at the railroad tracks. Nothing much to burn out there so - "

A lone figure had wandered into view on the courthouse lawn, shuffling uncertainly, clutching a Sponge Bob backpack and wearing a baseball hat.

"Fuck!" Corban said and bolted back into the Sheriff's office.

"Isn't that—" Titus was saying while squinting at the figure.

Corban charged through the office, down the hall, and out the back door into an alley. A truck with police lights on top and a Pikeburn city logo on the door was parked here, alongside a silver Prius and a red Jeep with mud splattered up the sides. Corban threw the AR-15 into the back. He stomped on the gas as soon as the engine was running, jumping the truck too fast out of the parking area, and clipped the side view mirror against the Jeep. He hit a No Parking sign as he exited the alley, bounced off the curb, and floored it straight for the courthouse.

The young man with the Sponge Bob backpack and cap heard the truck engine. He tilted his round face at the rapidly approaching vehicle. He smiled as it hopped the curb and tore tuffs of grass from the green lawn. It slewed sideways in an arc that ended before him.

"Eli!" Corban shouted. "Get in!"

Eli Crewler grinned broadly at Corban. "Sheriff, you are on the grass in your truck." Eli had Down Syndrome.

"Now, Eli! We have to see your dad!"

"Okay," Eli said. He went to the passenger door and carefully got in.

Corban fishtailed across the lawn, hit the road again with a protesting screech from the tires, and sped down the deserted street.

"Did you talk to Deputy Luke, Eli? At the school? Why aren't you on a bus?"

"I was not in school today. I was helping Mr. Ortega at the cat food place."

Corban twisted his hands on the steering wheel in frustration. He spared a glance at his watch. 3:11. He tore around a corner too fast and side swiped a UPS truck with its hazard lights going. Just as he managed to keep the truck from ricocheting into another parked car, he saw movement. He locked up the brakes just as the moving object burst from between two cars. The truck ended up inches away from a pair of stunned teenagers, a boy and girl holding hands. Without asking, they rushed around and jumped into the back of the truck. Corban floored it again.

The little window behind his head slid open. The boy put his face into the cab and shouted, "Where are you going?"

"East!"

"North is closer!" the boy said, shaking his head in panic.

"North is where everyone else is going, damn it! Now sit back and shut up!"

Eli was no longer smiling. He held his backpack tight to his body and was chewing on the end of one of the straps. "Why are you mad?" he asked. His eyes seemed unable to settle on one thing out the window.

"I'm not mad, buddy. I'm not mad. Bad things are happening and I need you to do as I say. Do you know what Red Diamond is?"

"No."

"It's a monster, Eli."

"Like from the closet?"

Corban nodded even though Eli wasn't looking at him. "Exactly. Something big and mean and deadly. Pikeburn is this year's sacrifice."

From the bed of the truck the boy shouted, "It's an experiment!"

"I know what the hell it is!" Corban fired back. "I'm talking to Eli!"

"Well okay, chill," the boy said.

Corban looked at his watch. The main bulk of the town was suddenly behind them, the road a straight black arrow before them toward rising hills and faded mountains beyond.

Several miles ahead was a clutter of unmoving shapes and colors in the road, shimmering as the sun heated the asphalt.

"You can't be here when the walls go up or you might be killed by the monster, Eli. I'm taking you to your dad. You'll be fine."

"Why is there a monster?"

"It's how things are. They make a monster every year and a town gets picks to be the testing ground. Pikeburn got picked for some reason. Dumb fucking luck."

"We aren't going to make it," the boy in the back said, pointing his arm through the window toward the mass of two dozen blocking cars, trucks, vans, and buses, none of which were rolling. On the other side of the collection of stopped vehicles was a line of tanks and armored trucks. These were all black and bristled with turrets, machine gun barrels, and radar dishes. Figures in blue jumpsuits and bio-hazard prevention style helmets milled about the area, some armed with bulky machine guns, some with clipboards and pens.

"They'll shoot us," the girl squealed, pawing at the boy's arm.

"Not yet," Corban said. "Not if we get across the line in time."

"Sheriff, there are cars in the road," Eli said without alarm.

"Yes. I see them."

"They aren't supposed to stop us," the boy said. "It's a road block! God damn it, that's cheating!"

"They didn't make it!" Corban said. Once more he risked a look at his watch. 3:16.

"Turn on your siren," Eli suggested.

"Hang on back there!" Corban shouted over his shoulder. Without letting up on the gas, he steered off the road to the right. The truck bucked, alive with the rise and fall of the field. The knee-high prairie grass and scrub brush slapped at the front bumper in ecstasy. The truck slowed with the shift in driving surface, wheels spinning up shredded grass and clods of fresh dirt. But it was still dangerously fast across the uneven surface. The teens in the back held each other and the edge of the bed and were launched several times higher than the cab but came down safely. Eli wasn't belted in and didn't take a hand off his Sponge Bob backpack to brace himself. He was bashed against the ceiling, the door, and the window but made no sound of protest.

To the left, a pack of empty vehicles blocked the road. Three were tangled together at the front of the blockade in a heap, their entwined steel bodies effectively shutting the road down. An obvious panic had resulted in shutting down any escape. Others had tried to go around the wreckage and been stuck in the soft prairie soil, creating even more of an obstacle. A few deep lines in the grass showed the path some lucky vehicles had taken to go around and ultimately cross into safety.

Corban swung wide of all of this chaos and aimed for a sixteen-foot-tall metal column jutting incongruously from the field. He watched a turret on the closest military vehicle track him. A man in blue was pointing at him, talking with his other hand touching his throat. Two different blue suits began jogging toward the spot he would cross.

The moment the truck went by the metal column, Corban brought it to a shuddering stop, banging the teens against the back of the cab a final time. Both were sobbing as he jumped free. He leaned into the bed and looked around. The AR-15 was gone.

"Shit," he muttered. He grabbed the boy's foot. "What's your name?"

"M-Micheal."

"That's Eli in the cab, the Mayor's son. He's yours until the Mayor gets here. Keep him safe. That's important."

Corban sprinted for the open field, retracing the truck's path through the grass toward Pikeburn. He glanced back and saw the two blue suits almost casually jogging toward the truck and its occupants. No one was following him but they were watching carefully.

A voice on a bullhorn called out, "Sheriff Corban! That stanchion is high voltage! Do not attempt to interfere in the Red Diamond event! You will be terminated!"

Corban veered slightly away from the gleaming metal column, running hard with his hands held up at his shoulders and fingers splayed. He passed it by, noticing the grass below him was burned to ash in a straight line from the metal column off into a stand of trees. Another metal column was embedded among the trees on the blackened path.

It was the wall.

He kept running another dozen yards before stopping. Gasping for air, he turned. Just beyond the military staging area filled with black tanks and blue suits was a pack of civilians and their transportation. They stood with the stunned expressions of helpless survivors. They watched the road, the trickle of people even now still arriving and hurrying to make it across. The military personnel did nothing to help or hinder this flow of humanity.

No one else was trying to drive across the field. The line of cars stretched back over half a mile now. People were lugging heavy suitcases, or dragging dogs on leashes, or running while talking into cell phones. Corban saw a few people suddenly abandon all they had labored with to get this far, just dump it with horrified understanding on their faces, and run for all they were worth.

He checked his watch. 3:21.

When he looked up, the wall was there, stretching upward sixteen feet, extending in both directions for eternity. It looked like it was composed of floating energy hexagons of various sizes overlapping each other millions of times. He could see through them but the color was gone from the world on the other side. Like watching on an ancient TV set, Corban saw the men in now gray bio-hazard suits help the teens from the bed of the truck. The girl was limping, crying, and the boy was trying to be the one to carry her, his mouth moving animatedly as he yelled at the gray suits. No sound made it through the wall. It was a TV set with a mute button.

People were screaming, though. Back at the road, near the pile up of cars that had stopped the flight of so many, Corban could see a woman on her knees next to part of a man. The back part. His legs, ass, and lower back. The rest of him was on the black and white side of the wall. No one moved to comfort the woman as she wailed over the dismembered man. Most were simply standing, staring at the wall.

One of the wrecked cars had been on the line and now was an amazing display of internal motor workings as the hexagon wall had sliced it in two as easily as a laser through paper.

One young man picked up a rock and tossed it at the wall. The rock pulverized into a cloud of fine particles and drifted away with the wind.

A booming voice issued from the wall. "Tampering with the Red Diamond wall carries a punishment of termination! This is your only warning!" On the other side of the wall, three machine gun armed gray suits converged on the point across from the young rock thrower.

The young man bolted for his car. A few others went as quickly. The rest of the gathered crowd who had failed to escape Pikeburn retreated slowly, or sat down, or wandered off in a daze to stand in the fields. Some were weeping and shouting, some blinking rapidly or muttering to themselves, some clinging to each other.

As Corban turned to walk away from the wall, something blue caught his attention about fifty feet down the wall toward the patch of trees. A blue suit was standing close to the wall on Corban's side, talking into his throat mic and waving his hand toward some gray suits on the other side.

"No! You're not listening! Please, I am calm, sir. I am calm. It's just that I am on the wrong side of the wall! I'm on the wrong side, sir!"

The man yanked off his helmet and flung it to his feet, revealing his sweat-streaked face and wild hair.

"Sir, you sent me to check on the stanchion C45 tremor sensor. You gave me that order yourself. I can't do that – you don't check the sensor from your side of the wall! You didn't - no one told me it was going up! Someone should have told me!"

Corban put his hand on his revolver at his hip.

The blue suit saw the movement. He lowered his voice but Corban could hear every syllable. "Sir, I need the wall section between stanchions C45 and C46 brought down for thirty seconds."

To his Corban's left, a ghostly gray Eli appeared close to the wall and was walking toward Corban. He reached out his hand toward the hexagon wall, a grin on his face. Even as Corban's mind spun helplessly at the sight of Eli headed for the wall, a gray suit ran up next to Eli, gently leading him away. They turned after a few steps, almost blurred out of existence by the rapidly twitching hexagons. Both waved at him. Corban took his hand off his revolver and waved back. He shook his head as if to wake up from a dream.

"God damn it," the trapped blue suit hissed into his mic. "I'm not asking for — God damn it, Sir. You sent me here! You told me check on — This is your fucking fault! Open the fucking wall! Open the fucking wall! I'm in here with these people and that fucking thing Harlow built!" The man pulled the mic out of the lining of the collar on his blue suit. Holding it in both hands he screamed into the bulb. "You fucking asshole! You did this on purpose! I'm going to kill you! I'm - "

He froze in mid rant, wide eyes fixed on Corban.

"I need to talk to you," Corban said.

The man dropped the mic and fled. In less than a minute he had reached the trees and vanished into the shadows of the underbrush.

Corban closed his eyes for a moment. "This can't be real," he muttered.

He began backtracking over the trail of crushed grass his truck had made. A few more cars arrived down the road from town, but they all quickly left when the occupants saw the wall and knew running was no longer an option. He was halfway to the spot he had turned off the pavement when a black Lexus came speeding up the road. It abruptly stopped with a protest of rubber on pavement. Corban could see a white-haired head moving dramatically behind the wheel and a fist hammering at the dashboard. The driver spied Corban and his mouth twisted into a snarl. The Lexus jolted forward, turned off the road, and drove right at him.

As Corban took a final step to wait for what was about to happen, his foot struck an object in the grass. He looked down and saw he was standing on his missing AR-15. He frowned at the assault rifle, then looked up and watched the car come at him.

The Lexus halted less than ten feet from him, sliding almost sideways on a layer of bent grass stalks. The door flung open and a man in his sixties wearing a tennis outfit jumped out.

"This is your fault, Sheriff!" he shouted. His tall frame showed no sign of being limited by age as he came at Corban stiff-legged in anger. "You insufferable little chink bastard! How could we be so stupid as to hire you! You just killed my family and - "

Corban bent down and came up holding the long black AR-15 in one hand, the hollow barrel pointed square at the raging man's belly.

"Get out of my way, Clark," Corban said. "I'm still Sheriff in this town."

Clark stopped where he was and seethed. "God damn you, chink bastard."

"Very clever. I knew you were a racist piece of shit, Clark. Glad to see you have embraced that side of yourself before the end."

"Highway 30 South was blocked! Your God damn deputy wouldn't get off her ass to move the stalled bus."

"A school bus? Was it a school bus?"

"No, it wasn't a God damn fucking school bus!" Clark said. "It was that ugly purple church bus from Forever Unity full of old people! And no one was getting off! They wouldn't move and I couldn't get around and I took off to get here and now it's too late!"

Corban shook his head. "How is that my fault, Clark? Maybe you should have stayed put or crossed on foot like other people. You panicked, that's all. Now go home. Get safe before it starts hunting."

"I'm not the only one who thinks you're a disgrace to this town," Clark said through clenched teeth. "You better hope that thing gets you. You are done in Pikeburn! I'll make sure..."

"Shut up," someone said from behind Corban. "Just shut your rich, ugly mouth and leave before I shut it for you."

Clark started to reply, but his eyes snapped to something the interloper was holding. His mouth hung open and he took a step back.

Corban turned but kept the assault rifle trained on Clark. A small group had marched from the jumble of cars bottle necked at what had once been the way to freedom. In the lead was a man built tall and wide. His maroon jumpsuit was stained with dirt and grease. His wide hands were caked with motor oil, brake fluid, dust and grime from a hundred car engines. In those hands rested a single, blood-soak shoe, a child's shoe. There was a severed foot inside the shoe, the flesh and bone sliced by the wall even easier than a metal car.

"My God," Corban said. "James, is—"

"No, it's okay," James said in a voice so calm it made Corban's arms rise with goose bumps. "I saved Benji. I threw him. I could tell the wall was coming up. I could tell from how the soldiers moved away. I threw my little boy as hard as I could." He looked at the shoe. "It almost worked. It got his right foot. That's all. He won't die. A missing foot is pretty easy to adjust to, you think?"

"Yes," Corban said, forcing himself to look James in the face instead of at the bloody shoe. "I guess it would be."

"He's four. He probably won't even remember by the time he gets into college. He's going to be All State, you know that? He's going to be as big as his old man but twice as smart. He's not going to change oil for rich assholes all day. He won't have oil under his nails, in his hair, smell of antifreeze and spilled gas."

"You people," Clark said in hushed wonder and disgust. He went to his Lexus. He slammed the door, gave them all the finger from behind smoky glass, and drove off over the uneven field to the road.

"That's bad for the frame," James said. "Lexus isn't a great off-road vehicle."

Corban touched James on the shoulder.

"No, I'm okay, Sheriff. I – I just want..." He looked at the little shoe. "I'm going to hang on to this a bit longer."

"That's fine. But get back to town. Get somewhere safe. For Benji, okay?"

"Sure, sure."

Corban looked at the ring of faces around him, haggard and scared and lost. "That goes for all of you. Get away from this place. It's too open. Hurry back to town. And don't leave anyone behind. Help each other out."

"What then?" a woman asked.

"I don't know yet." Corban slung the AR-15 over his shoulder. "Keep our heads down. Stay calm. Make a plan, I guess. I need a ride back to the station."

A man nodded. "We saw what you did with Eli and Michael and his girlfriend. You got them across."

"You saved them kids," another man said and a few others muttered affirmation.

"We all saw you come back, too, Sheriff, when you didn't have to," the woman said. "Clark Masterson is full of shit. You didn't leave. You can ride with me."

The short ride back to town was silent and uneventful. Evidence of the exodus from Pikeburn diminished as they got closer to the town itself. A few stragglers walked the road, headed back from the wall, lugging the same suitcases that had slowed them down in the first place. An abandoned car was in the ditch with wisps of smoke rolling from the grill. An old man was standing in the soccer field with a shovel at his side, waiting alone and taking gulps from a bottle. A frantic man tried to flag them down and the woman next to Corban didn't pause or acknowledge as she kept on driving. Once in town, she stopped at the stop signs and obeyed the speed limit until they were at the Sheriff's office.

"Did you want to know what happened back there?" she asked. "Why the cars were all piled up?"

"I think I know. People racing for their lives, they see the tanks and the guns and hit the brakes, others behind them try to pass in a panic. It only takes one mistakes and you have a blocked highway."

"Yeah," she said softly. "Someone was trying to get the soldiers to clear out the wreck. He got himself arrested when he grabbed one of them."

"Lucky he wasn't shot dead."

"I'm sorry. I didn't vote for you," she said suddenly.

Corban shrugged. "Someone did, I assume."

"I'm sorry Janet left you for that asshole in Vermont."

This time Corban laughed. "Small town grape vine, huh?"

"We love to talk."

Corban got out. "Thank you for the ride. What's your name?"

"Janet. Not kidding. I'm Janet, too. Sorry."

"Find a safe place, Janet. People need to hide until this is over."

Her face was red and tears threatened to spill down her cheeks, but she managed a smile. "You aren't going to hide, why should we?"

"I'm stubborn that way," he said. He closed the car door and walked into his office.

Alice was wearing a pair of over-sized headphones plugged into the CB. She was listening and nodding. The phone on her desk was silent and the previously blinking lights dead. The pump shotgun he had placed beside the coat rack was now behind her desk in easy reach.

A young man in a denim jacket was sitting on the wooden bench, leaning forward eagerly and staring at Corban. He had a replica army messenger back on his lap that was about to burst. He gave Corban a nervous smile and pushed his glasses up.

The young man said, "Sheriff, can I - "

"No," Corban said and turned away. He tapped Alice on the headphone.

She pulled them down to her neck. "Well?"

"I got Eli out, and some teenagers. The walls are up."

"I gathered that."

"Can you map them out if I bring you a map from my office?"

"The phones have gone down," she said.

The young man drew in his breath at that. Corban frowned at him before looking back to Alice.

"Cell phones still work?"

"Yes," she said.

The young man shook his head. "For now. Make any calls you need to make right away."

"Who are you?" Corban asked.

"My name is Adam Dorchet."

"Good. Now be quiet please a minute."

Adam slowly rested back in the bench with effort. He took out a square of fabric and polished his glasses.

"Alice, any of the deputies come back here?"

She shook her head.

"Any of them call in?"

She shook her head.

Corban picked up the handset. Alice flicked a switch and pointed at him.

"This is Sheriff Corban. Any deputy reply."

He waited thirty seconds in silence.

"This is Sheriff Corban inside Pikeburn. I'm at the station. Any deputy reply."

Another minute of expectant silence went by.

"Any deputy reply from any location. If you're outside, let me know. You still have a job to do."

When nothing was heard, Alice said softly, "I can't believe it."

Corban pressed the button again. "If you can hear me, you are still deputies of Pikeburn and I expect you to act like it. A lot of people got out and have nothing but the clothing on their backs. You rally those people. Find a place to gather.

You prepare for coming home. You—" He had to stop and steady himself. "You be ready to clean up this mess when it's done."

He put the handset down.

Alice leaned close and hit the button herself. "And you all should be ashamed of yourselves!"

Corban went to the water cooler and downed a cup. When he turned around, Adam was standing behind him.

"I don't live in Pikeburn," Adam said.

"You do now."

"I understand that. I'm not stranded. I, um, wanted to be here for this."

Corban started walking away toward his office and suddenly spun back. "What did you say? You knew this was going to happen?"

"Sort of. It's wasn't a sure thing. I used fifty years' worth of data to narrow down the choices. It was Pikeburn or South Hern or Girard or Pucket. I had to pick one and I got lucky."

Corban advanced on the young man until he was backed into the corner with the coat rack. "Who the hell are you?"

"I'm a Red Diamond researcher. I've been a follower since I was a kid."

"God damn nutcase then."

"No, it isn't like that. Sheriff, give me a chance. I can help."

Corban looked him up and down. "I don't think so."

"You're going to lose cell phones and power and soon."

"Why? They've never done that before."

"Yes, they have. Back in 2005 and 2004. In 2007, they hit the town with an electro-magnetic pulse on day three. In 1995, they tainted the water supply. In 1996, they let—"

"Okay, stop. I don't follow the Red Diamond, so I don't know what's true or not. I've seen some of the shows and the documentary segment on 60 Minutes. You can't get away from it this time of year, but it's all hogwash anyway. There's no telling the truth from fiction in Red Diamond." He pointed at the bench. "Just sit down."

Adam nodded briskly. "Yes. sir." He planted himself on the bench and hugged his messenger bag.

"Sheriff," Alice said. "Something brewing at the court house. People are talking about a gathering on the radio."

"That's stupid," Corban said.

"Sounds like Billy Voltrane started it."

Corban shook his head. "I better go see what he's up to now."

Alice wagged her finger at him. "You watch your back, Sheriff. Billy is a snake and now is the perfect time to settle old grudges."

"I know. Lock the doors after I leave."

"A glass door won't stop whatever is out there," she said.

"It'll stop people. Do you want something smaller than that shotgun? We have pistols."

"I'm good, thank you. Take the expert with you."

Corban eyed the young man on the bench for a moment, then sighed. "Well, come on."

Titus was in the street looking toward the town square and court house. Corban and Adam joined him. Now the parking lot was full and several trucks were pulled onto the grass. A crowd was gathered in a semi-circle around the front steps of the courthouse.

"It's a strange time for a party," Titus said.

"Billy Voltrane."

"I guess he wouldn't run, would he? I heard a few gunshots, too. Probably firing into the air, but just so you know they are armed."

Corban started walking for the square. Adam and Titus flanked him. The crowd saw him coming. Weapons were everywhere. They parted enough for him to make his way to the front steps of the court house. It was not Billy on the top step. A man in a Captain America T-shirt and an orange hunting vest held the crowd's attention, but he wilted as Corban took the steps without hesitation and stood next to him.

"Sheriff," the man said in greeting.

"I don't know you," Corban said. "You live here?"

The challenge brought some whispers and chuckles from the crowd.

"I— I'm Warren Steven's cousin."

"So, a trapped visitor. Bad luck."

"Yeah." The man looked down.

"I'll take it from here." Corban looked across the faces. Five men were standing on the tops of their trucks, rifles and shotguns held with a casual familiarity. Corban met each of their eyes and nodded. Three nodded back. One smirked. One turned his head and spat over the side of the truck.

"Billy," Corban said to him. "I heard you called this meeting. What do you have to say?"

The man rubbed spittle off his lower lip. Billy wore boots and jeans, a black T-shirt, and a camo baseball cap. He held a rifle with an extended magazine, had a pistol on his hip, and a long knife on his belt. "Just trying to be ready, Sheriff."

"I can understand that," Corban said. "Don't expect me to stop you."

"It's open season!" a man yelled in the crowd and a few people hollered back in agreement.

"On us," Corban said. "Open season on us, you mean. Or don't you get what's about to happen?"

"I think," Billy said loudly, "I think we're all eager to defend the homes we've lived in all our lives. We were born here, you get that? We're not going to hide in the basement."

"I never said otherwise."

"You've been telling people to hide."

"Did I tell you to hide, Billy?" Corban waited, fixing Billy with an unblinking eye. He waited until Billy drew a breath to speak and then he interrupted, "Because I don't want you to hide, Billy. None of you. Right this second, there's a monster on the loose in Pikeburn. It's got one goal. Kill everyone in town. We've got one goal. Kill it first. You want to make this into something it's not? You'll get people killed, Billy."

"I ain't—"

"Because I can't save all of you," Corban said. "It doesn't work that way. Right now, that thing is prowling for food. Right now, that thing might be creeping toward a back door.

Right now, a family might be dead. A family that was born here, or moved here for work, or was driving through and stopped for lunch at the Cowboy Cafe. And I can't do a damn thing about that! You want to hunt it? Go right ahead. I need you to hunt it. Just don't expect it to care who lives here and who doesn't. We've all been demoted on the food chain."

"Thanks for the permission," Billy said with a smirk.

"But let me ask a question that's pretty important. Do you have something bigger than that rifle, Billy? Because I'm not caring what it is or where you got it. I heard tales your father ran a meth operation before disappearing. I heard you might be doing the same and I don't give a fuck right now. I'm not going to arrest you for having bigger guns. We're going to need bigger guns."

Corban tilted his head and waited and everyone looked at Billy.

Billy scratched at his chin stubble, tried to be relaxed and shrug off the eyes, but finally he glared at the crowd. "What do you fuckers want?"

"Do you?" someone asked. "Do you have machine guns?"

"Fuck off," Billy said. "You don't believe the little bastard, do you? Monster or not, he's got the badge and the jail and I'm not going down for the bullshit he's throwing around. You people are all stupid. He's a lying bastard. He ain't one of us."

"I've seen the M-16 in your house," one of the other men on the hood of his truck said. He was older than Billy, sporting a full beard and wearing a pale cowboy hat.

"Shut up, Chambers," Billy said.

"This isn't a game," Chambers said. "You think he's after you for littering? He don't care if you pulled out a bag of crack right now. He's not Sheriff in Pikeburn. He can't be. Once the walls go up, there is no law."

The eyes of the crowd pivoted to Corban for a reply.

"That's only half true," Corban said. "And only if I want it to be."

"Told you! He's going to be arresting people for jaywalking," Billy called out and laughed, but no one joined him.

"I don't have time to arrest any of you," Corban said with a raised hand. "The truth is all my deputies ran. I'm alone and I have bigger things to deal with than you, Billy, and your meth business. Or you, Chambers, and your dog fights out by the tracks. Or you, Don Frakes, and your passing bad checks in Tullware County. I don't have time for that petty bullshit! But I'm not going to tolerate lawlessness ruining this town because some of you see the opportunity to become monsters yourselves. Cross that line and I'll just shoot you."

"You go ahead and try, chink," Billy said softly. His finger curled around the trigger of his hunting rifle but the barrel stayed pointed at the sky.

Corban smiled at him. "You're not doing anything wrong yet, Billy."

"What now?" Chambers asked.

"We go hunting!" Billy said.

"I'm setting up a command station inside the courthouse," Corban said. "I could use a bunch of men with guns to help secure this location."

"I'm not waiting around here," Billy said. "I say we go find this thing before sundown and beat the fastest kill record."

At the foot of the steps, Adam raised his hand as if in Grade school and said, "Excuse me." His quiet voice carried over the crowd at exactly the right time, dropping into the silence between shouts. Everyone heard and looked his way. "Go to the hospital," Adam said.

"What?" Corban said.

"Statistically speaking, that's one of the first targets."

"Who is this guy?" Billy asked.

"Our expert," Corban said. "But I don't understand why he's here."

Adam cleared his throat. "The fastest kill record was three days back in 1977. The government was really unhappy with that result. The entire design team was fired. In 1978, they built what is now called Berhooven's Beast, and it killed almost an entire town. That event lasted twenty-eight days. The longest event was thirty-seven days, in 2001."

"Jesus," someone muttered.

"But you don't need to hunt it. You are — um — being hunted. The monster has to eat human flesh. It is incapable of digesting any other animal or plant matter. It doesn't care about fair or being decent. Hospitals have the sick and the old and the young. It's an easy meal It knows how to hunt us because it's been hunting prisoners in mazes while growing this last year."

"That was a hoax," Titus said in a hollow voice.

Adam shook his head. "No. The proof it was a hoax was the hoax. You only see what they want you to see. The government didn't want the public outcry over feeding criminals to the monsters. They started hiding it better, that's all. Some national watchdog group made a stink by calling it cruel and unusual punishment."

"You think?" Chambers said.

"So, what is this thing?" Billy asked.

"I don't know. That secret is too guarded even for me. They grow a new monster every year to test new theories and strategies. It's all for the war effort. We can't lag behind Brazil or Russia or Japan. We have to have better monsters to fight for us when the war heats up again. That's what they say, anyway."

"How can we kill it?" Corban asked.

Adam looked surprised. "I don't know. How could I know? It could be anything. It could be immune to bullets. It could dodge bullets. The possibilities are endless. But you need to be thinking of other ways to attack it. Guns are too common. The scientists know you have lots of guns in a small town like this. They didn't build this thing so you could take it out with a hand gun. They don't want you to win."

People shifted nervously and looked at their weapons, so proudly displayed a moment ago.

"I came here to see it for real," Adam said. "There's all this talk online, hundreds of forums and chat groups, but hardly anyone has seen one with their own eyes. The government edits all the videos and documentaries for security purposes. Even the leaked footage is leaked by the government. The only way to know the truth is to be here. Now. Live or die, I'm going to see it." Little blooms of red had appeared on his cheeks with the excitement. Then he shrugged. "It's okay if I die. I put my affairs in order."

Corban could see the realization creeping into the gathered faces. Fingers were removed from triggers. People started taking casual steps for their cars, glancing at their neighbors for support.

"I'm heading for the hospital," Billy said. He looked at Adam. "That's the first place, right, genius?"

"Traditionally, one of the first places."

"Then where?"

"Here," Adam said. "Center of town, crowd of people. It's not afraid of us unless it has to be. Right now, we haven't given it a reason to be afraid. It could probably kill us all if we stand here like this."

Now people were heading quickly for their vehicles or off down the deserted streets at fast pace. Billy shouted out a few orders and three trucks of armed men sped off for the hospital. Corban stood on the steps and watched them go. Adam and Titus joined him. In a few minutes, everyone was gone except six men waiting anxiously for his command at the foot of the stairs.

"Okay," Corban said when the sound of engines had faded. "I left my truck on the outside of the wall. I'm going to need to borrow one, if you have a spare."

"I'll call my boy," one older man at the foot of the stairs said. A moment later he was staring at his phone. "Um, Sheriff."

"Phones are dead," Adam said. "And look." He pointed to the dark windows around the square, the blank neon signs in the Cowboy Cafe, the previously moving display in the jewelry store, the sudden absence of faint rock and roll that had been drifting from the open door of the Sud Place Laundromat.

"They cut the power," Corban said. "God damn them."

"They did or it did," Adam said.

"It can do that?" Titus asked. "It's just an animal."

Adam pulled out a small notebook with a pencil on a cord strung through a hole in the cover. He wrote down something in a code next to the time and date.

He looked around the square. "It's a well-trained animal. That's the point of all this." He slipped the notebook away. "It's not about who can be more vicious. Humans always win that contest. It's about who can be more *clever*."

"Then we start being clever, God damn it," Corban said. "I want you men to get camping supplies from anywhere you can find them. Loot the businesses or homes, I don't care. And as many weapons as you can find. Generators, lanterns, food and water, and some building supplies to turn this place into a fort. Bring it all here to the court house. Start barricading the rooms. And get Alice from the Sheriff's station right away. Knock before trying to barge in, though. She's armed and probably unhappy about the power being out."

The men nodded and pulled into a huddle to make a quick plan.

"Titus and Adam, come with me. Titus, you drive your Jeep. I want to check Ross Farms before we hunker down for the night."

"What for?" one of them men asked.

"Something is in the corn."

CHAPTER TWO

When they got to the muddy Jeep in the alley behind the Sheriff's office, Titus excused himself to run into his shop. Corban pulled out his pistol and offered it to Adam.

Adam looked from the pistol to Corban. He shook his head.

"Do you know how to use this?" Corban asked.

"I took a two-week course on gun safety once."

"Good enough."

"It won't do anything against what's out there. It's just a handgun."

"Do you want it?"

"No."

Corban put it back in the holster on his hip.

Adam cleared his throat. "You did a good job shutting down that guy, Billy."

"I thought I was going to throw up or get shot. He wanted to. We have a history, so he may still do it."

"He's going to get killed. The hunters always do. In 2000, they let five professional hunters into the town after two weeks and the monster seemed impervious to anything the locals could throw at it. Only one hunter survived and he was seriously wounded."

"Did he kill it?" Corban asked.

"No. Nancy Nefram ran it over with a moving van on day nineteen. It killed one hundred fifty-six people before that. It wasn't a strong year."

"Excuse me," Corban said. He went into the Sheriff's office. He found the bathroom door by feel as the interior hallway was a black tunnel. Once inside, he bent over the sink and emptied his guts in a single spasm. Slowly, he looked up at where he knew the mirror was. Nothing but darkness reflected back.

He ran water in the sink before leaving.

In the alley, Titus had changed into jeans, a faded green T-shirt, and a rumpled jacket with a digital camo design. He was nodding and muttering to himself. Adam was already in the back seat and buckled in.

"Are you okay?" Corban asked.

Titus froze, as if caught doing something inappropriate. "I'm fine. Hey, is this a good idea? Driving around looking for it?"

"I'm checking on Ross. He was shooting at something in the corn. If he's shooting, there's a damn good chance he's hitting something. He doesn't panic. You don't have to come along. This is my job, not yours. Give me the keys."

"Well, ok," Titus said, but didn't move to hand over the keys. "I'm just..."

"What is it?"

"I drove convoys as a contractor in Iraq," Titus said. He looked away and blew out his breath.

"So?" Corban said.

"It's hard for me to drive people. This - this has gotten some things stirring in my head. Shit I never wanted to think about again. Things I saw. Things I did." He looked at his feet.

"Give me the keys, Titus."

"No, sir," Titus said softly. "I got this. I just thought you should know."

"Are you sure? Because I don't need stranded at Ross Farms for the night."

Titus brought up his head and looked Corban in the eye. He slipped his unlit pipe between his teeth. "I've got this, Sheriff."

"Do you want my gun?"

"Nope. Give it to Roger."

"Who is—"

Titus pointed a thumb at Adam in the back seat. He frowned and shook his head. "Only that's not Roger. That's Adam, right?"

"Right. How about we get going."

They got into the Jeep and Titus turned to him again, pipe dipping as he spoke. "Roger was a reporter with us a few weeks. Got blown up. I saw that happen. I know that's not Roger back there."

"Who's Roger?" Adam asked.

"Okay," Corban said to Titus.

Titus put the Jeep in gear. "Just wanted you to know I'm not going soft in the brain."

"I'm glad for that. Head north out of town."

"Got it."

On the way north out of town, Titus steered them through a residential area with the name Stonebluff Estates. Each house was very much like the one before, squeezed together like they were afraid long before a monster came to Pikeburn. Corban saw doors left wide open, a suitcase left behind with a sleeve hanging from its partially closed zipper, a mailbox flattened by its owners, fresh tire marks on lawns and curbs. He glimpsed a single face gazing at them from behind a wide front window, and it disappeared like a startled fish in an aquarium.

"It's like a war zone," Corban said.

Titus gave a harsh laugh. "I'm sorry. Didn't mean to laugh at you, but this isn't a war zone."

"It will be," Adam said.

"I've seen a war zone and this is not it."

"Yet."

"Sorry I mentioned it," Corban said. "Let's stay focused."

As they turned left toward the highway out of town, a man could be seen on the roof of his little house. He had a pair of binoculars and a rifle. He was scanning the area to the west.

"How did it empty so fast?" Titus muttered.

"Fear," Adam said. "And training. This is also part of what they are studying. Can a city evacuate in a real emergency? How many will stay no matter what? How many grab possessions, pets, food and water? How many have a plan before this happens? Think how useless a bombing run will be against civilian targets if they have been trained to drop everything and leave."

"It's control," Corban said.

"Yep," Titus said. "You went through basic. You know."

"No," Corban said. "I was not in the military."

Titus frown. "Oh yeah."

"Kids are the biggest factor," Adam said. "Fear of having your kids eaten. Almost any family with kids gets out right away."

As they exited town, the last business was a small car lot festooned with bobbing balloons. The ten cars lined up facing the road had smashed windshields.

"Hey, does insurance cover shit like that?" Titus asked Adam. "Do we have monster insurance?"

"The monster didn't do that," Corban said. "That's a baseball bat. It didn't take long for old grudges to get settled."

"No," Adam answered Titus. "You're supposed to accept the loss like a good citizen. Doing your part to strengthen our nation."

"Really? They say that?"

Adam shrugged. "I read it in a pamphlet."

Titus laughed as he dodged a foot locker in the road.

"The monster didn't smash those windshields," Corban said. "That's a person settling an old grudge while he can. I was hoping not to see stuff like that."

"Doesn't take long," Titus said.

The road north from town quickly left behind the urban and turned into fields of corn. On both sides of them corn reached higher than they could see over. The conversation died. Corban tightened his grip on the AR-15.

They topped a rise in the road and Titus eased off the gas. Less than a mile ahead was the hexagon wall, slicing across the corn fields and into the distance. A pile up of cars was at the road where it passed through the wall. Titus brought the Jeep to a halt.

"What is it?" Adam asked.

"That's the wall," Corban said. "Ross Farms is out another few miles. He wasn't shooting at the monster. Couldn't have been."

"Want to head back?" Titus asked. "I'm getting a bad vibe here."

"No. Something is wrong with those cars. Drive up slow."

"Copy that," he said softly.

It wasn't a traffic jam like Corban had seen at the other road from town. These cars were wrecked, but not against each other. Glass and shredded metal lay scattered across the road. The frames were bent, tipped over, warped into frightening new shapes.

Adam stuck his head between the front seats. "Did the soldiers fire on them?"

"No," Titus said. "No bullet holes or blast marks."

"It was here," Corban said.

Titus look at him. "It did this? It tore up cars? It can do that?"

"They usually are quite powerful physically," Adam said. "Reinforced bone structures, muscle fibers dense enough to stop bullets, enlarged adrenaline glands. That's just the ordinary improvements. The really secret breakthroughs won't be given to the public for twenty years. It's not surprising it can rip a car apart."

"But why would it attack cars?" Titus asked with a look of pure dismay. "It can't eat cars!"

"It eats what's in the cars," Corban said. He pointed toward the windshield of a doorless sedan. Blood streaked the glass.

"Permission to about face this fucker and get out of here," Titus said.

"Do it."

Titus managed a quick three-point turn, but hit the brakes again instead of driving away. In the road, about fifty yards from them, was a woman. She was walking away slowly, weaving down the center line toward town. She was barefoot, her hair and clothes in tatters, blood smeared on her.

"Titus," Corban said, "what are you doing? Drive! Go get her!"

"That's a trap," Titus said, biting the pipe stem hard enough to make his jaw tremble.

Corban looked back at Adam. "Is that possible?"

Adam tore his eyes from the injured woman. "Maybe."

Corban took hold of Titus's arm. "A trap for us, Titus?"

"We go to help and we get ambushed. Seen it before."

They watched for a moment as the woman kept shambling toward town. A breeze rustled the tops of the corn. Corban turned his head to see both Titus and Adam staring at him, waiting. Corban looked again at the woman shuffling along on bloody feet.

"We are going to get her," Corban said emphatically.

"That's - "

"Titus, I'm going to ride on top, keep a look out and my gun ready. Adam, you lean out that window. As Titus drives by, grab her around the waist and don't let go. She's not a big woman, you can handle that. Titus, you drive like hell once her feet are off the ground. Any questions?"

"I— I—" Adam stammered.

"Adam," Corban said sharply. "If we sit here, that thing will spring the trap anyway. We don't stand a chance if we wait for that. What are my odds of killing it right now with this weapon? Come on, what are they?"

Adam swallowed. "You don't have any."

"But we aren't leaving that woman."

"Right," Titus said. He gripped the wheel tighter. "We don't leave anyone behind."

Corban opened the door but did not get out. "Adam, we're going to spring the trap early and run like hell. If it can outrun a car while I fill it full of bullets, we never stood a chance anyway."

Adam rolled down his window. He put his messenger bag next to him. He nodded to Corban.

"Wait for my signal," Corban said. He swung out and climbed to the Jeep's roof. He stood up, AR-15 ready. To his right, the corn was a gently undulating mass of green. To his left, the corn ocean was marred by trails made by something big that had moved through it.

"Shit," he whispered. There were enough trails to confuse his eyes. "It could be anywhere."

"What's going on?" Titus called up.

"One second. And don't throw me off when I say go. Take it easy but get there quick."

Corban went to his knee, then reached down and grabbed the roof rack.

"Titus, now."

The Jeep tires chirped as Titus laid his foot on the gas. Corban kept his eyes trained on the corn trails. Nothing changed as the Jeep barreled toward the woman. The Jeep veered slightly to avoid her, then braked hard enough to almost take Corban off the roof.

In the field, corn began to thrash as a new trail was made. Corban brought up his weapon, but hesitated when he saw it wasn't coming straight at them. The trail was heading away, toward Pikeburn, parallel to the road.

"Got her!" Adam said.

"Wait!" Corban yelled down.

"What for?" Titus shouted back.

"It's—" Corban watched the trail come to a stop. The corn grew still. "It's ahead of us! Waiting for us!"

Adam opened the door and dragged the woman inside the Jeep. She didn't make a sound or move to resist. Once the door slammed shut, Adam said, "She's safe. Oh God! Her fingers are gone! Her hands - oh God!"

"Wrap her hands up," Titus said. "When we get back to base someone more qualified than you can sew them back on."

"I don't have them! Oh God her hands are all gone!"

"I've got bungee cords in the back. Make a tourniquet. And stop screaming."

"It's waiting for us," Corban said. He looked to the right, at the pristine tops of waving corn. "Titus, how big is your engine?"

"My what?"

"Go right when I tell you."

"You want me to drive into the corn?"

"Yes. Try to lose this thing in the corn and get back to town."

Titus turned the steering wheel to the right until it stopped. "I'm ready."

"Won't we get bogged down?" Adam asked breathlessly. "She doesn't have much time."

"My Jeep? She can take it. You better climb on down, Sheriff."

Just as Corban started to move, he heard an odd crackling from the corn. He jerked his head up. There was a new trail blooming, this one headed straight for them. Corban fell flat on the roof and wrapped his left hand around the roof rack.

"Drive!" he yelled. At the same time, he raised the rifle and fired three shots at the hidden form creating the trail.

The Jeep lurched, hit the ditch, and tilted wildly. It amazingly righted itself and plowed into the corn with a roar. Corban pivoted on his stomach so he was facing behind them. He wedged his feet beneath the roof rack, ignoring the painful protests from his ankles. The jolting ride abused his ribs, but he didn't try to regain a more comfortable position. He sighted down the barrel of the rifle and held it steady.

The Jeep left behind a flattened trail of smashed corn stalks and ruts where the knobby tires clawed forward. Titus cut to the left after fifty yards. Corban could no longer see the road. The corn blocked everything from his sight accept for the trail in a straight line before him.

But he heard something. A guttural call just above the engine's roar and the corn being crushed aside. The sound made his flesh rise with goosebumps.

The Jeep hauled left again. Once more Corban's view was reduced to a receding corn wall. He braced his left arm under his chest against the metal roof. When the Jeep erupted from the corn and slammed over the ditch he managed to keep from knocking the wind out of himself, but his arm throbbed with the impact.

Titus swung the Jeep toward town and floored it. The hefty V8 pulled the vehicle forward, throwing corn debris and dirt clods in its wake. A shape, large and undefined, appeared behind a single row of corn, racing to catch up to them. Corban fired the clip dry at the bounding shape, sure he hit at least once, yet the shape did not alter its course.

The Jeep gained speed and started leaving the shape behind. The monster broke away, turning deeper into the corn, vanishing from Corban's sight. All he could do was hold on as Titus sped into town, veering around corners at unsafe velocity.

After several minutes, Corban glimpsed a white-haired man in T-shirt and Bermuda shorts walking a panting Dachshund with a gray muzzle, walking each other in a deserted neighborhood. The man stared open-mouthed at Corban on the roof of the Jeep tearing down the road.

"Go home!" Corban shouted. He started to say more, but the Jeep zipped around a corner and the old man and his old dog were gone.

They reached the courthouse and things had changed dramatically. The parking lot was full to capacity. The lawn was now being used for the over flow of cars and trucks. A flatbed truck was backed up close to the front doors and a line of people were passing supplies from the bed to the interior. A few of the narrow courthouse windows showed lights on inside.

Titus brought the Jeep to a shuddering stop in the street. He jumped out and opened the back door. He and Adam lifted the injured woman and began hustling for the courthouse. By the time Corban had pulled his feet free and gently climbed down on stinging ankles, they were inside. He leaned against the Jeep and closed his eyes.

"Hey," someone said.

Corban opened his eyes to see the blocky figure of James. He had pulled down the top part of his coveralls and tied the arms about his waist, revealing his sweat-stained white t-shirt. The severed foot was not in his hands.

"I'm sorry I sort of lost it out there," James said. His eyes were shiny and his face had clean streaks down his cheeks, but his voice was steady.

"It's okay."

"You might want to know while you were gone some stuff has happened."

Corban looked toward the activity at the courthouse. "What now?"

"Clark Masterson has taken over the courthouse. He's got all his workers in there, too."

"Okay," Corban said. He noticed the flatbed truck had the "Masterson Construction" name and logo on the side. "I'll deal with that later. I need to reload."

"Um, they took the bullets."

"From the Sheriff's office?" Corban pushed away from the Jeep.

"They've been grabbing stuff from all over town. Um, Clark said it was our only chance. He's got a lot of his guys with him. They don't seem to be angry or hurting anyone." He shrugged. "No one is telling him he can't do it."

A figure appeared at the glass doors of the courthouse, hands on hips, watching over the men carrying in supplies. Masterson had changed into jeans and a flannel shirt. A large pistol was strapped under his left arm. He was grinning.

"This guy," Corban said and shook his head. "James, the monster is north of town, in the corn. It could be here in minutes. Get these people off the lawn."

"They've posted guards," James said. "With rifles."

"They're going to need rocket launchers. Tell people to get inside, James, okay?"

James looked down. "What if they won't listen?"

"You don't worry about what they choose to do. You just tell them it's out there. Then get inside yourself. Benji is going to need his dad when this is over."

James nodded and shuffled away toward a group of people chatting like they were at a fair.

Corban got behind the wheel of the Jeep and felt for the keys. They still hung from the ignition. He started the Jeep and jerked it though a U turn. He sped north. Only a few minutes later he saw the old man and his old dog coming toward him. Corban left a pair of black lines as he braked hard near the old man.

"Get in, Mr. Deet!" he said.

"Tucker doesn't like to ride in cars," the old man said.

"I don't care, Mr. Deet."

"She will probably throw up."

"It's not my car."

Mr. Deet shrugged. "Come on, Tuck." He lifted the panting Dachshund up and carried her to the Jeep. They both got in the back and settled in. "Mighty grateful, Sheriff."

"Why aren't you hiding at home?" Corban asked as he hopped the curb in a wide turn.

"No one told me it was Red Diamond time. I heard the sirens and thought it was a tornado test. Just a test because it's not going to storm until next week. I've been thinking a lot about my daughter and her husband in Utah. She's not doing so well."

"I'm sorry to hear that. We need to make a stop before I take you to the courthouse."

"I suppose that's okay."

As Corban drove down a side street full of little brick houses of the same general size and design, a pick up loaded with people and guns turned out from an alley and headed toward them. Corban waved for them to stop as he got closer. Once the two vehicles were side by side the driver of the truck recognized Corban and he palmed a joint in panic.

"Sheriff," the passenger said quickly, "We didn't come out for trouble with you and - "

"The monster is in the corn north of town. Either go get it or get somewhere safe."

The men stared at him.

Corban rolled his eyes. "It's not going to kill itself, is it? If you want to go play with it, at least I see you've got enough guns. But if I were you, I would hold up in the courthouse with a lot of other people doing the same. It has to come to us, remember?"

"Okay," the driver said. He timidly offered the joint to Corban. "Want a hit?"

"Not yet, maybe later." Corban sped away.

Mr. Deet sniffed. "You should have ordered them to go home. I would have!"

"I'm not sure anyone would follow my orders today."

"I did."

Corban chuckled. "I suppose you did."

He swung down a dead-end street and stopped at the final house, a quaint 2-story house with red siding. He got out, leaving the Jeep running. He leaned back in.

"Mr. Deet, stay in this car. Do not let that dog out. I don't care if she pukes or needs to pee. I'll be back in a minute."

"Getting your dog, aren't you," Mr. Deet said with a smile and a nod. "You're a good man."

Corban ran for the house and up the six steps to the door. He reached behind a lantern hung on a peg by the door and found the spare key. He opened the door and stepped into a living room with empty book cases, walls with photo hooks but no photos, and a stack of pizza boxes on the coffee table. For a moment he looked about, waiting. When nothing happened, he whistled.

The dog was big; a full grown Great Dane. It appeared in the door to the kitchen with clatter of nails on hard wood and woofed as if asking a question.

"You're a terrible watchdog. Come on, King!"

At the sound of Corban's voice, the dog bounded two steps and jumped up, placing its thick paws on Corban's shoulders. It looked down at him and licked his forehead.

"You're so gross," Corban said, doing nothing to stop the bath. He roughed up the animal's ears. After another couple of moist licks, he moved the dog back to a standing position. "Okay, get off. We're going for a ride. You want to go for ride!"

King did a whole-body shiver and barked loudly.

"I need your food."

Corban went into the kitchen. He grabbed a plastic bag from a wall-mounted container, snapped it once to make it open, and moved toward the fridge. He stared inside at the dark interior, feeling the last bit of cool drift from within. Pushing aside a leftover container and a jar of olives, he pulled out the lone beer that had fallen sideways against the back.

The beer had a sticky line of some escaped and partially dried liquid down its length. Corban pulled the tab and sighed at the sound of hissing air. He drank slowly, eyes closed, downing half the beer before drawing a breath.

As he was licking his lips, a low growl came from behind him. He turned his head and saw King stiff-legged and arch-backed. He was staring at the large window that looked into the backyard. The growl came again, low and serious. The hairs rose up on Corban's arms. He slowly sat the beer on the table. He came around the table and looked outside with his dog.

The yard was small and neatly trimmed. A patch of black dirt for a garden was showing tiny green weeds. Stepping stones were arranged about the garden. A seven-foot tall privacy fence shut out the neighbors and the alley. The fence was not tall enough, however, to block the hump of something gliding down the ally, as slow and sure as a fin through bloodied water. Through the gaps between the boards he glimpsed the shape he had seen in the corn, a four-legged beast the size of a full-sized van.

King barked once, loud enough to make Corban jump as if prodded with a needle in the ass. He spun about and grabbed the dog's head. He looked back through the window. The hump had stopped gliding. A reply growl issued from behind the fence so deep Corban felt it in his gut.

Corban wrapped his hand through King's collar. He could feel King quivering beneath his hands. The dog was starting to strain against his grip, wide eyes locked on the unmoving hump of the monster.

"Easy, King," Corban whispered. "Just leave it alone."

The monster leaned against the privacy fence and the sound of splintering boards pierced the kitchen. King instantly tore free, jerking Corban off his feet. King planted his front feet on the window and let go a rapid-fire barrage of challenging barks.

"Stupid dog!"

Corban seized King and bolted for the front door, half dragging the startled Great Dane along. Something in the alley roared amid more breaking of boards, and King was suddenly dragging Corban out the door. They reached the Jeep and Corban yanked open the door. As King leaped onto the passenger seat, Tucker let out a yap, the small Dachshund eager to defend Mr. Deet from anything and everything. King ignored the old dog and sat rigid in the seat, looking back at the house with the front door still open.

"What was that sound?" Mr. Deet asked as Corban got in.

"The monster!" He slammed the Jeep into gear and stomped the pedal. He fishtailed into a neighbor's lawn and blasted through a flowerbed before hitting the street properly. He was quickly doing 60 down the residential street, abandoned cars and green yards flashing by.

"That's a big one," Mr. Deet said. "Not as big as last year, of course. Glad we don't have that one. But don't slow down to gawk."

Corban looked into the rear-view mirror and only saw a wall of gray. King had swiveled his wide head to also watch the monster and was blocking Corban's view. Corban looked at the side view mirror, but it was set for Titus and all it showed him was sky. He reached to adjust the mirror and the Jeep rocked to the left amid the shriek of grinding metal.

"You hit that car," Mr. Deet said.

"I know!"

Corban fixed both hands on the wheel and concentrated on going straight. After tearing through several blocks of residential homes the buildings became businesses. The courthouse came into view up ahead.

"Is it behind us?" Corban asked.

"No. It turned a while back. I think – I think it saw someone. I think it was Howard Kane in his yard. He was watering the grass."

"God damn it," Corban said. "Did it get him?"

After a slight pause, Mr. Deet said, "Yes. It was right on top of him when we hit that car and I lost sight of them both after we crossed Dun Street."

"That idiot. Watering his lawn during the Red Diamond. What the hell is wrong with everyone? You people watch the show and you don't understand how this works?"

They entered the town square. More cars had arrived since Corban had gone to save Mr. Deet. Someone had started a bonfire. Men and women with guns milled about. A pack of leather vest wearing bikers had claimed a spot off to the side and were being given plenty of room. An ambulance was parked near the front, the back doors left open and the inside ransacked. The flatbed truck was gone and the front doors of the courthouse were wide open.

"Are you kidding me?" Corban shouted. He locked up the brakes and slid to a stop in the street. He jumped out and ran toward the milling crowd. "Get inside! Now! Go find a place to hide!"

A young woman at the bonfire said, "They are hunting it north of town in the corn, Sheriff. It'll be over in an hour."

"They made a stupid one this year," a man standing next to her said.

"It's not in the corn! It's right behind me!"

"We heard it on the radio," she said.

"The CB," the man corrected her.

Corban pulled his revolver and fired into the air. Now all eyes were on him.

"I just saw it and it's following me and if you don't want to become a red stain on this lawn you better get inside that God damn courthouse!"

Mr. Deet managed to extricate himself and Tucker from the Jeep. He wobbled a few steps before gaining his stride. "I would listen. It just ate Howard Kane not seven blocks back." He made a beeline for the front doors of the courthouse, Tucker panting in his arms. Half the people immediately followed. The others started looking among their group for someone to take the lead.

"Idiots," Corban muttered.

He went to the Jeep and helped King down. With his hand tight around King's collar, he started walking the dog to the courthouse. The bikers were waiting for him at the steps. A bald man with a long, red mustache held up his hands in a peace gesture.

"Hey, we didn't come to town looking for trouble."

"You won't find it with me."

"We just came here to buy some meth from Billy or somebody who knows Billy and that's all."

"I don't care," Corban said. He looked over his shoulder at the street he had just driven down. The sun was starting to slide behind the distant hills. Without any electricity, the normally cheerful streets bathed in yellow-white at dusk were becoming ominously dark, the shadows as solid as stone.

"You have a problem with us leaving the bikes on the grass like that? I don't want them messed with and I don't want no tickets. I know how small towns can be."

"The monster doesn't eat motorcycles."

The man blinked in surprise. "Yeah. Yeah, that's true."

The lone woman of the gang spoke up. "You got room in the inn for us, too?"

"Go on in."

"There's been some white-haired dude, looks like some asshole, likes to be giving orders. I don't think he likes us here. He said we needed to wait out here. He's in charge?"

"No one is in charge."

"That's cool," she said. "I like your dog."

"So do I."

As they all started up the steps, she peeled back her left sleeve and showed him a tattoo of the Japanese flag, the red ball and red stripes faded with time. He looked her in the eyes.

"I'm not Japanese."

As her smile faded into a red blush, the other bikers burst out laughing, calling rude names and giving Corban many compliments on his take down of their member. She yanked her sleeve down and gave each of them the finger.

They had to walk through a shower of sparks to get inside. Two men with welding gear were adding metal bars to the frames around the front door and glass windows.

"That ain't going to hold," a biker said. "I used to weld for a living out in California and I know that's pretty worthless."

"Jump in and help," Corban told him, but the biker shrugged.

The open lobby was piled with assorted supplies and equipment. Mixed in with the logical selections of food, water, tools, and camping gear were the inexplicable: a banjo, a floor lamp, a stereo, a steamer trunk, a crib. There were no people in the foyer, and just as Corban was opening his mouth, a man in a Masterson Construction windbreaker appeared from a hallway.

"You people need to find a place to be," he said with the flat tone of something he had repeated many times. "No one in the lobby."

"You got power?" a biker asked as he pointed to the globes on the wall that were obviously on.

"Yes, we have generators on the roof. Courtesy of Mr. Masterson. Leave any supplies you have here and they will be counted and distributed."

"What?"

"Otherwise, please find a room to wait in and someone will be around after we seal up the doors for the night."

The biker leader looked at Corban. "Is this guy for real?"

"My name is Henry Goslein and I'm for real in charge of getting refugees put where they can be safe. We have to be organized, so please do as I say."

The front door flung open and people came rushing in.

"Something's out there!" the man from the bonfire shouted at Corban.

"Oh my God, my Dad said they had it in the corn," the young woman said. "I'm so pissed!"

Corban grabbed the young man by the arm and squeezed his fingers into the soft bicep until his eyes were locked on

Corban. "Take my dog. He's sweet and harmless and you're going to take him to Mr. Deet."

"Ow. Okay, yes, let go."

"King, go with this idiot."

The dog tilted its head in a lack of understanding.

"Hey," the young man protested.

Corban took the man's hand and put it on King's collar. He walked outside into the settling night. There were six people at the foot of the steps. Four were the lookouts that had been at the four corners of the courthouse lawn, now collected in one place. Titus and Adam were with them. Adam had blood stains on his jeans and hem of his shirt. His hands were still wet from scrubbing.

"Captain, you'll want to see this," Titus said. He paused and shook his head. "Sorry, Sheriff. Didn't mean to call you - "

"I know. Where is it?"

Titus pointed down the street Corban had arrived down minutes ago. "Heard a big noise, like a car wreck without the brakes. Glass and steel."

Corban pulled his gun. He eyed the weapons the lookouts had. All carried large caliber hunting rifles with scopes. "It's getting dark. You won't be able to hit anything vital in the dark."

One of the lookouts patted his rifle with affection. "You don't hunt much, do you? I don't need to hit vitals. I'll leave a hole the size of a bowling ball and it'll bleed out in a few minutes."

"They've thought of that," Adam said. "I'm guessing if it has vital organs, they are encased in bone or even steel."

"Steel?" the lookout said. "What do you mean steel?"

"They've been using mechanical augmentation since 1989."

"Well, shit, I'll just blow off a damn leg and it'll bleed to death."

"They don't bleed."

The man smiled at Adam around a toothpick in his teeth. "Like hell, son. Everything bleeds."

"Not if your blood is filled with coagulants that can clog a fire hose in three seconds. Not if your circulatory system is designed to prevent serious blood loss by rerouting or even running backwards. I'm sorry this makes you angry. I didn't build it. I don't want to die here tonight but you have no chance with that gun and that mindset. If you blow off a limb, it most likely will run off to regenerate."

"Like some kind of lizard," another lookout said. "I've seen that episode where it grew a new spine or something."

"That's not what happened," Adam said. "That was 2009 and it didn't even have a spine. It used imbedded fiber optic cord made from spider web and liquid glass to conduct nerve impulses. That's why it was hurt so badly with the electric charge from the super-sized taser they built."

"Fuck me," someone muttered.

"What kind of thing is this one?" asked the lookout with the toothpick.

"I don't know. It's got a lot of physical strength. It tore apart several cars at the north road out of town. It shredded them to get at the people hiding inside."

"Killed them?" a man asked. "Who was it?"

"We didn't see bodies," Corban said.

"It ate them," Adam said, then frowned. "I don't want to be rude, but what part of 'monster' aren't you understanding?"

"All of it," Corban said. "You men get inside. We can't kill it tonight."

"Hold on a minute, Sheriff," the toothpick chewer said. "My name is Lou Gilespi. I think we ought to have a crack at this thing. I don't care what this guy says about - "

"Do what you want," Corban said. "Masterson is sealing the building soon. I don't have time to argue."

Another loud crash came from the now heavily shadowed street. The crash faded to a rattle that grew closer. From the shadows of the street, a car appeared, rolling slowly toward them, the trunk caved in by some terrible blow. They watched in a fascination as it drifted to the left and finally bumped into a mailbox.

Lou swallowed with a gulp. "That's—"

"There it is," Adam said.

Something big moved in the street draped in shadows, a form that seemed to birth from the dark itself. Slowly, almost gently, it crossed a line of shadow and emerged into the twilight.

"Mother of God," Titus whispered.

"No way," one lookout said and bolted for the courthouse.

No one else moved.

What glided out toward them was a massive yet narrow head, bisected by a bony crest that ran from the chin to the crown. As the monster turned to look down the street, they saw the crest was jutting forward and ended in a wedge like a vertical hatchet five feet high. Four powerful legs moved with uncanny precision, each ending in a wide paw that was tipped with a single hooked claw. A short tail with a flat end jutted straight behind it for balance.

"That must be a tiger bone structure," Adam said in hushed reverence.

"Shoot it," Corban said. "Aim for the eyes. Blind the thing."

The monster had black and red stripes, but the stripes looked like they rippled slightly even as it stood still.

"It's got no eyes," Lou said.

Corban grabbed Adam's arm. "Where do we shoot it?"

"It doesn't have a weak spot like that."

"Yes, it does!"

"Why is it just standing there?" a lookout asked.

"It ain't afraid of us," Lou said. He put his rifle to his shoulder. "Let's make it afraid."

The other two raised rifles and almost on cue the roar of gunfire filled the air.

The monster charged before the slugs tore into it, going from a standstill to a sprint in a burst of power that left lines carved into the pavement.

"J-J-Jesus," a lookout panted. He dropped his rifle and turned to flee.

Corban held his pistol in both hands and began firing at the approaching engineered terror. He sensed Titus grab Adam and pull him toward the courthouse. Beside him, Lou was blasting away as fast as he could work the bolt on his rifle.

Corban realized he was pulling the trigger on an empty gun. The other lookout broke and ran up the steps.

"Let's go!" Corban yelled.

"Nope," Lou said and began walking to the left, away from the courthouse and into the parking lot. He was firing as he moved and the monster swerved to meet him.

Corban ran to the top stair and turned to watch.

The monster hit the line of parked cars and its wedge crest tossed them aside like a train through packed snow. Lou, standing in the middle of the parking lot, fired twice more, then it was on him. The true scale of it became horribly apparent when it dwarfed a full-grown man standing defiant. Lou swung the rifle in a gesture of hopeless anger. The bony crest hit him and threw him across the lot. His already lifeless body landed on the hood of Toyota and blood sprayed the windshield. A moment later the monster plowed into the Toyota and ground Lou into two pieces. It shoved with its thick legs and the Toyota was moved along with a screech of tires. It gathered speed and kept going in a display of rage and power, twisting its wedge into the already desecrated corpse, peeling apart the hood. The Toyota was driven across the street, up onto the sidewalk, and through the plate glass front of the laundry.

Above Corban, gunfire rang out. He looked up. From open windows and the roof people were laying down a hail of bullets. He looked back at the monster still engaged in slamming the Toyota into wreckage. Corban could see the results of the barrage as the surrounding walls developed holes and the remaining glass shattered. Bullets that struck their intended target left small dots of jelly-like blood. The monster remained undisturbed.

"Get in, Captain!" Titus was at the front door, beckoning wildly.

Corban ran his eyes along the front doors of the courthouse. They were basic double glass doors, with two side panels of tall glass, and a larger glass panel above. Maybe an inch of some kind of bright metal between the panes was the only real support. The welders had managed to put up a few steel bars, but it looked far from done. He looked at the monster across the street, ramming the car deep into the interior of the laundry.

"That won't hold," Corban shouted. He jumped down from the stairs.

"What are you doing?" Titus yelled.

Corban first went along the wall until he had put the ambulance between himself and the monster. He rushed to the open back doors and leaped inside. Stepping over the discarded boxes and bins, he made his way to the driver's seat. His hand felt the cold metal of the key still in the ignition and he let out a breath of relief. He turned the key and the engine came to life. He put the ambulance in reverse and immediately the warning beep of a backing up vehicle pierced the air.

The shooting came to a halt as everyone looked down at the ambulance in surprise.

The monster withdrew its bone crest from the blood-smeared ruin of the Toyota that had now been shoved through the stands of washing machines and dryers and was against the back wall. It turned its head toward the sound. The bone crest was aimed right at Corban as the shrill backup alarm screamed on.

"Shit," Corban muttered. He slipped the ambulance into drive and the beeping stopped. He looked back over his shoulder through the open doors of the ambulance. He could see the steps of the courthouse, the slightly reinforced glass doors, and Titus standing half outside chewing nervously on his pipe. When Corban turned around the monster was half way across the street going at a dead run toward him.

He pressed down on the accelerator and the big engine jerked the ambulance forward. For a moment, the two were on a collision course, monster and machine. Corban twisted the wheel to the right just before he was about to leave the grass, putting a line of parked cars between himself and the monster. The monster mirrored his move and ran parallel to his route.

It pulled ahead and swung its bone wedge against a two-door economy car. The vehicle was thrown into the ambulance's path. Corban's tried to veer away, but the lawn was covered in haphazardly parked cars and trucks. The ambulance clipped the tossed car and fishtailed to a stop.

The monster went on a few giant strides, then leaped over a car to get onto the lawn. Corban had to watch in morbid fascination as the monster displayed an Olympic grace in the move. It pivoted quickly on the lawn, its long talons tearing up gouges in the grass.

Corban put the ambulance in reverse. The loud beeping started up again. Looking through the wide open back doors, he went back the way he had come. He felt a jolt and heard bending metal from the front of the ambulance, but he didn't look at what was happening. He felt the ambulance speed up as it was pushed along by a bigger force.

He spied the sidewalk that led to the courthouse front doors. He twisted the wheel and turned his head forward. For a single heartbeat, he was staring at the bone crest, its jagged edge, the smears of fresh blood and clumps of caked old blood. Then the front wheels angled the ambulance in a tight turn. The vehicle lurched sideways with the combined power of the sudden turn and the force of the monster's attack. With a howl from the tires it turned ninety degrees and was backing down the concrete sidewalk while the monster was moving to Corban's left as it kept mindlessly shoving in a straight line. The front of the ambulance had a cleft in the hood and puffs of smoke were coiling around the torn metal.

Corban stared ahead at the sidewalk, carefully adjusting the racing ambulance to be as centered as possible. He let out a long breath. His arms locked on the wheel, bracing himself into the padded seat. The impact rattled the air from him and blurred his vision. The ambulance shook wildly as it went up the courthouse steps backwards. It destroyed the glass doors and lodged neatly in the opening. The engine rattled a last gasp and stalled. The piercing beep ceased.

Corban was out of the seat and moving. He stumbled and had to crawl toward the voices calling him. He made his way unsteadily on the slippery flooring, grabbing the cabinet doors on the sides to make headway. He paused to take a breath and shake his head. The ambulance was tilted ass up, the back doors now open to the lobby. A small crowd of people were just within the lobby, shouting and gesturing.

"It's coming for you!" Titus yelled.

Corban surged up and leaped the last step, landing and almost falling onto the glass-strewn floor. Titus had his arms about Corban's chest and helped him deeper into the lobby.

"Where's King?" Corban asked.

"What? The king? What are talking about?"

Corban waved the topic away. He turned to survey his work. The ambulance had bounced up the steps backwards and rammed its way into the courthouse lobby. The doors and glass panels had been obliterated and lay scattered into every corner. The gathered people were staring at him in shock.

The ambulance shook suddenly, rattling against the stones on either side. A great smashing and tearing sound filled the lobby. The monster roared from the front of the ambulance as it savaged the engine. People screamed and ran, but not all of them. Four men formed a quick line and started firing rifles and shotgun. There was no missing at this range as the monster's head had breached the dashboard and it was either trying to crawl through the ambulance or burst it to fragments to get to the food just beyond.

One after another the guns fell silent as all ran dry of ammo. The monster pushed and the ambulance broke several more feet into the lobby.

"It won't die," a man whispered as his eyes filled with fearful tears.

"G-Get more guns," a man said and rubbed sweat from his bald head. Someone else ran from the room.

Corban drew his pistol. He ejected the spent clip to clatter at his feet. He pulled a fresh clip from his belt and slapped it home. With a quick three steps, he jumped into the back of the shaking ambulance.

This time he was close enough to touch the bone wedge if he wanted to. He could smell the hot, meaty breath of the monster filling the ambulance. Aiming around the slamming bone crest, he fired all the rounds in the gun at the spot where eyes should have been. He saw flesh burst and blood fleck the white and blue interior of the ambulance. As the pistol went empty and the slide stayed back and smoking, the monster wrenched away, leaving a jagged hole Corban could have walked through. He could barely see the injury he had given the monster.

It turned and loped away from the courthouse. The firing from the windows and roof returned, having the same disappointing result. With a casual disdain, the monster went across the street and simply walked through the store front of Ocean Insurance as if the wood and glass where tissue paper. It disappeared inside the building.

The gunfire trickled off.

Corban made his way back into the lobby.

"Where is it?" Titus asked.

"Ocean Insurance. Can't see it now."

The bald shooter asked, "Is it...dead?"

"No. Not even close."

"You maniac!" The piercing voice of Clark Masterson came from the hallway and the man himself stomped into view brimming with fury. Goslein followed at his heels. "You drove the ambulance through our doors!"

"I had to keep it away," Corban said evenly. He looked down at the shattered glass and empty bullet casings under his feet. "It was coming for you."

"We had it where we wanted it before you fucked things up again. We could have killed it."

"Not with these guns. It doesn't care if we shoot it."

"That's bullshit," Masterson blurted out. "We hit it maybe a hundred times. It was bleeding!"

"Not that it noticed," Corban said. "Look, someone needs to keep a close eye on Ocean Insurance. It can be at this door again in twenty seconds or less. Set a lookout now. Find ropes or chains or whatever and secure this ambulance to block the hole or next time it's coming in."

"A hole you made trying to escape from it," Masterson said. "This isn't your office or your town and you don't give orders."

Corban ran his hands through his damp hair, feeling the layer of grit already building on his scalp from all the destruction he had been close to.

"Then don't listen, Clark. I'm not giving you orders. I'm telling these people what they need to do to have a chance to survive until dawn." He shrugged. "Not that dawn is going to help much. Unless we get lucky and the damn thing is nocturnal. Does it even sleep? Where is Adam?"

"In the CB room with Alice," Titus said.

"I need some answers. Take me to him."

Masterson blocked the way. "You hold on a God damn minute."

"This thing between us can wait, Clark. We don't have the time for petty bullshit. I need to talk to Adam about what we've learned."

"I should have you thrown into the street."

The bald shooter whispered, "Asshole."

Masterson looked at the people watching the encounter.

"Hey, Clark," Titus said, "we just need to talk to Adam."

"Then I'm coming with you."

"Suit yourself," Corban said. "I'm not trying to keep secrets."

Masterson led them down the left hallway. Some doors were open, revealing offices and courtrooms that had been changed into the refuge of the hunted. Office furniture and computers were piled against the walls to make room for cots and bedrolls. Every room had at least one person, and most had whole families. One doorway framed a boy of about ten wearing pajamas and a football helmet.

"Sheriff," he said, "is it over?"

"Not yet," Corban said. Behind the boy was a six-year-old girl and a haggard, white-haired woman clutching a child's ABC book like a talisman. "But we're working on it."

"Cool," the boy said.

"Help with your sister."

"I will."

In the next room, a makeshift cafeteria was taking shape with folding tables and chairs. Three people were bent over camp stoves. Already the scent of warm food was floating into the hallway, making Corban's gut remind him it needed filling.

The last door was propped open by a bowling trophy. Inside was a war room. The big map from his office was tacked down onto a round table. Two desks were against the wall: one covered in papers and maps and pens, the other with CB gear.

"Thank God you got out alive," Alice said from the CB station.

Corban broke into laughter. "Is that your desk from the office? Did you have them bring your own desk over here?"

"I certainly did. I may as well be comfortable."

"Only you, Alice."

Adam gave him a brief wave from a chair in the corner. His other arm was wrapped around his messenger bag. Two more men stood in the room looking over the map.

"Jacob," Corban said to a young and intense looking man with Native American features. His black hair was wrapped into a coil down his back. Jacob gave him a nod but did not smile.

The other man was weathered and tanned and probably in is late 70s. He leaned on a cane as he studied the map.

"I don't know you," Corban said.

"My name is Mitchel DePaul." He ran his watery eyes up and down Corban. "You got a plan to get us out of this mess?"

"I think Clark is doing pretty good here. I don't plan on interfering."

DePaul's eyebrows rose. "Is that so?"

"It's a lie," Masterson said. "You don't spend much time in Pikeburn anymore, DePaul. You don't know what he's really like."

"I have my ear to the ground," the old man said. "Jacob here does more than manage my properties."

Corban tapped the map. "I'm assuming the blue lines are the walls."

"They are." The entire town and some of the surrounding country were embraced by a rough rectangle scratched into the map with a blue ball point pen. Near the center of the rectangle was a circle labeled 'courthouse'. Another circle to the south was labeled 'Gunner's'.

"We don't need you here," Masterson said. "Goslein, throw him out."

Goslein reached behind his jacket and produced a pistol, but he kept it pointed at the floor.

"That's not right," Titus said. "Stop right there."

"You can keep quiet, mercenary," DePaul snapped at Titus, a sudden and fierce anger in his eyes.

Titus slipped the pipe back in his mouth. "I forgot for a moment. No one else's war is as good as yours. I've seen my share of hell, old man. I've got my scars, too."

DePaul didn't reply, but kept up a steady glare at Titus, who did not flinch from the assault.

Masterson moved around the table and stood in front of Corban. "I made this happen and I'm in charge here. All this is my equipment. The mess hall, the generators, the gasoline to make them run. My men hauled them up there. My men stand on the walls. Hell, they were making this place unbreachable until YOU destroyed it trying to save your yellow skin." He looked at DePaul. "He drove the ambulance through the front doors. Ever hear of something that stupid?"

"It was going to come through those doors and be inside if I didn't plug the hole. You underestimated it. You still are, all of you. It's not trying to insult you, Clark, or steal your car or fuck your wife. It's trying to kill you for food."

"I've had it with you. Don't play tough with me. You're not strong enough to take me. I worked for a living. And I know you're out of bullets."

Corban reached out his left hand straight at shoulder height and snapped like a firecracker. Masterson looked over involuntarily at the movement and the sound. At the same time, even before Masterson looked away, Corban's right hand was reaching. He grabbed the prominent handle of Master's gun under his left arm. He wrenched it free and had it pressed against Masterson's chest before the startled man understood what had just happened.

"You've got plenty of bullets," Corban said softly.

Jacob snatched up a revolver from the table and aimed it at Corban, "Drop that!"

Goslein had produced a pistol from the inside of his Masterson Construction jacket. It was pointed at Titus, who was chewing on his pipe but otherwise not showing any emotion.

Masterson's face went from unbelieving shock to triumphant sneer.

"Jacob Longtree, I will cut you in half."

Every eye turned to Alice, the frumpy woman with the reading glasses on the end of her nose. She was holding the police issue pump shotgun leveled at Jacob. She was the picture of calm resolve and her finger was on the trigger.

"Grammy?" Jacob said in slow surprise.

"No," she said. "I've taught a lot of kids to read and none of them would dare point a gun at the Sheriff of this town. You call me Mrs. Ulton."

Jacob looked like he had been slapped. He lowered the gun and his head. "I'm sorry."

"Now you, Mr. Goslein," she said as she pivoted in her chair to aim the shotgun at his gut.

He carefully put the gun back inside the jacket.

"Get his gun," she said.

"I don't want his gun," Corban said. "The only gun I'm taking is this one." He shoved the gun harder against

Masterson until the man was forced to take a reluctant step back.

"You don't have the balls to shoot me," Masterson said.

"I don't want to shoot you. I'm going to let you keep doing what you need to do. Clark, you've got this place running better than I thought anyone could, including myself. But you're letting me get in the way. I'll be leaving in the morning as long as we have an understanding."

"A what?" Titus said. "You're leaving?"

"I'll go with you," Adam said and stood up.

Corban shook his head. "Don't get excited. It's too dark to be running around out there. I'm waiting for morning. Can you stomach that, Clark?"

Masterson nodded, his face turning redder by the second. "Give me my gun."

"Not just yet. Like you pointed out, I'm out of bullets, and you might be mad enough to do something stupid."

"And you might be a psychopath," Titus said to him.

Corban lowered the gun. He stepped back. "You took a bunch of equipment from my office. I want the guns and ammo and radios. You give me that and a night's rest, you'll get rid of me in the morning."

"You don't want to make any hasty calls, Sheriff," DePaul said. "You were just in a fight. We all were. Now take it down a notch before we get someone killed. That means you too, Masterson. Last thing we want is a shootout."

"We need to have a meeting," Corban said.

DePaul shook his head with emphasis. "Don't do that. You'll make hasty decisions when we need cooler heads to prevail. Go to the armory and get your gear back. Take some food. Get a coffee for me while you're at it. I'm serious about this, Sheriff. You and Masterson don't have to start clawing at each other just because that beast is out of sight for a minute. We won't tolerate that, will we, Alice?"

"No, we won't." She put the shotgun back beside the desk and turned to the CB radio set up. "I have a job to do and I don't need to be throwing cold water on any more dog fights."

Corban pressed the palm of his hand to his forehead. After a moment, he placed Masterson's gun on the map. "Fine. Where is the armory?" he asked.

Goslein cleared his throat. "Second floor, office 2E."

"Fuck you people," Masterson said. He stormed from the room.

"Let him go," DePaul said. "The man needs some room."

Corban went to look down the hallway. "I wasn't going to stop him. I just want him to get away from the stairs." Masterson turned into one of the offices close to the lobby and slammed the door. "Okay, DePaul, I'll be back in an hour."

When Corban reached the lobby and started up the main stairs, he saw a pack of men working to solidify the ambulance into the wrecked entrance. Some of them stopped and watched him climb the stairs with blank faces.

There was a guard at door of 2E, a burly construction worker with a shotgun and a stool. He stood up quickly when he saw Corban coming. Most of the doors off the hallway were closed, but Corban heard voices from behind them.

"H-Hey, Sheriff. I saw you driving that rig. That was some sick shit."

"Thanks. I need inside."

"Oh. Um, I'm not allowed to let anyone in here. Mr. Masterson was real clear."

"Does the monster want the ammo, Danny?"

"Um, no. I saw it from the window. It doesn't need any ammo. It's really fast for a big thing, ain't it?"

Corban nodded. "Okay, move aside. I don't want to argue."

Danny gave him an embarrassed smile. "Sure thing, Sheriff."

Inside there were three desks with a small assortment of ammo boxes, a crossbow, several backpacks, and a stack of first aid kits.

Corban looked at Danny. "Is that it?"

"Yep. Not much of an armory, really. We already passed out all the guns we could find. We sent a truck to get more from Gunner's but they didn't come back. I figure they were eaten or stayed with the guys locked in Gunner's."

Corban dug around in the backpacks and found one with gear from his office. He dumped out the contents and reloaded the backpack. He ended up with a few ammo boxes and spare clips for his 9mm and the AR-15, road flares, two first aid kits, a box cutter, a roll of duct tape, and two walkie talkies.

"Need a machete?" Danny asked.

"No." Corban stood up and slung the backpack. "Maybe. How big is it?"

Danny held up a basic machete with a rust-pitted blade. "It's mine but you can take it."

Corban frowned at the offer. "I'll end up needing a tetanus shot just from looking at it. Keep it in case you need it."

"Okay. But after seeing that thing kill Lou, I don't think I want it, either. Kind of dumb."

"Do you know if there are any dogs on this level?"

Danny tilted his head, unwittingly looking very dog like. "You know, I heard barking from the third story and thought I was crazy! Did they bring dogs here?"

"I brought mine."

"I bet you have a German Shepard."

"Great Dane."

"Well, I was close."

Corban slapped Danny on the arm. "Take care of this place. I'm leaving in the morning."

"Going hunting, huh?"

"No."

The smell of dog urine lingered in the third-floor hallway. Here the faint sound of the generator on the roof was a constant buzz. Corban started down the right side, opening doors and peeking in rooms. The first one had a man with a rifle at a shattered window, and he gave Corban a nod before returning to his vigil. The second room was empty, but the window was wide open. The third one had a person sprawled on their face.

Corban rushed inside. When his hand touched the person's shoulder he let out a sigh at the unmoving, cold flesh. He slowly rolled the man over.

"Who is it?" someone asked from the doorway. Corban looked over and saw James.

"Mr. Deet. Looks like his heart or something. I just brought him in here half an hour ago."

"Oh damn. He taught chemistry at the high school. Why is he in here?"

"No idea. Shit. We can't leave him like this. James, can you find a sheet or blanket or anything? Cover him up. We'll need a morgue."

"I can deal with it. Sorry I didn't get the people to come inside. They didn't think I was serious. Someone pointed a gun at me and told me to get lost."

"You did your job, which is more than some are doing right now. Do you know where the dogs are?"

"Sure. I was just playing with them. Some of the kids from the high school are taking care of them. Want me to take you there?"

"Are they fed and watered?"

"Yes."

Corban put his hand on Mr. Deet's chest. It felt solid, like he had turned to stone in death. "No. I need to get on with this." He stood up. "Thanks, James. I'm going downstairs. You want to come?"

"Let me cover him up."

James found a suit jacket in the closet and gently covered Mr. Deet's face. For a moment, the two stood over the body and said nothing.

"I'll be going out into Pikeburn in the morning. I want you to stay in the courthouse," Corban said.

"Not going to happen."

"I need people here to watch things."

"And don't throw my son in my face to try to keep me here. I can't do a thing here. This is where people come to die for nothing."

Corban could only nod.

He looked at the body under the suit jacket. "I'll take care of Tucker for you," he said to Mr. Deet. Then he left the room and went downstairs.

CHAPTER THREE

In the war room many chairs had been brought in around the map. Alice stayed at her desk to monitor airwaves. Around the table were Corban, James, Adam, Titus, Jacob, DePaul, Goslein, and Masterson.

"Have we seen the monster move yet?" Corban asked as they all took seats.

"No," Masterson said tersely.

DePaul gave him a stern look.

Masterson grimaced a moment before saying, "Lookouts have reported no movement and no way of even knowing it's still in there. It might have plowed through the back of the store and be anywhere now."

"That's what I'm guessing it did," Corban said. "Before we go any farther, we need to share the info we have. Here's what I know. I'm alone in this. Every deputy took off. I have a job to do and I'm going to do it. I know some of you have volunteered to help me and that's greatly appreciated."

"What's your job then?" Masterson asked.

"The way I see it, there are three things you can do in a Red Diamond: run, hide, or fight. Running is over. If you didn't get out before the walls came up, you can't run. Unless it's in circles. I think the majority of people are hiding. That's what this place is for."

"It's for survival."

"Easy, Clark," DePaul said. "The man didn't insult you or anyone. Now hear him out."

Corban took a sip of bitter coffee and made a face. "Okay, when I said hide I didn't mean that in a bad way."

Jacob said, "The third way is hunting."

"Exactly." Corban put his finger on the circle marked 'Gunner's'. "Gunner's Hunting Supply. I know who is there. Billy and his outfit."

"We have them on CB if you need to chat with him," Alice said.

"I don't. Not yet. Billy and a bunch of hunters, armed to the teeth from Gunner's, ready to fight a war. I have nothing to add to that. Have they encountered it yet, Alice?"

"Not that I know of," she said. "Billy says they ran to the hospital but it was cleared out already. I guess the hospital staff had a planning meeting not two weeks ago for emergencies and Red Diamond was one of them. All patients and staff loaded up and gone."

"Except Ben Hooper," Corban said. "That's his ambulance, isn't it? He leaves the keys in it all the time. I've told him someone will steal it someday. Didn't expect it to be me."

"You knew the keys were in it!" Titus said with a grin. "And here I thought you just got lucky. That's crafty, Captain."

"Is Ben here?" Corban asked Masterson.

Masterson pretended he was thinking. "I do believe he is."

"Is that woman I brought in his patient?"

"Yes," Titus said. "He's got a small field hospital set up in office 1G. She's...not well. She's got bad injuries." He had to look away. "No fingers."

"Is she awake? Can I ask her some questions?"

"Not really. Ben didn't seem too optimistic about her chances."

Corban shook his head. "Okay. She's getting the best help we've got."

"So, what is your job?" Masterson said. "Spit it out, Yan."

"Run, hide, or fight." Corban looked at them and no one disagreed. "I think there's another option. I was elected to protect the people of Pikeburn. I'm going to go out into town at dawn and do just that. I may bring people back here. I may bring supplies to people stranded. I may end up running messages. I'm not going to hunt that thing because I don't think I can kill it. But if I see a good opportunity, I'll give it hell, maybe get lucky."

"Stupid little man," Masterson whispered.

DePaul banged his cane on the floor. "One more God damn comment from you and I'll have you gagged! Cut the shit! The man has the right to fight this his way!"

"You can't tell me— "

DePaul said, "Shut your mouth." Not loud but very serious.

Masterson grew quiet, his lips in pale little lines.

Corban spread his hands. "That's all I know. I'll be gone in the morning. I'm leaving a walkie talkie with Alice. If you need me, you can call. You'll want to secure that main door even more than it is. Park a tow truck in front of the ambulance or something. There are three other doors into this building but they are all too small. That's one way in for it. Block that good and you should be safe enough. Just leave a side door unlocked for me if I need back in. I may be running."

Masterson had to fight to stay quiet but he succeeded.

"Well," DePaul said, "thanks to Clark we have power and food and water. His men brought in Ben Hooper. They ransacked the local stores for camping gear. We can last here a long time."

"It's good work," Corban said.

Masterson scratched at his chin with his middle finger.

Corban turned to look at Adam. "I want to hear from you."

"Oh? About what part?"

"The monster. You know more than any of us. You've seen it now, just like you wanted to. What do you think?"

Adam stared at him for a moment. "I think it's magnificent."

"You little shithead," Masterson said. Others in the room gave him distasteful and offended looks.

"I'm sorry you don't like my opinion," Adam said. "It is magnificent. It's better than I even imagined. I've never been more frightened or certain I'll die. You can't stop it."

"Holy shit," DePaul said. "What in the hell is wrong with you?"

"He's nuts," Jacob said and slid his chair away from Adam.

"I'm not in love with it," Adam said. "I want to kill it. I'll do whatever I can. But, well, let's be honest. I saw your men hit it more than once, more than twenty times, and it didn't care."

"Stop," Corban said. "I need facts, Adam. Tell us what you saw. Tell us what this thing is made of."

Adam frowned in thought. "It's like a cross between a big cat and a rhino, only bigger than both. It charges, but it has a feline grace. The bone wedge it has can tear apart steel, we all saw that."

"Is it nocturnal?" Corban asked. "What's the opposite of nocturnal?"

"Diurnal. I can't tell what it is. It's probably never seen the sun or the night sky. It may not need to sleep. Anything is a guess."

"What else? What can you tell about behavior?"

"It sets traps," Adam said.

Titus nodded vigorously.

"It uses people as bait. It knows how to stalk. It knows how to use terror. It's also not afraid to use brute force."

"It doesn't have eyes," Titus said.

Corban held up his hand. "Hold on. It doesn't have eyes. What does that mean to us? Is it blind?"

"It could have eyes in a protected and shielded spot," Adam said. "It's probably not blind like you are thinking. It might be able to see in ways you and I can't. Infrared or electromagnetic."

"But I just remembered something, Adam. My point is it reacted violently when I was backing the ambulance up. It was homing in on the damn beeping." He glanced around the table. "It went nuts trying to get to that sound. If we can get it to chase that sound, we can draw it anywhere we want to."

For the first time, everyone was paying close attention.

"It can't be that easy," DePaul said, but he was nodding.

"It wasn't easy the first time," Corban said with a grin. "It's an advantage and we need one of those."

"Did you see the stripes?" Adam asked him.

"Yes. Black and red. And they could sort of move. How did that work?"

"They can't move. They flip over. It has a form of scale as protection and camouflage. It can flip the scales, sort of like a deck of cards laid out overlapping. Ever see that trick? The gambler turns the first card and all the others turn over, too. That's what it has. The black and dark red is for night. It probably has something brown or green for the day. I'm trying to say don't expect it to be easy to find even though it's really big."

"Noted," Corban said. "It can camouflage itself. Anything else?"

"I think..." Adam pulled out his notebook and looked at some pages. "Whoever trained it was very good. This one, that monster out there, is a lot smarter than it looks. I would be very cautious around it. Don't make any assumptions. A true animal wouldn't have walked away from the ambulance like that. This one made its point and simply left."

"And how are we doing?" Titus asked.

"What do you mean?"

"The humans. Us. How are we doing? I think we're doing okay so far."

Adam looked perplexed. "I don't pay much attention to the humans. They don't seem very exciting to study. Humans do the same thing every red Diamond. And weren't we pointing guns at each other five minutes ago? An interestingly high percentage of people die during the Red Diamond from other people, even when they are all safe."

"Is it going to attack again?" DePaul asked.

"Of course, but I can't tell you when or how."

"We can't do anything about that tonight," Corban said. "If it does attack, we fight it off. Maybe we can get lucky and kill it this time. I have to tell you guys, I'm done. I can't think straight. It's been...a hell of a day. Tomorrow is going to be the same. Let's get some rest."

There was general murmur of agreement. Masterson left quickly with Goslein at his heels. Adam moved his chair into a corner and hugged his messenger bag and watched the others. DePaul and Jacob bent their heads close to hold a private conference. James studied his wide hands.

"I'm going with you," Titus said. "I'm getting old and slow, but I want to go. Plus, I'm a hell of a driver."

"If it homes in on sound, it'll chase a car. I'm going on foot."

"I can walk. Usually do. I've lived here a lot longer than you, too. I know the back alleys."

"I've been here my whole life," James said to his hands.

"Don't make this decision now. When the sun comes up, you can reconsider. Now get some food and some sleep." He put his hand on James's shoulder. "That's an order."

James looked at him and half smiled. "You got it."

At dawn, as the sun banished the shadows to start a brilliant, cloudless day, the east side door of the courthouse opened just long enough for Corban, Titus, Adam, and James to slip out. It closed with a faint click and Corban reached back to test the handle. It was locked. Titus shrugged at him.

Corban said, "I want you three to get over by that black truck at the corner. Get under it and wait for me."

Corban drew his pistol and offered it to Titus. As soon he started to refuse the pistol, Corban aimed his thumb at the red Jeep in the street on the south side of the courthouse. "My rifle is in that."

"Okay then," Titus said and took the weapon.

"You know how to use it?"

"You bet, Captain. Aim for the soft bits."

"It doesn't have any but good luck."

As Corban skulked his way through the dew on the grass, he kept his eyes on the caved in Ocean Insurance. He was almost at his Jeep when the hole in the back wall became visible. The interior was wrecked but empty.

Corban turned to the courthouse where faces looked out from the windows and the roof. He pointed at the hole and shook his head. Jacob waved his understanding from a second story window and disappeared. On the roof, the lookouts spread out to the four corners to expand their watch.

The AR-15 was still on the passenger's seat. Corban took a moment to slide in a fresh clip. He jogged to the black truck with the three waiting members of his band. He motioned for them to come out, and they did so without making a sound. He led them away from the square. They stayed close to the walls as they moved. Corban tested each business door until he found one left open. He held it open as they filed into a flower shop.

The inside was packed with the stinging scent of flowers rapidly turning into weeds. They made their way into a back office without any windows. The air was warm and unmoving.

"We won't stay long," Corban said. He keyed his walkie talkie. "Alice?"

"Right here, Sheriff," she said. "Just like old times."

"The good old days. Patch me through to Billy."

"Give me a minute."

Corban started opening desk drawers at the desk he was sitting at.

"What do you need?" James said. "Here's a pen and paper."

"I'm looking for anything useful. Another gun would help."

"I don't want one," Adam said.

In the bottom right drawer Corban spotted a slim bottle of clear alcohol. He put it in his backpack. James began poking around the office as well, looking in drawers, opening cabinets. Adam and Titus stood to the side.

A bit of static burst from the walkie talkie, and then a clear voice. "Sheriff?"

"Hello, Billy."

"Damn if I never thought hearing your voice would make me smile."

"Yeah? You get hit on the head?"

"Just feeling nostalgic, I guess. Glad to hear from anyone, you know?"

"How are things going with you and your group?"

"Oh, you know. Same shit, different day," Billy said and laughed.

"I'm on my way to see you."

"What the hell for?"

"It's my job."

After a slight pause, Billy came back on. "Did you see it?"

"Yes."

Titus snorted. "Up close and personal."

"Anyone get a clean shot into it?" Billy asked.

"More than one."

"Us too. Damn thing is big. It came running down Heart Street and we let it have it. I know I didn't miss. Some of these other guys swear they didn't, but who knows. It's too big for everyone to miss, I'm thinking."

"What happened?"

"Not a damn thing!" Billy cursed, then laughed. "I'm not sure what to do next. It didn't even care that we shot at it. We're in the shit now, huh?"

"I think we are."

"But seriously, Corban, don't come around here. I've got my piece of land and you've got yours. Why - "

Suddenly someone was shouting in the background on Billy's end. All that came through to Corban were the words "hurt bad" and then silence. He tried to raise Billy for five minutes and no one replied.

"I think he's gone," Alice said. "I'll keep trying but you don't need to waste that battery."

"Okay. Thanks, Alice."

After the walkie talkie was clipped back to Corban's belt, Titus asked, "Now what?"

"Same plan as before. We're going to Gunner's."

"Do you think they got attacked?" James asked.

"I aim to find out."

"How far to Gunner's?" Adam asked.

"It's not a big town. We're going nice and slow, though. Maybe thirty minutes."

It took over an hour before the four of them were peering around a corner at a stand-alone, gray brick building. A black and red sign reading "GUNNER'S" in a savage font was nailed above the door. The two sides of the store were filled with cars and trucks and a few motorcycles. The front parking lot was almost empty. A semi-circle of trucks enclosed the front of the store, each of them pointed outward. Three of the truck beds had men with rifles propped on the cab as lookouts.

"Smart enough," Corban said.

"It would only slow it down," Adam said. "It can even push the trucks back into the store."

"They haven't seen it in action. Give them a break."

A single car was in the front parking lot, both doors left wide open. On the driver's window was a smeary, red hand print.

Corban got on the walkie talkie again. "Alice, is Billy there yet?"

"No, Sheriff. No one at Gunner's is picking up."

"Tell them one more time. I'm coming in and not to shoot me."

"I'll do it, but no one may be listening. Good luck, Sheriff."

Corban looked at the others. "We're just going to walk on up. I'll have the rifle slung. No one shout or run or do anything stupid. I don't think they are jumpy enough to start shooting at people walking up in broad daylight."

"And if they are?" James asked.

"Find cover," Titus said.

Corban said, "That's about the truth."

Slowly, Corban stepped out and started walking. He was quickly spotted by a lookout and they all perked up. One shouted over his shoulder toward the interior of the store. Sure, they had all been noticed and no one was aiming a gun at them, Corban picked up the pace and jogged across the deserted street. He stopped ten feet from the front bumper of the truck in the middle of the lineup and looked up at Chambers in the bed.

"Hell of a thing," Chambers said. "You've got brass balls to be running around if you've seen it. Why not drive a damn car?"

"It's attracted to noise, we think. It doesn't have eyes."

Chambers raised his eyebrows. "Well, ain't that a surprise. Come on in. We don't bite."

They sidled between trucks and into the dark interior. Gunner's had two big windows up front covered by thick bars and nothing else for natural illumination. Lanterns were set up about the store enough to drive away most of the shadows. Corban quickly counted over twenty-five men and women in little clumps here and there. Some of the shelves had been cleaned out. A long rack of rifles and shotguns behind a glass counter still had a quarter of the slots full.

From the back of the store came the sounds of muffled screaming.

A woman with her hair tucked under a black beret approached them down the aisle.

"Sheriff Yan," she said with a smile. The smile faltered when he didn't reply immediately. She pulled off the beret to let her brown curls fall in place and once again smiled for him.

"Janet," he said.

"Oh, thank God. You had me scared for a minute."

"What are you doing in here?"

"I hunt. Or I used to. It's been a while. But I know how to shoot and I'm not sitting at home waiting to die."

"Who is screaming?" Titus asked.

She looked toward the back. "I really don't know. I think — I think the monster got some people and this guy is a survivor, but he's chewed up."

"Lost his hands?" Corban asked.

She looked back at him quickly. "How did you know that?"

"We've seen it before."

"It must be a trained behavior," Adam said. "That's amazing."

The muffled screaming softened, then cut out to silence.

"I've got to deal with this, Janet." Corban looked at Titus. "Go outside and tell Chambers to be ready for an attack. He's the guy we talked to. James, go with him. Adam, with me."

As Corban approached the back-office area where the screaming had issued, a pair of men with shotguns jumped up from a pair of chairs. Corban pointed at the guards and shook his head and did not slow his march for the back. They glanced at each other before sitting back down. Three closed doors to offices were in front of them and Corban hesitated.

Adam pointed to the one on the right. "Bloody handle."

Corban went in without knocking. The storage room had been turned into a makeshift ER. A motionless man lay on a cot. He was strapped down with rope. An IV bag was duct taped to the wall over his head, the clear tubing entering his arm at the elbow. His hands were abbreviated bandages of white and red. Blood was on everything.

Billy stood in the corner with his arms folded. A muscular man in a black T-shirt, stained jeans, and combat boots was sitting on a stool next to the injured man. He had a syringe between his fingers.

"That'll keep him quiet or kill him," the big man said. "Out of my hands either way."

Billy rolled his eyes at Corban. "God dammit, Yan. What do you want?"

"What happened?"

The medic stood up. He grabbed a biker's vest off a stack of boxes and slid it on with practiced ease. He looked Yan up and down, then chuckled.

"Bill, you got some mighty small law in this town."

"Bigger pain in the ass then you think," Billy said.

"This guy put your Dad away?" the biker asked with disbelief.

"No. The previous guy did."

"How about the history lesson waiting," Corban said. "We've seen this before. The missing hands. I picked up a woman north of town, in the corn, and she had the same injury."

"So?" the biker said. "You got something important to say?"

"Yes." Corban kept his eyes on Billy. "I brought her back to the courthouse and we were attacked not long after. I thought it was bad luck. I thought we got out of the trap back in the corn. Now I'm thinking the trap was never meant for the corn."

Billy's face was dubious. "It's that smart?"

"Smart isn't a good word," Adam said. "This behavior is trained into it."

The big biker laughed. "A fucking trained monster. I love it."

Corban turned his gaze to the laughing man. "What is your name?"

"Me? Hell, buddy, you can call me Grease."

"Grease, you came to town to sell meth to another biker club, and Billy is your go-between. Now you're stuck in this, like it or not. I don't care about your meth or your deal or your fake bravado. I need you to shut the fuck up right now because something you should be very afraid of is quite possibly coming through that wall at any second."

"We've got enough guns to kill a tank," Billy said.

"Too bad you don't have a tank," Adam said.

Grease wasn't laughing. His face had grown pink as he loomed over Corban, but the smaller man remained unmoved. "Whatever, lawman, you win." Grease muttered a few curses and turned half away from Corban as if dismissing the confrontation. He picked up a leather satchel that had matching stitch work to his jacket. His hand started to casually dip into it.

"You don't want to do that," Billy said. He unfolded his arms.

"Oh yeah?" Grease said.

"Yeah. Go out there and mingle with the others, Grease. I'm dealing with the Sheriff alone."

"Oh yeah? Didn't know you two were lovers."

"If you start some shit, I'm going to hog tie you in the street. Make you squeal even, just for kicks. Leave you there for that thing. You didn't see it, Grease. You don't know what I'm talking about yet. Unless you want to see it real soon, take a walk."

Grease opened his mouth slowly, then gave a deep laugh. He slung the satchel over his shoulder. "Fuck me! You boys around here are comic gold!" He shoved his way between Corban and Adam and kicked the door closed as he left.

Adam went to a stool and sat down. He pulled out his notebook and started scribbling.

Corban and Billy stared at each other for a minute. Billy finally threw up his hands. "Not even a God damn thank you. Typical, Yan."

"Don't pretend you did that for me."

"Whatever. I saved your life. You fucking owe me."

"That guy is the real deal, hardcore and lethal. He's not just making a simple meth deal, and you know it. He's looking for new territory for his club to invade. If you look soft today, you won't be here next month. That's why you jerked his chain. You had to prove your dominance of him and me."

Billy rolled his eyes again. "Alright, fuck off then. I won't help you next time."

Corban looked at the wreck of a man on the cot. "What did Grease give him?"

"I don't know. Grease is the only one we got with some kind of medical training. I didn't have time to check his license. He said he could keep the man quiet and it looks like he can. I hear your group has a paramedic."

"Not my group. That's Masterson's set up."

"What an asshole. Why did you let him take that over?"

"I'm too busy to fight with him. Now tell me what happened here."

Billy settled back against the wall and folded his arms again. "Dean went on patrol with some guys and never came back. I sent Stallis out to look for Dean and he came back with this guy. He was in his yard just turning in circles. Stallis never found Dean."

"It was watching," Corban said. "It knows where you are now."

"Bullshit." Billy ran his hand over his stubble for a moment. "Okay, maybe. So why isn't it attacking?"

"Timing," Adam said. "And it doesn't need to come get you yet. Are you sending out more patrols?"

"Yeah. Last one to Q&A Grocery. We need food and shit like that."

"They won't come back," Adam said. "You need to stop sending people out on patrols like this is a movie. Keep them here. I think you'll be safe here for now. There are plenty of other, softer prey out there. But wait a few weeks when it gets really hungry and people aren't easy to find. That's when it'll burst through the walls."

"I fucking hate this guy," Billy said to Corban.

The door opened and James stuck his head in. "Um, guys? Chambers says something is moving outside."

As they hustled through the store, Corban tapped Billy on the arm. He pointed to the row of weapons behind the counter. "My crew needs some firepower."

"What's in it for me?"

"Nothing," Corban said.

Billy looked like he was in pain. "God damn it, Yan, you just don't know how this works."

"No, I don't."

"Fine. Help yourself," Billy said. "But you owe me one."

A minute later Corban handed a scoped rifle to Titus who was standing behind one of the trucks. He took it without a word and began inspecting the weapon. Corban and Billy joined Chambers in the bed of the truck.

"Okay, check this out," Chambers said. He pointed down the street. "You know there's an alley over there, runs behind the pool hall?"

"Yes," Corban said.

"Well, you can't really see the alley from here. But you can see that big window where Ink Heart Tattoo used to be. If you look hard, it's like a mirror. You can sort of see down the alley over there. You can see...something. This helps." He handed a pair of binoculars to Corban.

Using the binoculars braced on the roof of the cab, Corban could see a quivering and distorted image in the dark glass of the closed tattoo parlor. The bony crest was all that he needed to recognize.

"Damn it," he muttered. He handed the binoculars to Billy. "It's there."

"I can't see a thing," Billy said. "What the hell am I looking for?"

"It's got a big bone hatchet on its head. Looks prehistoric, like a nightmare dinosaur or something. That wedge can tear cars apart and plow through walls. And people."

"I can't see shit." Billy thumped the binoculars down and turned away.

"We should go kill it," Chambers said. "We know where it is. We can surprise it."

"Very bad idea," Adam said. "I would assume it wants you to see it. It wants you to come for it."

"Let's trigger the trap," Billy said. "It's not faster than a car, right? Someone drive by and we hit it with some heavy artillery and drive off. Shit, we can use multiple cars and just keep doing drive-bys on its ass!"

Adam was shaking his head. "I think if you provoke it, it will attack this building. It knows it's victim, the guy with no hands, is here. It's clever, but it has a lot of rage."

Billy hopped off the truck and stood chest to chest with Adam. "So, what's your fucking bright idea? Huh? All you do is tell us how badass that fucking thing is. Telling us why we shouldn't even try. What are you doing here? Who the fuck are you?"

"I— I want— I don't mean to make you mad. I don't want to die here." Adam swiped at his eyes that were tearing up. "You have to try to understand. No one has ever killed one in the first three days. Why is that? Don't you think it has to be because the people who built it already know everything you might try for three days? Guns, fire, running it over with a truck, trapping it in a collapsed building, gassing it with a chemical."

Corban joined them on the ground and gently put his hand between the two of them. "We have a bigger problem, Billy. Let it go."

"Let him come up with a plan for once," Billy said loudly. "Come on, genius, what would you do?"

"Wait. Study it. Find the weakness. Then kill it."

"And how many of us get to die while you study that thing?" Billy asked. "All of us?"

Adam shrugged. "I don't know. I hope not."

"How about right now? Do something right now!"

"Okay," Adam said. He turned on his heel and marched into the hunting store. He went to the left and directly into a small selection of archery supplies. He picked up a compound bow. He stood like that, looking at Billy.

Billy pushed his camo ballcap back on his head with one finger. He looked at Corban.

"Is he joking?"

"I am not," Adam said.

"Why a bow?" Corban asked him.

"Because it's never been done before. You have all the guns, but no one has managed to kill the Red Diamond with a bullet for over fifteen years. You get so angry when I suggest your guns won't save you. If you don't change your thinking, you'll all be killed."

Angry muttering came from the gathered hunters.

"Okay, okay," Titus said while moving to shield Adam. "What has worked the most times?"

"The government hides this information for a reason. They can't be giving the other countries an easy way to stop our monsters if a war breaks out. What I am going to tell you is truth picked out of a lot of misinformation. People don't kill monsters. Most of the time the monster dies of either hunger, predetermined cellular break down, or from pure accident. Organized planning rarely works."

Billy pointed at Corban. "You and me need to talk in private right now."

They walked to the rear of the store next to a stand of fishing poles away from anyone else.

"What is it?" Corban asked.

"You trust that guy?"

Corban looked at Adam still holding the bow and talking with Titus. "I don't know. He seems harmless."

"He knows too much about this stuff."

"He's a fan, a monster groupie. This is his best vacation ever. But I don't think he wants to die here."

"He's making people nervous."

"I think he's saved a few of you today. I've seen that thing in action. It's not like some animal you're tracking. We're the prey."

Billy sneered. "Shut up. Save that speech for someone who cares."

"Okay," Corban said. "Let's talk about something else. Do you really have a full auto M-16?"

"Sure. It was my Dad's and I never asked where he got it."

"Do you have any more?"

"A whole room full," Billy said dryly. "Hunting rifles is what we've got, Sheriff. Shotguns and handguns and some fishing poles. Come on! Stop panicking. Your little buddy is getting to you. We're not helpless."

"Glad someone feels that way." Corban walked away from him. "Titus! Get what you need. James, find a gun." Corban stopped as he set eyes on Adam. He was still holding the bow, and now wore a quiver over his shoulder. Adam had a goofy smile on his face.

Billy came up beside Corban. "So, what's your next move, Yan?"

"I had wanted to get some more guns to the courthouse, but we can't move them if it's watching this place." Corban turned his head and looked at Billy. "Do you want to combine forces with the courthouse group?"

"Move in with those idiots? Hell no."

"Then will you deliver a load of weapons and ammo to them?"

Billy folded his arms. "Do they have something to trade?"

"That's going to be between you and them. They have generators, gas, food, a real medic. You should talk to DePaul, not Masterson. I think he's cracking."

"Shit," Billy said. "You said we can't move anything. This is dumb."

"I'm going to draw it away from you. You can get stuff to the courthouse then. Do you have a car I can borrow?"

Billy laughed. "Are you nuts?

"Yes. Do you have a car? You won't get it back, probably."

"You've got some serious balls. Yeah, I got a car. Smells like a dog's ass, but it can roll like a freight train." Billy eyed Titus, James, and Adam. "You dorks going, too?"

"I'm a nerd," Adam said. "A dork is someone—"

"Yes, we're going," Titus said. "But I don't know where we're going."

Corban nodded in thought. "Courthouse and Gunner's. People have holed up in those two places. I'm thinking there are a few more gathering places. And then a lot of people shut in their homes, watching from cracks in the curtains. These people need help, too."

"We've only heard from the courthouse and the Moon brothers out by their repair shop," Billy said. "You might want to check them out."

"I'm more concerned with people without a CB right now. The Moon brothers are tough and a little crazy. They can handle themselves for a while. Our first stop is Capricorn House, see if everyone got out okay."

A man near the wall suddenly jumped up. "Sheriff!" When all eyes fixed on him, he swallowed nervously. "Um, well, could you..." He looked around at the people watching and then settled his resolve despite their stares. "My name is Henry Scoppe. Could you check on my father?"

"He was at Capricorn House?"

"Yeah."

"They have the same evac plan as the hospital. It should be empty. I was just going to see if anyone new had moved in."

"I know, I know. But, well, Dad doesn't move. He's been sick a long time. I don't think he could make the trip anyway." He gave a small, helpless shrug. "Probably kill him to move him across the building, let alone in the back of a truck."

Corban pulled out a pocket-sized notebook. "What's his name and room number?"

"Don Howard Scoppe, Room 27. And..." He looked around. He grabbed a pair of wool socks off a shelf and tossed them to Corban. "He's always got cold feet. If he's there." He had to sit down and stare at the floor. Another hunter next to him laid a hand on his shoulder.

"If he is, want me to bring him here?"

"No," he said softly. "He wouldn't make it. Just the socks, you know, to keep him warm."

"Okay." Corban looked about the store. "Anyone else?"

People started whispering and glancing about. A young man with the beginnings of a scruffy beard cleared his throat. "You – you willing to check on my dogs?"

"Sure am. What's the address?"

From the deep shadows in the back someone began to laugh. Grease said, "I've got a dog you can check on right here, pig."

Henry Scoppe stood up fast. "Shut your fucking mouth, trash, or I'll shut it for you!" Several voices joined his in calling the biker out. Grease made a show of acting surprised, but fell to more laughing.

"Forget him," Corban said. "I'm heading out in five minutes. If you want me to check on anyone, that's what I'm doing. People or pets, that's my job."

Five minutes later, Corban had a list of names and addresses in his pocket. A few people shook his hand. A few called good luck to him and his crew as they prepared at the front door. James had found a semi-auto shotgun he liked and held it awkwardly in front of him. Adam had his bow slung over his shoulder and the messenger bag on the other. Titus looked relaxed with his rifle on his shoulder and unlit pipe in the corner of his mouth.

Billy dangled a key in front of Corban. "It's a rusted out, blue, 1999 Lincoln Towncar. I think possums lived in it until a week ago. The windows don't roll up. It stinks. It's a car you love to hate."

"Why do you even own it if it's that bad?" Titus said.

"Makes me laugh. It's not my daily driver. Take it and be blessed."

Corban took the key. They went outside into the small open area in the front of the store's parking lot. Chambers was scoping out the monster with his binoculars again.

"It's still there," he said.

"Okay," Corban said. "Billy, you're going to have trouble with Grease. Don't let him get these people killed. They are counting on you."

"I hear you. Good luck out there."

Corban paused, looking at Billy.

"What?" Billy asked.

"You're turning out to be what this town needs."

"Yeah, well, it's not like I planned it to be this way. Now get lost."

"Keep someone on that CB in case I need to talk to you. Janet might be a good choice."

"I know how to run shit. Go!"

Corban led his group to the Towncar behind the store. The seats were covered in blue tarp and held down with duct tape. It had dents and gouges in the metal, the blue paint faded and scorched. A sheen of dust lay across the pitted windshield. Someone had written the words Big Fist on the hood with a marker. The smell rose as soon as they slid into the seats.

"Damn," Titus said. "He wasn't kidding."

"It's like a litter box," James muttered. "A very big one."

"We just need it to start," Corban said.

One turn and the engine blasted to life. Corban slapped the car into drive and the tires screeched as he shoved on the accelerator. He came around the back of the store and through the front parking lot. As he neared the street, he drifted to the left. Titus pointed in that direction and started to yell a warning but it was too late.

The big Lincoln clipped a black and gold three-wheeler motorcycle decorated with skulls and flames. The Towncar rattled only a little from the impact, but the motorcycle spun about as the front tire and forks were destroyed. The car hopped the curb with a grinding of steel and tore off north.

Adam stared at the savaged motorcycle as it was left behind. "Was that Grease's trike?"

"No one else drives something like that here," Titus said. "Damn, Captain!"

"Accident," Corban said.

Titus and James started laughing, and soon Adam was joining in. Corban couldn't fight the smile that grew on his face as he sped through the silent town, ignoring stop signs and crosswalks.

CHAPTER FOUR

J ust as they pulled into the parking lot of the nursing home with a stomach churning left turn, the walkie talkie beeped. Titus scooped it up and said, "Go ahead, Alice."

"Got word from Billy. He says it's on the move. Watch your backs."

"Copy that, Alice."

Corban parked the car in front door of Capricorn House under a pale green awning. The front door was a sliding door wide enough for easy access with a gurney. A plastic waiting room chair had been placed to keep it open.

"Looks deserted," James said.

Corban nodded. "Someone was here not too long ago. Someone had to prop that door open after the power was cut. We need to check. Everyone with me. We don't split up."

The lobby had papers strewn on the floor, a knocked over plastic palm tree, and an unsettling quiet. Adam moved the plastic chair and shoved the glass door closed on oiled bearings. With the door closed, the quiet deepened.

"I hate this place," James said.

Corban pulled his flashlight out and sent a spear of light down the main corridor. All the patient doors were open. Evidence of the rapid exodus was on the floor: papers, a blanket, a medicine bottle, a shoe.

"Why does it always smell like this?" James asked.

"It's a law," Titus said.

Corban moved down the main hallway, glancing into empty rooms. Heavy blinds were drawn in all the rooms. On one bed, he noticed a bulky yellow flashlight. He stepped in and picked it up. A powerful beam filled the room when he pressed the rubber button. He handed this to James.

The main hallway turned left. A pair of double doors to the right led to the kitchen and activity center. Corban followed the hall deeper into the nursing home.

Room 27 was a short distance from the turn. As soon as Corban aimed his flashlight inside he saw the body. A shriveled little man on his back, eyes closed, tucked in neatly. The four came into the room with a respectful silence. After a moment of looking at the peaceful scene, Corban pulled up the end of the blanket and checked Mr. Scoppe's feet. He was wearing thick socks with rubber soles. Corban set the socks Henry had sent on the bed.

"The commotion must have killed him before they had the chance to move him," Titus said.

"He's the second one I've seen like this," Corban said. "Mr. Deet died from a heart attack at the courthouse. God damn them."

From the distance came the tearing sound of metal.

"Oh shit," Titus said.

"That was the car," Corban said. "It followed us."

"Does it—"

A louder sound of smashing glass sounded and they all felt a tremor through the floor.

"It's in the building," Corban said softly. "Don't make a sound."

Adam said, "Maybe it can scent us."

"Out the window," Titus said. He pulled apart the blinds and the sunlight blinded them. He felt around the window and turned to the others. "It doesn't open."

James lifted a padded chair from the corner. He charged the window and the chair blasted out the glass. Careful of the glass shards, they slipped from the nursing home onto a stretch of lawn. Beyond was an empty street, a vacant lot with weeds and blown trash aplenty, then a neighborhood. The sound of rising destruction came from behind.

"Where?" James asked.

"We can't make those houses," Titus said.

Corban's eyes went to an iron grate set into the street. "We need in the storm drains."

He ran for the gutter. He pointed at the rectangular cover. "James?"

"Got it." The big man heaved the cover off and tossed it aside. Corban was the first down into the darkness. He found himself in a circular concrete tube five feet in diameter. There were piles of leaves and sticks and trash along the bottom, but no water. He motioned for the others to follow. James came last into the tunnel and he had to crouch just to fit. They moved down the tunnel a dozen steps before stopping in a huddle.

"Damn, that was close," Titus said. "It followed us here. It must have been after the sound of the car, like we thought."

"We knew it would," Adam said.

"It attacked the car first," Corban said. He sat down on the sloped side. "It's done that several times now."

"Why isn't it attacking every car?" James asked.

"They haven't been used yet," Adam said. "It goes after our ability to travel. It's locking us in place."

"Damn it," Corban said. He rubbed his face. "It locks us down by taking out the cars we are using. It uses wounded people to find where we are holing up. It knows where we are hiding and congregating. It doesn't attack Gunner's because it doesn't have to. They will run out of food before it does. How smart can this thing be?"

Behind them the shaft of light from the open grate disappeared. The tunnel darkness pressed in on them.

"It's right there," James hissed.

"I know." Corban put his hand on James's arm. "We're safe for a bit. I don't think it can even fit down here if had the power to chop through the concrete."

"But we aren't going to sit here, right?" Adam asked.

"No. I think we can get closer to downtown by using the tunnel, if I remember right."

"Can we use the storm drains as roads to get all over town?" Titus asked.

"Not really. There's only this main line that is big enough for a person to walk through. The rest of the town has smaller tunnels, smaller openings. I'm not keen on crawling through them."

"I won't fit," James said.

A splashing sound reached them from the grate they had come through. Liquid spattered the dry leaves and concrete inside the tunnel. Moments later an odor struck them. Titus immediately turned and threw up. Corban fought his guts down and motioned for them to move down the tunnel.

"Amazing!" Adam said, then gagged.

They waddled away as fast as they could. It was twenty minutes later that they stopped under the light from another grate.

"What was that?" James asked as he rubbed spittle from his lips.

"Another weapon to drive us out of our hiding places," Adam said. "A gland like a skunk's spray. If it can't get to us, it can force us into the open."

"How do we fight that?" Corban asked. "Some kind of painter's mask?"

"I doubt a normal mask will work. My eyes were starting to water before we left. It could be far worse than a bad smell. It could be an actual chemical poison. We're lucky we got away like we did."

"I don't feel lucky," Titus muttered. "Can we get out of here?"

James pushed the grate away. He carefully looked around. "I can see houses. No businesses. No people. Nice houses. Two stories with garages and privacy fences."

"Do you see one with an open door?"

"Sure."

"We head for that. No one will be there so we won't be scaring anyone when we burst in. As soon as you're free of the tunnel, run like hell."

They all helped James get out and he reached down and lifted the rest up one by one. Corban was the last to run across the street, up the lawn, and into the house. He closed the door quietly behind him.

"Anyone know who lives here?" he asked.

Adam was holding a framed photo he had picked up from the coffee table. "These people."

Corban nodded. "Okay. I know them. I can't remember their names right now. No looting but we're taking what we need. Go find food in the kitchen. We're taking a break."

"And keep quiet," James said.

Titus headed up the carpeted stairs. "I'm washing this stench from my hair." His face was pale, his eyes red and watering.

Corban made two peanut butter sandwiches and found a stash of orange soda cans. While James and Adam stayed around the kitchen table eating from a bag of chips, one lost in thought and the other writing notes in his ever-present notebook, Corban took the food and drinks upstairs. He wondered around and could not find Titus in the bathroom or any bedroom.

"Titus?" he said softly, then louder. "Titus?"

"Out here."

A window was open and an arm waved at him from the roof. Corban peeked out. The slant of the roof wasn't too steep to keep Titus from crawling out and sitting to one side of the window. Titus had his wet hair flat against his skull, giving him a demented undertaker look, but his color had returned. Corban carefully came out and sidled over to join him. Titus took a sandwich and a drink.

"I saw a car go by way over there," Titus said around a bite.

"There's a lot of people trapped in here with us."

"And if you look over that fence, the backyard is really torn up. I think it went through there at some point, really after someone."

Corban squinted at the damage. "I think that's my house."

"Oh yeah?"

"I saw it break down the fence. It was a new fence, too."

"They don't make them like the used to," Titus said. "Hey, Captain?"

Corban sighed. "Yes?"

"Why are you here in Pikeburn?"

"You think I lost a bet or something?"

Titus looked at him to see if this was a joke. "I know you showed up and ran for Sheriff and won. Some people in town don't like you because of that."

"Then they should have voted against me." Corban opened the orange soda and winced at the loud crack hiss of releasing air.

"Were you a Sheriff somewhere else before this?"

"No. I was a deputy in Florida. My boss told me about Pikeburn and said he had friends who would help me get elected, said the ton needed a new start and I was just the man for the job. Sure enough, as soon as I was in town there were signs on lawns with my name on them. It was pretty weird. My boss was a good man, so it's not like I owe people for getting me this job. No strings attached, they said. They didn't want to see more of the same."

Titus nodded in understanding. "More of Sheriff Bull's legacy. You know about him?"

"Heard the name once or twice. Bad news from the sound of it."

"He was three or four Sheriffs ago and his methods are still here." Titus finished his orange soda. "Before my time, too, but I get along with some of the old people in town and I hear about it. Every Sheriff since him has just been Bull Junior, if you know what I mean. I guess some people got tired of Bull running the show from a grave."

"I feel very wanted," Corban said.

"No offense meant," Titus said.

"Don't sweat it. I know why I'm here. I'm the bleach you put in a really dirty bowl. I probably can't win the next election, though. Bull's fans are pushing back. Assuming anyone survives this nonsense to hold an election."

"I figure we've got a good chance," Titus said. "I'm feeling positive about it."

"So, what's your story? Why are you here?"

A loud snapping sound made them jump. A few feet to the right a hole had appeared in the black shingles. Even as Corban was staring at the hole, Titus was shoving him and yelling, "Sniper! Move! Inside!"

Corban jumped up and nearly lost his footing on the slanted roof. He managed to pinwheel his arms and lean forward to grab the side of the window. Another snapping sound came from above them. This time Corban also heard the report of the shot floating in the air several moments later.

They tumbled into the bedroom just as a third bullet hit the outside. A fist-sized hole blasted into existence next to a painting of a sailing ship. Titus held Corban down.

"Sniper, Captain. Stay low."

"Okay! Get off! Let's get out of this room!"

They crawled into the hallway and down the stairs. James and Adam were waiting at the foot of the stairs.

"What is it?" James asked. "What is that sound?"

"It's a sniper," Titus said. "He's not military, though. Missed us by a mile three times. He's probably not even a good hunter."

Another snap sounded from upstairs.

"What is he shooting at?" Adam asked.

"Us," Corban said.

"But no one is up there now? Why keep shooting?"

"I know who it is. We saw him on his roof yesterday. God damn nutcase."

"I can take him out," Titus said. He patted his rifle.

"No," Corban said. "I'm going to talk to him. If that doesn't work, you can take him out."

James held up his hands. "Are you sure about that, Sheriff? He's already shooting at us."

"I'm sure. Get your stuff." He looked at his pocket notebook. "Looks like we can stop and feed Pepper the cat along the way, too."

The man was on his roof, binoculars to his eyes, slowly turning and scanning the town. He was balding with a ring of brown hair. His gut hung over his shorts and his Hawaiian shirt barely covered it. The rifle was slung over his shoulder.

James snapped his fingers. "I know him! Mr. Marsh. Greg or Gary Marsh."

They were hiding behind a shed in a neighbor's back yard, close enough to study Marsh but not draw attention.

"Any idea why he's shooting at people?" Corban asked.

"No. He gets his oil changed every month, that's all I know about him."

Corban looked around. While well shielded from the sniper, they were easily seen from the road or the backyards of the area.

"We can't stay here. Titus, put a crosshair on him. If he raises that rifle at me, put him down."

"Yes, sir."

"I'm going to circle around and – "

"Too late, he sees us," Adam said.

They all looked over and Marsh was waving at them cheerfully.

"Damn it," Corban said. "Same plan, Titus. I'm going to talk to him."

Corban crossed the neighboring lawn and ended up next to the flat-roofed house. "Mr. Marsh?"

The man came over and looked down at Corban. "Good morning, Sheriff."

"Want to explain why you were taking shots at us?"

"No reason, really." Marsh looked around the area. "I've been hitting birds all day but that's getting boring."

"I need you to come with me."

"I can't do that. My wife is counting on me to protect the house."

Corban glanced at the windows. He couldn't see into the dark interior. "Is your wife inside the house?"

"No. She's off in California doing her thing."

"Is anyone in the house?"

"Nope. I'm living alone these days." He smiled at Corban. "Have you seen her?"

"Your wife?"

"Hell no! I'm talking about her! The glory that hunts Pikeburn!"

Corban slowly moved his finger to the trigger of his AR-15. "I have. What makes you think it's a she?"

"I saw her drag off some poor bastard last night. An animal only does that to bring food to the nest. She's got young somewhere near the chair factory."

A chill ran up Corban's spine and he shivered. "Okay. Marsh, I could use your help. I need to find that nest."

Marsh stopped smiling. "Help you? For what?"

"To stop her."

"To kill her," Marsh said. A red flush was starting at his neck. "You want to kill her."

"I do," Corban said.

"Screw that." Marsh threw himself backwards.

Corban swung the AR-15 and aimed at the ledge but saw nothing. From behind him came the boom of Titus's rifle. Corban backed away, sweeping the roof with his weapon. The roof was empty.

Titus jogged up to him. "I missed, Captain. He jumped down on the other side as I was pulling the trigger."

Corban motioned the others to him. When they got there, he said, "This man is a danger to others and we have to disarm him. I am officially deputizing you three. Don't wait to be fired on. If he points that rifle at anyone, you have a duty to put him down."

They all nodded. Adam looked pale and shaky. He looked at the bow in his hands.

"You didn't pick that to hunt men, did you?" Corban asked.

"No, I did not."

"Stay behind me. I'll need an extra pair of eyes. Marsh isn't the only trouble we might run into."

They went around to the other side of the house with weapons ready. They found a ladder and a sofa next to the wall.

"He was prepared for a quick exit," Titus said. "He could just jump down!"

A dog set to barking down the street, drawing their attention. A moment later Marsh bolted from a backyard and ran down the street, thin legs pumping.

"Idiot," Corban said. "After him."

They began chasing him. Corban motioned for them to scatter. James and Titus went to the sidewalk. Adam stayed next to Corban in the street, giving him an uncertain smile. Corban nodded back and they kept running.

Marsh looked back and his mouth worked in a series of unheard curses. He spun about and fired from the hip as he tried to keep moving backwards.

Corban dropped prone. Adam froze in place, looking from Marsh to Corban.

"Do I shoot him?" Adam cried out.

"Get down!" Corban said.

Adam went to his face next to Corban.

Titus and James fired at the same time from the sidewalk. Marsh did not appear hit by either attack and kept running awkwardly backwards. He worked the bolt on the rifle and fired again in their general direction.

Titus and James took cover behind a thick tree.

As Corban drew a bead on the Hawaiian shirt, something huge moved behind Marsh. Through a stretch of tall bushes emerged a head crowned with a bone wedge. The camouflage scales were flipped, making the body a tawny color instead of the nighttime red and black. The monster tilted its head as if listening. Marsh was backpedaling right toward it.

Corban shifted his aim and began firing at the monster. He saw the impact points on the head and neck of the monster, saw the multi-colored scales flinch and blood trickle. The monster remained impassive to the attack.

Titus and James had also seen the head appear through the bushes less than half a block away. They were crouched down and holding position.

Adam stood up, bow held before him with an arrow notched. He drew back and released. The arrow was followed by everyone's eyes, including Marsh, who smiled at the rainbow arc of the projectile. The arrow ran out of momentum and landed in the grass at the talon-tipped foot of the monster. Marsh screamed as he saw what was near him. Even as he raised his rifle, the monster pounced.

Corban jumped up and grabbed Adam's arm. They reached the tree and kept going, Titus and James falling in behind them. They went to the nearest house and tried the door. It was locked. James pulled back to kick it down and Corban stepped in the way. He waved toward the back and put his finger on his lips.

In the street Marsh was wailing and thrashing. The monster held him down on his back with one huge paw. It lowered its head slowly.

Corban led them around the side of the house to a detached garage that had a side door wide open. James pulled the door shut and flipped the lock for good measure. The garage main door had a row of dusty windows that gave them just enough light to look around. The place was empty in the center where a car would park and packed to the ceiling along the sides with boxes and plastic storage bins.

Corban crept to the windows and looked out.

Marsh was holding up his hands, pushing at the enormous head uselessly. The monster began opening its mouth under the bone wedge and moving it around, almost playfully. Marsh kept trying to ward it off, hitting and pushing. A thin, black tongue languidly coiled down from the open mouth. It tightened around Marsh's wrist and pulled his hand behind the row of glistening teeth. Then it bit off his hand.

"I can nail it right in the head from here," Titus said. "It's just standing there!"

"Keep quiet. You'll hit it. I don't doubt that. It won't care, and it will know where we are."

"I bet it has subdermal plating," Adam said. "Possibly a type of internal chain mail or scale mail. It doesn't even flinch when shot. I think pain suppression. Maybe no pain receptors at all."

The ribbon of tongue lashed out and drew in Marsh's other hand. In a spray of blood, the hand was chewed off. The monster swallowed both hands. The tongue dropped from the open mouth and flapped at Marsh's face, leaving red lines of his own blood.

In a burst of speed, the monster bolted back through the bushes, leaving the disfigured victim behind. Marsh sat up and screamed at the sky, holding his arms before him, blood bubbling from the savaged stumps.

"Are we going to help him?" James asked, then shook his head. "No. That wouldn't be smart. It's waiting, isn't it? Another trap?"

"Yes," Adam said. "And it's not hiding where we saw it go into those bushes. It could be right next to this garage. As long as it can sense Mr. Marsh, it could be anywhere."

Titus looked down. "I could, you know, help him along."

"The shot will give us away," Corban said. He turned from the window and the grisly scene of Marsh bleeding out in the street. "Search the garage. I want to build a bomb."

James sat down and cradled his head. "What is this thing?"

Adam and Titus moved with extreme caution to the wall of stacked junk. It wasn't long before they found a metal gas can that sloshed when they moved it. Titus stuck his nose into the cap and nodded.

Titus said, "We saw some nails, Captain. We can make a nice improvised claymore. If we can get it close, we can peel the skin right off the thing. I don't care how armored its guts are, it's not going to live long without skin."

"I want noise, not shrapnel," Corban said. "Too many people might get hurt if we go building bombs like that. How soon after you stuff a lit rag down that can before it goes boom?"

"Not long," Titus said. "I think. I know the theory, but I've never done this stuff before."

"Get it started." After Titus started on the bomb, Corban turned to Adam. "Did you hear Marsh saying it had a nest?"

"Yes. That's impossible. He was wrong."

Corban studied Adam's impassive face. "Because if he was right and there's a God damn family of them, we're all dead."

"They can't breed. Does that thing look like amateurs put it together? Do you think the same scientists that made that monster are also so dumb as to give it a womb? Let it get pregnant? This isn't a town anymore, Sheriff. It's a lab. They would never corrupt the experiment with a pregnant monster. Besides, it's probably male judging from the way it aimed that chemical attack into the storm drains."

James looked up. "That— that was piss?"

"Probably, yes. Mixed with some kind of glandular secretion."

Titus stood up from the gas can. A shop rag was hanging from the mouth of the can. The scent of gas was filling the garage.

"Can we set it on fire?" Titus asked. "Will that work?"

"You can try," Adam said. "Most animals have an instinctive fear of fire that won't be deprogrammed. And fire burns most things."

"So, where's the problem?" Corban asked.

"Human error. The problem with building bombs is no one here is an expert. You're just as likely to blow yourself up or set yourself on fire."

"I know an expert," Corban said. "Two of them."

"The Moon brothers!" Titus said. "Billy said they were at their shop!"

"How far to the shop?" Adam asked.

"Across town. And we can't lead it to them. Their shop is a sheet metal building. Paper thin to that thing. So first we get out of here clean and find a new place to hole up."

Titus pointed to the gas can. "Where do you want it?"

"Put it right in the driveway and light it up. We all take off east before it blows. We're not going by street. We go through yards, over fences, that sort of thing. We stay out of sight and as quiet as possible."

Titus hurried the gas tank into the driveway. He used a long BBQ match he had found inside the dome of a rusty smoker to get the rag going. It caught with a flash and he fell to his back. He was grinning as he scrambled up and ran with a limp to the others.

"Are you hurt?" Corban asked as they took off across the backyard.

"No. Don't worry about it. That's going to be good. Wish I could stand around and watch it."

They went through a gate, into an alley, and into another backyard. They passed between the houses and raced hard across the open street into another set of houses. That was when they heard the gas can explode behind them. Daring a glance back, a puff of black smoke was rolling into the sky. Then they set to running.

They bolted through three more neighborhoods before Corban raised his hand for a halt between two houses. Corban looked back as they caught their breath. A single strand of black smoke reached for the clouds.

"Doesn't look like it caught the house or garage on fire," Titus said.

"Good," Corban said. "I don't think any firemen stayed behind to help out. We need a place to hide and where we can watch our trail." He looked around.

"Speaking of firemen, why not the fire station?" Titus said. "It's just down the street over there."

"Good enough, let's go."

The station was a cinder block building with two bays for trucks. A smaller second story of wood was settled to one side of the main building giving the structure a lopsided look. The front door was open and the bay doors were up. James and Adam set about manually bringing the steel doors down while Corban and Titus swept the building. On the kitchen table was a binder of emergency procedures still spread open to a detailed plan in case of a Red Diamond event.

"Looks like it worked," Titus said. "No one home."

"Titus, get to that second story window and watch the street. Especially the way we came. If it's following, I want to know before it gets here."

"We were pretty quiet. I doubt it can follow our footsteps over a gas can explosion."

"Humor me and I'll relieve you in a bit."

Titus gave him a quick nod and headed upstairs.

Corban settled into a chair. He pulled out the walkie talkie and checked the charge. He keyed the button. "Alice, come in."

"I can hear you, Sheriff."

"Billy told me the Moon brothers have a CB. Can you raise them?"

"I'll try. Give me a minute."

Corban pulled the binder toward him. He flipped through colorful cartoon depictions of airplane crashes, forest fires, earthquakes, floods, and monster attacks. The advice on Red Diamond was brief. Convince as many people as possible to get out, then get out yourself. Corban closed the book and shoved it away.

James and Adam came in from the truck bay.

"Tight as a drum," James said with a smile. "I always wanted to be a fireman."

"Did you bring extra shotgun shells from Gunner's?"

James groaned. "That lady Janet handed them to me and I put them down to grab a granola bar. I'm so stupid! I'm sorry!"

"Don't get upset. I wouldn't matter anyway. That thing is bullet proof."

James sat down and shook his head. "I should know better."

The walkie talkie crackled and Corban picked it up.

"Alice? Go ahead."

"I have the Moon brother's frequency but they aren't picking up. By the way, Janet says hello from Gunner's."

"Alice, is everything okay there?"

Alice cleared her throat. "Okie dokie here, Sheriff."

"Great. I'm heading to the Moon brothers. If you get them, let them know I'm coming."

"Will do. Look after yourselves."

Corban put the walkie talkie down. He laced his fingers and bent his head.

"What's wrong?" Adam asked.

"I don't know yet. That word she used, okie dokie. That's our code word. It means she can't talk safely." He stood up and started to pace the kitchen.

"Are we going back?" James asked.

"No. I need to speak to the Moon brothers. Of all the people in town, they might stand a chance of killing this thing."

He turned aside and climbed the stairs. He emerged into a bunk area lined with beds. Titus was hunkered down on a pillow next to a window. He had a bottle of warm sport drink in his hand.

"Anything?" Corban asked.

"A raccoon, if you can believe it. Damn thing waltzed across the road like it owned the place."

"There's trouble of some kind at the courthouse. Alice can't tell me about it but she's still able to use the CB for now."

Titus shook his head. "That fool Masterson, I bet."

"It could be. Or the bikers. Or lots of things."

"What's the plan, Captain?"

Corban sat on one of the beds. "What time is it?" He eased back and settled his head on the pillow.

"Almost three," Adam said.

Corban sighed. "We're taking a rest. Titus, keep watch, then wake me in about an hour. I slept on a floor last night with my dog."

Titus nodded. "I've got it. I'll tell the others, too. You guys get some sleep."

One minute later Corban was shaken from the depths of dreamless slumber.

"What is it?" he muttered.

"It's out there," Titus said.

Corban sprang up. Adam and James were by the next window. The light had changed and Corban looked about in confusion.

"Titus, how long did I sleep?"

"Almost two hours."

Corban patted him in the shoulder. "Okay, thanks. Did you sleep?"

"I slept last night on a couch in a lawyer's office. Very comfy. Don't worry about me." Titus pointed out the window. "Over by that brown house. Look under the tree."

For a second the image was innocent. Then the monster shifted a little and the camouflage was broken. It was crouched under the wide boughs of the tree in shadow, patiently waiting.

"That's where we came from," Corban said. "Give me the rifle a minute." He took it from Titus and used the scope to get a better look at the monster. The black ribbon tongue was flicking the air.

He handed the rifle back.

"It's scenting the air like a snake. It can smell us."

"Like a snake?"

"We were marked in the tunnel," Adam said. "We're leaving a perfect trail."

"You've got to be kidding?" Titus shouted, then slapped his hand over his mouth.

"We need a way to get rid of this scent," Adam said.

Under the tree, the monster rose and started moving carefully, daintily forward.

"To the kitchen," Corban said.

They all ran downstairs. Corban pulled open cabinets. "I need vinegar. As much as possible. Check the fridge for pickles or that lemon juice concentrate. Anything acidic and pungent."

A minute later there were a handful of bottles on the kitchen table. They had located apple vinegar, pickles, tomato juice, lemon and lime juices, and a small vat of olives.

"Well," Corban said, "let's take a bath."

Each man grabbed a bottle and began splashing it on themselves. They rubbed it in their hair and on their faces. They poured it on their clothing and stomped on it to get their shoes covered. When all the bottles were empty, Corban took stock of the men.

"You guys are a mess. Let's get out of here while we still can."

"Won't it just follow this new scent?" James asked. "Anyone could follow this scent."

"If it's following a scent trail it marked on us, that trail ends here. It has to. We've got to put some distance between it and us."

They used a back door that opened to a training area. Keeping the fire station to their backs, they ran across the flat expanse and into a small apartment complex. On the balcony of one apartment stood a couple having drinks as if the world hadn't been turned upside down. Corban waved for them to get inside, and they cheerfully waved back. Corban turned right and into a strip mall with most of the shops for rent and weeds growing through the sidewalk.

The roar of an engine made them all freeze. Down the street barreled a big sedan, the driver wearing a black cloth over his nose and mouth. The rest of the car was full of TVs, stereo equipment, cases of beer, CDs and DVDs. The car flashed by them before Corban could raise a hand in warning.

"It's going to get him," Titus said. "Fool is driving right into it."

"Maybe he will get lucky," Corban said. "Now let's use his stupidity and find some cover."

"And a shower?" James asked. "This pickle juice stinks like hell."

"I know where to get that and some cover."

They kept at a steady jog as they wound through town. Occasionally they spotted people watching them from behind windows. No one tried to interact. They also saw a few shredded cars. One home looked like a freight train had barreled through the front door and out the back, scattering debris and belongings in a trail.

On the southern outskirts of town, they found a patch of tall grass and gravel lots. The sign for Orleans RV Park was flattened in the grass. There were no RVs left in Orleans RV Park, though. The office building was a shack with broken windows and artless graffiti. A nasty mattress was up against the wall.

The only other building in the abandoned park was a squat concrete structure. It was a public laundry, bathroom, and shower set up for the park occupants. There never had been a real door, just a doorway to a right angle turn that blocked anyone from looking in from the outside. The machines were long gone, but the plumbing was still in place. Each shower stall was a concrete alcove with a rusty shower head pointing downward.

Once they were inside, they sagged to the ground or leaned against the wall. James held up a fist full of granola bars and they were passed around. Warm orange soda washed the crumbles down.

Corban got up. He turned a handle in a shower stall. The water trickled out brown, but soon became clear. He held his hand under the water, then rubbed at his face. The brisk splash made him shiver.

"I'm going to watch our backs at the door. You guys get showered. Clothes, too. If that thing is following the scent of pickles and tomatoes now, we're leaving it here."

"Wish we had some soap," Titus said.

Adam withdrew a plastic bottle of green dishwashing liquid from his messenger bag. "I took this from the house to wash my hands with later."

"My man!" Titus said and offered him a high five. Adam returned it awkwardly.

Corban took the scoped rifle and sat down just inside the door where he could easily see their path from the nearest block of houses. He pulled out the walkie talkie again.

"Alice? Can you talk?"

"I'm here," she said.

"How are things? Still okie dokie?"

"About the same, Sheriff."

"Shit," he said to himself. He pressed the button again. "Alice, I think this thing is stalking me. That's good news for you and bad news for me. Tell people it can also track by smell. I'm not sold that it's completely blind, either. I'm still heading for the Moon brothers, but I can't risk bringing it to them on my heels. I need to hunker down here until someone can spot it. Can you pass this info to Billy?"

"Sure can, Sheriff."

Corban studied the row of houses across the empty RV park.

"Anything else, Sheriff?" she asked after a moment.

"Yes. This is important. I need to know where it is before I move again. This falls to Billy's crew, like it or not. They have the trucks with CBs. I'm staying here until I hear from you again."

"I'll tell him the good news."

"Do you need anything from me?" He closed his eyes while he waited for the reply.

"No," she said after a long pause. "I think I'm fine. Don't worry. We've had a few more stragglers come in. Some of the people have started patrols to get supplies. So far everyone has come back."

"Billy's crew isn't as lucky. Neither will yours if you push your luck."

"You better save that battery if all you've got to say is stuff I already know."

Corban smiled. "Okay, Alice. Signing off."

He settled back against the cool concrete. He watched as the breeze played with the tall grass. Other than the sound of nearby trees rustling and splashing water behind him, the town was unearthly silent. The blue sky was stained by three black smoke trails from local fires, none of them very big. The sun was fading, drawing shadows from their hiding spots, giving life to pools of darkness.

It was two hours later before the walkie talkie chirped to life again. Each man had taken a shower with their clothes on, scrubbed their hair with the soap that smelled of lemons. Now they waited as best they could in damp clothes.

Corban picked up the device. "Alice?"

"Sheriff, Billy just called in. Someone saw it near the duplexes on Deer Street. Said it was tearing into one like it was after someone."

"Good job. I'll call when we hit the Moon brothers. Have you gotten them on the CB?"

"No, Sheriff. Neither has Billy since this morning. Maybe those boys have moved to a better location?"

"Not if I know them," Corban said. "They wouldn't leave that shop unless they had to. Signing off, Alice."

"Good luck, Sheriff."

Corban got up and brushed at his damp jeans.

"Deer Street isn't too far from here," Titus said.

"Yep. But it isn't here and that's important. Last push. We can be at the Moon brother's repair shop inside of an hour. You ready?"

They all nodded.

Corban led them into the night.

CHAPTER FIVE

The Moon Brothers' repair shop was alone on a dirt road. Long before they could see it, they could hear it. A motor was running and it sounded like a dozen soup pans rattling together. They had to top a small rise and look down at the shop building. A rusted and many-times painted Quonset hut was centered in the middle of a courtyard surrounded by high walls of corrugated sheet metal, chain-link, and debris. Broken cars and trucks and piles of various parts littered the inner courtyard. Lights were strung to each corner of the wall and spread a weak yellow illumination into the scrub brush and tall grass around the shop. It resembled a post-apocalyptic fort.

Beyond the shop was an eerie blue glow that hugged the ground and ran into the distance.

"Adam," Corban said. "Is that the wall?"

"Yes. At night, you can see the energy output. It looks dull in the sunlight but at night it's like a small version of the Northern Lights. It's beautiful."

"Seriously," Titus said. "Can we get down off the ridge before the entire world spots us?"

They moved up to the front gate and found it chained and locked.

"They can't expect this to hold it back?" James asked as he pushed against the metal wall and it flexed.

"It's all they have," Corban said. "Climb over the gate and let's go inside."

"Are they the type that shoots first?" Titus asked. "I ask because we've been shot at once today for doing a lot less than breaking into a fort."

"The brothers are pretty calm unless they get behind the wheel of a truck." Corban slung his AR-15 and began the climb.

"What about dogs?" Titus said.

"Never seen a dog in here before."

Titus looked back toward town and saw nothing in the darkness. He sighed and started over.

Corban went straight to the front door that sported a CLOSED sign. He pulled the door open and walked right in. More lights blazed within. The interior was surprisingly empty. Two trucks occupied the floor area that could have held six. Each was a modified tow truck. The windows were covered in metal grate. The doors were reinforced with steel beams. The front of each truck was decorated with a row of medieval spikes. Welding rigs, steel saws, and piles of material were scattered about the floor near the trucks.

"Holy shit," Titus breathed.

"I knew it," Corban said.

Sitting on camp chairs to the side of the main floor were two men wearing coveralls and filthy shirts. A folding table set with pizza and beer was between them. They waved the new arrivals over as if they had expected visitors. A jukebox in the corner was sending out classic rock, but the generator filled every space with the sound of grinding gears.

"Hey there, Sheriff Corban," one of the Moon brothers said. He pointed at a cooler near his feet. "Help yourself."

"Am I speaking to older or younger?" The men looked identical in their faces, down to their haircuts and beards. One wore a red shirt and the other wore green.

"Older by a year and a day!" He wore the red shirt.

"Terry, we've had a hell of a couple of days. We need your help."

James took out a beer from the cooler and handed it to Titus. Adam shook his head when the next beer was offered to him.

The man in green went over to a microwave and pulled out another pizza. He snapped open a pocket knife and swiftly cut it into parts. He flopped it on the table. "Dive in, boys."

Terry looked at his brother with a grin. "They need help, Tom."

"I say we give it to them," Tom said as he settled back into his chair. "Shit, I didn't spend all day welding that truck into a war machine for nothing."

Terry clapped his hands once. "Sheriff, you came on a good day."

Corban studied the savage looking tow trucks. "What do they weigh?"

"What, those things? I don't know," Terry said. "Tom?"

"About eight thousand pounds."

Corban turned to Adam. "What do you think?"

"Vehicles have been used before. But...not like that. That's impressive."

"Nothing could survive a hit from one of those!" Titus said. He offered a fist bump and Terry completed the move.

"Yeah, if only we had some gas," Terry said and sighed.

Then he burst out laughing when everyone was staring at him.

Corban forced a laugh out before leaning closer. "Terry, if you're done working on them, I would advise you to turn off that generator."

"Huh?"

"It's attracted to noise. If it gets here early, it can come right through the walls. You need to listen to me on this one."

Terry glanced at Tom. "Well, I guess. You wanted another hood ornament, Tom."

Tom shrugged. "I don't need the power for that, Terry. My good luck charm can function anywhere. I'll hang it from the spikes by a chain."

"It might bounce off, brother."

"I don't care. It's not that lucky."

With a grunt, Terry rose and strolled toward the back.

"We were going to roll out at dawn," Tom said. He drained his beer and set it on the folding table. "You want to ride along?"

"I'll think about it," Corban said.

"Might be fun, Sheriff. I've ridden in your truck a few times. Now you get to ride in mine."

"A few."

"Can I get you to excuse my speeding tickets for this?"

"Yes," Corban said.

The rattling stopped with a tired wheeze and the lights faded to darkness. A flashlight turned on in the back and worked its way forward. Terry found his seat and pressed a button on the flashlight that turned it into a lantern. He set it on the table. Above them, plastic sheets over squares cut into the round roof began to brighten as their eyes adjusted. They located more chairs after a search and everyone had a seat around the table.

"Looks like we finally out thought the bastard," Titus said.

"No," Adam said. "Don't think of it like that. It doesn't think. This isn't a chess game. It can't adjust a strategy to counter yours. It simply is."

"Programmed," Corban said. He yawned. "Like a computer."

"Trained like a computer. Keep in mind, it can only have so many situations trained into it. After that, it's random."

"I don't think that's true," James said.

"It doesn't matter," Corban said. He crossed his arms. He was certain James was talking, but his mind was full of fog and waves. His chin dropped to his chest and he was sleeping.

Very close to his ear a voice said as softly as possible, "It's here."

He opened his eyes. The fresh light of predawn was filtering down from the skylights. He could see Terry and

Tom sprawled in their chairs, mouths open in identical slumber. James was on the floor, head on a dusty coat he had found. Titus was next to him, chewing on his unlit pipe.

"Where's Adam?" His voice sounded garbled and raw.

Titus pointed toward the front. Adam was at the door, peering through a small window at the brightening day. He had an arrow notched in his compound bow.

Corban levered himself up. "Did you see it?"

"Something big is circling the outer walls. Can it still smell us?"

"I don't know. Wake the brothers. Looks like we won't have to hunt it down today."

Corban picked up his backpack and slipped it on. He checked his AR-15, then quickly moved to Adam at the grimy window.

Adam whispered, "It's gone around us twice, I think. It can break through at any spot it wants."

"Why isn't it?"

Adam looked at him. "Maybe it knows we're up to something."

"How the hell would it know that?"

"Because we aren't running away anymore."

"Adam, this thing is acting a lot smarter than you keep making it out to be."

Adam shrugged. "It's a great build. One for the record books."

"How many records will it break if we kill it this morning with a pair of spiked up tow trucks?"

"It doesn't matter. I'm telling you, the top scientists are opening champagne already. We've seen pure rage and clever tactics from the same monster. It's using humans against each other. It's not afraid of us, but it's wary of falling into a trap. I've never seen the like before."

Corban glimpsed a shadow moving beyond the corrugated walls where two sheets of metal left a gap. The chain-link tinkled as the monster pushed, then backed off.

"It did that at my house with my back fence. It's testing the strength. Now it knows it can get through."

"Yes," Adam said. "Don't expect it to wait long."

A roar of mechanical might jolted them. The tow trucks were firing to life. Terry and Tom were behind the wheels, grinning like demons.

"That's bad," Adam said mildly.

Terry waved for them to join him in the cab and they ran for it even as the sounds of chain-link and sheet metal being ripped apart sounded behind them. Adam got in first and Corban slammed the door shut.

"Now what?" Terry asked. He laid his palm on the horn and shivered the air with a challenging call.

The monster came through the front bay doors, peeling them apart like tin foil. It slid to a stop and cast its head around, searching for a target.

"Good God damn!" Terry shouted. "Look at that thing!"

"Kill it!" Corban said. He brought up his AR-15 but didn't fire.

Both tow trucks lurched forward. The monster lowered its head as if to meet the charge, but then it turned away with amazing agility and fled through the hole it had made.

"It wants to play!" Terry yelled. He drove through the ruined bay door and into the dirt courtyard. The monster was racing around the corner to his left.

"There!" Adam said.

"I can see the monster just fine, professor," Terry said.

Shifting gears, he turned the corner and the monster was waiting. It slammed into the front of the tow truck and blood flecked the windshield. The truck shuddered to a halt and the engine died.

Corban was staring at a fist-sized chunk of bone wedge that had broken free and was resting on the hood of the tow truck. The monster slowly stepped away. The spikes had gouged the bone wedge in several places. The black and red scales had been peeled back where the spikes had managed to stab the monster's narrow face. It shook its head as if stunned.

Corban opened his door and stood on the seat. He fired the clip dry into the monster's neck and side.

Terry grabbed at a CB mic on the dashboard. "Tom! Are you coming round?" At the same time, he was cranking the engine over and tapping on the gas pedal.

"On my way!"

"You've got the big spike! It's right in front of me! Nail this ugly fucker!"

Corban got back into the cab. He fished around in his backpack for another clip, cursing under his breath.

"Save the ammo," Terry said. The tow truck fired to life again. "This bitch is done for!"

Terry put the tow truck in gear and rumbled at the monster. It backed away from the spikes that had damaged it. From around the corner of the repair shop came the other tow truck. Corban stopped looking for the clip when he saw the big spike, a ten-foot-long metal spear at least three inches in diameter. It thrust out from a mess of other spikes like a middle finger. Chained to this spike was a much-abused stuffed bunny rabbit, an absurdity that had to be Tom's good luck charm.

Tom was laughing as he bore down on the monster. Titus and James were with him but they weren't laughing. They were bracing their arms and legs for the impact.

The monster pivoted on its hind legs, trying to bolt from Terry's truck. Also sensing the approach of Tom, it pointed its bone wedge toward town and raced toward the wall.

"Let's get him, Tom!" Terry shouted to his brother but there was no way he could be heard. Even without the encouragement, Tom instantly veered to stay with the monster. The monster blasted through the wall and chain-link. Terry and Tom aimed right for the hole it had made.

And then Corban saw the monster turn left to race along the outer wall. Corban looked back at Tom's truck barreling toward the hole. He grabbed the mic from Terry's hand.

"Drive through the wall! Tom! Drive through the wall NOW!"

The tow truck veered left. Its engine let out a roar and a plume of black smoke and it sped forward. The wall came apart under the onslaught, hardly slowing the tow truck. The monster was exactly where it needed to be. The big spike caught the monster on the side of the head just behind the bone crest. The monster shrieked in madness as the tow truck's mass punched the big spike through whatever bullet-proof protection it possessed. The big spike erupted on the other side, slick with gore.

Tom kept his foot to the floor, dragging the unfortunate monster. The tow truck hit a junked car and bounced up and over the hood. It clawed its way higher and suddenly lodged in place, high centered on the abandoned vehicle. Smoke billowed from under the stranded tow truck as the engine self-destructed.

Terry slammed on the brakes. As people jumped from both tow trucks Adam was shouting, "It's not dead! It's not dead!"

"It will be," Tom said as he backed away from the high center tow truck. "It's going to cook!"

Flames started to appear under the tow truck.

Titus grabbed Corban's arm. "Captain! Did you see that shit!"

James stumbled and sat down in the dirt.

Black smoke rolled into the air, blocking everything from view.

"Bring more gas!" Corban shouted and both Moon brothers ran for their shop.

Corban slapped in a new clip. He started moving around the truck, rifle aimed at the rolling smoke and flames. He reached the spikes and could barely make out the shape of the monster wiggling on the spike. He aimed the AR-15 and waited for a clear shot. But as he watched, the solidity of the monster faded, became mixed with the smoke from the burning tow truck, a figment of imagination.

The big spike was gone and so was the monster.

"Fucking impossible," he said.

Titus joined him with his own rifle raised. "Where is it?"

"Gone!" Corban looked around. There was a slight ridge that blocked the repair shop from the view of town. He had to scramble to get to the top. Once there, he immediately saw the monster heading for town. Its head was waving in an ungainly fashion as it tried to run full speed sporting an enormous arrow protruding out both sides.

"No way," Titus said. "It has to be nearly dead."

"Let's go make it deader."

They ran down the slope and headed for Terry's tow truck. They both met at the driver's door and reached for the handle at the same time.

"Move, Captain," Titus said, not taking his hand off the door handle.

"I'm driving," Corban said.

"You don't know how to drive this beast and I don't know how to shoot out the window."

"Point taken."

Corban went to the other door and climbed up. Titus jammed the gear into place and the tow truck leaped at his command. He steered it back into the shop courtyard, startling Terry and Tom who each had a gallon bucket.

"What the fuck?" Terry yelled.

"It's alive and running!" Corban managed to shout over the engine's roar. Titus didn't slow down. He drove right through the front gate, leaving it flattened and twisted in the dirt.

In the distance was the shape of the hobbling monster. It had reached the first row of houses.

"Don't lose it," Corban said.

"I'll be on it in a minute."

They lost sight of it before they reached the first street in town. Titus cranked the wheel and the tow truck groaned. They rumbled through a neighborhood of small houses with peeling paint and leaning fences. There was no sign of it. Titus slowed down to crawl ahead at ten miles per hour.

"It has to be dead in a back yard," Titus said. "It has a spear through the head."

"I'll believe it when I see it. It just ran half a mile with a spear through the head."

"There!" Titus stopped the truck.

A shattered picket fence left a debris trail behind a house with a faded For Sale sign in the front. Corban got out and stood in the street. The tow truck sputtered and died behind him. Titus limped up, holding onto the truck.

"Are you hurt?" Corban asked.

"What? Oh, it's nothing. Bent not broken." He slapped at his leg. "I've got another one at home."

"Okay," Corban said. "You stay - "

"Don't start that shit, Captain."

Corban frowned at him. "Stubborn ass. Okay. Let's go."

"Maybe I should stay here," Adam said from above them. They spun around so fast, Titus nearly fell over and Corban had to steady him.

"I will God damn shoot you if you do that again!" Titus yelled.

Adam was standing next to the towing arm, a smear of black grease on his face. He climbed onto the roof of the cab and stood up. "I can be a lookout. But I dropped my bow back there when you took the corner."

"What are you doing here?" Corban demanded.

"I have to see the end," Adam said with sincerity.

"It's not dead yet!"

"That's why I'm up here."

Titus shook his head. "Let's go, Captain."

"Shout if you see it running away," Corban said. Adam gave him a thumbs-up.

Amid the debris of the fence were footprints and splashes of brilliant red blood. They advanced carefully toward the back yard with weapons raised. Behind the house was another flattened fence section. A mangled swing set led them into another yard. Then the sounds of banging brought them to a detached garage nestled behind a house. The garage wide door was up. They came at it from the side, giving the shadowed interior as much distance as possible.

"It's still bullet-proof," Corban said. "Don't get its attention. We just watch it die."

"Good with me."

The monster appeared in the doorway of the garage. It stood unmoving, head held regally up toward the rising sun with it's impossible injury. It tilted its head until the big spike tapped the driveway. Slowly, it put its front foot up on the metal. From there the foot groped higher until the hooked talon sank into its own neck. It slashed through the scales and flesh and blood poured onto the driveway.

"What the hell?" Titus hissed.

Corban waved him to be silent.

Again and again, the monster slashed its own throat and neck. Chunks of scaled skin started to pile up below it. It was completely silent during this process.

Titus raised his rifle to fire and Corban caught the barrel. He pulled it down. Titus looked pained, but kept it pointed low when Corban released it.

The monster's head flopped forward and struck the ground. Now both front feet were engaged to tear itself to pieces. Digging in deeper and deeper, the head began a loose thrashing that caused the big spike to knock at the driveway in a bizarre rhythm. Then bone could be glimpsed, thick vertebrae slippery with hot blood. The talons found purchase amid the gaps in the spine. The length of the monster's body spasmed as it set to work.

"My God," Titus breathed. Both men had unconsciously lowered their barrels in dumbfounded amazement.

The spine gave way, the last muscle and sinews shredding, and the monster's head flopped forward and lay like a discarded toy. What remained was something still alive despite any logic. Where the head had once joined the body, a new face in the meat of the torso stared at them, a face revealed by the self-beheading. The mouth was a pulsing circle filled with inward pointing teeth that had the gleam of steel needles. The black tongue was still there, only now much longer, slipping through the air like a banner.

"No," Corban said through numb lips.

Above the new mouth, striated bands of exposed muscle flexed and rearranged. Two eyes popped open between two layers of muscle, as big and white as cue balls, their surface smeared with the blood of violent birth. The eyes rolled about in the muscular slits as the newly exposed flesh crawled into a final shape. They fixated suddenly on Corban and Titus.

A rattling howl issued from the maw.

"Run," Corban said, but he couldn't move. Titus was also still, captured in his fear like steel chains.

The monster spun from them and jumped over a tall privacy fence into the neighboring yard and was gone.

The severed head lay on the driveway concrete amid a puddle of blood and flayed flesh.

Corban felt his nerves coming back to life. In slow motion, he raised the AR-15. He had to take several deep breaths before looking at Titus. The other man was visibly shaking.

"You - you okay?"

"I'm fine," Titus said, sounding amazingly normal. "I want to go back to the truck now."

"Let's do that."

They started toward the street.

"What just happened, Captain?"

"I can't imagine. I don't even have words for that."

"Here's what I think."

The monster came over the privacy fence in a blur, landing just before them. Corban was pulling the trigger before the AR-15 was fully raised and bullets sparked of the driveway. The monster plowed into them with a single pounce. Corban went flying straight backwards. He landed against the bone crest of the severed head. He lay there, blinking and stunned, seeing Titus on the ground, hearing him call for help. He managed to sit up. His back was coated in the blood and flesh of the severed head. He lifted the AR-15 but his hands were empty. He started looking around, sure he once had a rifle.

The black tongue whipped toward Titus and latched onto his left leg. It yanked him down the driveway and into the street like his weight was nothing.

Corban was somehow on his feet and running. He drew his pistol. He turned right after the monster and pursued. He put his arm out straight and fired over and over. He saw the impacts on the body, the shattering of small colored scales and pulverized flesh and faint trickles of blood. The monster ignored his attacks and began to distance itself from Corban, taking Titus with it.

The monster reached another street and Corban fired his last bullet to no effect. It turned to head down the street and for a second Titus was lifted off the ground and shaken. Then he tumbled away from the monster, his leg missing. The monster bounded away with the limb sticking from its steel teeth.

Corban dropped his pistol and increased his speed. He grabbed at Titus as the other man was struggling to come up on his elbows.

"Stay down," Corban said. He pulled off his belt.

"Captain?"

"Be quiet," Corban ordered. He spared a glance down the street and the monster had gone. "I'm making a tourniquet and—"

Corban had pushed back the torn pant leg and was staring at a stump that had healed over many years ago. He looked from the stump to Titus and back. He looked at the street, empty of monster and severed leg. He frowned at Titus.

"It got blown off ten years ago in Iraq," Titus said. He pulled his pant leg down over the stump.

"You - you've got a fake leg?"

"Yeah. I told you it was bent. The ankle on that model makes walking easy but it can fold up if you put too much pressure on it."

"Are you fucking kidding me?!"

Titus took hold of Corban's shirt front. "I don't like to talk about my leg with people, okay!"

"Why didn't you tell me?"

"Because I'm not a fucking cripple!"

"I thought it was killing you, you ass!"

"Well, excuse the fuck out of me!"

They stayed locked together, glaring, and Corban said, "A monster just ate your fake leg."

"I know."

They fell away from each other and laughed hard enough to dredge tears from their souls. It was a brief but intense fit of laughter that left them gasping and holding aching stomachs.

"Well, come on," Corban said. He helped Titus up. "Back to Adam."

"It was taking me, Captain."

"I tried to stop it."

Titus shook his head. "No, it was taking me for something. Where was it taking me?"

Corban ground his teeth. "A nest. A God damn nest."

They retrieved the tossed pistol first, then the hunting rifle Titus had lost, and finally the AR-15 next to the severed head. When they hobbled into view of the tow truck, Adam jumped down and ran to them.

"You got it!" he exclaimed. "Where is it? I have to see it before it melts!"

"Calm down," Corban said. "Titus is fine."

"I'm fine," Titus said. "It's not my blood."

"What?" Adam stared at them. "I need to see the body! They start to decay!"

Corban helped Titus into the tow truck. "It's not dead, Adam. I— I don't know how. I can't even explain it. It doesn't have a head now."

"Show him the head," Titus said. "I'll stay here."

Adam gasped as he noticed Titus was minus a leg. "What the hell happened? We need to get to a hospital."

Titus wearily pulled up his pant leg. "Old wound, Adam. I'm fine."

Corban put his last clip into the AR-15. As he was doing this, he caught his reflection in the side mirror. He was a mess. Drying blood and bits of shredded flesh stuck to his arms and neck. He could feel the sticky mess soaking through his uniform. He tore the shirt off, sending buttons scattering. He threw it down.

"We have to hurry," Adam said.

"Don't push me right now, Adam."

The front door of the nearest rundown house opened on creaky hinges. A teenage boy came out holding a black shirt. He walked to the curb and smiled hesitantly at them.

"Get inside," Corban said. "There's a monster lose around here."

"Sheriff, you need a shirt?"

Corban looked the young man up and down. They were about the same size and he was holding out a wadded shirt.

"Yes," Corban said.

The young man handed it to him. "I wore it yesterday, but there's no monster blood on it."

"Good." Corban pulled it on and looked down. The T-shirt was blank. "I thought it would have a middle finger or something."

"Or a marijuana leaf," the young man said.

"Thanks. Do you live here?"

"With my mom. She took off when the sirens went off. I slept through it. Too late now."

Corban shook his hand. "Get inside, okay. It's dangerous out here."

"Yes, sir. Do you have a spare gun? I know how to shoot."

"No," Corban said sternly. The young man gave him a had-to-try shrug and went back inside his dilapidated house.

"Okay, now?" Adam asked. "It's really important."

Corban led him to the severed head. Adam stopped him from getting close.

"Don't go near it, Sheriff. It's probably got a rapid decay protocol. It's melting. Plus, it might give off a chemical poison, odorless and tasteless. Anyone trying to recover the remains for study ends up dead."

"They think of everything."

"They try. Where's the rest of the body?"

Corban looked at him. "It ran away."

Adam recoiled. "You were serious?"

"Yes, God damn it! I saw that thing tear off its own head and run away! It tried to carry Titus off to its nest, too, so you better rethink everything you know."

Adam had his hands on his head. He walked in a circle, muttering and casting glances at the severed head. After a minute, he stopped. "Sheriff, it was on the CB. I heard it on the CB in the tow truck. People think it's dead. The Moon brothers are telling everyone it's dead."

They ran back to the tow truck. Corban got behind the wheel and Adam shoved Titus over. Corban took the CB mic.

"This is Sheriff Corban. Anybody reply."

"This is Alice."

"And this is Janet."

Corban waited another moment to gather his wits. "Listen carefully. It's not dead. I repeat... it's not dead."

"You said it was dead," Janet said.

"No," Alice corrected her, "Terry Moon was the one talking, saying he put a spear or something through its head and the Sheriff was finishing it off."

"It's not dead!" Corban shouted. "It... I don't know how to explain it."

Adam took the mic from him. "Hello? This is Adam. I can explain it."

"Go right ahead," Alice said.

"It sloughed off an injured part to prevent the injury from killing it. It may not store its brain in the head. It may have more than one brain, or no brain we would recognize."

"It has no brain?" Janet asked.

Corban took the mic back. "It tore off its head. It has another head between its shoulders. For God's sake, I don't know what to tell you. It's not dead!"

"A bunch of people left here," Janet said. "Oh my God. I've got to go!"

"Alice," Corban said.

"Do not come here," Alice said. "I've got ten seconds. Do not come here, Yan."

"Masterson?"

"No! Now stay away."

"Alice?"

There was no reply. He hammered his fist against the wheel. He flung the CB mic onto the dashboard. He leaned across Titus to look at Adam. "Start talking, Adam. This is insane! What kind of animal can do this?"

"None," he said flatly. "This is all new. This is something...alien."

Titus snorted with laughter. "Like *alien* alien? Like from another planet alien?"

"Um, probably not," Adam said. "Alien as in didn't come from nature. I'm thinking...maybe...this monster isn't based on anything. Someone sat down and created a new entity from scratch. What couldn't it do? Without any constraints of nature, you could build it any way you wanted. It would take fantastic skills, though. Way beyond anything I've heard of."

Corban sat back a little. "Did Harlow make this?"

Adam slowly looked over at him. "Where did you hear that name?"

"I'll take that as a yes."

"Who is Harlow?" Titus asked.

"He's a dead scientist," Adam said.

Corban turned the key and the tow truck rattled to life. "I'll bet money he's not dead."

"How do you know that name?" Adam asked. "That's not a name you should know."

"Later. We're heading to Gunner's."

"Can we swing by my apartment first?" Titus asked. "I have—"

"You have another leg in your closet."

"I did tell you. South Spire Apartments."

Corban turned the tow truck around and headed that way. "Were you military?"

"Nope. Contractor. Made a pile of cash before some mortar shell landed next to my truck. I'm pretty lucky to be alive. Four other guys didn't make it."

"So that's why DePaul hates you."

Titus stuck his pipe in his mouth. "Yeah, I'm just a merc for hire in his eyes. But I don't know how he found out. I don't tell anyone."

CHAPTER SIX

The parking lot in front of Gunner's was different. Quite a few trucks were gone, leaving the fortification thin enough to be useless. Someone had moved the wrecked trike to one side into some grass. As they pulled in, Billy and Janet hustled out.

"What the hell is this about?" Billy said before the engine died with a last cough.

Corban jumped down from the cab. "I told Janet. It's not dead."

"The Moon brothers say they put a fucking three-inch pipe through its head. How alive can that be?"

Corban was about to shout in Billy's face when Janet pointed behind him. A car was speeding down the street at them, weaving side to side. It hit the curb at full speed in a crash of sparks, blowing out both tires and flopping the hood up over the windshield. It didn't stop until it slammed into the back of the tow truck.

A man with blood on his face and arms kicked open the door and staggered toward Billy.

"There's another one!" he shrieked.

"It's the same one," Adam said.

"Where?" Corban said.

"The Fireball." He went to his knees. Billy and Janet rushed to his side and started picking him up. He shook them off and spun on Corban. "We went there to have a drink! We was celebrating your victory! But then a second one came through the windows! It got everyone! It got everyone!"

"What the fuck is going on?!" Billy shouted. "Make sense, Yan!"

"I can't make it make sense! It's the same monster, but different! I never said it was dead!"

"We should get inside," Titus said. "That thing is faster now." He leaned on a wooden cane as he walked toward the door. The pants of his left leg were slashed up and his metal prosthetic was easily seen.

"What happened to you?" Billy asked in shock.

"Lost a leg in Iraq," Titus said. "I don't like to talk about it."

Billy looked at Corban. "Seriously, Yan, what the fuck?"

"Later. Do you know where the Moon brothers are?"

"Probably doing donuts in a parking lot. How should I know?"

Corban stopped at the threshold of Gunner's. He looked back at the street, at the wrecked car pushed against the tow truck, at the blood on the ground.

"What's wrong?" Adam asked.

"Did you see it?" Billy asked. "Is it out there?"

"No," he said softly.

"Oh shit," groaned Billy. "You're going to the Fireball, aren't you?"

Corban looked at him. "It's my job."

"You've got a screw loose, man."

Titus sat down on a display of insulated sweaters. "Enough, Captain. You'll get killed this time. Before, we didn't have much to go on. Now we've got nothing. Nothing at all. You and I saw it. I don't think—" He paused to take a steadying breath. "I don't think it can be killed."

"He's right, Sheriff," Adam said. "If what you are saying is true, you've got no chance against it. Not with that gun. Not alone. Not without some kind of plan."

For a minute longer, Corban lingered in the open door. Grimacing, he finally stepped inside and pulled it closed. He flipped the lock before walking away. He sat in the corner and hung his head. Three times people came to the door, banging and yelling. They came in with stories of horror and bloodshed. The monster was rampaging. The population of Gunner's rose to nearly twenty.

A while later someone came over and kicked Corban's foot.

"Time to get to work again." It was Billy.

"Have you gotten in touch with Alice?"

"Briefly."

"Do you know what's going on there?"

"It's DePaul." Billy sat next to him. "I deal with bad guys, like Grease, and some worse than him. My dad had deals with very bad dudes from Mexico when I was a kid. I would get sent out of town when they rolled in for a meeting. But my dad told me there was one guy he wouldn't deal with at all. That's DePaul."

"Why was that?"

"Dad said DePaul lost his soul in the war. Said he was flat out the scariest guy he ever met. I bet DePaul has gone wacko over there. He doesn't take no for an answer."

Corban got up and rubbed life back into his legs. "I'm going to steal some new clothing."

"Help yourself. Then come into the back office. We've got a pow-wow going on you don't want to miss."

Corban striped down and put on fresh blue jeans and a tan shirt. He stuffed the old clothes in a trash bin. Finding the bathroom, he washed as best he could by the single candle that burned on the back of the toilet. Then he joined the others in a supply room in the back.

There was a green-felted card table in the middle of the room. Billy was leaned back in a chair with his feet propped on the edge of the table. Titus, Adam, Chambers, and Janet were there. The man from the Fireball massacre was sitting and nervously chewing on his nails. It took Corban a minute of staring before he connected the pale and sweaty face with a name.

"Grease?"

The man flinched. He looked at his nails with intense concentration.

"Titus has filled us in," Billy said. "What you guys saw. It sounds nuts."

"You didn't see it," Grease whispered. "Killing and stuffing people into that mouth. You didn't see. No fucking head. White eyes seeing everyone. It herded people to a corner and they couldn't get out."

"I get that," Billy said with a sigh. "Moving on..."

"What about the Moon brothers?" Corban asked.

"No word."

"We left James with them," Corban said. "It's all gone to hell."

"I've been thinking, and I have a theory," Adam said. "If you hurt my hand, really cut it up, the pain and blood loss and fact that I have a useless limb to haul around makes me less of a perfect organism. I don't function at peak efficiency. Now what if I could yank off this hand?" He held up his left hand and everyone was looking at it. "You damage it and I discard it. But under the hand might be something else just as useful to me. A bone spur. A claw. Even an already sealed up stump. No offense, Titus."

"None taken."

"But that's not enough," Adam said. "Just breaking off the wounded part isn't good enough to get a fully functioning monster again. You need it to change how it thinks of itself."

"Is this monster psychology?" Chambers asked.

"Exactly."

"I was joking."

Adam frowned. "I'm not. There are plenty of fast two-legged animals. Why can't you take a four-legged animal, cut off two of the legs, and have it be just as fast as any other two-legged animal? Because inside it knows it once had four legs and it will always favor that form."

"I had a three-leg dog that could outrun a car," Billy said.

"That's stupid," Adam said with rising emotion. "Don't you get what I am saying? Why don't you understand this?"

"Try again," Corban urged. "Billy, shut up."

"It doesn't just shake off a body part that could slow it down and then try to compensate for that missing part. That's why this monster is attacking differently! It's got a whole new brain. It doesn't have to compensate for the injury we dealt it. To that monster, it never had a head with a bone crown that could tear steel. It's always been fast and aggressive. It's always pulled people into that round mouth and chewed them up." He shook his head in frustration. "We have to start over. Everything we know is wrong."

Chambers reluctantly raised his hand.

Adam stared at him.

"Can I ask a question?" Chambers asked.

Adam nodded.

"How does it have a brain now that it doesn't have a head?"

"Because it's not like anything you've ever seen before. That reminds me, no one go near that head it pulled off."

"It's leaking poison into the air," Corban said.

"Not just that," Adam said. "I don't think it's completely dead. It might bite you if you pick it up. Or something worse. We should leave it alone."

"Alien," Titus said. "I'm starting to understand that word."

"I'm sorry," Adam said. "I can't help any more. I don't know what this thing can do. No one does."

Corban raised his head suddenly. "I think someone does." He snapped his fingers. "Billy, I need a map."

Soon a map was unfolded on the green felt and everyone was standing close around. Corban found the east road out of town. He marked where he estimated the wall was.

"That wall is pretty straight." He drew a line south. It struck a green area on the map. "And there's the trees he ran into."

"Who?"

"A man in a blue suit."

"One of the soldiers?" Billy said.

"Yes. He got caught on our side of the wall. He wasn't too happy about it. They wouldn't open it for him and he ran into this big stand of trees."

Chambers ran his finger along the length of the narrow thicket, the tip of which pointed toward the east side of town. "If he came out here, he will be in the Red Hills neighborhood. I'm guessing he went to ground in one of the abandoned houses. Food and water and shelter."

"House to house search," Billy said. "I don't like that. Was he armed?"

"Not that I saw."

"But he could have found something," Chambers said. "Lots of guns in town in closets and under beds."

Corban touched the map where the thicket met the hexagon wall. "He's not in town. He wouldn't leave sight of the wall. Adam, would they open a part of the wall for him eventually?"

"Never."

"But he still would stay close, just in case they did. He followed the wall." He moved his finger alone the pen mark that was the wall. It left the thicket, crossed open ground and a creek, and entered in a cluster of squares with what the legend explained was a dirt road leading from the highway. "What is that?"

Billy looked at Chambers. "Is that your uncle's old place?"

"Looks like it. I haven't been there is ages."

"What is it?" Corban asked. "Does it have buildings?"

"It did. Uncle Bowett had some shacks put up a long time ago as a hunting lodge or some crazy shit. He's been dead for ten years. No one goes out that way. There's no water and no electricity. His wife still owns the land, though, and won't sell for nothing less than a truck of gold bricks."

"He's there," Corban said. "I'm going to pay him a visit."

"What about the monster?" Chambers asked.

"It can follow me if it wants. Despite what Adam says, I think it's a little weaker. I was afraid of meeting it in a car when it had that big bone wedge. I'll be driving a tow truck covered in spikes this time and if it wants to play, I'm game."

Adam stood up. "When do we leave?"

"I'm in," Titus said.

"Hold on," Janet said. "That truck only holds three. I want to go, too."

Corban looked at Titus, glanced at his cane.

"Don't do it, Captain. Don't leave me behind."

"I'll just jump on the back again," Adam said. "Or run all the way after you. I'm not being left behind either."

"Titus," Corban said, "can you drive okay?"

"What? Oh, hell yeah, I can drive. I drove you all over creation yesterday." Titus beamed at the group. "Even with a missing leg."

"Adam can ride in the middle." Janet's face was darkening and Corban held up his hand. "And Janet and squeeze in, too."

"What if you need to bring that blue guy back with you?" Billy asked.

"He can ride on the back. I have no sympathy for him. He's part of this God damn horror show."

"We all are," Grease said to his hand. "Every single time you watched the show on TV, this is what you were rooting for. Hell, I had a bet on how long the humans would last this year. Now I find I was betting against myself."

"That's a philosophy topic for another day," Corban said. "You better snap out of it, Grease. We don't have time to coddle anyone."

Grease forced his eyes up to meet Corban's. "Okay," he whispered. "You ran over my trike."

"Yes, I did."

Grease looked away with trembling lips. "Don't sweat it, Sheriff."

As the others were loading up with weapons and ammo, Corban stood with Billy.

"You should move," Corban said.

"Yeah, it knows we hide out here. I guess it's coming sooner or later. Maybe that's what I want. Everyone else has had a crack at this thing but me."

"If you do," Corban said, "I don't think it's new face is as bullet-proof as the old one."

Billy laughed. "So, I have to be looking it in the face? That's easy enough."

"If you hear from the Moon brothers, see if James is with them."

"Good luck." Billy slapped him on the shoulder and walked away.

The group made a quick dash to the tow truck and jammed in. Janet ended up on Corban's lap instead of wedged between him and Adam. She gave him a "sorry, do you mind?" look. He shrugged. Then she gave her ass a little wiggle against him and winked. He looked at her like she was quite possibly insane.

"What? A chubby girl can't have fun during a monster attack?" She put one arm around his shoulder and settled against him.

"Um, you two need a room?" Titus asked with a grin.

"Drive," Corban said.

The dirt road came to an end at a ring of tall trees. The entire lodge area was covered in shade from the interwoven top branches. Not a blade of grass grew under the canopy. Four concrete pads of various sizes were all that was left of buildings, even the basic materials long since scavenged. A long RV had been parked here off to the side and was joining in the slow decay of forgotten machines: the tires were flat, dust covered all the windows, and rust was eating away at all the metal.

About three hundred feet away was the shimmering hexagon wall. The ugly shapes of tanks could be faintly discerned through it.

Titus stopped the tow truck before entering the dirt-covered area under the trees. Dust billowed behind them. Corban opened the door and helped Janet get out. She quickly swung up to the top of the cab, put her rifle to her shoulder and scope to her eye, and watched the way back to town.

"Clear so far," she said.

"Okay," Corban said. "No way Blue didn't hear us coming in that rattletrap. If the monster still has ears, it heard us too. Adam, keep watch with Janet."

Adam joined her on the cab. He adjusted his messenger bag. "I didn't pick up another bow. Sorry, Janet."

"Now we're in trouble," she said.

Titus was using his cane in his left hand and carrying an intimidating silver revolver. Corban still had his AR-15, but he had it slung over his shoulder. He moved to the middle of the lodge area. The cooler temperature from the shade made him shiver.

Titus sidled up to the RV door and carefully peeked in. He came over to Corban. "Gutted. Not a splinter left inside. He can't be hiding in it. And it smells like a dead raccoon is under it."

"You can come out," Corban shouted, "or I can come and get you. I've had a really bad three days, so my patience is damned thin."

"Hey, we just want to talk," Titus called out. "You're in this with us."

Corban kept looking at the hexagon wall, its sliding and locking patterns drawing his eyes despite his efforts to ignore it. A voice called down from above.

"Leave me alone!"

Corban and Titus look up. A man was straddling a branch twenty feet above their head. He wore gray pants and a brown T-shirt. His blue suit was not in sight.

"I'm Sheriff Corban."

"I know who you are. Now go away."

"I can't do that. People are being killed."

"No kidding. That's what happens during the Red Diamond."

Titus raised his revolver and aimed at the man. "That's a shitty attitude. Get down or I blow you off that stupid branch."

"I think he means it," Corban said. "I think I'm going to let him do it. But how about we start slower. What is your name?"

The man laughed. "I'm not telling you shit."

"I'll call you Blue."

"Oh, for the suit. Very original."

"Someone put you here," Corban said. "Sent you in here with us to die. I'm beginning to see why. You're an asshole."

"That's not my fault! I know he's been fucking his Chinese translator and he's got it in for me!" The man sagged. "It's hopeless. I can't get out and survival is never going to happen. Have you seen it?"

"Yes."

"It's unstoppable. We're all dead."

"Harlow thinks so, huh?"

The man reacted so violently he almost fell. Then he laughed nervously, looking around. "You're a lot more informed than you should be. People are going to get fired. Damn, how did you get that name?"

"We have a better chance together, Blue."

Blue shook his head. "You think you have any chance?"

"We're going to kill it eventually."

"Not this one. Shit, you don't know anything."

"Come down and tell us about it," Titus said. He lowered his revolver. "I'm sorry about the gun. It's been...tough. That thing has killed some people I know."

"You need to pick a side, Blue," Corban said. "And they obviously don't want you on their side."

"I'm pretty safe up here, alone. I don't need you."

Corban looked back at Pikeburn, a small jumble of squares and colors. "It's been chasing me and Titus from the start. Can't seem to shake it for long. I bet it's coming here next. Why is it chasing us?"

"I - I don't know. What do you mean coming here?"

"What part of 'chasing us' don't you get?" Titus said. He looked at Corban. "Captain, let's go. This guy wants to starve to death up a tree."

"Last chance, Blue," Corban said. "I have trail mix and a warm Sprite."

Blue laughed some, then started to sob, but that didn't last long either. He looked stupefied, washed out, staring at the distance. He gave the hexagon wall the finger. With some difficulty, he climbed down from the branch. Five minutes later he was standing before Corban. Through his dirt-streaked face he was obviously quite young.

"How about your name?" Corban asked.

"Blue. May as well."

"Okay, Blue. Do you have a weapon?"

"I found an old rusted ax."

Leave it. Anything else we can use?"

Blue rubbed snot from his upper lip. "No. Nothing. I'm so hungry. Do you really have food?"

"Hell, we got a whole town full of food," Titus said.

A sharp whistle from the tow truck got their attention. Adam was waving at them. "Hey! We've got company!"

When they reached the tow truck, Janet said, "It's not the monster. I saw dust and thought... you know. But it's another truck."

"Like this one?" Corban said.

"Could be the Moon brothers," Titus said. "And James."

"No." Janet hadn't taken her eye off the scope. "A big pickup but something's wrong. I'm seeing... I don't know. There's something tied to the hood."

"Spread out," Corban ordered. He pulled his pistol and offered it to Blue.

Blue took it slowly. "Are you sure?"

"You picked a side. Now get into cover."

Janet stayed on the roof of the cab. Blue and Titus went to the tall grass in the ditch and crouched down, not really hidden from view but harder to target. Adam was busy scratching at his notebook. Corban waited by the front of the tow truck, AR-15 within easy reach.

Corban watched the other truck arriving. He had to process the image several times before he understood. There was a big chunk of some animal tied to the front hood of the truck. Corban studied it a moment as the driver slowed down and stopped in front of him. It was the front half of a horse.

The truck pulled forward slowly until the driver's window was even with Corban. It rolled down to reveal a man wearing a black and white checkered bandanna around the lower half of his face and sunglasses. A passenger was hidden in shadow.

"What are you doing out here, Sheriff?"

"Checking on things. That's my job as Sheriff. Who am I talking to?"

"You need to get to the courthouse. That's the only safe place now. This new monster is worse than the first one."

"Okay, thanks for the advice."

The man looked up at Janet. "You people out of Gunner's? That place isn't safe. No place is safe."

"What's with the dead horse?"

The man looked at the carcass on his hood. He seemed to think about it for a moment. "Just protection. We're all trying to be safe. We can ride this out. Five days more is all we need. If everyone gets into the courthouse, we win."

"Oh yeah?" Corban got closer to the truck and the driver dipped his hand to his lap. Corban ignored the obvious move for a gun. "What makes you think five days?"

"We have information from the outside."

"Bullshit," Blue called from the grass.

Adam jumped from the tow truck and ran around to stand next to Corban. "How do you know that? What information are you getting? Who is giving it to you?"

"Calm down," Corban said quickly to both Adam and the startled driver. "All that can wait. You know my name?"

"Yes," the man said, keeping his eye on Adam.

"Now tell me yours. We can't have a conversation without knowing names."

The man took some time to debate the request in his head. "Okay. I'm Miller. That's all you're getting for now."

"Okay, I know some of you Millers. I'm friendly with Ada Miller. Did she get out before the walls came up?"

"Yes," Miller said grudgingly. "I'm not here to talk about my aunt. So—"

"Pete Miller," Corban said. "She's talked about you."

The man pulled down his bandana. "God damn it! Stop doing that! I came out to tell you to get to the courthouse! That's all!"

"DePaul sent you?"

"Yes!" The man gunned the truck's engine. "Now I've told you and I'm done!"

"Why the horse?"

The man back the truck away at high speed. He did a fast three-point turn in the dirt road and drove away in a plume of dust.

"Janet," Corban said. "Keep that scope on them. Make sure they actually go back to town."

Titus and Blue walked up. Blue said, "What was that about? What the hell are you people doing?"

"I don't know yet. Titus, what do you know about Depaul?"

"Nothing, really. Retired military. Fought around the world. People say don't mess with him. Looks normal but has a few cards shy of a full deck."

"Great," Corban muttered. "And he's got the courthouse."

"That horse was some kind of trophy," Blue said. "Like demented post-apocalypse movie shit. Are you people eating each other in town?"

"I don't think so," Adam said. "I mean the trophy part. I bet they are trying to mask their scent, kind of like we did with all that food we rubbed on. Why they are using a dead animal is confusing."

"See anything, Janet?" Corban called up.

"Looks clear to me. The truck didn't slow down until town and then turned. They went toward the courthouse, I think. I don't see anything else moving out there."

"Good. We can talk more at Gunner's. I want to get inside. Blue, you can sit on Adam or ride in the back."

"I'm not riding in the back of a truck. Which one is Adam?"

When they pulled into the parking lot and Titus killed the engine, Corban grabbed at his wrist before he could step out. No one moved. The front door to Gunner's was open. No one stood guard. No one could be seen inside and no one appeared to greet them.

"Well?" Titus asked Corban.

"Feels like an ambush," Blue said. "Get us out of here."

Titus put his hand on the key. "We drive on, Captain?"

"To where?" Janet asked.

"We need to check it out," Corban said. "Something is wrong, but I don't think it was the monster. It doesn't use doors."

They spread out from the tow truck, weapons up and ready.

Corban called out, "Billy! Chambers! Anyone in there?"

There was a reply, but it was faint and coming from behind them. He turned his head and saw Billy a block away peeking out from a doorway amid a line of downtown businesses. He was waving frantically.

"Over there," Corban said. As the group started back for the tow truck, Billy waved even harder and shook his head.

"Run for it," Blue said and took off at a panicky sprint.

Adam and Janet started after him and Corban took up the rear with Titus. They all moved in formation until they hit the doorway. A narrow flight of stairs went up to a landing with open doors on both sides. The left door opened to a wide-open room with mirrors on the walls; a dance studio. The right door was a storage room filled with banker boxes labeled Cannerholt Accounting. There were people camped out from Gunner's in both rooms.

Billy was by a row of windows in the dance studio, looking down at the street. He had a clear view of the front of Gunner's as well.

"You got the guy? Is that him?" Billy asked and looked at Blue.

"Yes," Corban said. "What's happened at Gunner's?"

Billy took off his hat. "That thing. That thing attacked us. It hit the back door, kicked it right off the steel hinges. It couldn't get in but...but...damn. It sprayed something into the room before we even had a chance to shoot it. That smell was unbelievable. And it burned, like pepper spray, man. People got sick and ran out. It was waiting for us. Six dead. I hit it a dozen times, I swear, at close range, too. Nothing happened." He looked at them with bright eyes. "And don't get into a car. It took Frank Kent and his daughter from their car as there were driving away. Fucking thing was on the roof, reaching in with that tongue, and pulling out pieces. That's when it ran off, after it got all it wanted from the bodies. We didn't chase it off. It just decided that was enough and bolted."

Chambers came in from a back room. He joined them at the window. "Billy, Grease dosed the injured up pretty good. He's starting to shake it off, whatever he saw in the Fireball."

Billy nodded his thanks. "We hightailed it over here after the attack. It doesn't know we're here."

Chambers started to talk. "We have—"

"Do you have any food?" Blue said.

"Yes," Chambers said slowly with annoyance. "Who the hell are you?"

"I'm Blue. I— I haven't had any food for three days." He looked at Corban and Titus. "I found a couple of water bottles in the RV. At least I had that."

"God knows how old it was," Corban said.

"It was fresh enough. Not that I cared."

"This is the guy you went after?" Billy asked, his face clouding with anger. "Hey, Blue, I got some questions for you, soldier boy."

Corban stepped between them. "He needs some food before we get to that. That's not too hard, is it?"

Billy glared at Blue a moment. "Feed him. Whatever. Ten minutes." As soon as they had turned to go Billy said, "Now you have two experts, Sheriff. Think you can kill this thing now?"

"I'm trying."

Titus leaned forward. "I'm going to get the truck and park it closer."

"What are you, deaf?" Billy snapped. "Didn't I just say it was dragging people out of their cars in pieces?"

"It's not far!" Titus shouted back. "Then we don't have to run the hundred-meter dash just to get inside the damn thing later!"

"You won't make it fifty feet! It's on the God damn roof over there watching everything on the street!"

There was a long stretch of stunned silence.

"What did you say?" Corban asked.

"It climbed the wall like a spider and we see it peeking over the roof every once in a while." Billy started walking away and Corban caught his arm.

"Why didn't you say that in the first place?"

"It's kind of crazy around here is why?" Billy jerked his arm free. "I don't want to sit around here and talk about it. I'm sick of this hiding bullshit. I know where it is. I'm going to set up shop on this roof and when it peeks over again I'm blowing it away. Janet, you got the chops to hit it. You used to be a hell of a shot. Better than your old man. Chambers and me and Luke McCall are killing it. You want in?"

"Well, okay," she said. "If that's okay with you, Sheriff."

"Great," Billy said while glaring at Corban. "Some God damn sense in the group." He stormed off to another window to keep watch.

"Give him some time," Janet said. "Something really bad happened while we were gone."

Corban turned to Adam. "First it goes on a rampage. Now it's watching, waiting. What is it doing?"

"It makes some sense." Adam pulled his notebook out and flipped to pages in the front. "It seems to be cycles. Attacking, herding, waiting, striking."

"What's next?"

"If I had to bet on a behavior?" Adam closed his notebook. "It will strike anything that it sees moving on the street for a while, force us back into our holes. It will use some people as a type of Judas goats, biting off their hands and releasing them to find help. I don't think we should bring those people to our hiding spots anymore. I know that sounds horrible, but we can't let it know where we are."

Corban looked around the repurposed dance studio. A few sleeping bags, lanterns, boxes of trail mix and dehydrated food, a pile of guns and ammo. The people, perhaps fifteen, staring at hands or walls, no longer enthusiastic, no longer even afraid. Waiting with the patience of death.

"Get some rest," Corban said. "Let's all get some rest."

Adam opened his mouth.

"Just rest for a few minutes, Adam. Sleep if you can."

Corban drifted across the landing and into the room full of accounting boxes. About ten people were here, each camped out in an area away from the others. Corban stacked a few boxes into a cot and laid down on it. He stared at the ceiling and did not sleep.

There was almost no conversation going on around him. A few people whispering. A few people weeping quietly. The shuffle of feet as someone moved around. Gradually, a new sound wormed into Corban's ear. He sat up, tilting his head. He walked deeper into the stacks of boxes and found a closed door with a light underneath it. A garbled, mechanical voice was coming from behind the door.

Corban opened it slowly and looked inside. A narrow closet had been converted into a radio room. Five car batteries were arranged on a shelf with cables going from their terminals to a truck CB duct taped in place on a desk. A man was at the CB and talking.

"It's still on the roof as far as I know. You can drive all over town getting what you need."

A Moon brother's voice replied. "Shit, we've got all we need right here. Trouble is - "

Corban reached over the man's hand and seized his wrist. The man looked up with an angry retort on his lips, and froze when he saw Corban.

"Give it to me," Corban said. The man quickly did so. He pressed the button and said, "Is this the older or the younger?"

"Who is that? Is that you, Sheriff?"

"Yes, I'm still here."

There was a pause, then laughing from more than one throat came through. "This is Terry! Older by a year and a day! Hot damn, Sheriff. You're a lucky son of a bitch."

"I don't feel lucky, Terry." He looked at the CB operator. "Get my team here now." The man hurried off to do as ordered. "Is James with you?"

"Yep. He's on the other side of the shop, bending some metal for me. The guy knows his way around tools and he's strong as Tom and me together."

"Glad to hear he didn't try to follow us."

"Oh hell, Sheriff," Terry said, suddenly quieter. "I'm sorry about telling people it was dead. I – we - "

"You put a spike as thick as my arm right through its damn head. It should be dead. It's not your fault."

"Well, we didn't finish the job. We got to drinking and celebrating. We could have helped you kill that thing good."

"Or gotten killed. It wasn't wounded like a normal animal. Think out if it...like a butterfly. You made it leave its cocoon. That's all. There was nothing anyone could have done."

"Okay, but we won't make a mistake again. Now we're trying to figure out the next step."

"I came out there the first time to have you build me a bomb."

"Great minds think alike," Terry said, back to his jovial self. "That's what we've been doing! But, well, Tom says it won't work."

Tom shouted from the background, "It won't! I know what I'm talking about!"

"Why won't it work?"

"Tom doesn't like my fuse."

"You'll get yourself blown to pieces!" Tom shouted.

Titus and Adam barged into the narrow space, forcing Corban into a corner. He waved for them to be quiet. Janet stood in the doorway. Billy looked over her shoulder.

"Shit, they're alive," Billy said. "We haven't heard a peep from them for so long I assumed they were dead."

Corban activated the mic. "Lot of people excited to hear your voice. How about you keep checking in more than once a year?"

"Yeah, sorry about that. We can't hear the CB over the genny. I'll try harder next time."

"Now about your bomb..."

"Bomb?" Janet and Billy said together.

"I need less shrapnel and more fire," Corban said. "Can you rig something like that?"

"More fire?" Terry said. "I didn't think we needed that when I built Hilda."

There was the sound of brief arguing and what sounded like the same voice came on. "This is Tom, the younger Moon."

"Year and a day!" Terry hooted in the background.

"Go ahead, Tom," Corban said while shaking his head.

"You want fire? You want to catch it on fire? Burn it real good?"

"I do."

"I can do that, but it's not going to be very portable. It will have to be big."

Corban sighed. "Can it fit on a truck? A normal truck?"

"Yeah, sure, I can rig a truck. But you'll have to get it to come to you. Chasing it down with a bomb-filled truck is a terrible idea." Tom drew in a quick breath. "You're not going to do that, are you?"

"If I have to, but I have a better idea." Corban could see the relief in the eyes around him.

"Because I can make it boom and send flames everywhere, but you won't like being near it."

"Have you heard from the courthouse or Alice or Depaul?"

"Nope," Tom said.

"See any trucks with...dead animals on the hood?"

Tom laughed at the question. "You're the last visitor we had. Like real dead animals strapped to a hood? A hunting trophy?"

"Sort of. I don't know what it's about. But don't worry about it. Tom, I need that firebomb."

"Would be easier if I could steal a truck, you know?"

"So, steal one."

"Cool!"

Corban looked at his group. "Anyone have a question for the Moon brothers?"

They did not.

"I'm signing off," Corban said. "Tell James he's doing great. Check in at the top of each hour, Tom. It's kind of important."

"Will do, Sheriff. Good luck!"

Corban set the mic down with care. He rubbed the grit from his eyes.

"You okay?" Janet asked.

"I will be." He dropped his hand. "Let's go talk to Blue. Billy, is there a good place for an interrogation?"

"I think I know of one."

At the back of the dance studio was another narrow stairway. This one didn't end in the street, but a landing with three doors. One was to the alley. The other two were businesses: a quilting supply store and a travel agency that hadn't booked a trip in years. Even though the travel agency had a pair of wide windows, they were completely covered with posters for exotic locations that the sun had degraded to sepia versions of once popular destinations.

Billy put a lantern on the corner of the table that occupied the center of the travel agency. He dragged up a dusty office chair and got comfortable. Everyone else found office chairs, plush waiting room chairs, or red plastic chairs that looked like they belonged on a deck. It was Corban, Titus, Adam, Janet, Billy, Chambers, and Blue around the table. Billy dropped the map on the table, billowing dust particles into the air. He unfolded it and tapped a location near the center of downtown.

"Us," he said.

"Where is it?" Corban asked.

"Over there."

"Be more specific."

"I can't," Billy said with annoyance. "The map doesn't show details like that. Remember where the dance studio windows looked out on? Summer Street. Across the street and up about half a block. It's on the roof there. It can see all of Summer and Heart Streets and Gunner's. It can hit Gunner's in a second if it wanted to." He swung his feet up to the table. "And why are you grilling me? I've told you everything already. Ask this asshole a few questions."

Blue looked straight ahead.

"I will in a minute. Is someone watching that monster right now?"

"Luke has his eyes on where it was last seen. If it moves, he will let me know."

"But he can't actually see it. Only when it looks around."

"Yes!" Billy said. "Are we done yet, Sherlock?"

Corban eased back in his chair. He slowly turned to Blue.

"I know what you want," Blue said. "I'm just a tech. I don't know anything about that monster."

"That's not what I heard."

"From who?"

"You."

Blue shook his head. "I never — oh, wait a minute. You heard me at the wall?"

"You were shouting." Corban made a helpless shrug. "I understand. You were a little upset."

"You would be, too."

Billy slammed his palm on the table. "We are! A little upset!"

"Hey," Blue said, "this is how red Diamond works. I'm sorry. I didn't make the rules. It's just a lousy job I don't like."

Chambers stood up. He went to stand in the filtered light by the windows. He stared out at the street through a slit in the posters. He had his rifle across his chest and his finger on the trigger.

"Now," Corban said, "before things get out of hand, tell me who Harlow is."

"He's—" Adam started, then clapped his mouth shut. "Sorry, Sheriff."

"He's a scientist." Blue shuddered. "A very creepy guy. Most of the big names in Red Diamond are off in the head, you know what I mean? You get used to it if you work there. But this guy seems less than human. The way he looks at people. I don't know. It's not right."

"He built our monster?"

Blue nodded. "It's all him, I think. About ten months ago he walked into a meeting – this is what I heard – and slapped papers in from of General Attics. Said he had finished the first stages of something big. Attics kicked everyone else out right there and the two of them have been best friends ever since."

"He's supposed to be dead," Adam said. "Executed for espionage years ago."

"I'm not lying to you," Blue said. "I've seen him. Right after he barged in on General Attics, the place shifted gears. The thing that was supposed to be Red Diamond this year got executed. They brought in this metal shipping box on a semi. We were required to wear all kinds of safety gear around it. It can spray you and you'll die."

"What else can it do?"

"Look, I'm just a tech. I work with the wall. All I know is this thing is major. I heard people saying if this one kills the entire town, they wouldn't be surprised. Maybe...maybe even breed them for an army of monsters."

"A nest," Corban said to Adam.

Adam was writing as fast as he could in his notebook and still talking with excitement. "It's never been done before. How could that be done? It's already lightyears ahead of other monsters. Imagine if it could produce offspring!"

Billy gave the table a sudden kick, jolting Adam from his scribbling. "We are imagining that, dumb ass."

"It's the Holy Grail of design. Maybe we get lucky and kill this one. Then four more show up. Then sixteen more. You can wipe out a country with a single monster at that point."

"That's not fucking fair," Janet said. She blushed when everyone looked at her. "I mean, how are we supposed to win against something like that?"

"You don't," Blue said.

"No more negative bullshit from you," Titus said around his pipe. "Okay? Start helping around here."

Blue shrugged.

"If..." Chambers said without looking away from the street. "If it has a nest, it isn't guarding it. Some animals lure predators away from the nest by using themselves as bait. Maybe that's why it's on the roof over there. It's letting us see it. It wants to be seen."

"Fucking hell," Billy muttered. "It's distracting us from eggs or something."

"We don't have any proof there is a nest," Adam said.

"But if there is?" Corban asked.

"Then we're all dead. One of those things is tough enough."

"Does anyone have any real evidence of a nest?" Corban asked them all and no one spoke up. "Well, we're going to look for this nest anyway. We have to know for sure. We can't walk up and ask politely to see baby photos. Adam and Blue, put your heads together. Billy, walk them through this map. Where would it hide? Where would it lay eggs? It can't be live young, right?"

"Right," Chambers said. "It's been gone too long for live young."

"We can't assume anything normal about this monster," Adam said.

"It did tear off its own head," Titus said. "That was pretty surprising."

"It doesn't matter," Corban said. "We look for a nest because not doing that might be suicide." He pulled the map closer. "Titus, when it grabbed you and took off, it was heading in this direction. What's over here? Where could it be going?"

Blue cleared his throat. "They kept it wet. I know that much."

"It lived in water?"

"No. Like they had misters or something. Water hoses that we had to set up on timers that sprayed its cage. Wet and dark. Especially when it was young."

Corban looked at the group. "Anything?"

"I don't know," Billy said. "The swimming pool is here. But that's drained for repairs, right?"

"It is."

"No lakes in town."

"No water treatment plants," Corban said. "Hasn't rained in two weeks. There's no water. What else do we have to go on?"

For several minutes, they stared at the map and each other.

"The nest could be anywhere," Titus said. "Maybe it was taking the scenic route with me in its mouth."

Corban was staring hard at the glass of water in Blue's hand. "Where did you get that water?"

Billy looked from Corban to the glass, then to Chambers. "Hey, Chambers?"

"Out of the bathroom sink," Chambers said. "It's a clean cup. I didn't spit in it."

"Stop drinking that. Stop everyone from drinking the tap water now. Now, Chambers!"

The man blinked at Corban in surprise, but headed out the door as told.

"It's in the water tower," Corban said. "We can't find it on the map because its inside the water tower!"

"Son of a bitch," Billy said. He stood up and kicked a trashcan against the wall. "Son of a bitch!"

"We have it," Titus said.

"No," Adam said quickly. "If there is a nest and it is in the water tower, all we're talking about is stopping more of them from coming. The mother is still out there. It won't be happy if we kill the young."

"Or it won't give a damn at all," Janet said.

"It's too much speculation," Corban said. "I'm going to take a look."

"Hold on," Billy said.

"We already know where the monster is. We know where the water tower is. I'll just run over and look."

"Not without me." Billy folded his arms. "I'm not staying in this fucking prison any longer. If anyone gets to run around, I'm going with them."

"Okay," Corban said, locking eyes with him. "I can't stop you, Billy. I'm leaving in ten minutes."

"I'll get my shit." Billy left the room.

"Damn, Captain," Titus said and chuckled. "As fun as it might be going with you just to watch you and Billy snipe at each other, I need to rest a while. This back up leg isn't made for running around like the other was. My stump is set to start bleeding if I do much more today."

"That's fine." Corban stood up. "What about you two?"

"I'll go," Janet said.

"I'd kill to see what kind of offspring that produces," Adam said. He stuffed his notebook away.

Titus inclined his head toward Blue.

Corban understood. "Blue? You coming with me or staying here?"

"I don't see as I have much choice. If I stay here they might kill me. That guy Chambers pretty much said as much. They see me as the enemy."

"Because you are," Janet said. "But you're also right here, right now, so stop being a pussy and get ready to go." She left the room.

"Right," Blue said softly. He stood up. "I guess I'm going."

Back in the dance studio a knot of people near the front door were having a whispered and animated conversation. Corban came up and stood next to Billy. The CB operator was talking and his face was distressed.

Billy turned to Corban. "Because things can't get any weirder, right?"

"What's the problem now?"

"We got a call on the CB from DePaul."

"It wasn't really just for us," the CB operator said. "It was a broadcast to the entire town. DePaul says he's got it all figured out."

"How many people could he be reaching?"

The operator shrugged. "Us, the Moon brothers, some old guy in his basement named Troy. That's all I know of for sure, but there could be more listening in."

"What does DePaul say?"

"Check this out," Billy said. "The old bastard says he's got a line to the outside world. He's in contact with a man who owes him and that's where he's getting his info about this year's Red Diamond."

"Impossible," Adam said.

"Never in a million years," Blue said. "You have no idea the security level going on."

Adam held up his hand. "I know I've been wrong on some things. I know this is a Red Diamond like no other. But, Sheriff, this is flat out impossible."

"He's batshit crazy," Billy said. "That dead horse on the truck hood? That's his idea. He's saying dead animals drive it away. It only eats human flesh, so a dead animal is something it can't handle. He's telling people to kill their pets and throw them in their front yards! Sick fuck."

Corban had his hand wrapped in the operator's shirt and he had pulled the startled man inches from his face.

"You get back on that CB and you counter that line of bullshit with a message from me. You tell everyone that can hear that I'm saying it's crap. Absolute crap. It won't work and don't you dare do it. We are working - "

Titus put a hand on Corban and he knocked it away.

"Listen to me! Tell DePaul we are working on several plans and we've got experts and the Moon brothers are building a firebomb and this thing is going to die. When it's dead, I'll deal with any bullshit he's caused. I'm still the Sheriff of Pikeburn and I will lock his ass in a cage for inciting a riot. I'll make it stick no matter who he knows." He let the man go and tried to bring his voice down. "Tell DePaul he's a lying sack of shit and I'll be along to make sure he isn't hurting..."

Corban trailed off. He went to stand with his fists clenched at the window, the afternoon sun warming his face. Janet joined him and just stood shoulder to shoulder, watching the rooftops across the street.

"And I thought Masterson was going to be the problem," Corban said through his teeth.

"Let's get the water tower taken care of," she said.

He looked at her. She was at least two inches taller and when they stood close he was looking up. "Yeah. One monster at a time."

CHAPTER SEVEN

Someone had rigged a rope out a window away from the monster's last known position. The group held there until word came from the lookout. The monster was still on the same roof, still peeking out every half hour or so to look for targets. Then Corban, Adam, Janet, Billy, and Blue slipped to the alley and ran as quietly as possible for the water tower across town.

Corban had his AR-15 and sidearm. Blue had been given a different pistol and hip holster. Janet carried her hunting rifle. Billy was carrying his M-16, but had ditched the pistol and long knife. Adam had picked out an archaic double barrel shotgun loaded with solid slugs that would pulverize concrete.

Corban and Janet led the way, keeping to the shadows and avoiding open areas as much as possible, while Billy brought up the rear with a constant eye on their trail. They passed a looted liquor store and paused to grab a few bottles to take back to the dance studio. In an intersection, they found a running motorcycle, bright red and purring, a thing that was more high-tech beetle than a vehicle. They left it as they found it. They passed a house with a dead cat suspended by an extension cord from the porch eave. Corban borrowed Adam's pen to write down the address on his palm before continuing.

The chain-link fence around the water tower had a section knocked flat. The group looked at each other knowingly. Janet spent time on her scope looking over all the roof tops and corners in the area. Adam and Corban studied the metal ladder that rose up one of the four legs that held up the white UFO shape of the water tower.

"Trouble with high places?" Corban asked.

"No. Trouble with being so exposed for so long. If it can see the nest from where it is squatting, we're going to get picked off that ladder like snacks for that thing. Should someone stay behind?"

"If you want to," Corban said.

"Well, not me. I'm going. I have to go."

"Okay, Adam, calm down." Corban waved them into a huddle. "Janet, you come last in case we get a surprise visit from the monster. If we hear her shooting, reverse course immediately. Blue, you lead the way."

"Okay, Captain."

Corban stopped him. "Why did you call me that?"

Blue looked at the others, then at Corban. "That other guy with the missing leg keeps calling you Captain. I just figured...you were military."

"I'm not. Titus thinks he's back in Iraq."

"Okay. Sorry."

Corban let him go and he rushed across the open ground to the ladder. Billy slung his machine gun over his shoulder and followed. Adam leaned his shotgun against the wall of the building they crouched near. He ran after Blue and Billy.

"I think it's cute," Janet said. "Maybe I'll start calling you Captain."

"Start by watching my back."

She winked at him. She put the scope to her eye and began sweeping the horizon for trouble.

The ladder went up one hundred and sixty feet. Corban kept glancing over his shoulder as the town of Pikeburn opened up to him. At the top of the ladder was a balcony that ran the circumference of the tower. Corban peered over the rail and waved down. Janet gave him a thumbs-up and started her climb.

Pikeburn sprawled before him, silent and oppressed. Nothing moved on any street except leaves that were being blown around by the wind. There was also destruction. There were black marks where fires had sprung up and burned themselves out. Fences laid down or torn apart, vehicles reduced to parts in the street, holes in homes big enough for the tow truck to drive through. The silence was unnerving.

"Captain," Blue said. "You've got to see this!"

He followed Blue around the balcony. On the opposite side from the ladder was a tear in the white metal of the water tower above his head.

"That's it," Blue said.

"It can't be. It's too small. A man could get through that easily, but not that monster we've been fighting."

"Unless," Adam said. He pulled out his notebook. "Unless it just laid eggs and didn't even go inside."

"Boost me up," Billy said.

Blue and Corban locked hands and boosted Billy up. He peered into the darkness for a while, then motioned for them to bring him down.

"I don't see anything," he said when he was standing with them.

Janet came around the curve. "Well, thanks for waiting, boys."

Adam dug into his messenger bag and held up a keychain flashlight.

"Give it here," Billy said.

"No," Adam said and closed his hand around the flashlight. "I'm going to see."

Billy's face grew angry, but it quickly faded. "Whatever, genius." He and Blue formed their hands together and lifted Adam. Wedging himself into the tear in the metal, he took all his weight off their hands. They could see his lower half wriggle around as he moved the light.

"I— I don't see anything. Maybe we're wrong again."

"Up," Corban shouted.

"What?"

"Look up!"

There was a pause, then they barely heard a whispered, "Shit."

Adam threw himself from the tear, away from the steel side of the water tower and into open air. He struck the rail with his waist and flipped over, legs together and straight up like an Olympic diver. He was plunging off the side.

Billy and Corban reached him as he started the drop. Billy wrapped his arms around the upthrust legs. Corban had him from below the rail around the waist. For a moment nothing moved, then everyone was shouting orders. With a great deal of care and fuss, Adam was brought under the rail and laid out on the balcony.

Billy grabbed his M-16 and covered the tear.

"What's up there?" Corban asked.

Adam was on his back, blinking rapidly. He was taking tiny, gasping draws of air.

"Should I slap him?" Janet asked.

"Please don't," Adam wheezed. "I'm hurt is all."

"Should I blast it?" Billy asked.

"No. Well, maybe. I don't think that would do any good. It's a—a sack. Some kind of egg sack and it's empty. I need to look again."

Corban picked up his weapon and clicked off the safety. "Empty? Is it in the water?"

"I don't know. It's too dark to see to the bottom." Adam sat up and gave a small giggle that was bordering on hysterical. "That was interesting. I dropped the flashlight, too."

Corban's eyes widened. "I got it covered." He found the four road flares in his backpack. "These burn underwater, right?"

"Yeah," Billy said. "Is that going to be enough?"

"I'll find out. Boost me up."

"Hold on," Blue said. "I wouldn't go sticking my head into a hornet's nest and then light a firecracker."

"What?" Corban asked.

"Why not light the first one and throw it in. You don't have to have your head over the water like some kind of shark handler at Sea World. You'll get bit in half."

"Well, when you put it that way," Corban said. He struck one of the flares into life and even in broad daylight it was a raw piece of the sun in his hands. He stood on his toes and flipped the flare into the water tower. The faint sound of a splash was heard.

"Just wait a minute," Blue said. "The bottom curve of the tank will put that burning magnesium against anything resting in there. And - "

A weird skittering sound echoed within the tower.

"Fucking hell," Billy said.

"I don't like this," Blue said.

Weapons were aimed at the tear and no one moved.

The skittering increased. Something landed hard against the metal under the tear with a gong-like boom. At the bottom of the tear, a wet tendril of flesh poked out. It was pale, dripping, probing the air. When the sun hit it, Corban could vaguely see the diminutive bone structure holding the sagging flesh in place.

Blue vomited over the rail at the sight of the thing.

Billy pulled the trigger on the M-16 and did not let up. True to his word, it was fully automatic and chattered away in his hands. The tendril vanished in a puff of pink moisture. Billy walked a line of bullet holes down the side of the tower. Everyone else hit the ground.

There was a moment of quiet and people slowly started to rise. Billy blew on the smoking barrel of his weapon. Something hammered at the inside of the tower walls and water jetted from the bullet holes. The balcony shivered from the impact.

"We're leaving!" Corban shouted. He shoved Adam toward the ladder. Janet hauled on Blue and took him around the curve. Billy was fixing another clip into his M-16.

"Billy! We are leaving!"

"No shit!"

A shadow bulged from the tear, a thing that barely held a shape, more expanding plastic membrane than skin.

Corban fired a single shot and the brass casing jammed in his weapon. But his one shot plowed a rippling line through the jelly of the bulge. It recoiled from the attack back into the water tower.

"Now!" Corban shouted.

"I swear to God, Captain!" Billy shouted back in his face as he ran by.

They made the ladder as they heard metal bending. Billy jumped onto the rungs and started down. Corban took a knee. He dropped the AR-15 over the side and drew his pistol. He cocked it and aimed for the curve of the balcony.

The rending metal could be felt in his knee as the entire balcony structure vibrated in sympathy. He kept looking from the point something would appear around the bend, then down the ladder to where the others were. A bead of sweat stung his eyes and he had to squeeze tears away.

The rending stopped, but the vibrations increased.

"It's free," Corban said. He suddenly felt cold and an uncontrollable shiver went down his spine.

The odd skittering sound came again. It was getting louder, but he saw nothing. He looked back along the other side and still saw nothing. The skittering was even louder, the only sound now louder than his heartbeat.

Corban looked up... and the mass of pulsing flesh was coming over the top of the water tower.

Corban jumped.

He flung the pistol away as he dropped off the balcony. In front of him the ladder rungs started to blur by. He counted one, two, and grabbed for the rungs. The first one slapped his hands so hard they burned. Fighting the impulse to bring them back, he thrust them forward again. The second rung was easier but his fingers would not close. The third rung he grasped and cried out in triumph and pain as he was swung into the ladder.

Someone was calling his name from below.

Corban was aware he hurt. His hands were on fire and his knees were filled with glass shards. Just hanging there was all he could do for several moments. He slowly brought one foot up and found a rung. He took the weight off his hands and grimaced as new pain in his wrists flared to life. Ignoring it, he started down the ladder.

Below him gunfire was popping. He didn't look down or up. He fixed his eyes forward and climbed, getting faster as the pain and shock subsided to manageable levels.

A pair of hands seized him around the waist and he was physically lifted from the ladder. Blue put him down only after they reach the corner of a building and joined the others.

"That ugly fucking thing almost had you," Billy said. He was pale and sweaty.

Janet grabbed him in a bear hug that he had to force himself out of.

"It's started down one of the tower legs," Adam said. He was peeking around the corner at it. "It's amazing."

"L-l-let's get out of here," Blue said.

Even as the other moved to obey, Corban said, "Not yet. We're not done."

The others exchanged glances.

Janet squeezed his arm. "It's slow but it's coming for us."

"No," he said. "We came here for it. We came here. For. It."

Billy was shaking his head. "You were busy nearly falling to your death, but we just put a lot of lead into that thing and it didn't stop."

"I saw it up close. I saw through the damn thing. It has organs. We can kill it."

"You, um, don't have a gun," Blue said.

Corban walked around the corner. Something that appeared to be made from thin plastic bags and pink jelly was halfway down the nearest leg of the tower. It was mostly cylindrical in body shape, but it undulated and quivered. A dozen small, bony legs clung to the metal, but the glistening, sticky body was helping it scale the tower, leaving a trail of clear goo. It had no eyes, nose, ears, or a mouth. There was no way of telling if it were scaling down head first or ass first.

The AR-15 was near the base of the ladder. The impact of the fall had cleared the jam, making Corban laugh. He slid the next shell into the chamber. By this time the group had joined him.

He pointed at the monstrous thing working down the tower's leg. "We came here to stop that obscenity. Well, there it is! We won't get a better chance."

"We tried that!" Billy said.

"It doesn't have blood," Adam said. "This one has the complete opposite defense than the first one. It's got some kind of gelatinous body that can ignore bullets, let them pass through or get lodged in it. I bet it's also got a very high resistance to heat. Fire won't be an easy fix."

"Janet," Corban said, "can you blow off those legs?"

Janet looked up in surprise. Her mouth formed a circle as she understood. "Hell yes!"

"Bring it to the ground."

"Yes, Captain!"

"Billy, take this." He thrust the AR-15 toward him. "My hands are shaking. Get to the other side and start taking off legs."

Billy swapped him his own M-16 and ran off.

Janet's first shot was dead on and the lowest leg spun into the air amidst a confetti of bloodless flesh.

Corban pointed to Adam, who was holding his double barrel shotgun like it was a broom. "Wait for it to fall. Wait for it to hit the ground. Then step up and blast holes in it. Can you do that?"

"I – I can. I know I can."

"Blue."

"Yes, Captain?"

"You're the last wave. If it's still twitching, wait for Adam to pull back, then you empty that clip into the center of it. It has some organs, I saw them, and they will explode."

"This is fucked up," Blue said. "I drank water that thing was growing and swimming in. Oh God." He retched again onto the grass.

Janet shouted, "It's slipping!"

The claws scrabbled at the metal but too many legs had been taken off by gunfire. It slipped from the surface and plummeted eighty feet to the ground. The outer membrane of the monster ripped down the side like a seam giving way on a tight pair of jeans. A gush of steaming semi-solid liquid burst from it all over the grass. The misaligned legs that remained waved in fits at the sky.

Adam strode over to the flailing creature, put his shotgun against it, and pulled both triggers. The concussive blast shredded what was left of it. When Adam stepped away, the monster was torn into two unmoving parts.

For a moment, they all stared at the steaming remains. Parts began to break down, oozing into the soil.

"Hey, did we just kill a monster?" Billy said. "Am I seeing that right?" He started jumping up and down.

Adam came to stand next to Corban. "I forgot more shells. I'm as bad as James at this."

Corban grabbed him by both arms. "You just killed a monster, Adam! It's in pieces! We did it!"

"Oh," Adam said. He looked back at it, tilted his head in surprise. "Wow."

"Stay away from the corpse," Corban yelled at Janet and Billy who were moving toward it.

"I need a trophy," Billy said.

"It's poisoning the air you're breathing."

Billy and Janet looked at each other. They hustled back to Corban.

"Nothing on that thing I want on a wall anyway," Billy said.

"Just throw a trash bag of water balloons on your wall." Janet said.

"Now what, Captain?" Blue asked.

"We go home. To the dance studio."

On the way back, Corban detoured at the house with dead cat strung up. He wrapped his hand in the cord and yanked it down. He pounded on the door and yelled, "Sheriff's office! Open this door!"

A face appeared in one of the small windows in the door, goggling at Corban.

"Open the door," Corban said.

Locks clicked and the door swung inward a few inches.

"All the way," Corban said.

The man did as ordered. He was in his late thirties, larger than Corban by a hundred pounds, and totally afraid. A woman and a 10-year-old boy stood on the first step of stairs to the second floor.

"Don't drink the water," Corban said. "It's been tainted. Not sure how bad. We'll have to wait to find out. Don't shower or clean with it."

"But what are we supposed to drink?" the man asked.

"I don't care." Corban dropped the cat at the man's feet. "How did you hear about this? Do you own a CB?"

"Well, n-no. Some guys in a truck. They saw my son in the window and they came up. They said DePaul was in charge. Said..." His eyes filled with tears and quickly spilled over to his cheeks. "They said we had to. It was the only way. My God, they were driving about and nothing was happening to them. They had a horse's head on their hood. They weren't being attacked. Doesn't it have to work?"

"No. It doesn't work. Stop panicking. Bury your pet in your backyard or I'll come back here and make you. Good day."

As soon as they climbed back into the back room of the dance studio, Corban pointed at Chambers. "Have you seen the monster recently?"

"Yes," he said. "Lookout said it was acting antsy about the time you guys showed back up."

"It heard us coming but couldn't spot us," Billy said.

"It didn't need to spot things before," Titus said. "Maybe it's lost some senses without a head."

"Don't you even want to know what happened with us?" Janet asked.

Chambers looked at them carefully. "I, uh, assumed nothing since you aren't covered in blood."

"It didn't have blood," Corban said. "But we killed it anyway."

"Seriously?" Chambers asked Billy.

"Not here," Billy told him. "Let's get to the table downstairs and we can talk there."

Corban nodded. "Bring ammo for all of us, find some clean cups, and stop people from drinking any water from a tap."

Fifteen minutes later everyone around the table was sipping whiskey from plastic cups and soaking in the details of the attack on the water tower. Billy had taken up the chore of reloading clips and cleaning guns.

"Are we all poisoned?" Chambers asked. "I didn't taste any difference in the water. I don't feel any worse."

"Let's not worry about that right now," Corban said. "There might be more of them so we need to do another search."

Adam raised his hand. "I have something to say about both those issues."

"Go on."

"I don't think poison is the problem. Poison is easy. It's not any challenge for the people who run Red Diamond."

"What the hell are you saying?" Billy asked.

"If the goal were to kill a town, poison would be a great choice, but it wouldn't advance science at all. The best poisons were invented hundreds of years ago."

"Plus, no revenue from TV viewers," Janet said. "Did you know you can buy a plush doll of the wolf monster that tried to eat the train depot town?"

"Yes," Adam said. "So that's why I don't think it was poisoning the water supply. That doesn't fit the rules."

"And what rule are they breaking for dropping a pregnant monster in here?" Corban asked.

"I have an idea on that, as well. It was never pregnant. I stand with my first statement. The thing we killed was not an offspring. They share almost no characteristics."

"Then explain it being exactly where a nest would be." Billy challenged.

"Oh, I think we logically found the place the first monster liked, but not that the two are related in any fashion. I think that thing in the tower is... a parasite of some kind. What they released into Pikeburn was a main monster with some kind of embryo inside it or attached to it like a tick. Plus..." He took a moment to scan his notebook. "Okay, plus, it was a very poorly designed. Hideous and really unpleasant, that's for sure, but not really that dangerous. I get the feeling it was supposed to be something else. It was so malformed it could hardly chase us. It sure did freak us out, though. If Sheriff Corban hadn't stood up to it, we would have that thing crawling around Pikeburn looking for whatever it eats."

"It eats people," Chambers said.

"There were no people in that tower."

"Well maybe you didn't look hard enough."

"Have you tasted any decaying flesh in your drinking water?" Adam asked him pointedly. "No? Because it's very noticeable to have a decaying animal in the water supply. This entire town would be puking blood in the streets."

Chambers glared but remained silent.

"That still leaves a question of where it's been taking people," Corban said. "If not a nest, then some kind of den."

"A larder," Janet said.

"Keeps getting better," Billy said to Chambers. The other man nodded, still eyeing Adam with his jaw muscles tight.

"And we need to get a handle on Depaul," Titus said. "He spent half an hour ranting on the CB about doomsday and knowing what was really going on. Was there a military hospital east of town?"

Billy looked to Janet questioningly, and both shook their heads.

"We were born here," Billy said. "No hospital was ever out there."

"I don't have time to deal with him," Corban said. "His time will come but right now I have something bigger to fry. Any words from the Moon brothers?"

Titus snorted in disapproval. "No. Not even at the top of the hour. They just aren't made for responsible behavior."

"That's good news for us," Janet said. "I can't make a bomb."

"Someone here might have to try," Chambers said. "If they're dead."

Corban had been studying the map. He looked up. "Do the soldiers monitor our CB broadcasts?"

"Yes," Blue said.

"So, they listen to us?"

"Yes, but they can't reply. I know because I disabled some of the radios in our company to prevent even accidental contact. No one is talking to DePaul."

Corban held up his hand. "I understand that. But we can talk to them."

"What good does that do us?" Billy asked.

"I don't know yet. Adam, don't they have to follow rules, too?"

"To a degree. There is a Red Diamond document, sort of a mission statement. It details the goals of Red Diamond. Most people never read it. It does specifically state only one monster is to be released upon a town. Keep in mind what's going on here in Pikeburn isn't being broadcast live to the world. It's got a few hours delay and they can edit it to look like anything they want. Some parts will be scrubbed from any documents. I doubt that tower monster will have a plush doll."

Blue shuddered. "I hope not."

Footsteps on the stairs alerted them to a new arrival. Grease came through the door. He had somehow returned to his normal size and swagger, but didn't look at Corban.

"Chambers, that guy is getting worse. Ain't no way I keep him alive without a real doc."

"We don't have a doc," Chambers said.

"So, go get one." When no one spoke up, he shrugged. "Makes no difference to me. I'll keep him juiced up. I brought plenty with me."

"The courthouse has the only medical help," Corban said. "Is it worth trying to get him there?"

Grease didn't acknowledge Corban. He left the room and went back up the stairs.

"What was that about?" Blue asked.

"Trouble in paradise," Titus said.

"Why is it just sitting up there?" Billy asked. "Yesterday the damn thing was running all over town eating people, breaking into homes and ripping people to pieces. Today it's..." He pulled off his ballcap and slapped it on the table. "God damn it."

"That's exactly why." Adam jotted something down in his notebook. "Confusion. If it had a pattern, we could lay a trap."

"I want to see it," Corban said and stood up.

Chambers held up a restraining hand as everyone rose. "One at a time, damn it. It doesn't know we're here and we don't want to let it know."

"It knows," Adam said quietly.

Up on the roof there were plenty of places to hide behind in the form of air conditioner units, mechanical sheds, and vent pipes. To one side was a dilapidated pigeon coop. Next to this collapsed coop was the lookout man. He glanced at them before waving them forward. Chambers and Corban rushed over and dropped behind the rotting boards.

"Saw it looking around not sixty seconds ago," the man said. He spat into a beer can with the top cut off and rubbed at his mouth. "It's still there."

Chambers carefully pointed across the street and down the block. All the buildings along both sides of the street were two stories with flat roofs. Some had signage on top in addition to the usual rooftop scattering of equipment of unknowable purpose. "Right above the book store. It's got itself squeezed behind the billboard."

"Something else," the lookout said. "I swear I saw a face in the window of the apartment right below."

"That would be Mr. and Mrs. French," Corban said. "They own the book store and live above it. I didn't think they would leave. I hope they keep quiet."

They heard rapid footsteps from behind and Billy and Janet joined them at the crumbled coop.

"Why don't we wave some red flags, too," Chambers said. "Turn on the tunes and have a cook out, invite everyone up."

"Shut up," Billy told him. "You're turning into an old woman."

"Fuck you. It's not supposed to know we are here."

"Boys," Janet warned. "Don't raise your voices."

Billy looked at Corban. "We don't have any water supplies. Someone needs to get to the store. If that thing is just squatting there, we can bust out the back again and make the gas station on Hooper Street. They always have stacked cases of bottled water in the window."

"How many people do you need?"

"Four, I figure. We may need more than one trip."

Corban looked at the sky, judging the lowering sun. "I think..." He squinted at the horizon. Something was in the sky at the edge of town. It was moving. It was getting closer.

Something in his face alerted the others and everyone turned to the west. The object defined itself into two, one atop the other. A low throbbing beat started to reach them. It grew louder and deeper as they waited.

"Is that a helicopter?" Janet asked.

"Damn right it is," Billy said. "About time we got some air support." Then he frowned. "But that's not for us, is it?"

"Hell if I know," Corban muttered.

"Not with our luck," Chambers said.

The two objects solidified into a big twin rotor helicopter and a black box on steel cables strung below. It came fast and low over town, shaking windows and setting dust and leaves billowing in its wake. It passed right over the group on the roof.

"It's moving!" the lookout shouted.

The monster had come out from its hiding spot and was staring with white, blank eyes at the flying machine. Janet put her rifle to her shoulder. Before she fired, the monster sprang backward from the passing helicopter and scaled down the other side of the building.

"Well, fuck me," Billy said. "Now it's on the move! Assholes!" He shouted his frustration at the helicopter.

Corban was on his feet. "Come on! We have to see where it sets that box down!"

All the roofs of the block were connected so they raced along to the east. They reached the end of the block that overlooked a street and small buildings on the other side. The helicopter was hovering now about a quarter mile away.

"Where is it?" Corban asked. "Is that Stonecut Park?"

"Yep," Billy said. "I think it's dropping that in the tennis court."

Motion caught their attention to the left. The monster was galloping across the street and into the residential homes outside of downtown Pikeburn.

"Whatever they are dropping off is going to have company real soon," Janet said.

"That's not our problem," Corban said.

More people had come to the roof and made their way to stand with them.

Adam was shaking his head in disbelief. "That's not possible."

"I saw a big chopper off in grid 71 before the wall came up," Blue said. "That has to be it."

"What about that box?" Corban asked Blue.

"Never seen that before. I have no idea."

"Adam?"

"You've got me, Captain. At this point, it could be a snow cone shop and I wouldn't be surprised."

The steel cables released tension under the helicopter and it leaped higher into the air. It turned away from them and flew away rapidly. They couldn't see the black box from their vantage point.

"A third monster?" Titus asked no one in particular.

"They wouldn't," Chambers said, his voice cracking. "They fucking wouldn't. Why not just firebomb Pikeburn and be done with it?"

Corban slapped Billy on the shoulder. "We've got another four hours of daylight. I'm going to see that's in the box."

"Yeah, okay," Billy said absently, staring at the leaving chopper. "I'll come along."

"What the hell for?" Chambers asked. "Why not leave it alone?"

"I don't like surprises."

"Look!" Titus shouted. He was pointing.

About six blocks away down the street, the black pickup was driving like mad away from them. On its tail bounded the headless monster. It was gaining as the truck pinballed between parked cars on the narrow street.

"They've had it," Billy said.

Janet had the scope on the developing chase. "I see blood on the driver. Jesus, it's spraying the windshield."

"It got them through the window," Corban said. He looked at the others. "It'll be busy. Now's when we get shit done. Chambers, pick a good spot for the survivors and move there immediately. A place with food and water and defenses is ideal."

"And where the hell am—"

"Do it! Janet, take Blue and anyone else fast and sharp-eyed you want. Follow that monster. See if it will take the truck driver to the larder. Do not engage it! You don't have the firepower."

"I know that," Blue said while tapping his hip-mounted pistol.

"Go now before you lose it for good."

Janet motioned with her head and Blue took off with her. She did a quick spin, blew Corban a kiss, and followed Blue down the stairwell.

"Billy, Titus, Adam. You're with me."

"You bet, Captain," Titus said. He stuck his pipe in his mouth and chewed on the stem.

Corban turned to Chambers. "Where are you taking these people? Pick a place, Chambers."

"The High school. It's got food and bottled water in the cafeteria."

"Good enough." Corban motioned for his men to follow and he ran for the stairwell.

The black box had come down in the tennis court, ripping the net from the posts. Ten-foot-high chain-link fencing encircled the court. The two gates were shut but not locked. The court was on the edge of a small park, a colorful sign proclaiming it Stonecut Park. The black box was visible from all the surrounding area.

Corban and his group were crouched on a porch behind a trellis that was burdened with an acre of winding vines.

"We circled it twice now," Billy said. "What else you got?"

"I guess get closer," Corban said.

"We could shoot it from here," Titus said. "You can't miss something like that."

The black box was a perfect square, each side being twelve feet across. It appeared without decoration, seam, or door. It did not reflect any light.

"What kind of game is this?" Corban whispered.

"I'll go and look closer," Adam said.

Corban thought for a moment and nodded. Adam adjusted his messenger bag. He cocked his reloaded shotgun. With a little wave, he jumped off the porch and walked on stiff legs across the street, careful to pause and look both ways. Corban followed him a moment later, motioning for the others to spread out.

Adam lifted the latch on the gate, the sound of scraping metal on metal unbearably loud. Adam let it swing open. He moved to the black box and stood there, staring at it. After a full minute, he waved them over.

As he got closer, Corban saw what Adam was staring at. There were three words at eye level right in the middle of the black wall. They were small and he had to get within three feet to make out his own name. The words read "Sheriff Yan Corban?"

"Are you kidding me?" Billy said.

"Someone sent you a present," Titus said.

"Insanity," Corban said. He looked at the others. "Should I?"

"Go on," Titus said. The others nodded.

"I am Sheriff Yan Corban," he said firmly.

The black wall changed color from black to gray to stark white. But it wasn't an empty white. It was a room. A room with white walls and a white chair. On the back wall was a white bench with white cushions. The man was the only color in the room.

"Hello, Sheriff," he said with a pleasant smile. He looked like a college professor, relaxing in his khaki slacks and maroon sweater. He even had the salt and pepper beard and wire-frame glasses.

Corban reach out and touched the box. The image wavered where his hand met cold steel.

Billy had taken a quick jog around the box. "It's on every side, like some kind of Jumbo-tron."

"This is not a recording," the professor said. "I can see you just as you can see me."

"Why are you here?" Adam blurted out.

"What's your name?" Corban asked.

"I am Doctor Regent. I have been selected to converse with you about this historical Red Diamond event." His smile broadened. "As you have surely noticed, this is a record breaking year."

"Excuse me," Corban said. He motioned the other over. They went to the chain-link fence and huddled.

"What gives?" Billy asked.

"I have no idea. Regent wants to talk for some reason. My God, this can't get any weirder."

"This could be a lure to get us in the open," Titus said.

"At least get some answers," said Adam. "If you can."

"He won't tell us anything," Billy said. "This is some kind of trap."

Corban led them back to the box.

"You have ten minutes, Regent, then we leave," he said.

"Don't be afraid. When I am broadcasting to you, the box is also sending out a sound too high pitched for you to hear. The monster will stay away because that's what it's been trained to do."

"You'll excuse me if I can't trust you on that."

"Naturally." Regent's eyes went to Adam. "Hello, Adam. It's been a while since we've talked."

"I have never talked to you before," Adam said. He wrote something down in his notebook.

"Oh, we have. Not in person, of course."

"Online? What is your screen name?"

"Where is the monster's lair?" Corban asked.

Regent laughed at the question. "Do you think I came here to help you?"

Billy stepped closer to the wall. "I think you came here to help that fucking thing, Doc. Because we've been kicking its ass."

Regent continued to smile. "Really? I don't see it that way. I see a town locked down, under siege from within, unable to perform even the most basic tasks. I see a town all but paralyzed, soon to be dead."

"We aren't done yet," Corban said.

"Your firebomb won't work. Terry and Tom Moon aren't half the mechanical geniuses you treat them to be. A single misstep and they die. Poetic, to burn at the hand of your own creation."

"This is bullshit," Billy said.

"I know," Corban said.

"And from a psychology point of view," Regent said, "what is happening to the power structure in Pikeburn is nothing short of fascinating." His eyes glittered. "A deranged veteran with a god complex. A pack of cowards willing to believe anything. People looting when they should be hiding. People hiding when they should be fighting. People fighting when they should be running. And so many families silently bidding their time, getting one step closer to desperate measures every minute. It only takes a rumor in Pikeburn to cause casualties now."

"None of that explain this," Corban said. He slapped the side of the box. "Why drop your fancy TV set here? You don't need to hear our side of the story. What's your true business in my town?"

"I wished to observe less and participate more."

"From a TV in a tennis court?"

"This remote unit has some astonishing capabilities. This location is ideal for... observation."

Adam raised a finger. "Why are core rules for Red Diamond being broken in Pikeburn?"

"Because you don't understand the rules, Adam."

"How do you know his name?" Titus asked.

Adam looked at him. "I'm on a watch list. It's not surprising he knows me. And he's right, I might have spoken with him online many times. I can't tell without a screen name."

"This young man can be quite persistent and annoying," Regent said.

"Are you Bakerwood66 from the Kansas City Red Diamond Forum?" Adam asked. "Because that whole mess with the key was not my doing."

"No," Regent said with a toothy smile. "But I was around for it."

"Don't you have enough data on Pikeburn now?" Corban said. "Call it off. You can't learn anything more by changing the rules midgame. Just call it off."

"Actually, Sheriff, I can. Despite Adam's copious knowledge of Red Diamond, I am the only person here who has been in a Red Diamond more than once. My whole career, actually. You are in no position to judge this event or demand it to end early. There's so much more yet to happen. You can't even imagine."

"We're leaving," Corban said. "Time's up."

"Going to the High school? I shall warn you, there's a man there with a gun. He's not going to want visitors."

"He knows where we are going?" Titus said. "Come on! That's not fair!"

"Ignore the fucker," Billy said. He took Titus by the arm and led him away.

"Hide while you can, Sheriff," Regent said. "It's not over. Not by a long way."

Corban pulled his pistol and fired a shot at the wall. The bullet left a thumb-sized distortion in the image. Corban ran his hand over the mark, feeling the slight indention. "What is this made of?"

Regent shook his head at Corban. "You do know it's trained to investigate gunfire, don't you? At least tell me you've figured that much out. Now you really better run."

As the group headed away from the box, the walls faded to solid black again. Regent's voice spoke from the black walls. "Come back and chat, Corban. I am very interested in your opinions on this."

Once they were around a corner and out of sight of the black box, Corban called a halt in the recessed doorway of an antique shop.

"Damn, Captain, I don't know what to think about that," Titus said. He leaned his head back against the big glass display window.

"I know when someone is playing me for a fool," Billy said. "Fuck that guy. It's all a game. He's sipping tea with his buddies and watching us on a big screen like a football game."

Adam hung his head. "This isn't how I envisioned it going. I thought I would be dead by now, day four, but that I would finally understand everything." His voice was quivering. "None of this makes sense."

"Maybe it never did," Corban said.

"Then it sucks," Adam said as a single tear fell to the ground. Then he laughed and looked up at them. "But it all sucks, doesn't it? Experiments, monsters, patriots, plush dolls."

Titus squeezed his shoulder. "Sure does."

"Just figuring that out, genius?" Billy said. But he was smiling and he punched Adam on the jaw in slow motion. "Shake it off. You got a job to do."

"We all do," Corban said. "There's a man with a gun at the High school. I plan to make sure Chambers doesn't walk into an ambush."

CHAPTER EIGHT

T wilight had taken hold of Pikeburn when they crouched behind a minivan looking up a slope of lawn to the sprawl of red brick and glass that was the High school. The grass was thicker at the bottom of the slope. A riding lawn mower was stopped half way up, a straw hat on the seat. The parking lot was empty except for a black SUV parked on the sidewalk near the front doors.

"I bet the owner is inside," Billy said.

"He might not be alone," Corban said. "Just because Regent was telling the truth doesn't mean he's telling all the truth."

"That's a family car," Titus said. "Who else knows to run to a school than a man with a kid in school?"

Behind them in the maze of neighborhood housing, a dog started barking furiously.

They looked at each other nervously.

Corban waved them closer. "No power, so the halls will be dark. If he knows we're coming, he can hide in any shadow and sniper us. Go careful. Go slow. But we have to get inside now. I don't know what held up Chambers, but he could be running around that corner at any second. Billy and Adam, I want you circle to the south side of the building, come in through the gym if you can. Titus and I will come in the front, make a lot of noise, draw his attention, and head for the main office. That's where we all end up. Got it?"

They all nodded.

"Let's go."

As soon as they broke from cover, a popping sound came from the school and Billy grunted, falling over. Adam straightened up and fired off the shotgun. Brick fragments flew up from under the window he had fired at. Three more times the popping sound rang out and Corban could almost feel the projectiles whipping by. He reversed course, snagging Billy by the hand and pulling him back to the cover of the minivan.

Titus lined up his revolver for a shot. He stumbled backwards in a spray of red.

"No!" Corban yelled.

Titus stood there. He looked around, blinking. "I'm okay, Captain."

Adam fired again and the window shattered.

"Get down!" Corban ordered. He rolled Billy over. "Where are you hit?"

"In the fucking balls," he moaned.

Billy's crotch was green. Corban had to stare, trying to figure out what was going on. Titus squatted next to him. Red paint was splattered over his chest but he wasn't bleeding. Corban wiped his finger through the red paint.

"Paintball?" Corban asked in shock. "It was a paintball gun?"

"Still hurts like a bastard!" Billy said. "Fucking hell, Captain, go get the guy!" Billy laid out on the pavement. "I'm gonna puke."

"Adam, stay here with Billy."

Corban and Titus raced across the street and up the lawn. A blue paintball exploded on Corban's shin. He saw a person in another window, the characteristic paintball gun silhouette in his hands.

"Stop shooting!" he yelled out.

Something whizzed by his ear as the shooter kept at it.

"Moron!"

He was struck twice more in the chest before reaching the front doors. Titus pulled on them and they only opened a few inches. The doors were chained shut on the inside. Without pause, Corban fired twice into the chains and they burst apart, sending shattered links dancing down the hallway. Inside, Corban sprinted down the hall, past lockers, trophy cases, and posters for events never to happen. He turned left down a side hall without any caution. After a dozen steps, he slid to a stop just as a person ran out of a classroom right in front of him, popping out so fast they almost collided.

Neither moved.

The man was covered in black and white motorcycle pads and a full-face helmet. The paintball gun hung from his hand.

"Where's my shirt?" the man said in a muffled voice.

"You idiot," Corban said. He reached over and flipped the visor up on the helmet. It was the teenager from the rundown house across town.

"I'm sorry," he said. "I-I didn't know what to do. I broke my glasses two weeks ago and I can't see anything. I've been skipping school, too. My mom is trying to get my dad to buy new ones but he's not going to. He lives in Denver and—"

"Shut up."

Titus came up, favoring his fake leg and grimacing each step. "This guy again? Kid, are you alone here?"

"No. There's another guy in the cafeteria who has a gun. Waved it at me when I first got here. He's really crazy. Don't go near him."

Corban pressed his palm to his forehead. "Titus, get the others. I'm going to talk to the crazy man."

"Be careful, Captain."

The kid frowned at Corban. "Aren't you a Sheriff? Why did he call you Captain?"

"Long and stupid story. Stay here. I mean it."

The hall to the cafeteria was pitch black. At the end was a thin slice of light where the double doors joined. He went to the left wall and edged his way forward. In a few steps, something caught at his ankle and he stumbled. A wild clanking filled the hall. A cord was tied across the hall and strung with tin cans. Corban pulled free of the alarm.

"Smart!" he called out. "Okay, you know I'm coming in. This is Sheriff Corban. Do not shoot. I'm just going to talk."

He waited, listening. He could hear Adam and Billy entering the building somewhere behind him. The kid was jabbering to Titus. No sound came from the cafeteria.

Even more carefully, Corban moved toward the doors. He noticed another cord tripwire and stepped over it. At the doors, he took a deep breath. He knocked.

"This is Sheriff Corban! I'm coming in! I want to talk!"

He eased the left door open and looked inside. The main area was full of red tables, steel and plastic chairs, and faded light from a row of sky lights. Even the dim of near dark was more than he had adjusted to in the hall. On the other side of the cafeteria was a serving counter with a wide pass through window to the kitchen. A folding metal gate was down to block off the window, but it wasn't closed all the way down. Corban could see light flickering in the kitchen through the inch-high gap between counter and steel gate.

He also saw a push-through door to one side of the counter with a round window. He crouched down and moved through the red tables until he was at the door. He put his back against the wall next to the door.

"This is Sheriff Corban. Who am I talking to?"

There a small sound, a click and hiss. Someone had opened a can of pop or beer in the kitchen.

"I don't want to hurt you, or take what is yours, or get into a fight. I just want to talk about what is going on."

The voice that answered was low, just above a whisper. "I know what's going on."

"Can I come in?"

"If you want."

"Are you armed?"

"Aren't we all?"

Corban slung his AR-15 so it rested across his belly. "No. I have my hands empty. I would appreciate it if you did the same."

"Fine, very neighborly. Come on in."

Corban used his shoulder to open the door and slid into the kitchen with his hands near his shoulders. A small fire was going in a pot on the floor. A man was sitting on one of the plastic and steel chairs over the fire, slowly feeding it pages from a pile of textbooks. The light reflected off the barrel of a rifle aimed straight at Corban's heart.

"I've had this moment in my head a long time," the man said.

Corban squinted at the figure lit from below. The face was dirty and the white hair in a frenzy, but he recognized the man. "Masterson? Clark? What the hell are you doing here?"

The rifle barrel lowered to point at the floor as if it were too heavy to hold up. "Exiled." Masterson's face was demonic from the dancing fire below him.

Corban lowered his hands a touch. "Exiled? From the courthouse?"

"DePaul has... issues. That's funny, coming from me, isn't it?"

"No. Not really."

"You do find it funny, though. I deserve this, right?"

"Are you injured?"

"Oh, a little here and there. Not like my foreman, Goslein. He was a good man and wasn't going to sit by while DePaul did bad things. He couldn't take what DePaul was starting to sound like. He said he grew up in a cult and knew the language too well. He stood up to DePaul, maybe thinking that would be enough, and he didn't see who shot him in the back."

"Who did it?"

"Some biker. I wasn't even watching. It happened so fast. After that, I— I just got carried away in what happened next. I made threats. I went a little crazy. So..." He sighed. "They exiled me. Stripped me naked and threw me out the door in front of everyone. Didn't take me long to find clothes. The stores are full of clothes."

"And you came here?"

Masterson put the rifle on the ground. "You want some food, Sheriff? I'm warming up some kind of chicken patty. The freezer is full of them. Course the freezer isn't cold anymore, but these things are made with a ton of preservatives."

"Maybe later," Corban said. He dropped his hands. "Where did you get the rifle?"

"In some home. I knew there had to be one. I went door to door. I thought I would have to kick down the doors but most were wide open."

"What's going on over there at the courthouse?" Corban came in all the way and squatted down opposite Masterson with the fire between them.

"Not long after you left DePaul locked himself in with the CB. He came out talking like he had been visited by God." Masterson dropped a curl of paper into the fire and watched it crisp to ash. "He claims he knows what Red Diamond is really about."

"A mental hospital."

Masterson blinked in surprise. "How did—? Oh, never mind. Yes, a mental hospital. I've lived here damn near forty years, Sheriff. I turned this town around when it was sliding into hell. I made deals with Pegasus Cutlery and Verdonn Jackets, made them put factories here instead of Mexico or New York. I brought a sense of pride back. But I can tell you, there's no Goddamned mental hospital. He's the one who needs a mental hospital."

"I think—"

"I get the irony," Masterson said loudly. "Me, being here. And you finding me. Don't think I can't appreciate the irony of me being here eating mushy chicken patties after being run off like a dog! He was smiling as he threw me out, Corban. Smiling because he's the big man now. And my men didn't do a fucking thing!"

There was a clatter of tin cans in the hallway and Billy set to cursing.

Masterson reached down for his rifle and nothing was there. Corban had beat him to it by a heartbeat.

"Of course," Masterson said.

Then Corban slowly swung the butt around and offered it to him.

"You're kidding?" Masterson said.

"If you didn't shoot me when you had the chance a minute ago, I don't think you're going to shoot anyone today. We've had our issues but now we have a shared problem."

Masterson slowly took the weapon. He wrapped his hand around the grip, put his finger on the trigger. The barrel was inches from Corban's chest.

"I have never liked you," he said.

"We've established that."

"Are you going to kill DePaul?"

"If he forces me to."

"Can I kill him?"

Corban thought about the question a few seconds. "Clark, I've got bigger things to worry about right now than your goals."

The gun was lowered for a second time. "I'll take that as a yes."

"Captain?" Titus asked from the cafeteria.

"I'm in here. I'm fine." He turned to Masterson. "We have a lot of people about to show up. Do you have water here?"

"Stacks of cases in plastic bottles." He got to his feet. "I'll put on more chicken patties. Did you know my first job was a cook in a deli? That was a long time ago but I still love to cook."

Corban went into the cafeteria. Adam, Titus, Billy, and the kid were around a table. The kid had his helmet off. He was holding a wad of paper towels to his bleeding nose.

Billy glared at Corban. "Kid deserved it."

"As long as that's the end of it."

"I shaid I shorry," the kid said.

"He'll survive," Billy said.

Corban pulled out his walkie talkie. He tried to get Alice for a few minutes and was rewarded with silence.

"What's with the guy in the back?" Titus asked.

"As crazy as it sounds, that's Clark Masterson. And he's cooking up some food. Be nice and eat whatever it is he brings out." Corban quickly retold the story as he knew it. When he was done, no one spoke.

The cafeteria had one wall that was all windows. It looked out into a courtyard where students could eat at stone picnic tables. It was a mass of black shadows as the sun vanished.

"I need to get to the Moon brothers," he said. "We have to kill this thing."

"Tonight?" Billy asked.

"We need to take a rest," Titus said.

"I'll go with you," Adam said and immediately stood up.

Corban looked at them and realized the darkness had stolen their faces and expressions. "Maybe not tonight. But not right now no matter what we decide. This location is terrible. It can come through these windows without thinking twice. Kid, what's your name."

The teenager took his hand off his nose. "Kevin Pesh."

"You know the school. What's a good location with no windows?"

"I don't know. The gym. It has locker rooms, too."

"Take us."

The double doors to the hallway swung open and a light slashed the room into brilliance. The light played on their faces, then went to the floor.

"You look like a bunch of kids caught with their daddy's dirty magazine stash," Chambers said.

"You asshole," Billy said. He got up and went to the doors. He clapped Chambers on the shoulder. "What took you?"

"Just some stuff I handled. This is like herding cats, but we made it. I've got people bringing in supplies. I also found a generator so we can have a little light around here. Did we find water?"

"Yes," Corban said. "Kevin here says the best place to defend ourselves is the gym."

"Sounds good. You need to know not everyone came with us. Grease stayed behind with the guy we found all chewed up and some old lady who doesn't have much brain left. Some others figured they could do as well on their own and decided to go home. On the way here, we spotted lights in houses. Flashlights, lanterns, and a few that looked like fireplaces. I knocked on doors and told people what the plan was. Now we have a few new faces."

"People just came to the door?" Titus asked.

Chambers shrugged. "Monsters don't knock, I guess. So, what was in the black box?"

"It's a TV set," Corban said. "A monitoring station of some kind. Have you heard from Janet and Blue?"

"No. CB seems dead, too. We're flying blind."

Corban sighed. "Good job, Chambers. Get your people settled in."

After he was gone, Corban looked to his group. "I can't stay here. I need to check on our plan. They might be sitting on the firebomb and waiting for me to give the green light. I can give you two hours of sleep, if you want to join me."

"Let's go now," Billy said.

"I'll get us water and whatever food I can find," Titus said and walked off.

Adam sighed. "Is there a coffee shop in town? I would love a hot cup of coffee."

"I'll take mine black, genius," Billy said. "You want to make a coffee run in the dark? We're stuck in a High school." Then he raised his head. "They have to have a coffee maker in the teacher's lounge! Come on, man!"

"We don't have power," Adam said morosely.

"Chambers will have that generator going before we can find the lounge. Come on!"

Corban was left staring at the shadows in the courtyard. He sat down and gently eased his head to the table. He slept with his hand on the AR-15.

"Captain? Captain?"

"I'm awake," Corban said without lifting his head or opening his eyes.

"A group of people just wandered in," Titus said. "About twenty or more. One of them...has a story."

Corban sat up, wincing with every inch. "How long?"

"Over an hour. That's something."

"It is these days. Did you get some sleep?"

"About an hour." Titus placed a mug in front of Corban. "Fresh and warm."

Corban picked up the mug as he stood. He took a gulp of the coffee and felt it hit his empty stomach. "Can I get some food first?"

"No," Titus said. By the light of his flashlight, his face was twenty years older.

Corban motioned for Titus to lead on.

The faint sound of the growling generator tickled his ear as they walked down the hall. Lights shone from around the gym doors, but Titus turned a different direction. He handed Corban a small flashlight as they went. The moved deeper into the school where no light existed but what they carried.

Ahead was a body covered in a sheet and shoved to the side. Titus walked by it without a glance.

"Titus, who is that?"

"We don't know yet. Found the guy in the hall. Looks like someone hit him with a bat a few days ago. He's...kind of ripe."

Now Corban noticed the nasty smell of decaying meat. "We should bury him to at least get rid of that smell."

"Here we are."

Titus turned into the library. Four flashlights were stacked together on their ends, firing light at the ceiling tiles and spreading it around the circular table. Billy and Adam were sitting with a man with a damaged face. He had recently been on the wrong end of a beating.

"What's your name?" Corban asked before he reached the table.

"I'm Oliver Tellman. We met at the picnic on the 4th of July."

"Yes, I remember. I can't say I recognize you now, though. What happened?"

"A biker thug."

Corban looked at Billy. "Grease?"

Billy shook his head. "Let him talk, dammit."

Oliver said, "DePaul took over the place a few days ago. He's gotten weirder by the hour. Someone said he had a stroke, too, since he's walking funny and his arm stays next to his chest like a broken wing."

"You're from the courthouse," Corban said. He put his mug down and found a seat at the table. "Tell me."

"He's saying—"

"Leave out the crazy talk. Give me what he's doing."

"Just tell him why you're here," Billy said with exasperation.

"DePaul said this evening he was going to draw names for a sacrifice."

Corban settled back in the chair. "That's his word or yours?"

"Well, mine. It's the same thing."

"But what was his word, Oliver?"

Oliver had to look away. "Gift."

Billy pointed in the general direction of the courthouse. "He's going to stake some poor bastard on the lawn and ring a feeding bell. Says an offering will keep it away long enough for help only he can summon arrives."

"That won't work," Adam said.

"We know that," Corban said. "How serious do you think he is, Oliver?"

"He's serious," Oliver muttered.

"And the bikers are with him?"

"Not all of them," Oliver said. "Only one, really. Mean son of a bitch." His voice broke and he started to cry. "He did this to me."

"I need some more answers, Oliver, so pull it together. People are still being hurt out there."

Oliver rubbed snot and tears off his face with his sleeve. He sniffed loudly. "Okay. I'm okay."

"How many people does DePaul have that will fight for him."

"Maybe four."

"Jacob Longtree?"

"No. He's been loyal to Alice. When she got sick, he's been—"

"Sick how?" Corban demanded.

Oliver pulled away from the intensity of the question. "Well, she fell over at the CB station. No one did anything to her. No one hurt her but she isn't well."

"They have the only medic in town," Titus said to Corban. "She's got better care than we could give her."

Oliver looked down and his shoulders started shaking again.

Corban was on his feet. He seized Oliver by the shirt and yanked him from the chair to look at him.

"But she's not getting any care, is she, Oliver?" Corban hissed.

"It's not my fault," Oliver begged. "The ambulance guy is locked in with all the medicine. No one gets anything without DePaul giving it."

"He's crowned himself king," Billy said.

"It's not that uncommon," Adam said. "In 1999, a man and his five sons did the same. Well, worse than this, actually. They lasted two weeks while the monster ravaged the south side of town. Then it came north and finished their compound. But he was king for two weeks."

"He's not getting two weeks," Corban said. He dropped Oliver back to his seat. "I'm dealing with him tonight. You coming with me, Oliver?"

The beaten man shook his head and could not look at any of them.

Corban looked at each of the others. "Gear up. DePaul has become a priority."

"Copy that, Captain," Titus said.

Billy picked up his M-16. "I'm ready now."

"I have one stop before we head out. Won't take long."

"What are you going to do?" Billy asked suspiciously.

"I'm going to tell DePaul we're coming."

Chambers had the CB set up in the announcer's booth looking down at the gym. Corban, Titus, Adam, Billy, and Chambers were the only ones inside the glassed room. Below them on the gym floor flashlights waved and moved about like overgrown fireflies in a meadow. The ranks had swollen since he last saw the refugees.

He lifted the handset and paused to collect his thoughts.

"No one has answered in a long time," Chambers said.

"He's listening," Corban said. "He's not talking, but I think that's about to change. If I start to lose it, pull the plug on me."

"Lose it how?" Chambers asked.

"I don't know, Chambers. Use some common sense on it."

"You really want to do this, Captain?" Titus asked.

Corban pressed the button. "This is Sheriff Corban calling the courthouse. DePaul? Are you listening? Can you hear me? I have some things to discuss with you. You really want to hear what I'm going to say. It might save your life. I know you or some goon can hear this. I'll only be waiting five minutes before I get started on what I have to do tonight." He put the handset down. There was a slight tremor in his fingers. He quickly made a fist.

Chambers sighed. "I've got a new subject to talk about. Someone is going through town saying we are holing up in the

High school. Going house to house. I can't get a good description, but that's why we are getting new people. Paul Revere of Pikeburn."

"The monster doesn't have a head hatchet anymore," Titus said. "It can't blast through walls like before. Maybe this place is safe enough."

"It has other ways," Corban said. "These doors couldn't stand up to a determined man, let alone something that size, hatchet or not."

There was a chirp from the CB set, as if someone had clicked the button on the other end, and everyone grew silent. Corban picked up the handset again.

"DePaul, this is Sheriff Corban. I'm hearing a lot of bad things about you. You want to comment on them?"

"Hello, Sheriff," the old man said.

"He sounds chipper," Titus said.

"Thanks for talking," Corban said into the mic.

"Why don't you drop that act, Sheriff? We both know you're pretty damn angry."

"I can control my anger. It's part of my job. Whatever you think you've done, DePaul, I've seen worse. I wasn't always a small-town Sheriff, you know. Why don't you explain to me why I'm hearing rumors of you killing animals?" As calm as he sounded, Corban was standing rigid.

"Oh, you and I both know they aren't rumors."

"I haven't seen much more than a dead house cat, so I have to treat this as a rumor."

"Take my word for it."

"If that's true," Corban said, "it's a pretty strange response to what's going on in town. Where would such an idea come from?"

After a short pause DePaul came back. "I have friends."

"People outside the wall? That's a little hard to believe, DePaul. You're not that special. Who would break a federal law like that? What is his name?"

"I'm telling you I have friends," DePaul said with rising volume. "I'm in contact with people. With a man whose life I saved. You don't understand the power, the bonding of brothers in combat."

"I'm starting to," Corban said.

"Oh, bullshit! Don't get cute. You running around with that disgusting mercenary for hire and that halfwit monster fan. I was with men, Corban. The God damn finest men in the world. Long before you were born I was learning lessons you won't ever learn."

"Is that who are talking to on the outside, a buddy from your unit?"

"I'm not explaining myself to you," DePaul said, calming down. "That's fine if you don't believe me. I'm not going to get eaten. That's my proof in the end. You die and I don't."

"This unnamed friend told you the secret is killing animals?"

"Don't be an asshole, Corban." DePaul chuckled. "You can't begin to understand what is really going on here. They didn't pick us at random. They never do. They target people! They want me dead!"

Titus swirled his finger next to his temple. Corban nodded.

"DePaul, can we stick with the animals?"

"This is an interrogation? Are you being clever and using your law enforcement training on me? I know all about that training. I've had more than you, I assure you."

"Okay," Corban said evenly. "But I'm the Sheriff and you aren't, so how about we talk about why you have this idea the monster is afraid of dead animals?"

"But you want to know about something specific, don't you?" The voice had filled with a goading lilt. "Yes, you do. That's something you can ask me about. Go on. Don't be shy."

Corban had to swallow before he could answer. "I'm only interested in why you think killing animals will keep this thing at bay. I can almost see some logic in it. How long before you made the leap from animals to people? You want to talk about that gift?"

"Grow a pair of balls and ask me," DePaul said.

"No. It's unimportant. Tell me about this gift you want to give."

"I killed your dog."

"I know." Corban had his eyes closed. He unclenched his fist and put his palm on the cool glass of the booth window. "I've known for a while. It's unimportant. Another personal tragedy in a greater tragedy that is this town right now. Others have lost so much more. Now tell me about your plan for tomorrow."

"You don't fool me," whispered DePaul.

"End this," Chambers said. "He's baiting you."

"Be quiet," Corban said. He pressed the mic button. "What about tomorrow? Who gets to be the gift?"

"It's a lottery."

Titus touched Corban on the shoulder. "Give it up. There's nothing to gain by dealing with this guy."

"Are you in it?" Corban said to DePaul. "What happened? Did you run out of animals? Too afraid to leave and hunt the monster so you'll just kill whatever else you can?"

DePaul laughed into his mic. "You're pathetic at this, Sheriff! I should have expected as much."

Corban pressed the button to reply and Titus said, "You have to hang up, Captain."

Corban let go of the mic and dropped it to dangle by the cord. As he moved for the door, DePaul's voice sounded from the speaker.

"Captain? Who the fuck is calling you Captain?" Something in DePaul's tone caused all of them to freeze. "You don't have that rank, mister."

Billy pointed at the mic with enthusiasm. Corban lifted it slowly.

"You hear me?" Depaul said. "Don't you pretend you walked away from me."

"They started calling me Captain. I never thought about it. Just a nickname for the man in charge. I was never in the military, never felt the need."

"That's disgraceful. You're a fucking embarrassment. You wouldn't last a minute in a uniform. You hear me?"

"Is that a uniform like the one I wear every day for my job? Or a uniform that I run around the jungle in? You need to be more specific."

"You know God damn well what I mean," DePaul seethed. "How dare you pretend to be a soldier? Men ten times as deserving as you died for that rank. I'm glad I killed that dog. You hear me?"

"Is this about you being a Captain as well? Are you pissed because I'm stealing your thunder?"

"He was a Sergeant!" Billy yelled.

"Oh yeah?" Corban said. "That's something. Nothing to be ashamed of there."

"Bastards," DePaul said. "You fucking bastards. You get to mock my service to this country because I made it possible for you. I did hard things, lost brothers, watched people die, just so you can sleep in soft beds and call soldiers names. I put a gun in my own mouth too many nights, all because you wanted to burn flags and spit on me."

"Tell me about the gift tomorrow."

"You think this is the first time I sacrificed people? You think I didn't kill innocent people in Vietnam? You think it was a movie over there? I killed your people, Yan. Your kind. I shot them by the truck load, whole villages, burned buildings and fields and didn't even look back at the smoke. You come here, you gook fucker, and I'll stack you next to the ashes of your family I killed in 1968. I've still got a few teeth in a bag I'll bring down and tuck into your dead mouth so you can be closer to your cousins I dusted for looking at me the wrong way."

The group in the announcer booth were frozen in uncomfortable silence, staring at Corban, waiting for his reaction. Corban didn't hesitate with his reply.

"Well, I know you wish you were back in the jungle all hale and young, raping innocent women and killing babies like the good old days, but I'm really just a Florida-born

Sheriff of a small town. I've never been to Vietnam. But you sound more than a little crazy, so I'm afraid I'm just going to come over and kill you tonight. No hard feelings, Sarge, okay?" He kept his finger on the button as he pointed to Titus and spoke loudly. "You ready, Titus?"

Titus leaned toward the offered mic and crowed, "You bet, Captain!"

"Yes, Captain!" Adam shouted.

"Fuck yeah, Captain!" Billy said.

Chambers stared at them all and didn't speak, his mouth hanging open.

Corban released the button and the air was filled with an unhinged bellowing that had some words mixed in. Curses, racial slurs, threats, and promises were flung with vehemence. Corban reached over and clicked off the CB.

"Now we go to the courthouse."

Billy elbowed Chambers and grinned. "You ever see anything that cold in your life?"

"He knows you're coming," Chambers said.

"I want him to know," Corban said. "I want him beyond angry. I want him blind, deaf, and dumb with anger. And when we finally get around to showing up, he won't be ready no matter how ready he feels."

"What if he takes it out on the other people?"

Corban shook his head. "He can't. He's not in as charge as he thinks he is. If he oversteps whatever position he's made for himself, the folks crowded into the courthouse will take him out for us. Oliver said only four were following him without question. I bet that means only two. It doesn't really matter, though. We're going."

Ten minutes later the five of them were gathered by the front doors of the school. A woman was standing as lookout with her face against the narrow side window.

"When do you think you'll hit the courthouse?" Chambers asked.

"Not soon, but before dawn at the latest. I want to stop and check on some people between here and there. Do you want me to try to convince Grease to come over here?"

"Whatever," Chambers said. "The guy is nerve-wracking. I'm glad he's got the skills to drug up the wounded, treat a few injuries, but he's kind of mental. Good luck out there."

The woman whispered, "I've seen nothing moving. It's all clear."

"I doubt that's true," Titus muttered.

They bolted across the street and waited under the low branches of a tree to get their night eyes. When they could see enough to move out again, they jogged in single file with Corban in the lead. No one questioned him when he turned from their route to the dance studio and headed toward Stonecut Park.

He called a stop along the corner of a building. Before them was the tennis court. The black box was a shape cut from obsidian, somehow even darker than the night.

"What gives?" Billy asked.

"I want another word with this guy."

"But why?"

"He's got something up his sleeve. He already knows all of us, I'm sure of it. We know nothing of him. So, we can't lose by giving him a little more info he already has. We might find something useful in what he says, though."

"He's a liar," Titus said.

"He wasn't lying about the man with a gun in the High school," Adam said.

Billy squinted into the night. "That makes him more dangerous. Always tell a lie between two truths. If we start thinking he might help us, we're screwed. He's just as dangerous as that monster."

Corban left the cover of the building, moving quickly to the interior of the tennis court.

"I'm Sheriff Corban. I want to speak to Regent."

The others took up positions spread out from him, watching the nearly impervious night.

Corban knocked on the black box. "Hey, I want to talk to Regent. He said he would talk. Where is he? Let's talk."

The black box remained silent and still.

"Shit," Corban muttered. "Let's get out of here."

They reached the street and Titus spun about, revolver raised. Billy went to one knee next to him, aiming the M-16 toward the left side of the tennis court cloaked in total darkness.

"I heard something rattle the chain-link," Titus hissed.

"Let's not stand around," Corban said.

"I heard footsteps," Billy said.

Before they could run off, a blazing white light exploded from the black box as the walls lit up. The illuminated tennis court and surrounding park were empty.

"Hello, Sheriff," Regent said. He waved at them from the two sides of the black box they could see. "It's safe to chat with me."

Corban looked at his men. He nodded to them before going back to the black box. Billy muttered something under his breath as he fell in behind the rest, sweeping the now brightly lit park with his M-16.

"You've come back," Regent said. He seemed slightly out of breath. "I am surprised. I had to hurry over from another location at our base."

"You said I would come back."

"But, why did you?"

Corban shrugged. "I'm tired. Not thinking straight."

"Sounds awful. Why aren't you sleeping?"

"I have a job to do, not matter what you people have done."

"It's a town with no rules, Sheriff. No one blames your deputies for running away."

"I do," Billy said while scanning the area for movement.

"Tell me something," Corban said. "Who is Harlow?"

"Doctor Harlow," Regent said. "He's the man behind this year's Red Diamond event."

"Some people say he's a little crazy."

Regent raised one eyebrow. "That might be true. Who are you talking to about him? How do you even know the name?"

"Adam told us."

"I don't think that's true. His death was given full media coverage." Regent went to the perfectly white chair and sat down. He adjusted his sweater. "Care to enlighten me?"

"Nope. I like my little secrets. Makes me feel in control."

Regent dismissed the topic with a wave. "How are you faring against the monster? Tell me what you think of it?"

"It makes me sick to know someone built an abomination like that for no good reason."

Adam left his spot in the corner of the tennis court and hurried to stand next to Corban. "It's beautiful."

Regent smiled and leaned a little forward. "Yes, it is."

"It's something new," Adam said. "Something very new. Something that never existed and probably shouldn't exist now. How did he do it?"

"I don't understand all the science he uses. No one else does, either. It may as well be magic."

"It's not magic," Corban said. "It's a twisted animal shape and now it has no head."

"And it doesn't care," Regent snapped. He relaxed against the chair, smiling again. "It doesn't care. That's how powerful it is. Even when you get lucky, it matters not at all."

"That's genius," Adam said. "I wish I had seen it divest itself of its head. How many times can it do that?"

"It depends on the injury, of course. A head is not as important as it seems. Move around functions, make backup systems, alter the neurofiber layout to achieve maximum blank slate logic facilities. It's an easy target, so that would be the first choice to leave behind."

"Must carry its brain in its ass, then," Billy said and laughed at his own joke.

Regent gave him a sneer. "It is always the lower classes that mock the accomplishments of their betters."

"I've heard that before," Billy said.

"Can I talk to Harlow?" Corban asked.

"I don't think so. Doctor Harlow is busy interpreting the data gathered so far. He's got great new plans for next year. I'll tell him you asked about him."

"Tell him," Adam said, "tell him I'm in awe of what he built here. I know it's a monster that eats people, and it's probably going to eat me too. I know a lot of people look at it and cringe. I don't. I've waited my whole life to be a part of a Red Diamond event. To get to be a part of what will be a historic moment, a turning point in so many scientific fields, it's beyond what I dreamed of. I feel I've seen a future of untold potential." Adam touched the black box with his hand. "Tell him thank you."

Regent's face was blank, his entire countenance seemed molded from plastic. At last he took a breath.

"I will," he said. "And you have to leave now. It is coming. I want you to survive, Adam. There are greater things to see than this."

"You said we were safe here," Titus said.

"And you are, as long as I broadcast. It knows you are here, though, and is getting closer. Once I stop broadcasting, you will be hunted. Go now."

"Move!" Corban said. The black box continued to blaze with light as they ran, giving them light for several blocks. They kept running for a while, turning corners and staying close to cover, and suddenly Corban held up a hand. They halted and crouched in a recessed doorway together. Corban tried the handle of the business and it was locked.

"I can break it," Billy said.

Corban shook his head and pointed up. Something moved on the roof above them.

Titus mouthed the words, *"Oh Shit."*

The monster paced above them, at times seeming to stomp on the roof in agitation. Little moaning growls floated down to them. Slowly and quietly, they readied their weapons.

The faint light on the tops of nearby buildings winked out as the black box shut down. Immediately the monster was gone. They heard it running along the rooftops toward the tennis court. Corban peeked out and saw it leap from one side of the road to the other, hardly making a sound. He shuddered as he stepped onto the sidewalk. This time they ran harder and did not stop until they were in the alley below the dance studio. They stopped to catch their breath below the knotted rope to the open window.

"What was that about?" Titus asked. "Why did he tell us about the monster coming?"

"You tell them," Corban said to Adam. "You figured it out before I did."

"Regent is Doctor Harlow. His face is different, but that's him. He must have had surgery when they faked his death."

"So, the arrogant bastard built this monster and now wants to talk to the victims about it?" Billy asked. He slung his M-16 over his shoulder. "That's sick."

"So how does this help us?" Titus asked.

"It's one more thing we didn't have ten minutes ago," Corban answered. "And he's in love with Adam."

"Well, who isn't?" Billy asked and punched Adam in the arm. "Good job back there, genius."

"I wasn't lying," Adam said with a perplexed look on his face. "I may have hammed it up a bit, though."

"It got us out of there alive," Corban said. "That thing would have ambushed us from the roof on the way here."

"It still might," Billy said. He grabbed the rope and hauled himself up to the window.

There was darkness and silence in the dance studio. As each man came up, they instinctively grew quiet and waited with weapons ready. Once they all were up, Corban flicked on his flashlight and barely managed to banish the gloom. Three other flashlights did little more.

"Something ain't right," Billy said.

"Take point and be careful," Corban said.

They found Grease in the dance studio's main room. He was leaning against the wall, slumped so far down his chin was jammed against his chest. Blood was pooled around him. In his right hand was a pocket knife. Above him, written in blood, were the words: CANt KILL It CANt Go oN.

The big biker had slashed his wrists.

"Fuck me," Billy muttered.

In the other room, the injured man and the old woman had their throats cut. Blood here was sprayed on the walls, the floor tacky with it. Corban pointed to a leather bag that looked like a man's shaving kit. A couple of pill bottles and syringes were inside. Billy tiptoed into the room to avoid soiling his boots too much. He snagged the bag and retreated quickly. Corban closed the door on the scene. Without comment they returned to the storage room filled with accounting boxes.

For a while each man sat in his thoughts. Adam made notations in his notebook. Titus chewed on his unlit pipe. Billy leaned against the wall and checked his weapon. Corban went to the window and looked at the stars over the rooftops.

"Something bad happened to him at the Fireball," Billy finally said, breaking the quiet.

"Yep," Titus said softly. "Even the tough guy breaks. We learned that in Iraq. And sometimes it's only the tough guy that breaks. There's no telling who can handle stress like this."

Billy pushed away from the wall to stand with Corban at the window. "God damn this mess."

"Did you know him well?" Adam asked.

"What? Hell, no. He's a drug dealing psycho." He caught Corban looking at him sideways. "Oh, come on! I don't deal the shit. My dad did, okay? That's the truth. He's dead and he was a mean son of a bitch and that's the truth. I don't make it, I don't use it, I don't sell it to kids. I just move it around. Someone is always going to need shit like that moved and I've got a reputation for doing it cheap and clean. Grease isn't -

wasn't my partner in anything. I'm just the middle man on this. I don't even know what they were buying and selling, Captain. It could have been anything. I'm not my dad. He died in a cage. I don't want that."

Corban turned his face to the window. "Being the middle man also gets you a cage."

"Harvard turned down my application. There's not a lot going on in this town, in case you didn't notice. My mom worked like a fucking dog, two jobs all her life, and she never got her head above water. Some of us don't want to be a wage slave and die in a trailer park and have nothing to show for it."

"You've only seen two options," Titus said. "Deal meth like your dad, or become a working zombie like your mom. There are other options. Life isn't made of two choices."

"Oh yeah? Like what? You got a job for me in your art gallery? Choices, my ass. Fuck off."

Corban grabbed Billy's wrist.

"Get the—" Billy started angrily, and then noticed Corban looking across the street to the opposite rooftop. A bulk of shadows that had been there since they started looking out had suddenly developed twin gleaming eyes. Eyes that pulled the starlight into them and shimmered back. Eyes that could see very well in the night.

"Run," Corban said.

"What?" Adam asked, looking up from his notebook.

Billy grabbed him and shoved him for the door. "Run now!"

They raced through the hallways and turned into the storage room with the rope tied to an exposed pipe. Titus hopped out the window, awkward yet quick, and started down the rope.

Glass exploded behind them and something shook the floor.

"It jumped through the studio windows," Corban said.

"It's too big to get through the hallways without that hatchet," Adam said.

A great smashing sound echoed through the dance studio and the walls shivered.

"Don't bet on that!" Corban said. "Go, Adam!"

Billy went to look out the door and jerked back. "It's coming! It's digging through the walls!"

"Get out of here!" Corban said. He leaned out of the room and shone his flashlight into the hall. One of the walls was torn to pieces and something big was forcing its way through the hole. The light fell on its face, turning the two eyes to mirrors. The monster stopped with its front legs braced on either side of the hole it had made. The black tongue trickled out of the open, steel-toothed maw.

Corban opened fire on the monster's face. He dropped the flashlight to hold the AR-15 steady and it went out with a pop. The only light now was from the muzzle flashes. In strobe light glimpses, Corban saw the walls spread apart under terrible pressure and the monster force its way into the hall. Still too large to navigate the hall, it tore at the walls and floors and made headway one claw at a time.

In the flash of exploding gunpowder, Corban saw the effects of his firing. Flesh and muscle was cratered. One of the mirror eyes had been hit and turned into a gory flower of splayed matter. There was blood spilling from the monster's face, slicking the floor as it dragged itself.

The last round fired and the hall went dark. The monster roared, so close to Corban he felt the air move across his face.

He ran for it. Something touched the back of his neck as he swung his legs over the window sill. He dropped down and descended in a barely controlled hand over hand fall. He staggered on impact and sat down. Above him a taloned claw grabbed one edge of the window and began tearing it away with ease. Corban rolled away from falling bricks.

"Captain!" Billy shouted from the end of the alley, waving his M-16 in the air.

Corban ran to him and turned to look back.

"Just run!" Billy said and hauled Corban by the collar.

They left the businesses behind and came into houses. A flashlight was waving at the sky in front of them. Adam was standing in the back door of a van-sized RV. He ushered them in and slammed the door. He turned off his flashlight and the only light was a red clock on the built in VCR.

"The door was open," Adam whispered. "Titus is in the front now." Titus could be seen silhouetted in the driver's seat through a narrow doorway with a curtain shoved aside.

A howl lifted up from a distance away.

"You made it mad," Billy said, then stifled a laugh.

"I shot it in the face a few times. It isn't as bulletproof as it was."

"Poor thing."

Corban managed to put a new clip in his AR-15 in the dark. Adam opened a cooler on a seat and looked in. He tilted his head at the contents. He reached in and pulled out a wet beer. In silence, he passed one to Billy, then Corban, then Titus. They all opened their slightly cool beers and drank.

"Something," Titus said after a few minutes, "I think something is moving behind us. I can see something in the street in the side mirror."

"Is it the monster?" Corban asked, setting his empty can down.

"It's big... so, yeah."

"Tracking us again," Adam said.

"Only me, I think. I felt it—" He shuddered. "I felt it lick my neck. It has my scent. I'll break for the houses and loses it in the backyards. You three head for the courthouse. If you don't see me in two hours, make a new plan to get rid of DePaul."

"You don't go alone," Billy said. "We can draw straws or something."

"I'll go with the Captain," Adam said.

"I don't need babysitters and we don't have time for a debate."

The RV rumbled to life. Lights clicked on in the interiors, flooding their surprised faces with yellow illumination.

"What the hell, Titus!" Corban shouted.

"Keys were under the seat," Titus said. He slapped the gear shift into drive and floored it. The others piled on top of each other as the RV jolted forward. In moments, the RV was flying down the deserted street.

"You idiot," Corban said as he got up from the tangle of bodies. He sat on the small couch. "What's your plan, then?"

"Drive like hell, Captain. It's not as fast as we are and it can't track you from inside a metal box."

Corban glared at him. "Okay, you're right, but give a guy some warning next time."

"To the courthouse?" Billy asked.

"Give me a minute. Titus, is it following us?"

"Crazy bastard hasn't turned on his headlights yet so I don't know."

Adam and Billy burst out laughing.

Corban shook his head slowly. "Okay, wiseass, take us to the Moon brothers."

"Copy that."

CHAPTER NINE

The metal gate to the Moon Brother repair shop was still flat in the dirt when they pulled into the yard. Titus drove over them and gave the horn a double tap as he turned off the engine. The bay doors that had been flattened in the attack days ago had been propped back up and welded in place. A face appeared cautiously in the front door window. The door flung open and James came barreling out. He tried to grab all of them at once and almost managed to lift them off the ground.

"Oh man! Oh man! OH MAN!" He had tears in his eyes. "I thought you guys were dead!"

"Just putting up a good fight," Titus said. "How are things here?"

"Billy?" James said. "What are you doing here?"

Billy looked embarrassed, but he said, "I'm with him. I guess. Shit."

"That's cool," James said. "You'll want to see this. It's a bomb!"

"Oh good," Billy muttered.

Inside the shop was a small pickup that had been modified with steel grating and plates over the windows. A single spike had been welded to the front end. In the bed of the pickup were more than a dozen metal gas cans, all wrapped onto a bulky object with duct tape and yellow cord. Many of the gas cans had wiring going into their caps. There was a stuffed animal bear also duct tapped to the top of the contraption.

Tom and Terry were sitting at the table, feet up, casually eating chips and drinking cold beer.

"All done!" Tom said as the others walked up. "I've been calling for six, seven hours. Thought you wouldn't hear me."

"I didn't. No one has."

"Probably busted again," Terry said. "Stupid CB came out of Grandpa's big rig twenty-five years ago."

"Oh well," Tom said. "It's all done now. That thing will rain fire down on anything in a three-block radius."

"You don't know that," his brother snapped. "Sheriff, it's going to go boom, but it's not a nuke. What the hell is wrong with you?" He slapped Tom's leg.

Tom got up and stretched. "Let me show you how it works."

"Oh my God," Terry said. "It's a red button. Hit the red button and you've got about ten seconds to get out of Dodge or become bacon. It's not that hard."

Tom shoved Terry out of his chair. "You want a beating, bro?"

Terry was up and charging, but James was there before the two could land punches. He had each one by the shoulder and held them apart. He had the look of a tired parent as he waited for the cursing to stop.

Billy stepped up and cracked Terry across the knee with the butt of his M-16. Terry howled in pain and hit the floor. Tom froze at the attack, staring from Terry to Billy. Billy raised the rifle and made to plant the butt across Tom's face. Tom recoiled and shielded himself with one arm.

"What the fuck, Billy?" Terry shouted from below.

Do we look like we have time for this horseshit?" Billy shouted back. "You morons! That thing is tracking us. It might be outside right now. So enough with the sibling bickering act. I'm not dealing with it!"

"Okay, be cool," Tom said. "Here. Take the keys. It's like Terry said. You hit the button and run like hell."

Corban took the keys.

"Now we just need to find it and draw it out," Billy said.

"You really think it's not on its way here?" Titus asked. "It's coming."

"Just like last time," James said. He looked down. "It won't stop."

"But it isn't here yet," Corban said. "I'm going to drive, head back toward town."

"You aren't a driver," Titus said softly. "I am, Captain."

"Not this time and don't fucking argue with me. I'll have ten seconds to get clear. It'll be enough. I ran track in school."

Tom sat back in his chair. "Oh yeah? What was your best 100 yards? Because I was the fastest wide receiver this town ever had. I built it, I should drive it."

"I don't care. I'm driving. I want the RV following behind me." He looked at the pickup. "What about some noise? Can you strap a radio or CD player to that hood? And any extra lights you can nail down, too."

"I suppose."

"You've got twenty minutes."

"No problem." Tom got up again. He reached a hand down and pulled his brother up. He stepped nose to nose with Billy. "Hit my brother again, you drug dealing loser, and I'll bury you out back."

"Promises, promises," Billy hissed at him.

"Get to work," Corban said. "Billy, stand guard at the front door. Adam, take the back door. Everyone else help the Moons. We've got nineteen minutes."

The pickup had a flashing red light on top and a battery-powered boombox tied down with wire. The group stood around the pickup, flickering in the red light.

Tom offered Corban a plastic tumbler of water. Corban took it and sipped, then spat.

"Where is this from? Is this tap water?"

"You're not supposed to drink it," Tom said, taking the tumbler. "You're going to wear it. It's to keep you from burning to death on accident."

"Oh," Corban said. He pointed at his head. Tom slowly dumped the water over him and it trickled through his clothes and pooled at his feet. He shivered as it went down his spine.

"This is bad," Titus said. He folded his arms tightly. "This is really bad."

"It will work," Corban said.

"Well, it's too crazy not to work," Billy said.

James pulled his cap down tighter. "I don't like it, either."

"You helped build it," Tom said. He slapped James on the shoulder. "You need to come work for us when this is over."

"Okay," James said.

Corban got behind the wheel and slammed the door. Through the slats of steel plate, he could see the bay doors. Cables had been strung to their sides, and the cables tied to lifting motors in the rafters. When the Moons pressed a button, the doors would break free from the spot welds and swing to the ground. Corban started the pickup. The engine sounded smooth and ready. He looked at the red button, a piece taken from a tape recorder and affixed to the dash.

Billy tapped on the steel grate over the side window. "Give 'em hell, Captain."

Terry pushed him out of the way. "Move, asshole. Sheriff, we found these." He waggled two green walkie talkies. "They ain't much more than toys, but they work pretty well over short distances." He pushed one through the gap in the steel and Corban took it. Terry tossed the other to Adam.

"Can you hear me on this?" Adam said into the walkie talkie.

Corban nodded. He pointed at Tom, who pressed a button by the front door. Overhead winches tightened the cables and the bay doors popped free from their posts. They fell flat in a swirl of dust in Corban's high beams and red flashing light. He drove over them and into the night.

Corban waited for the others on the dirt road back to town. He could detect the bulk of town ahead because it was darker than the sky. Very faintly he could see two or three lights. Fires, or lanterns, or flashlights. It was people still alive. People still fighting and surviving.

The RV rumbled up behind him and honked.

Corban held the walkie talkie to him mouth. "Stay far enough back. Try half a mile or so. Do not come running in trying to rescue me."

"Okay," Adam said, sounding like a rebuffed child. "Good luck."

Corban pulled on a piece of kite string and the boombox turned on. Cranked to full volume, it still wasn't very loud. He shrugged and eased forward.

Closer and closer he rolled for town, only his headlights and the red flashing light giving the world any definition. He reached over and spoke again in the walkie talkie. "My name wasn't Corban when I was born. I was named Yan Pho. I changed it in college because I didn't get along with my dad. I'm not a doctor or a lawyer or a Nobel prize winner. I wanted to be a cop. That was disgraceful to my dad. So, one day when I was still only eighteen, I went and changed my name. I also did it to impress this girl. Neither was a good idea."

Corban backed off on the accelerator. He tapped the brakes a few times.

"I can't change it back now. My dad, for some crazy reason, suddenly decided to show me some support. Like my standing up for myself and showing him I didn't want to be his son if all he could ever do was shit on me in public, gave him a slap to the face. Or whatever. I swear he's crazy. He went and changed his last name, too. He has a wood carved 'Corban' name plate on the house, sends out 'Happy Holidays from the Corbans' Christmas cards, and loves to tell this story at every gathering."

He stopped the pickup. He could feel his heartbeat in his temples.

"I can't change now. He loves being a Corban. So does my mom. It's sick." He released the button.

"That's really funny," Billy said, and he sounded like he had been laughing it up, "but why are you stopping?"

"There's a single light ahead of me about a quarter mile. Not a light, really. It's reflecting my lights."

"A single light?"

"Yeah. I shot out the other eye in town."

"Oh. Well, shit. Change of plans?"

"Nope. I'm going to charge it."

For a moment on the line there was a set of voices talking at once, arguing and shouting. Adam came on and Billy was in the background complaining about "some grabby asshole".

"I have a better idea," Adam said. "Don't charge it. If it is as smart as we think it is, it's not going to take you head on again. The tow trucks taught it that much. Go slow."

"Just roll at it?"

"Yes. Go slow. The spike won't work anyway. You want it on top of you when it blows. Look at it right now. It's not charging. It's wary. Do something different or you'll miss it and all for nothing."

Corban closed his eyes and ground his teeth. "Okay," he said. "I can see your headlights behind me. Turn them off. I don't want it coming for you guys if I fail."

He left off the brakes and the pickup began to roll forward at a crawl. He eased a few more miles per hour into the approach. The song on the boombox restarted for the tenth time. He pulled the kite string and it cut off.

"I'm not dying listening to that crap again."

The pickup cruised closer to the single reflective eye. He couldn't judge distance very well in the darkness. He poised his hand over the red button. The eye did not blink or shift. It was as stationary as a distant star. Corban opened the door, causing the cab to fill with chiming.

The eye vanished.

He let off the gas and fought the urge to slam on the brakes. The truck kept rolling forward. He looked around through the slots in the metal covering, not breathing, hand shivering over the red button. The eye was nowhere.

"Jumped," he said aloud and hammered the red button. The monster came down on the cab at the same instant. The windshield pulverized and showered the interior. The metal plates popped off or bent aside under the weight. Corban managed to slide down to the pedals as the space above compacted with a grinding shriek. He grabbed for his AR-15 and it was gone from the seat.

Corban wiggled out the open door. He hit the dirt and rolled away from the coasting pickup. As he reached the ditch, he looked up. The monster was a huge, malformed shape on the cab, rending the metal apart, flinging pieces of the cab into the night. The red light burst and went dark. The steering wheel was pulled from the column. One clawed foot dug into the seats, popping springs and pale stuffing.

It paused in the act of destruction. The black ribbon snaked out and tasted the air.

"Now," Corban hissed, and somehow his timing was impossibly accurate.

The firebomb went off with a whomping roar. The blast forced Corban's head down, hot air slapping at his back. Flaming wreckage landed all around him. He looked up. A flaming chunk of metal the size of an anvil was an inch from his face. He backed away and stood up.

The pickup was a shell with four burning tires. Dozens of other smaller fires burned in a large radius. The grass of the area was ignited but not spreading.

In a heap further down the road, the largest burning object was starting to move. The monster was engulfed in fire. The flames rose in a twisting spiral above it. The body of the beast was a black silhouette in the inferno. And it was struggling to rise.

A hand landed on Corban's shoulder and he spun about swinging. Titus backed away quickly.

"Hey, Captain! It's me!" His voice was a small squeak in Corban's ears. He had not heard the RV pull up behind him, nor the approach of Titus and James.

"Look at her burn," James said. "That worked like a charm."

The monster was up on its legs now. It stood in the road, blazing like a gasoline-fueled bonfire.

"You did it!" Titus wrapped his arm around Corban. "That thing is roasted!"

"No," Corban said. He drew his pistol. "Get back to the RV."

"But she's burning," James said.

"It doesn't care. Look at it! It doesn't care!"

The monster widened its stance in the road. It began to shake like a dog covered in water. Only it wasn't water that was flung about to land burning in the grass. It was flesh. The seared flesh and muscle soughed off in flaming chunks as the monster violently thrashed. In a moment, the monster was no longer burning. It stood in a circle of flickering layers of cooking meat that had once belonged to it. A new form was revealed in blood-streaked glory.

"Mother of God," James whispered.

"Get to the RV now," Corban said. Titus and James ran for the RV. Corban couldn't tear his eyes away from what was before him.

The outer flesh had burned off and been discarded. What was exposed was a sculpture of ceramic and steel, a headless nightmare with a needle-toothed maw. It had no eyes yet it was staring right at him. He holstered his pistol.

Again, someone grabbed his arm. Billy was hauling on him, the M-16 chattering in his extended other hand. A few bullets hit their mark and glanced harmlessly off the armored monster. It took a hesitant step toward them.

Together they turned and ran for the RV. Once inside, Corban shoved to the passenger front seat. He grabbed Titus's hand as he was shifting into reverse.

"Go into town. Go forward. Lose it in the neighborhoods again."

"But...it's in the way."

"Go around and hurry."

"But..."

"Now, Titus!"

Titus floored it. He drove onto the shoulder around the burning pickup, one wheel in the ditch, tilting the RV to the right dangerously. They had to drive through piles of flaming skin, sending up sparks that skittered across the windshield. The monster slowly pivoted to keep its maw facing them. For a moment, the monster and the RV were less than ten feet from each other.

"What is it doing?" Billy asked, M-16 aimed at the window he was looking out of.

"It's adjusting," Adam said, eagerly pressing his face against the glass. "Like a computer doing a reboot. That's how it can function so well as this new entity. It's purging all instructions for the old one."

"It did that last time, too," Corban said. "After it tore of its own head, it just stood there."

"So, it's sort of paralyzed?" Titus asked.

"Not for too long," Corban said.

As soon as they were safely passed the monster, Titus steered back onto the road and gunned the engine. The monster took a step after them, then stopped. It raised a fleshless paw and licked at it experimentally.

"That thing is more machine than animal," Titus said.

"That bomb worked perfectly," Billy said. He punched a cabinet, caving the wood inward. "Why can't it die? This is bullshit!"

Adam was holding his pencil over the notebook, but not writing anything down. "That's not right." He folded the notebook away. "If it's just a machine, what's the point of all this? It can't be. No, it's an animal with machine parts. Layers of parts under the skin, that is now the outer skin. An endoskeleton that can become an exoskeleton. That's fantastic."

"I'm tired of you giving this thing a golf clap every time we fail," Billy said.

Adam sighed. "It's not that I want it to win... oh, never mind."

"You're saying there's another animal inside that plastic and metal suit?" James asked.

"It's ceramic, a very tough clay that's been cooked. It's not plastic at all or it would be melted. And yes, I think another animal is under that suit. It has to be there."

"Get to the High school," Corban told Titus. "We regroup and make a new plan."

"This is bullshit," Billy mutter, wringing his bruised knuckles.

The RV jolted forward, tossing those standing in the back to the floor. Corban caught himself before slamming into the windshield. Titus was stiff-arming the steering wheel. The entire vehicle settled back as a weigh pressed down. The RV was slowing.

"This isn't me!" Titus yelled.

"It's on the back!" Corban shouted.

Adam sat up. He braced the shotgun against his shoulder and fired both barrels at once. The boom within the RV confines made everyone cry out and grab their ears. Twin inch-wide holes appeared in the back door. Then the back door was pulled off the hinges and hurled away. The monster was clinging to the back of the RV, the weight of it forcing the back end to rub against the tires. One clawed paw reached in and pulled the stove from the wall and tossed it backwards. The next blow carved a chunk from the roof.

"Shake it off!" Corban said. Titus swerved violently left and right. The three passengers in the back were flung around, shouting and cursing. The monster was unperturbed by the maneuver and widened the hole it was trying to climb through.

Corban fought his way out of the passenger seat and into the back. He drew his pistol, but before he could fire it, the RV jolted again as it was struck from behind. Titus was unable to maintain control and the RV spun wildly into the grass. The world became a swirl of flying debris and tossed bodies. Corban hit the ceiling, the walls, the floor in a bizarre tumbling act on repeat.

When Corban opened his eyes, the RV was resting on four wheels and still running. He was staring out the back of the RV through a gaping hole where the door had been. The monster was gone.

"What the hell?" Billy said. He was propped up on the lopsided couch, blinking rapidly.

"We rolled a few times," Titus said. "But I think we're okay. We're still running. Can't find my pipe, damn it."

Corban got up and stepped over James and Adam. He jumped from the RV and aimed all around. Out in the grass something big crouched. He fired at it and in the flash from the shot he saw a beat-up flatbed truck, front crumpled in, steam coiling around the hood. His bullet had burrowed into the engine.

He holstered his pistol and ran to the wreck. Someone sat behind the wheel, slumped against the door. Corban yanked on the door and caught one of the Moon brothers before he fell. Blood was coating everything. A long and deep injury split the side of the Moon brother's head and neck.

"Get me towels!" Corban shouted at the RV.

"It's got Terry," Tom said in his arms. "I saw it take him."

"You idiots," Corban said. "You were supposed to stay at the shop! Damned if you didn't save our asses, though. You saved us."

"You can't have all the fun." Tom struggled to get up.

"Stay down, Tom. I'm taking you to the paramedic at the courthouse. You need a few stitches."

"Bullshit," Tom gasped. He suddenly pushed Corban away. He got to his feet and stood straight. He reached under the front seat and pulled out a greasy rag. From this bundle, he produced a heavy black pistol.

"It's got Terry," Tom said. "I saw it take him. It's right over there and I'm getting him back."

"He's dead," Corban said.

"I know that." The pistol waved at Corban. Blood spilled from Tom's face in a constant river, dripping to the ground like rain. "Don't stop me."

"Okay," Corban said softly. "I'm sorry, Tom. Go get your big brother."

"A year and a day. I've heard that line my whole life." Tom gave Corban a crooked grin as he backed away into the darkness. "Get out of here."

By the time Corban reached the RV, gunfire in the night started. He didn't look back.

James is hurt," Billy said as soon as Corban hopped into the disastrous interior of the RV. "A fucking kitchen knife from the drawer got him in the armpit when we rolled."

"How bad?"

"It ain't good."

"Titus, can we roll?"

"The engine sounds okay, but – "

"Take us to the courthouse."

"What happened back there?" Titus called out as he back onto the road.

"Moon brothers rammed us with a truck. Knocked the monster off us and got its attention. They're dead and it's busy. Drive."

"Copy that, Captain." He stuck his pipe in his teeth on focused on the road.

Adam was sitting on the busted couch next to James. Adam had a bloody towel packed under James's left arm. The big man was leaned back, eyes closed, sweat running down his face.

"How did you pull this off?" Corban said. "Monsters tearing around town, bombs turning trucks into junk, and bullets flying. And you, James, get stabbed by a flying steak knife." Corban squeezed his shoulder. "We'll get you help. Hang in there."

James nodded and bit his lip.

Corban went to the wide hole in the back of RV. Billy was on one knee watching the road disappear behind them. Debris from RV was falling off as Titus barreled onto paved streets.

"We're fucked," Billy said. "We blew it up and it didn't care."

"James needs help now. We're taking him to the courthouse for the paramedic."

"I heard."

"And DePaul is going to try to stop us."

"I suppose you're asking me if I'm ready for a fight."

"I am."

Billy was quiet a moment, listening to the wind through the busted windows and open back end. "I'm ready for anything."

Corban started for the front, kicking aside the assorted debris of RV living that had been dislodged in the rollover. He got back in the passenger seat and stared through the cracked windshield.

"Hell of a day, Captain," Titus said. "I found my pipe."

"Moon brothers are gone."

"That's a bad thing. I was counting on them to build a bigger bomb." He glanced at Corban. "It was a good plan."

"I don't think there are any good plans against this thing. It's two steps ahead of us, Titus." Corban looked at the dried blood on his hands. "We have to get ahead of it or everyone will die."

CHAPTER TEN

Half a block away and around the corner from the courthouse, Titus pulled over and looked at Corban. "It's a bad idea to roll up without a warning. Someone might just start shooting at a van that tries to park too close to a base of operations."

"This isn't Iraq," Corban said. "Keep it running."

Corban got out of the seat and worked back to James and Adam. The towel was soaked through. A gory steak knife was on the couch seat next to Adam.

"He pulled it out and made things worse," Adam said. A smear of red was across one lens of his glasses. "I— I didn't know what to do after that. He keeps bleeding."

James was pale, eyes flicking to imaginary objects.

Corban grabbed another tea towel and jammed it under James's arm. "Titus, we need to—"

"Company!" Billy shouted, still on guard at the back of the RV. "I saw our brake lights reflecting off something steel about two blocks down!"

"Titus!" Corban said.

"We're moving!"

The RV turned the corner and went on two wheels for a moment. Corban braced himself against the built-in cabinets. Adam screamed. Billy came a hair from falling out, somehow managing to pinwheel his arms wild enough to stay in the RV until it banged down on all four wheels.

"Sorry," Titus said, but he was laughing.

"I will shoot you in the good leg!" Billy replied.

Ahead, the courthouse had a stand of work lights set up on each corner. Despite the urgency, Titus let off the gas. The pipe fell from his mouth to his lap. Arranged in a warding circle around the lawn of the courthouse was a series of evenly spaced poles. Animals of all sizes were hung from the poles. Dogs and cats, family pets, strays, pieces of larger farm animals. All of it lit up by the floodlights. A single, larger pole was sticking up from freshly turned dirt behind the line of animal corpses.

"It can't be," Titus said. He looked back to Corban with a mix of outrage and confusion. "How did this happen, Captain?"

"Get us there and we will set it right," Corban said.

The RV rolled to stop against the curb. Billy and Adam helped James up and out the back. They started up the front sidewalk before noticing the savaged front end of an ambulance jutting from the double doors.

"To the west door," Corban said as he walked up beside them.

"Stay where you are!" a voice called from the rooftop.

Billy and Adam half carried James along the sidewalk, leaving a trail of coin-sized red droplets. Corban glanced at the row of people on the roof, but did not obey the command. Titus limped up next to him, revolver in his hands.

The man on the roof shouted down again. "I said stay where you are! We will shoot!"

"Don't aim that weapon at anything but the ground," Corban said. "Don't give them a reason to start a fight. Billy, Adam, you guys keep moving no matter what happens."

They made their way around to the side of the courthouse.

"This is your last warning!" the man on the roof shouted angrily.

Adam pulled on the handle of the door and it didn't budge. The side door was locked. Corban shoved before James and pounded on the door.

"This is the Sheriff! We have a wounded man! Open this door now!"

Someone on the inside started saying something in response and Corban slammed his palm on the steel again.

"This is Sheriff Corban and I have a wounded man with me who dies without immediate medical help! Stop fucking around and open this door!"

Voices rose from within, an obvious argument. The lock clicked and a woman pushed the door open. A man with a gun in his waistband held up his hand as they hurried into a hallway. He put his hand on Corban to slow him down and Corban struck him in the face with his pistol and the man sat down. A line of blood trickled down over his left eye as he tried to collect his wits. Corban picked up the man's gun and tucked it into his belt at his back.

"Thanks, Tracy," Titus said as he pulled the door closed. "That damn thing is out there looking for us."

"The animals will keep it away," she said in a wavering voice.

"That's stupid. I didn't know you to be stupid. You're a teacher, for God's sake. Why are you going along with this?"

Tracy put her hands over her face and began to sob.

"Come on," Corban said to him. "Now's not the time."

They walked quickly to the main lobby. People watched from open doors, or flattened themselves against the hallway walls to stare. Some of them were armed like sentries, but no one tried to stop them. At the foot of the main staircase, they finally met resistance. On the landing above stood DePaul, the red mustached leader of the bikers, and a man in a trench coat. DePaul had a pistol in his hand aimed at the ceiling. The other two had pump shotguns, readied but not aimed.

"Who let this rabble into our home?" DePaul asked.

"I have a wounded man and he needs treatment. Let them by, DePaul." Corban pulled his pistol with two fingers and dropped it at his feet. "You and I can talk this through in private."

"I'll do no such thing. Our supplies are limited. Only those who have earned them can have them."

"Okay," Corban said. "I was just trying to give you one more chance."

"If I were you—" DePaul said.

Corban smoothly drew the guard's pistol and fired. The bullet slammed into DePaul's chin. His lower jaw exploded, flinging teeth and blood to the air. He stood for a second, eyes wide and bulging, the stump of his tongue visibly flopping in the ruin of his face. A garbled scream tore from him as he toppled forward to land face first on the steps.

The biker raised his shotgun to fire, but the man in the trench coat was faster, turning his weapon against his former ally, and blowing a bloody hole in the biker's chest. The biker hit the wall and slumped sideways. The man in the trench coat raised the shotgun over his head in both hands.

"I surrender," he said.

"Take this man to the paramedic," Corban said.

The man laid his shotgun down and rushed to help Adam and Billy with James, who was now unconscious in their arms.

"Who else?" Corban said to the crowd of people in the hallways. "I was told DePaul had four followers. Where is he?"

"She," an old woman in a zipped-up parka said. "She's on the roof, I think. Misty Arrieta."

"Are you okay, Mrs. Franklin?" Corban said.

"I'm not hurt, Sheriff. But I really glad you're here now."

"Do we go to the roof?" Titus asked Corban.

"No. If Misty was on the roof, she had her chance at us. She didn't take it. We can deal with her later." He turned to Mrs. Franklin again. "Where is Alice?"

"Mr. Longtree is guarding her in the jail."

"A jail?" Titus said in astonishment.

"Not really," Corban said. "It's a holding cell on the third floor for criminal cases and such. Thank you, Mrs. Franklin."

Corban retrieved his pistol and put it back on his hip. He switched the guard's gun to his left hand. He looked at the slow-motion waterfall that was making its way down the marble stairs from DePaul's cratered face.

"Someone clean this up," he said.

Corban and Titus made their way up the stairs, passing many staring faces.

"This is officially giving me the creeps," Titus said. "I feel like we're going to be attacked and eaten."

"No one is going to do anything. It's over. DePaul never had control. These people are just broken."

There were eight people crammed into a ten by ten-foot cage of chain-link and metal poles that looked like it had been a dog run in a previous life. Word had spread quickly of their arrival and the jailer was already opening the door and stammering apologies to the people inside. Jacob Longtree was the first person out the door and he slammed the jailer against the wall and started giving him an angry piece of his mind.

Corban ignored the brewing violence and went straight into the cage. Alice was on a folding cot, looking small and helpless under a blanket.

"Alice? It's Yan. How are you feeling?"

She opened her eyes, looking around the room to see people leaving the cage, the jailer being manhandled, and Corban and Titus armed and in control. "Much better now, Sheriff." She swung her legs off the cot and dumped the blanket. "I was going crazy on my back all this time. Where's DePaul?"

"Are— are you faking being sick?" Titus asked.

"Well, of course," she said as she stood up. "DePaul needed to stop making those sick broadcasts over the CB. Without me, he doesn't know how to operate the thing. He's lucky if he remembers to turn the power on most of the time. I'll be damned if I help him become the Pikeburn emperor." She put her hands on her hips. "Have you dealt with him?"

"Yes," Corban said. He shook his head and smiled at her. "You are a piece of work, Alice."

"That's why I'm here. Did you see Janet?"

"Yes. What? Here? She's here?"

"Down the hall in another room. We got too crowded in here so the other prisoners were taken there. I'll show you"

She led them down the hallway to a closed door and stepped aside.

Corban tried the handle and it was locked.

"It's locked from inside," Alice said. "They have a guard."

Corban pounded on the door. "Open up! This is the Sheriff!"

A woman behind the door gave a startled yelp, then called out, "Corban!"

"Stay in the chair!" a man shouted at her. "Janet, I'm in charge here!"

"Fuck you, Danny!" Janet said. "Open the door or I'll kick your ass!"

"Well, give me a Goddamned second!"

Corban planted a kick on the door, but it was solid and the lock held. "I'm shooting this lock off in five seconds!"

"Hey," said Danny, now from right on the other side. "I need to talk to DePaul first. I've got orders."

"He's dead."

"Oh. Um. How about Clark Masterson?"

"He's making chicken sticks at the High school. DePaul exiled him days ago."

"Oh. Shit, no one tells me anything! I guess that leaves you in charge."

The door opened and Janet was in his arms, the force of the hug driving him back across the hallway to the opposite wall.

"I thought it got you," she whispered as she tried to crush him.

"What happened to you?"

She pulled away. She ran to Titus and gave him a hug, too, but not as emotional. "We followed the monster," she said.

"Is Blue with you?"

"No, we got separated," she said. "It chased him after we split up. I came here and DePaul said I was a spy and threw me in here."

Corban turned his eyes to the guard. "Danny Steiner."

Danny raised his hands. "I don't even have a gun, Sheriff. I was doing as I was told. After they shot that guy in the head, no one was going against DePaul."

"Keep doing what you're told, then. Come with me." Corban led him down the hall and into the holding cell. There were already two people behind the chain-link fencing. One was the man in the trench coat and the other was a woman in her late thirties dressed in a black tactical vest over a pink T-shirt. Corban shoved Danny into the cage and locked the door.

"This ain't necessary," the man in the trench coat said. "We weren't the only ones doing stuff."

"I'll sort it out when I have a free minute," Corban said. "Keep quiet and I'll try to get here sooner rather than later."

"I saved you on the stairs. Just pointing that out."

Titus scoffed. "Oh, bullshit you did. Saved your own ass, is more like it."

The woman's face was shaking with anger. "This is your fault," she said to Corban. "You did this to us. DePaul knew what was going on and you killed him in cold blood. Murderer. They told me you shot him in the face. Murderer!"

"Don't listen to her," Titus said.

Corban studied her red face. "I'm guessing you weren't going to be DePaul's gift to the monster in the morning. Did he pick someone to die, or was there a real lottery? Volunteers? What would happen the next day? Another and another and another gift? All to feed some lunatic's need to be a savior. I'm sorry he died. I'm sorry I had to shoot him. He didn't give me a choice."

"Because he killed your dog," she hissed. "That's why you did it."

"Misty, this isn't my blood," Corban said, looking at his fist that was mapped in the grooves with dry blood. "This is Tom Moon's blood. Some from his brother, too, I guess. And James. A lot of people, really. It's hard to get worked up when you've seen as much as I have this week. It's a shame King died." He looked at her again and she took a step back from the chain-link. "It's a shame you people got so panicked and unhinged you did something horrible. You and I both know it. Even if you survive all this, you'll know what you did here."

"Your fault," she whispered, wide-eyed and shaking.

"And they record everything we do here," Titus said. "So now everyone knows what kind of people you really are. Or did you forget this is broadcast all over the world?"

The man in the trench coat turned and kicked the chain-link wall. "That's great. Just great."

"I didn't even have a gun," Danny said. "I didn't hurt anyone."

Corban walked into the hallway. Alice and Janet were waiting for him.

"Well?" Alice said.

"I'm thirsty and need to wash my hands. Give me ten minutes. Meet me in the CB room. Titus, check in on James."

A man appeared at the top of the stairs. He spotted Corban and rushed to him.

"Sheriff! That thing is outside!"

Corban didn't bat an eye. "Where else would it be?"

"What?" The man looked at the others for help and got even more confused when they didn't speak. "But— but that thing... is... outside..."

"It's been outside for almost a week. What's your point?"

"It looks different."

"We burned the skin off it. Honestly," Corban said, "you people need to keep up."

"But— but— shouldn't you do something?"

"Like kill some more house pets?" Corban shoved the man. "Mutilate the bodies and hang them outside like Christmas decorations? Is that what you have in mind?"

"Easy, Captain," Titus said. "These people haven't been out there. They don't know better."

"They fucking should." Corban pinned the man against the wall with his finger. "You think someone needs to do something? Grab a gun and start doing it." He let his hand fall and shook his head. "Instead, I need you to spread the word we are having a meeting in ten minutes in the main courtroom. Make sure everyone knows. That's something you can do, right?"

The man bobbed his head.

Corban went back to the holding cell. He tossed the key through the fence and it rang like a bell on the concrete floor. The inmates stared at him, unwilling or unable to move under his gaze.

"Meeting in the main courtroom in ten minutes. Mandatory. If I see you armed, I'll kill you on the spot. Let yourselves out."

Corban found the upstairs restroom. The trashcan was overflowing with wadded paper towels. The mirrors had streaks on them. The sink counters were wet and smeared with soap. A few articles of clothing had been rinsed in a sink and now air dried on the metal frame of the two toilet stalls. The place smelled of urine.

Titus and Janet came in after him and locked the door. They did not speak to him. They rested and waited. He went to a sink and turned the tap. Water merely trickled out. He sighed and shut it off.

"We're losing water pressure."

"Judging from what was living in that water," Janet said, "I don't think that's a bad thing." She held up a mostly full bottle of water. "Let's see those hands, mister."

As she gave his hands a good scrub, he filled her in on the black box, adventure in the High school, the suicide of Grease, the run to the Moon brothers and their ultimate deaths. Then she scrubbed Titus's hands while telling them a more detailed version of trying to track the monster, being spotted by it, losing sight of Blue, and arriving at the courthouse alone.

She pulled a mostly dry T-shirt from the stall and offered it to them. "Don't spoil my good work by rubbing those clean hands on filthy jeans."

When they got into the main courtroom, Adam, Billy, and Alice were sitting at the front. They had cleaned up some too, but the blood stains on their clothing were still drying.

Billy stood up and grinned at Janet. "This is a surprise. What are you doing with these assholes?"

"Long story."

"Where's Blue?" Adam asked.

"I don't know yet. He ran one way and I ran the other."

The six of them were in the open area just in front of the judge's bench. The crowd that had gathered was staying behind the rail as if they knew it wasn't their territory.

"How is James?" Corban asked.

Billy shrugged. "Lost a lot of blood, but he's as big as a horse. The paramedic, Ben, was hooking him up with some of the best blood money can buy. Seems there was a blood drive going on while we were out. Masterson set up a good place."

"Until they threw him out," Titus said. "I don't trust any of these people, Captain. We should get back to the High school."

"In a minute. I'm going to do some rumor control first."

Corban stood behind the judge's bench and looked at the faces gathered before him. There was fear, and exhaustion, and anger, and apathy. Few people could look him in the eye. He simply stood there and stared at them and they wilted.

A man looking at his feet said, "We - we will get them animals down. We will cut them down in the morning."

"You will not," Corban said. "It's out there right now, waiting for you to do something stupid like that. And before anyone asks how many there are, there's only the one. It looks different because we burned all the skin off it. We keep fighting it and it keeps... evolving. Sooner or later it won't have anything left to evolve into and that's when this will be over."

"DePaul said—"

"I get why you followed him," Corban said loudly and the man shut up. He waited a second before going on in a quieter voice. "You're scared and uncertain what to do. DePaul was certain. He was insane, but he was certain. You need to forget anything he said or promised. Everything he believed was a delusion. Get over it. There is no help from the outside. We kill this thing or it kills us. End of story."

"How are we going to kill it?" someone asked in the crowd.

"We?" Billy asked mockingly. He shook his head at the man.

"Billy's right," Corban said. "You should stay inside here and keep this place safe. We need at least one safe place to fall back to. This is important." He took a breath. "I'm sending Clark Masterson back here. He built this place before DePaul took it from him. He's your best hope."

"He's crazy, too," a woman said.

"Well, that's okay with me. I'm not feeling so sane these days."

Janet pointed at the woman. "You've got some gall calling people crazy when you've got dead animal staked out like hors d'oeuvres! You people are fucked in the head!"

A few people looked shocked at her outburst. The woman she was pointing at glanced around for help, but no one was coming to her aid.

"Well, Janet - "

"Don't Janet me, Carla! You saw them lock me away and did nothing! I was out in the streets fighting this thing up close and personal and you repay me by locking me up and threatening to stake me out with those dead animals as some kind of fucking twisted offering!"

Alice took her by the hand and whispered in her ear.

Corban looked down at the line between his people and the courthouse people. Billy, Titus, Adam, and Janet were facing the crowd of more than one hundred like a battle was about to erupt. Weapons were still pointed at floors or ceilings, but the hands that held them were tight and ready. Alice was unarmed, but she bristled like a cornered badger.

"What time is it?" Corban asked. "Does anyone have a watch on?"   .

After a moment of uncertain silence, someone said, "About 4."

"I'm really tired," Corban said. "I expect all of us are. I want everyone to get some sleep. We're wired and angry and someone is going to get hurt. We've got no solutions right now. Go on."

The people were happy to be let go and quickly fled the room. Only the man in the trench coat stayed, leaning against the wall by the door.

"Are we safe here?" Adam asked quietly, keeping an eye on the man by the door.

No," Billy said. "This place is going to implode."

"Even without DePaul, we're the bad guys," Titus said sadly.

Corban sighed. "We still need rest. We find a quiet room away from things, block the door, and all get some sleep. We can fight this war tomorrow. They aren't going anywhere."

"Second floor," Janet said. "That's the quiet floor."

"Okay." Corban motioned for her to lead the way.

As they passed the trench coat man, he raised his hand toward Corban. "Can I talk to you?"

"Is it about DePaul?"

"Yeah. You might—"

"Not tonight. Rest or stand watch."

"But I—"

Corban walked away.

Predawn light was spilling into the room through the narrow window when Corban sat up. He was on the floor, his head resting moments ago on a couch cushion. The others were sprawled around the room with cushions for pillows and jackets for covers. Billy was slumped back in a chair that was shoved against the door to the hallway. He had one eye open.

"What was that?" Billy asked.

"Why am I awake?" Corban said.

"Shooting."

"Damn it."

Corban got up. He stepped over Janet to get to the door. Distant popping sounds reach them.

Billy took up his M-16. "Do I really need to move, Captain?"

"Yes. That's coming from the roof."

"So?"

"So, what could they be shooting at?"

Grumbling, Billy struggled up and moved the chair with his foot. Together they slipped into the hallway and closed the door. The hallways were deserted, the stairwell silent. They followed the increasing sound of gunfire to an open door filled with growing yellow light. On the roof, there was a row of gas generators thumping away. A line of people on the south side of the roof were firing rifles in bursts.

"Where is it?" Corban asked as he pushed between two shooters.

One man pointed toward an alley directly across the square. "It's about to walk across there."

On cue, a shape gracefully moved into the open, paused for a moment, prompting a volley of gunfire from the gathering on the roof, then strode across into cover of the buildings.

The men and women on the roof gave a cheer.

Billy tapped Corban on the arm and they feel back to the other side of the roof.

"What the hell now?" Billy asked. "They can't kill it. Why are they shooting?"

"Why is it goading them, that's what I need to know." He went back and grabbed a man by the shoulder. "How long has it been doing this?"

"Maybe twenty minutes," he said. "I've hit it a bunch of times."

"You got a mountain of ammo, right?" Billy asked him. "Or are you just dumb enough to waste all your shots at a bullet-proof target that is obviously trying to get you to shoot at it?"

"Hey, I'm doing what I have to do to protect my family."

"Is anyone in charge up here?" Corban asked loud enough for all to hear. No one answered. "Okay, then listen up. No more shooting at it unless it's a lot closer."

"But we're hitting it!" someone protested.

"I know that. I could see the impacts on the steel from here. It isn't caring about your bullets. It never has. It doesn't care about being on fire, either. Or getting its head cut off. So just stop and—"

"There it goes!" a woman called out. Everyone hurried to the edge to see. It was no longer skulking in the shadows of dawn. It was sprinting all out along the street in full view, a vision of liquid metal and ceramic plating gliding over each other as muscles deep within flexed. It had lost mass in the fire, but it had gained speed. It leaped a car with the ease of a cat over a shoebox.

"Holy God," the man beside Corban whispered.

No one fired a shot. They stared as it crossed the open ground in a diagonal line and disappeared around a building on the east side of the square.

"Yep," Billy said. He clapped the man who was just protecting his family on the back. "Keep up the good work, buddy. Soon enough you won't have any bullets to waste. You ever think that might be what it wants?"

Corban was looking about the roof. He held up a hand to stop the brewing argument. "Wait. What if that's not what it wants? What if—" He turned in a circle, taking in the group and the roof and the generators. "What if it was just trying to figure out where all the bullets were coming from?"

"It ain't that smart," the man said, but he was noticeably paler.

"Get off the roof," Corban said. "Now."

Half of the crowd did as ordered. The others hesitated, trying to figure out what direction the mob would take.

"We need to protect the generators," a different man said. "DePaul said they were the most important things we have."

"Don't waste the time with this guy," Billy said to Corban. "Let's get the others."

Corban forced himself to nod. As they walked away, the man called out to their backs, "It's just an animal, you know? And you two can't tell what it's thinking. It's not that smart!"

"Oh my God, shut up!" Billy burst out. He turned, kept walking backwards, and gave the lined-up shooters a proudly raised middle finger. Two people responded in kind.

On the stairs Billy muttered, "This town is stupid."

"Well, I wasn't born here," Corban said. "Unlike you."

"You can shut up, too."

They found the others had already woken up and located coffee and slices of bread with butter and honey.

"We need to draw it away," Corban said around a wad of bread in his cheek. "Nothing will drive it away, but we can make it chase us."

Billy shook his head. "Hell no, Captain. Did you see that thing move? You'll lose that race from now on. Don't even think about it."

"If it's preparing to attack here, we have to draw it away."

Titus cleared his throat. "Yeah, I agree with Billy on this one. I was awake and I saw it run by out the window. I know what you're saying about drawing it somewhere else. We should. But I kinda feel we might be stuck here. Anyone sets foot outside with it watching us is a dead man."

"Can we make it to the storm drains again?" Adam asked.

Corban shuddered. "If you like crawling around in tight spaces that might be blocked by an iron grate ahead of you. That was bad news last time we tried."

"What about—"

The dawning light streaming in through the window was blocked out, bringing the room to deep shadows. Through the stone wall they heard grinding of some kind. As they all stared at the covered window, the blockage moved up, flooding the room again in light.

"Too late," Adam said.

"It's going for the roof," Janet whispered.

The faint popping that had woken Corban and Billy started up again. And this time there were screams.

Corban started for the door and Billy caught him in a bear hug. "Don't! Listen to me! It's too late!"

"I have to try!"

Now Titus and Alice were next to him.

"Captain, those people are already gone."

"You're being a fool," Alice said bluntly.

The lights went dark. The background noise of humming generators was gone. The gunfire had ceased, too, but the screams were louder as some people had escaped into the courthouse. And something else was grinding and breaking.

"That's... what is that?" Titus asked.

Corban struggled free. "It's the roof! It's going to be inside the building in a minute! Get out of here and get to the High school!"

"We have to warn people," Alice said as they all rushed for the door.

"I'll do that! Get out of here! Billy, take her!"

"I've got her!" Billy said as he snagged her by the hand. "Don't waste time!"

Corban sprinted for the stairs. Above him he could hear the same shredding of materials that had preceded the monster's arrival in the dance studio hallway. It was burrowing through the building like a mole. He ran door to door, throwing them open, shouting to evacuate the building. Most of the people were already aware and moving. A few needed angry words or threats, but he made sure each room was empty.

At the stairs, he turned for another sweep of the second floor, and he saw people at the far end, framed by light from open doors. It was Alice ushering a young, weeping woman with a child in her arms. He motioned for her to move faster. She gave him a disapproving frown and mouthed, "I know."

A doorway between them bent outward, rupturing splinters and drywall and dust into the hall. The monster had dropped into the room from the third floor and was making the doorway larger with terrible blows from its metal-encased paws.

Alice did not run. Corban saw her lips move as she gave the young mother an order. The weeping woman fled away from Corban and the main stairs, back into a room and slamming the door.

The front half of the monster crashed into the hall amid a hail of broken boards and plaster. The maw, filled with steel needle teeth, was its only vestige of facial features. It turned toward Alice, a lone woman standing so close to it she could have hit it with a broom, and she did not run. She wasn't even looking at it. She was looking at Corban. Her brows were bunched together in a mass of wrinkles over unblinking eyes. Her lips were white lines she was grimacing so hard.

Corban was suddenly moving, running, aiming his pistol.

Alice stood straight as an iron pole. She was looking only at Corban as the monster tore completely free of the doorway. She pointed, gestured, down and outside, making the single motion a command. And she stood there, imperious, glaring at Corban, demanding he obey.

He staggered. He stopped. As the monster bore down on the unmoving woman, Corban retreated backwards to the stairs and ran down them. He looked back as his head went below the level of the floor. Alice was gone, one shoeless foot being pulled deeper into the maw, blood gushing forth to spray the walls and floors.

Titus and Janet were making their way up the stairs.

"Out!" Corban shouted. "Now!"

Outside, the sunlight was in full morning force, making a mockery of the horror they were fleeing. People were running from the courthouse, heading for cover in the surrounding businesses as fast as they could run. Titus's red Jeep was still in the street and Titus headed straight for it. Corban and Janet piled into the back.

"Where are the others?" Corban asked.

"I saw Adam and Billy hauling ass a few minutes before seeing you," Titus said. "I haven't seen Alice."

"Billy," Corban muttered. He put his head on the seat rest in front of him. "Alice is gone. Go to the high school, Titus."

"Go, Titus," Janet said.

He pulled away and headed for the high school.

The woman guarding the High school front door pulled then open as soon as the Jeep hit the lawn. She waved them inside and slammed the door behind them. With the doors sealed at their backs, the three stood and stared, at the walls and at their feet.

"What's happening out there?" the guard asked.

"Don't," Janet advised.

"Well, take some water. Here. We have plenty." From a case of bottled water by her feet, the woman produced a gleaming container. She pressed it into Corban's hands.

He threw the bottle down the hallway as hard as he could.

"Back off!" Janet roared at the woman.

Corban walked into the nearest classroom. There were bookcases along most of the walls. Parts of a sentence were spread out on a bulletin board. Thirty desks were arranged in neat rows, the same green textbook at each one. Corban sat at a desk in the back of the class. He pulled his copy of the green textbook closer. He opened the cover. 'Holly Faben' was written on the inside cover in purple ink. Corban shoved the book onto the floor, where it landed face down on bent pages.

"Did you see anyone else get out?" Titus asked.

He and Janet were at the front of the class, leaning on the teacher's desk.

"Alice..." Corban swallowed. He sighed. "Alice didn't make it. I saw it."

Janet got up and started for him. She changed her mind before she got there, finding a chair at a desk instead. "This is impossible," Janet said.

"We wait an hour," Corban said. "If they aren't here in an hour, we move on without them."

"Move on?" Titus asked. "Like, with a plan? Shit, Captain, we don't have a plan."

"I do."

"Oh," Titus said. He pulled out his pipe and tucked it between his teeth. "That's good because I'm all fucking out of ideas."

"We wait then," Janet said. "I'm getting something to eat. What I wouldn't give for a few cold beers."

She was at the door when the way was blocked by Chambers. He looked at her, then Corban, then Titus.

"Well?" he said.

"Courthouse is gone," Corban said. "It came through the roof."

"Is it coming here?"

Corban shrugged. "How can it not be coming here, Chambers?"

Chambers nodded to Janet. "Didn't think we would see you again."

"Why?" she asked. "I got separated from Blue while tracking the monster. I went to the courthouse and got myself jailed."

"Your buddy Blue came here by himself. He had a crazy story about you running off."

"Then I want to talk to him," Corban said.

"Too bad," Chambers said with a flare of anger. "He's dead. Killed himself, slashed his wrists in the principal's off. But he smashed the CB and generator before that because why not, right? I thought since you didn't come back with him, Janet, he had cut your throat in an alley."

Titus hung his head. "Things are getting tough."

"I can hear the generator," Corban said.

"Well," Chambers said, "he tried to smash them but he just made them uglier. Genny is working fine. CB works as far as I can tell. No one listening, though. Can't raise the courthouse or the Moon Brothers or anyone."

Voices rose up in the hall.

"Moons are dead," Titus said.

"No way," Chambers said. Someone in the hall was shouting. Chambers held up his hand to stop the conversation. "I'll be right back." He went to investigate the commotion. From his seat, Corban could see a sliver of the hall. A pack of refugees from the courthouse were coming in from the front door. It was Billy who was shouting, moving the stunned survivors deeper into the high school. He was also half carrying James, who looked drugged to the gills. A round man with a stained paramedic uniform was helping. Adam came behind them like a balloon on a string. Adam saw Corban out of the corner of his eye and quickly joined them in the classroom.

"Glad to find you all here," he said. He was clutching his messenger bag across his chest.

"Not all," Titus said. "Alice…" He shook his head.

Adam took out his notebook. He went to a corner and sat down, curling his legs around his messenger bag.

Billy appeared in the doorway. He had fresh blood on his right arm and his shirt was torn down the side. He was looking at Corban. Neither spoke. Billy looked down first. He came over and leaned against the wall near Corban.

"She told me…" Billy took off his hat and squeezed it in his fists. "She told me to save the wounded. She ordered me to do it."

Corban nodded slowly, staring at the desk top. "Sounds like her," he said after a moment. "You couldn't have argued."

"Maybe," Billy said. "I don't know."

"She told me to leave her. She stood there for that damn thing to eat so we could have an extra couple of seconds to get away. She told me to get to safe ground with all of you. And I did it." Corban closed his eyes. "I left her behind."

Billy examined his hat. He unfurled it and put it back on. "You couldn't have argued."

"Probably. No one could, really."

"So, what's next, Captain? Because I feel a mighty urge to rain hell on something."

"I think..." Corban stood up. He placed his fists on the desk top. "Let's have another talk with Regent. Or however the hell he is. Adam, I want you to rattle this guy's cage. He seems a little fragile to me. Can you make him lose his cool completely?"

"Probably. If he is Doctor Harlow. He had a reputation for being too short tempered to allow onto the Red Diamond forums. I guess that's why he was using a fake screen name."

"I need him to give us something to work with. Make him give us the upper hand for a change."

Adam closed his notebook. "I can make him angry, make him shout at us, but they might pull the plug on the broadcast if he's giving away any secrets."

Corban looked at the others. They all nodded.

"Are you people crazy?" Chambers was in the doorway with his arms folded. "You can't run off like this again. We need to hunker down. Every time someone runs around out there, someone dies. Enough!"

"What's up your ass?" Billy asked.

"You, motherfucker! You running around like this guy's best friend! You playing at the hero! When did you turn into Captain America's little sidekick? You're getting people killed!"

Corban walked over to stand before Chambers.

"I'm not playing," Chambers said. "Don't fuck with me, Sheriff."

"Did he leave a note?"

"What?"

"Did Blue leave a note?"

Chambers looked at him like he was crazy. "Okay, yeah, some scrawl on the wall behind him. I didn't read it."

"In his own blood."

Chambers frowned. "Well, yeah. How did you know?"

"Because he didn't kill himself. You've got a murderer in your house, Chambers. It wasn't any of us because we were out trying to kill this thing. You've got to—"

"Shit," Chambers said in exasperation. "Who cares? That Blue guy was one of them. It could have been anyone pissed off at being in this mess. I wanted to blow his head off! Fuck it. It doesn't change anything."

"And Grease? Because he didn't kill himself either."

"Scumbag biker druggie. No one cares."

"That old woman in his care was Harriet McCloud, and someone around here slit her throat."

"I don't care!" Chambers shouted.

"We," Corban said with careful enunciation, "are going out again. We are coming back here when done. You're worried we might draw it back here with us, but we don't have to bring it back here. It already knows. It will come for you because you're surviving and because it's hungry. It's that simple."

"We can—"

"No, you can't." Corban shook his head slowly. "No."

Chambers looked around and saw the blood-streaked, hollow-eyed faces arranged against him. "Fine," he said. He stepped back into the hallway. "But you'll go now. I've got work to do here and I don't want to babysit you."

"Titus," Corban said. "How is that stump doing?"

"Oh, hurts like hell. I'm going with you anyway."

"Any of you want to stay here?"

A chorus of negatives came from the others.

Corban pushed by Chambers. He paused at the front door to grab several water bottles and stuff them into his pocket. The others did the same. Then they walked into the morning light and headed off into a Pikeburn seemingly devoid of life.

"Don't come back here," Chamber said as the door closed. "You're just going to get us all killed."

"What's his issue?" Titus asked as they started to snake through the backyards and alleys.

"Hunters and hiders." Adam said. "He's now one of the hiders. You can forget what he was like before he started hiding. I don't think we should go back there."

"Fuck that idiot," Billy said. "Chicken shit coward."

"Pipe down," Janet said. "Or did you forget what's out here with us?"

CHAPTER ELEVEN

Corban led them toward the tennis court. They saw three houses that had been entered by the monster, gaping holes into living rooms and kitchens. On a screened-in porch, a man had hung himself from a support beam with a fluttering note pinned to his chest, but they didn't investigate. In a backyard was a smoker with some curling smoke rising from the vents, and the scent of cooked meat was a maddening distraction as they kept going with grumbling stomachs.

They reached the last building before the tennis court in single file, moving as stealthily as possible. Corban took a quick peek around the corner and immediately threw up his hand to stop the others. He jerked his head back and motioned them away. They moved into a small music shop with a shattered front door and crouched among the guitars.

"It's there," he whispered. "It's right at the black box."

"What the hell is it doing?" Titus asked.

"I didn't spend a lot of time figuring it out, Titus. It was... sitting there."

Billy pointed up. "There are apartments upstairs. We can find a window that overlooks the park."

"Should we just run for it?" Janet asked. "This doesn't feel right."

"I want to see what it's doing," Corban said.

Billy nodded and motioned toward a door in the back of the store. He tried the handle and it was unlocked. He winked at Corban and opened it to reveal a narrow set of stairs. They climbed the stairs and ended in an apartment that smelled of candles, spoiled food, and cat urine. As hoped, two open windows faced the park, lace curtains moving in the breeze.

Billy and Corban gathered at one window. Janet and Adam went to the other. Titus sat down in a faded recliner facing a dusty television set and sighed as he lifted his legs up.

On the tennis court, the black box was a surreal cube of abstract art waiting to be interpreted. The monster was sitting next to it, facing one of the flat sides. On the surface of the black box closest to the monster a circle of swirling light the size of a manhole cover was pulsing.

"Genius, you got an explanation?" Billy asked.

Corban was squeezing his hands into fists. "He's talking to it."

"No," Janet said. "With a colored light?"

"It doesn't have eyes," Billy said.

"Yes, it does," Adam said. "The lack of actual eyes does not mean it can't see. Its entire body might be capable of pulling in light and creating images. Couple that with sonar and even a type of seismic sense and it could be aware of everything in a one-mile radius. There's no way to tell for sure. Best to assume it can see and hear and smell better than any other living animal."

The light on the black box pulsed rapidly, then slowed to a pale green color. The monster turned in a circle like a dog finding a place to nap. It settled again to pay attention to the light.

"This just keeps getting better," Billy muttered.

"That's how it knew to attack the courthouse roof," Corban said. "How to track us to the Moon brothers. That's how it knew everything."

"It knows about the high school," Janet said.

"Guys," Titus whispered. "Help."

Corban looked back to the recliner. Standing over Titus was a frail, wispy-haired woman in a housecoat. She had a double-barrel shotgun and the twin openings were inches away from Titus's face.

"Stop," Corban ordered as soon as the others started to move. "Be calm."

The woman was leaning over Titus slightly. She did not speak. She just kept the barrel very steady.

"What's your cat's name?" Corban asked. "I had a dog named King, but I've never had a cat."

It seemed like ages went by before she spoke. "Cats are better," she said, her voice dry and cracked. "Her name's Tic Tac."

"Like the candy?"

"No. Like the game. No toe. Tic Tac with no toe."

"Funny." He got up from his crouch by the window. "I'm Sheriff Yan Corban. What's your name?"

The woman didn't respond.

Janet started to move and Corban shook his head minutely.

"I'm the Pikeburn Sheriff. Don't worry, I'm not here for a donation. I'm checking on local animals and owners. Some people have been hurting the pets. It's sick and I want to stop it. Have you seen your cat today?"

Her head pivoted toward him. She wore black-rimmed glasses that turned her eyes into enormous moist pools.

"My cat?"

Titus grabbed the barrel that had drifted from his temple and aimed it up. She pulled the trigger and filled the ceiling with buckshot. Titus rolled out of the chair and yanked the shotgun away from her gnarled fingers. She screamed like a bird and waddled down a narrow hall, waving her arms above her head.

"It's coming!" Adam shouted from the window.

"Heard the shot," Billy said. "Fucking great."

The monster was already over the chain-link fence and bounding for the apartment.

"Shoot it," Adam said.

Billy pushed him toward the door. "Won't do any good! Move!"

"I'll get the lady," Janet said and headed down a hallway plastered with photos in ornate frames. Billy and Adam hit the stairs just as the sound of claws scaling the brick exterior reached them. Titus was close on their heels. Corban took aim at the gently moving drapes and waited.

Three explosions rattled the apartment. Gunfire from down the hall. Janet staggered into the living room holding the right side of her face, blood smeared on her fingers. Corban grabbed her arms and moved her down the stairs.

Glass and wood shattered behind them.

"Old bitch has a handgun in her bathroom," Janet said.

"Are you hit?"

"I don't— don't know. First round might have clipped me."

They reached the music store and kept going into the street. The others rushed to help, but Janet waved everyone off her. "Just run! I'm fine!"

Corban put a finger to his lips and they all ran down the sidewalk in single file, followed by the muffled sounds of destruction and a final gunshot and scream. He didn't go far before he spotted a large delivery van in front of a business supply store. The back was open and the interior had leather executive chairs lined up like soldiers ready for inspection. Corban jumped inside. As soon as the others were in, he pulled the sliding door down and softly let it rest. Light came in from a plastic skylight in the roof and a narrow doorway that led into the cab.

Corban swiveled a chair out of formation and pointed at Janet. She sat down. The others found seats, except Titus, who went to gaze out the front window.

Gently, Corban removed her hand. She was facing the light from the front and he had a good view of the damage. He examined the wound for a moment. Splinters of wood stuck out of her cheek. Large pieces had torn away lines of flesh, but the gouges were shallow.

"Okay," he said. "It's just debris from the door. She fired through the door without looking, right?"

"Yes," Janet said. "I knocked to be polite, you know, and she almost took my head off."

"Almost. It didn't miss you by much. I'm going to, um, pull the splinters out."

"Go ahead. Hurts like a bitch already." She looked him right in the eyes. "Is it going to leave a scar?"

"Probably, if you know where to look. You might need stitches on some of these if we had an ER to take you too. You'll have to tough it out. It's going to make a hell of a story, though."

"If I live through this."

"Don't be a pessimist."

"Then kiss me."

And he did, soft and brief. And again, longer this time.

"Get a room," Billy said, "you're making Adam nervous."

"I'm not a virgin," Adam said. "Why do people assume that all the time?"

"Because you look like you're twelve."

Corban started plucking the longer pieces from Janet's face. She didn't flinch.

"There it goes," Titus said from the front.

Billy and Adam crowded forward and blocked the light flowing into the trucks interior.

"I need the light," Corban said.

"Keep your pants on," Billy said. He came back to his chair near Corban. "Damn thing was hauling balls down Cardinal Street."

"Which direction?" Corban asked as he returned to cleaning Janet's face.

"East."

"That's away from the High school."

"Maybe it was chasing us." Janet said.

"It's better than that. If it were tracking us, I bet it would be on the rooftops again. No." Corban finished up his task and touched the other side of her face in a gentle caress. "No, Harlow gave it a new target."

"It might be hungry and running off to eat from its lair," Adam said.

"That cheating piece of shit," Billy muttered. "Because fighting that thing isn't hard enough."

"It is an interesting development," Adam said. "If we could send out specific instructions over a simple video feed, we could have the flexibility to alter the monster's targets in almost real time. There wouldn't need to be a big black box, either. You could piggyback your instructions with a normal TV broadcast signal. Any TV, digital billboard, smart phone, computer screen could be a potential communication device for honing the monster's behavior."

"Shut up," Billy said.

"This truck has a CB," Titus said.

"So what? No one is listening," Billy said.

"We can call the high school."

"Does it have any keys?" Corban asked.

"No."

"Can you hot wire it?"

Titus had to think for a moment. "In theory. Why?"

"I may want to drive it to the high school."

"Okay." Titus stuck his head under the steering wheel.

Corban leaned back in his leather chair. "Adam, they could broadcast those signals from a satellite, couldn't they?"

"Yes."

"And they have ways of monitoring everything that we're doing right now?"

"Yes. They see and hear everything."

"Even right now, hidden in this truck?"

"Yes," Adam said.

"What are you thinking?" Janet asked.

"We keep saying no one is listening." Corban stared up at the foggy skylight. "But that's not true. Someone is always listening."

"Yeah," Billy said. "Doctor Harlow and his staff."

"His staff?" Corban muttered almost to himself. "His staff?" Corban sat up. His eyes flicked about the interior. "What if... he has no staff?"

Janet leaned closer. "What?"

Adam paused with his pencil over his notebook. "He's got a reputation as always working alone. Maybe he's alone in some trailer or in a bunker, surrounded by video and audio feeds, and all we see of that white room is a stage set up."

"No," Corban whispered. His eyes were fixated on a point far away from the dark delivery truck. "He already told us."

No one spoke as Corban stayed focused on the distant spot. He suddenly stood up.

"Grease," he said. "Blue. The smashed-up generators. The way it keeps tracking us. One step ahead! God dammit!"

"What?" Billy asked in frustration.

"You ever been arrested?"

"What? Are you kidding? You've arrested me!"

"So, what does that white room really look like?"

"I don't know!"

"Stop thinking random. Nothing is random here. Everything has a reason. The table is bolted down. The chair is bolted down. There is a long bench that looks like it could have storage beneath the cushions. A man could sleep on that bench. What is that, Billy?"

Billy's mouth hung open. "That's a jail cell."

"Or?"

"A place where he can't leave!" Billy was on his feet. "That motherfucker is INSIDE the black box!"

"But he can leave!" Corban grabbed his arm and Billy seized him back.

"Captain, he can run around town and not be attacked! He has the run of the town!"

"He killed Grease and Blue and God only knows who else!"

"He can see everything and tell his fucking pet monster how to win!"

"And he just sent that thing off on a mission." Corban grinned. "He sent it away."

Billy was grinning back. "He's alone."

"Let's go say hello."

"Guys," Adam said. "Do I have to talk to him? Make him mad? Is that still the plan?"

"No," Corban said. "I have a better idea. Titus? Are you done yet?"

"Almost, Captain."

The delivery truck flattened the chain-link fence and roared across the tennis court. Corban slammed his fist on the horn and held it there as he drove. The front bumper impacted the corner of the black box. The truck's side panel and hood crumpled, and the windshield became a mass of flying glass shards. The truck reeled with the strike, turning hard to the left, flinging the executive chairs all over the back in a cacophony of steel and plastic wreckage. For a moment, the truck balanced on two tires, creaking and groaning, before falling back to four wheels with a jarring crash. Corban slowly uncovered his head.

"Damn," he said. He turned off the laboring engine. He jumped out and stood on the seat to look over the cab at the black box.

The box had rolled like a thrown die and was entangled with the chain-link fence on the opposite side of the tennis court. One of the walls was flashing red and green in weird pulses. Another was crossed with jagged lines of fractured glass or plastic. The closest side to Corban was still all black, but not quite whole. An opening had been revealed, a secret door bent beyond the capacity of the frame it was set it. Now that the black box was on its side, the door hung open to reveal a glimpse of an all-white interior.

Billy was the first to reach the box and he dove straight through the door.

Corban hopped down. He staggered and went to one knee. Janet was there beside him as if she teleported.

"I banged my head. Am I bleeding?"

"Some on your arm. Damn, Corban, you're covered in glass. Stand up for a second."

He got to his feet. She slapped and brushed at his clothes and hair until all the glass was gone.

"Thanks," he said. He put an arm over her shoulder and let her help him to the black box.

Harlow crawled out. He sat on the tennis court asphalt, knees pulled up to his chest. He was moaning, holding his left arm close to his chest. When he saw Corban, he said, "I need a doctor."

"That's funny," Corban said. "Billy!"

"Out in a minute!"

Corban let go of Janet. He pulled his pistol. "Hello, Doctor Harlow. I'm Sheriff Corban. It's nice to get to meet you face to face."

"My arm is broken," whined Harlow. "I need to see a doctor immediately. I don't deal with pain well."

Corban whipped his pistol against Harlow's knee. The doctor howled in pain. He tried to scoot backwards and ran into the chain-link fence. Corban followed. He crouched before Harlow.

"You've made a very big mistake, Harlow."

The pain and fear slipped off Harlow's face. He glared with open hatred. "You will regret this." He leaned his head back and started yelling. "Attics! General Attics! I demand extraction! I know you can hear me!"

Corban stood up. He looked at Adam. "Where have we heard that name?"

"General Dan 'Smoker' Attics. Once the walls come up, he controls everything in and around the Red Diamond event."

Harlow continued to yell. "Attics! I demand to be extracted!" He looked at them with a rabid smile. "They will probably shoot you as soon as the helicopter lands. Your only hope is running away. Now! Run away! Go! Go home!"

Janet shook her head in disgust and amazement. "What the hell?"

"I guess we're stray dogs," Titus said.

"Attics! I know you can hear me! I know you! Send an extraction team and kill this man! Send them for me now, Attics!"

Billy climbed out of the black box. He was smoking a cigar and had an open bottle of wine in his hand.

As soon as Harlow spotted this, he drew in a slow gasp. "Those are mine,"

"Well, too bad for you, loser," Billy said. He took a swig of the wine and handed it off to Titus.

"You are the loser. All of you! Losing all your life. Go on then! Drink it!"

Titus raised the bottle in a mock salute and drank. He handed it to Adam.

"It won't matter!" screamed Harlow. "You're all dead! Go on! Drink it up!"

Adam took a sip, passed it to Janet with a scowl.

"It's too good for you! That's why you'll always live with your uncle, Adam! Did you tell your friends about your conviction? You're a pervert! A stalker!"

Janet took three big gulps. A trickle coursed down her chin from the corner of her mouth. She offered the bottle to Corban. He took it, but held Harlow's eyes.

"Drink it! Drink it! You savages!"

Corban tilted his head as if listening to something. "I don't hear choppers."

"You still have the engagement ring in your desk! You were going to propose and she ran off to fuck another man! Drink up! You're all dead! My beast will eat your hearts!"

"This guy's pretty entertaining and all," Billy spoke around the cigar, "but we might want to find cover."

"Where did you send it?" Corban asked.

"Savage," Harlow hissed.

"Not the high school. Has to be another group of people holed up somewhere."

"All of them are dead," Harlow said. He laughed with an edge of madness. He abruptly stopped and seemed about to weep. "Attics! I demand an extraction! You son of a bitch! I made you!"

"Hey," Corban said. He kicked Harlow's foot. "Hey, look at me." He tossed the bottle away and it shattered.

"Savage!" howled Harlow.

Corban leveled his pistol at Harlow's head. "Will it kill you?"

"No, it won't! It's mine! I built it! It's perfect!"

"So, I'll kill you instead. If that thing you built comes for us, now or later or whenever, I'm going to put a bullet in your head. You'll never see it kill us."

"Attics! I'm too valuable to the war effort! I know things! I haven't given you everything! You don't even understand how the prevariam cortex works! God damn you! Kill them now! I order you to kill them now!"

Corban bent down and slapped Harlow. The result was instant silence. Harlow stared at him.

"How dare you?" he whispered.

"I'll shoot you in the gut and you'll bleed out screaming in the street. Now I need your attention. Attics isn't saving you. No one is. Got it?" Corban emphasized the question with a jab of his pistol.

"You are insane."

"That's rich," Titus said.

"I have to know one thing," Corban said. "Do I kill you now? Because if I can't keep that thing at bay with you as a hostage, I'm going to end you right now. You deserve to die in pain. I can make that happen."

"Savage."

"Tell me now. Can you control it?"

Harlow swung his head wildly. "No! It can't be controlled like a toy!" He grabbed at his hair with his good hand. "Without the Kerheart system, I can't communicate at all."

"The what?"

"He means the lights on the outside of his cage," Adam said. "Doctor Linda Kerheart invented a way to use pulsing lights and colors to communicate simple information to dolphins." Adam's eyes widened. "Does it have a dolphin brain?"

"Idiot," Harlow snapped. "It is something so much better than a mere chimera."

Corban stood up and faced the others. "We can't use this guy as a shield. We need to get somewhere safe. Not the high school."

"It knows about the school," Harlow said. "It knows about a lot of things."

"So, let's put this guy down," Billy said.

"No. He's got a use left, even if I don't know what it is yet. Grab him. We need to move."

"Where?" Janet asked.

Corban pointed down the street. "Library. I'm guessing it doesn't like to read."

The library was a low brick building set back behind a row of bushes. A simple blue and green sign declared it the Pikeburn Public Library. The parking lot was empty. Corban pulled on the front door and it was locked. Before he could do something about it, the lock clicked, and the door was pushed from inside.

"Hey, Sheriff," someone said. "It's Andre Newcomb."

"Can we come in?" Corban asked.

"Sure thing." The door swung wider. Andre was a tall and thin black man wearing slacks and a pink collared shirt that hadn't been clean in a few days. He smiled at the Sheriff, but didn't give the others much more than a glance. "Good to see you. Is it over?"

"Not yet."

Andre nodded. "Okay. Okay. But getting there, right?"

"Right."

"Okay. Good news." He seemed to run out of things to say. He spread his hands. "What do you need?"

"A place to plan. Food and water. But not tap water. Don't drink the tap water."

"We ran out of water a few days ago. Nothing comes out of the faucets. Sorry about the smell. I've got my family here in the special edition room. We, um, can't flush the toilet any more. We don't know what to do." He laughed, but quickly stopped. "I tried to find some books on this subject. None of them discusses three grade schoolers and busted toilets. If we were in the woods...I have plenty of books about surviving out there. You would think the librarian could survive in his own library for more than a week before going nuts!"

"Why didn't you run when the sirens went off, Andre?"

He shrugged. "My car broke down the day it started. It seemed safer to grab what we could from home and hide here. We heard some things in the first days, cars and gunshots and a lot of yelling, and nothing since."

Corban touched Andre's arm. "Andre, we're going to set up in the lounge. You probably want to go away, be with your family. Keep them away from us. I am going to interrogate this man and it could be ugly."

Andre frowned at Harlow. "Howard Harlow?"

"No fucking way," Titus said. "You know each other?"

"Sort of."

Harlow was looking at the floor.

Corban tightened his grip on Andre's arm. "Explain, Andre."

"I— I— I—"

Corban let him go and raised his hands. "Take it slow. This is important."

"He - he came in about ten months ago. He wanted local history books, maps, population studies, local industries. I did my best to get him what he wanted. He said he was with the USGS."

"Well, God damn," Billy said. "Bastard has been scouting us out for a long time."

"That's how it works," Adam said.

"Nothing is random," Corban said. "What else did you look up, Harlow?"

Andre closed his eyes. "He went through a lot of older newspaper articles, too. April of 1984."

"How do you know that?" Titus asked.

"I can see it."

Harlow looked up and glared at Andre. "Because he's the smartest man in this entire town. He has almost perfect memory recall. You disgust me the most out of all the people in their stupid little lives here. You! How can you bear to be here when you have such a gift?"

Andre did not flinch from the verbal attack. "All my life I've wanted to be a small-town librarian. And that's what I am. It doesn't matter what I can remember. When you first came into my library you wore brand new jeans and a checkered shirt. Your left shoelace was looser than the right. You had a spot of food in the corner of your mouth. You faked every smile you gave me. But I didn't care. Remembering you is easy. Forgetting the stuff I don't want to remember is hell. I was four years old when my dad was killed by a truck. I was watching out the window when it happened. I see it again every day. Every single day, like a movie I can't turn away from or mute. So, yeah, being a small-town librarian where the most memorable thing that happens is a kid spilling a soda in the lounge, yeah, that's my perfect job. So, fuck you." He turned to Corban. "What do you want to know?"

"Everything."

"Go find a seat in the lounge. I'll bring it to you."

The lounge was a sunken area down three steps and cordoned off from the rest of the library by a wood railing. Comfy chairs and couches were arranged around coffee tables for easy reading and quiet conversations. The far wall was an expanse of the floor to ceiling glass. Corban and Janet exchanged knowing looks, but led the group into the area anyway.

Billy shoved Harlow down into an overstuffed chair and stood behind him. "You did a lot of research on Pikeburn. You know all the people and all the secrets, huh? What do you know about me?"

"Low life drug pusher with a reputation as a daddy's boy. I'm surprised you didn't run at the first chance."

"That's why you'll lose," Billy said. "You got me wrong. You got us all wrong. And now you're going to pay for this, one way or another. But don't get angry, boss. Not your fault you couldn't figure me out."

"You were there when your father killed Scott Mallow. You helped burn down Bart Hardware. You are a common criminal, a thug, a shadow of the man who really instilled fear in this town, along with Sheriff Bull."

Billy looked at Corban. "Captain, I'm not saying any of that shit he says is true—"

"I understand."

"—but this guy knows a lot more than he should."

"I'm beginning to see that." Corban pulled the coffee table in front of Harlow out of the way. He moved a few chairs around until everyone could sit in a circle.

"What does it mean?" Titus asked.

"That nothing is random," Corban said. He steepled his fingers and looked at Harlow over them. The other man kept his eyes on the floor. "Pikeburn was chosen long before this Red Diamond event."

"Has to be revenge," Janet said.

"Why do you say that?"

"Look at him. He's an angry little man. He's after someone. And whoever it is, is still alive."

"You don't invent a monster to go after one man," Titus said. "It's too much work."

"But if you already have the monster, why not dump it in your target's home town?"

Corban shook his head, wincing at the pain the motion started. "Maybe the target is just the town. All of Pikeburn. He wants to see it ravaged, eaten, destroyed. He wants to see it up close and personal, too, so he makes a pact with this

General Attics to drop him in here with us. Too bad the General isn't honoring his side of things. He must hate you."

"He's jealous," Harlow said to the floor.

"Why not tell us what is going on? Is it one person or the whole town? Are you from Pikeburn?"

"I was born in Seattle."

"Yeah? Brothers? Sisters?"

"That stupid cop trick of getting me talking might work on the yokels, Mr. Yan, but I am unimpressed."

"Suit yourself," Corban said. He looked at Janet. "So maybe little man here got beat up by someone from Pikeburn? He can't be that petty?"

"Pathetic," Harlow muttered.

"It's one person," Janet said. She walked to Harlow and went to one knee to be on his level. "All this to prove one person wrong."

"It was going to happen anyway," Harlow said.

"But you got to pick the town, didn't you?"

Harlow looked her in the eyes. "I got to pick everything, you whore."

"Better a whore than some kind of mass murderer prick."

"You don't get to judge me. I've been tested in ways you can't imagine. They cut off my face, bitch! They killed my wife and son! They killed my mother! I'm dead to everyone! I can't— I can't see a movie or eat something that doesn't come in a styrofoam box! I can't—" Harlow started sobbing but his fury was still forcing words out of him. "They made me a lunatic so they could steal my soul! No matter what I make for them now, I'll never be free! I will die with their chain around my neck!"

"Who are you after?" Corban asked.

"Go on! Kill me! Torture me! Tear out my guts and throw them on the floor!"

"Why Pikeburn!"

"Never! Never tell you!" Harlow lunged at Corban and was easily dragged back by Billy. He thrashed in the chair, kicking and hitting at the air. Billy popped him on the head with his fist and Harlow immediately grew still. "My arm isn't broken, you know," he said. "It hurts when I move it. Isn't that an old joke? 'Doctor, it hurts when I move my arm!' And the doctor says, 'So don't move your arm.' Right?"

Janet stepped away from him. She looked at the others and shook her head. "This guy is crazy. We can't get anything from him."

Andre appeared with a stack of books in his arms. He plopped them down on the coffee table. "These are all the books he looked at that day. Seventeen of them."

"Can we figure out who he is after from that?" Adam asked.

"It doesn't matter," Corban said. "We've got the upper hand now."

"You only think you do," Harlow said. "It can find you without my help."

"It never has before, though, has it? You've been holding its hand all this time. Now we get to fight it fair."

Harlow leaned forward in his overstuffed chair. "You can't beat it."

"I think I'm getting closer than you want me to."

Harlow sneered.

Corban went to the stack of books and looked at the first one. "Local history. Might explain how you know about Sheriff Bull. Billy's Dad is too recent to be in books yet."

"Yet," Billy pointed out. "The man was a grade A piece of human shit, but he sure made an impression on this town."

"I suppose that's true," Corban said. He ran his finger down the spines. "Adam, can you make sense of this?"

Adam looked at Andre. "Are you sure about the timeline?"

"Yes. I was vague at first because people don't like it when I am too specific. It was exactly ten months and five days ago."

"Okay, sorry. Give me an hour, Captain."

"No," Corban said. He was watching Harlow. "Don't bother. Come sit down with us. Andre, you want to join us?"

"No. My family is hiding in the special edition room. I can't leave them for long. Good luck." He paused as he was walking away to look back. "Are you military?"

Corban rolled his eyes. "No."

"It's a nickname," Janet said.

"Oh." Andre walked away with a curious glance back.

"I can get through the books in less than an hour," Adam said. "At least give you an idea of what he was researching."

"No," Corban repeated. "Harlow has a lousy poker face. He wasn't bothered by you going through the books. I was watching him. There's nothing there."

"So, what are we doing?" Billy asked.

"I'm sitting down and talking." He was staring at Harlow, and the scientist was staring back. "We don't need to outsmart the monster. We need to outsmart this guy."

Harlow gave a single cough of laughter. "You? You can't outsmart me!"

"Oh, you misunderstood what I said. I think you do that a lot, if you want my honest opinion. You think you're too smart, that people can't keep up, but in truth, you're just hearing the wrong things."

"Try me," Harlow said. He was smiling now.

"Again, you don't get what I mean. I'll have to explain it to you." Corban nestled into his seat as if ready for a long talk. "I don't have to outsmart you as you sit before me, captured and raging at your own weakness. I only have to outsmart the guy who was here, in this room, ten months and four days ago. That guy was a fool."

The smile on Harlow's face broadened slightly. "You don't know anything. You wouldn't even have a clue if we hadn't stumbled onto that librarian. You got lucky!"

"Luck is a part of police work. So is gut instinct. My gut tells me you left more behind than you wanted. I'm not lucky to find Andre. You're an idiot for finding him. You just walked in here, the town you meant to destroy, and you expect no one to notice? If you didn't have people like General Attics to clean up behind you, I bet you couldn't get anything done."

"Except I've been with the Red Diamond for almost forty years now. Back then, he was Private Attics and it was his job to clean up after me. Still is."

"Odd that he isn't helping you now?" Corban touched his finger to the side of his face. "That must be a shock to find out how little you matter."

"It isn't. I took control of this year from him, snatched it right out from his tired, little hands. Oh, he will suffer when they find out."

Corban leaned forward a touch. "Who are they?"

"The usual people. You wouldn't understand. Don't even try. Is this you outsmarting me?"

"What was your plan if we got you out of your black box? Scream to be saved? Didn't you even have a gun?"

"I didn't need a gun."

"Would have helped, don't you think? Put a round right between Billy's eyes when he jumped through that door. Keep us out until your pet comes back from that errand. Where did you send it?"

"I don't need a gun. You're laughable." Harlow crossed his legs. "I'm glad Attics didn't exterminate you. This is quite fun."

The others had grown silent and where watching the exchange as if the words were a tennis match.

"Laugh it up. The best part of this for me is I don't have to be clever. You can't stop talking. You aren't very smart. That's a bad combination. Sooner or later, you'll give me what I want."

"Even if I did drop some information, you couldn't identify the worth of it, let alone use it. Like a child playing with a calculator."

"I'm looking for something very specific from you." Corban winked at Harlow. "You want to tell me why you had to fake your own death?"

"Oh, that's far beyond your comprehension. Next question."

"You're pretty cocky for guy with one dead monster and one running wild he can't control."

"Do not lump that abomination in the water tower with my creation."

"Oh?" Corban said. "Well, I just thought..."

"It isn't mine! Didn't you see it? Useless effort."

"They made you bring that piece of shit in here, too?"

Harlow had to take a breath to calm himself before speaking. "It was a concession I had to make to a fellow researcher. Politics, you see. Disgusting. It was simple to train my creation to deposit that amateur parasite into the water tower. I did it to prove I could, with ease, adjust my creation to whatever was needed. Yes, it was an embarrassing failure, but it was never mine."

"You think your monster is much better?"

"You can't kill it," Harlow whispered in reverence.

"When the monster tore off its own head, did you – hey, did you get a chance to see that?"

"Yes." Harlow's eye twitched. "I did see it on one of our camera feeds."

"In person, it was something else. It was staggering around like it was drunk, making weird noises. Kind of sickening. But it's not your fault! How can you test something like this in a lab?"

"With multiple copies, of course. And it wasn't staggering drunk. It was unburdening itself of useless material. You wouldn't understand."

"Rebooting. Like a computer."

"Another very poor choice of comparison, but since you must speak in the simplest of terms, yes like - "

"Got it!" Corban shouted, jumping from his seat. "Got you! Reboot it!" He looked at the others. "We reboot it."

"How?" Titus asked.

Corban smiled at the stunned Harlow. "With Kerheart light."

Harlow started shaking his head. "No. That isn't how it works."

"And your protest proves it," Corban said. "It all makes sense." He jumped into his chair and pumped his fist. "It all makes sense!"

Janet took his arms and pulled him down. She was laughing with him. "Okay, brainiac, clue us in."

"Nothing is random! Why did they turn off the electricity?"

"To scare you, isolate you, panic you," Harlow said hurriedly.

"Wrong! To make sure your precious beast couldn't get confused by a blinking traffic light. To make sure only you could talk to it. You wanted to be the only one speaking that thing's language. Light!"

"No," Harlow said. He motioned for Corban to calm down. "Now that's an interesting theory. Sit down and I can explain why it's garbage."

"Holy shit," Billy said. "Captain's right."

Corban was almost dancing. "I've got more, too. Do you remember when I drove that damn truck bomb? It didn't attack me right away. I was shining lights right into its one eye! It hesitated! And when it did attack, it went right for the red light on the roof. It could have killed me, but it wasted time killing that red light."

Titus slapped his hands together. "And maybe it didn't attack the courthouse because the row of lights! It waited for morning, waited for the big lights to get turned off."

"It did attack!" Harlow shouted over them.

"Only when you told it to! Only when you had to cheat and yank that thing's chain. You didn't create a perfect animal! It's confused by flashing lights like a toddler!"

"No!" he howled. "It can think and attack without me! Kill me and it will devour this town! Kill me and this never ends! Your children and your parents and everyone you ever loved! Release me or hell will find you!"

Corban slapped Harlow hard. Blood oozed out from his split lip as he stared open-mouth at the dark fury on Corban's face. Corban slapped him again, sending a fine spray of tiny droplets onto the arm of the overstuffed chair.

"What was that color you used to make it sit still?" Corban asked softly. "Oh yes, pale green. A very nice shade of pale green."

Blood ran in a string down Harlow's lip to his chest. "You'll never get the pattern right."

"I don't have to. I only need to get it to stop for a few seconds exactly where I want it."

"It won't."

"It will. For you. Because that's the other thing you've let me know. This isn't your pet killing machine. This is your pet. It will come to save you. I'm going to make you scream, and it will come running to save you, you rotten son of a bitch."

Harlow had grown purple. He was trying to speak and nothing but garbled sounds were mixing with the spit and blood.

"Titus," Corban said, "I want this man bound and gagged. He's going to try something if we don't."

"Yes, Captain." Titus limped away to find material.

"Adam, find out if the library has their Christmas lights handy. I've seen them on before. Multi-colored chasers. Very pretty. Probably very confusing, too."

"Savages!" screamed Harlow.

"Calm down or I give you another knot," Billy said. "This time I'll use the rifle."

"I will kill you all! I will—I—and—and—and—" He clamped his mouth shut with his own hand to stay the torrent of words that couldn't stay in his brain. He stayed like that until Titus arrived with a roll of duct tape. Janet helped him strap Harlow's hands and feet together. They put one long strip over his mouth.

Adam came back with a large cardboard box labeled LIGHTS. "There's ten strings in here. They can connect end to end. We just need, you know, a place to plug them in."

And a place to make a stand." Corban sat down on a couch and sighed. "We can't do anything with them until night. We need to stay quiet and alert until then. I know we're all really tired. Someone has to stay up and watch him at all times. No nodding off. Our lives depend on it."

"I'll do it," Andre said. He had walked up and was leaning on the wooden rail. "All I do around here is sleep. If you all want to take a nap, I'll sit over this guy."

"I thought you had a family to stay with," Titus said.

He shrugged. "We heard almost every word through the wall. It's paper thin. My wife says I need to help." He looked at Harlow. "I need to help because this man isn't human and we can't let him win. Her words."

"Sounds like a plan," Corban said. "I'm going down right here." He let himself slump over until his head rested on the arm of the couch.

CHAPTER TWELVE

There was an ocean between waking and sleeping, and Corban was sure he was on a boat. No one was in the boat with him. A lazy moon was crossing the starless sky. He was content to sit and listen to the waves lap at the boat.

But someone was talking. It was Titus.

"What if we drive it against the laser wall?"

"It's not a laser," Adam said. "The wall uses a lattice of hexagon energy constructs—"

"Genius," Billy said. "Not now."

"It wouldn't work, anyway" Adam said. "The monster won't go near the wall. That's the highest priority in their training. And if you drove at the wall, they would blow you up long before you got there."

"Well, shit," Janet said. "We can make it hold still but we can't kill it."

Corban tried to speak. His mouth was sealed with cotton and wax. He could barely twitch his lips.

Billy said, "We can get some of the guys from the High school. All of us open fire on it. It has to have a soft spot, right?"

"That mouth has to go to a stomach," Titus said.

"It can't close it, either," Billy said. "It's just a hole with teeth. Okay. We're going to need as many guns as we can get."

"Chambers isn't going to like this plan," Titus said.

Billy snorted. "You leave that asshole to me. I'll get us some shooters. That was my group first."

"You'll need—" Janet started to talk just as a wave struck the boat and filthy water poured onto Corban. He gasped at the amazing cold, like a slap with a leather belt on his skin.

The waters around the boat remained weirdly calm, the rogue wave a nasty surprise visitor that was already gone. He settled back to his seat and watched the moon and shivered. Eventually the voices started back up.

"I should stay," Janet said.

"We need your aim," Billy said. "Half these guys are going to be spraying and praying. You know what I'm talking about. We're going to need to get lucky as it is. You have to come."

"Yeah," she sighed. "Okay."

"Take a look at this," Adam said. "It's called a UPS. Uninterruptible Power Supply. It's a fancy battery to keep power always on your computer. We can use it to power the Christmas lights if we have to move them off the car."

"Good," Billy said. "Take two strings of lights off the car now and put them with this battery thing. We can use it as a secondary decoy if things get hairy."

"Got us a ride," Titus said, out of breath. "Found it two doors down. Keys already in the ignition, if you can believe that."

"Gas?"

"About half full. Plenty for what we're doing." There was a long pause in which the only sound was the small waves against the boat. Titus spoke again, "Are his lips moving?"

A second frigid wave clapped Corban on the back and he was driven to his knees in the standing water in the boat. He climbed back to his seat, shaking so hard his teeth were clicking together. He pulled his feet up from the water. He looked around the ocean and saw nothing new or interesting. It was miles and miles of near freezing water and a moon orbiting the world.

"See you on the other side, Captain," Titus said.

"Rest," Janet said. "You've done enough."

"No shit," Billy said. "Time to let someone else have some fun."

Their voices faded. He was alone. The silence pulled at him from every direction. He tried to speak, tried to yell. He clapped his hands, kicked at the wooden sides of the boat.

Pure silence.

Corban stood up on his seat. The moon flickered in the sky, seemed to turn for a moment into an engorged eyeball watching him. Corban flipped the moon off. He took a single step to his right and plunged into water black and cold and somehow inviting. He swam down, down into deeper waters.

Down.

CHAPTER THIRTEEN

The world was dark. Corban sat up. Something wet fell off his head and landed on his lap. He picked it up. By the faint light from the moon through the library wall of windows, he could see it was a wad of paper towels. He dropped it. It landed on his bare feet and he kicked it away.

Standing up sent the room to spinning, but he did not sit back down.

"Janet?" he said. "Billy? Who's here?"

He made his way toward the front and tripped over a coffee table. As he lay across the coffee table, a light sprang up around him.

"Sheriff," Andre said as he rushed to help. "You need to be on that couch."

"Where is everyone?"

"Away. You hit your head in the crash. And then you passed out and we couldn't wake you. You need to—"

Corban seized Andre by the wrists. "Stop that. I'm not laying down. Where did they go? Tell me, Andre, or I'm walking out of here blind. Tell me."

"The soccer field."

"Do you have a car I can use?"

"My car broke down."

Corban let him go. He ran his hand over a throbbing lump on the back of his head. "I don't even remember getting hit."

"You've been out for most of the day, Sheriff. They tried to wake you a few times. It's best if you take—"

"When did they leave?" He grabbed the flashlight from Andre. "When?"

"Two hours, thirteen minutes ago. They took Harlow."

"They have to get to the high school first." Corban scanned the area with the flashlight. He found his shoes and started putting them on.

"How do you know that?"

"I was awake, sort of. I just was confused on where I was. I couldn't get my body to move." He stood up. He offered the flashlight back, but Andre shook his head.

"Sheriff, I'm asking you to stay."

"Can't do it."

"You're in no condition to run around fighting monsters."

"I couldn't agree more." He stuck out his hand. "Wish me luck."

Andre shook it and said, "Good luck."

Outside, Corban found a cool wall to lean his head against. "Okay," he said to himself. "Okay, Yan. One last push." He filled his left hand with the flashlight and his right hand with his pistol. He pushed away from the wall, put his head down, and started running in the middle of the empty, dark, and silent street.

A nearby gunshot made him look up from the pavement. He stopped running and looked around. He had left the houses and was at the outskirts of the park. The crumpled chain-link of the tennis court was next to him. Ahead was the wide and flat expanse of the soccer fields. Beyond was a small community center, a public swimming pool, and a gazebo big enough to hold an entire choir. Lights were flashing all over the fields and the community center. One set was moving so quickly away it must have been tied to a car.

He heard screaming. He heard someone laughing. Flares of yellow muzzle flashes came from the swimming pool, followed by the delayed sound of gunfire again.

Corban headed into the soccer fields. One of the soccer goals had been wrapped in the pulsing lights: red, green, blue, white. A car was parked nearby and a black extension cord connected the lights and car. The car had a crumpled hood and missing door. When he aimed the flashlight into the car, there was red on the seats.

He walked away, sweeping the light at the ground. There was a discarded shoe. There was a dropped rifle with a bent barrel. Then the light hit a body. Corban hurried to the face down man. He turned him over. The man's chest was caved in. His face was flattened, one eye squeezed shut and the other bulging unnaturally. By the clothing, it wasn't one of his group. Corban let him fall back where he was.

The flashlight picked up another body, but this time the legs were moving, slowly kicking at the ground.

Corban bent over the man. It was Chambers.

He frowned up at Corban. "You? What happened?"

"I just got here. I was about to ask you the same question."

"I— I can't see much. Is it night?"

"Yes. Where are you hurt?"

"I don't know. My neck feels weird."

"Then I am not moving you. Stay down and help will come."

"Aren't you help?"

"God, I hope not. I can barely stand."

Chambers grabbed Corban by the sleeve. "Something went wrong."

"I can see that."

"Take my rifle."

"Okay." Corban did not see his rifle around them. "Stay down and don't make any noise."

He took off in a crouch across the open field. He heard faint whispering and followed the sound to a truck parked in the field. He came around and spotlighted two people hunkered down near the back tire. They hissed at him to kill the light. He came over and crouched beside them.

One was a woman shaking with quiet emotion and tears. The other was Kevin, the teenager in motorcycle gear. He held a rifle now instead of a paintball gun. He had blood on the side of his face.

"Hi, Sheriff," Kevin said. "We were told you were in a coma."

"I'm not. What happened?"

"I was helping one of the guys—"

"Make it short."

"When we started shooting at it, it got real angry and attacked everyone. It's spooky fast."

"Did anyone hit it good?"

"I don't know. Probably not me. I play a lot of video games, but it's so dark out here."

"Are you injured?"

"My knee is sort of fucked up. Sorry. Messed up."

Corban had to smile. "You can call it like it is tonight. New orders. You're the medic. Get this truck going or find another. Get all the wounded back to the High school. Got it?"

"Yes, Captain."

"And don't run anyone over."

"What if—"

"Make it work."

Corban took off again while shaking his head. Looking around, he saw a big stack of flashing lights near the metal-sided community center. As he got closer, he saw a long shotgun in the grass. He went to his knees over it. He scooped it up, checked it, and carried it with him. Someone had driven a pole into the ground and used it as a scaffold for the stack of lights. At the base of the pile of shimmering lights was a severed hand. The bones of the forearm stuck out beyond the flesh several inches, unhealthy white under the flashlight's beam.

Corban went the rest of the way to the community center and put his back to the wall. He had stepped on something in the grass and it was attached to his shoe. He pulled it free and looked at it. Duct tape torn from Harlow and discarded. After a moment of staring at it, Corban flattened it out. He plucked off grass and dirt. He used it to secure the flashlight to the end of his shotgun. Jiggling the shotgun, the light did not fall off. Nodding with satisfaction at his handiwork, Corban went around the community center.

The double front doors were propped open. Corban shone his light inside and illuminated row after row of folding chairs. To the left were doors marked 'men', 'women', and 'storage'. To the right was a small kitchen set up and a counter to lay out food. A raised stage was along the far wall for productions and speeches. As Corban started to turn away, a voice floated from the deep shadows by the stage.

"Close the doors, please."

Corban's light danced around until it settled on Clark Masterson sitting on the floor, back against the wall, a rifle on his knees. He did not appear wounded or upset.

Corban stepped in, keeping the light on Masterson. He kicked the door stops away and the doors slowly closed.

"What the hell happened?" Corban asked as he approached.

Masterson shielded his eyes from the beam. "What has been happening for a long time. You make a plan and it fails. That's how life is working now. I thought you were gravely ill."

"I got a bump on my head. Where is my team?"

"I think they jumped into a car and tried to lure it away from me. Sort of brave of them."

Corban sat down in a folding chair facing Masterson. He clicked off the flashlight. The windows let in the flicker of Christmas lights, turning their faces into different materials every few seconds.

"Away from you?"

"Yes. Don't you understand?" Masterson looked out the window. "It's after me."

"You? Why?"

"I can hear the doubt in your voice."

"Why is it after you?"

"Because I ruined that bastard Harlow a decade ago."

Corban felt his finger tighten on the trigger of the shotgun. He had to let go of the weapon and run his hands over his hair.

Masterson sighed. "I made a lot of money building things for Red Diamond. All in secret, of course. Masterson

Construction working only in little Pikeburn can't make me a millionaire. I made enclosures for the monsters. Habitats. I built safe transportation containers. Did you know they build a new facility every three years? Just to make sure the newshounds have a harder time finding us. It was all I could do to keep up with demand. Those were the days."

"None of this matters." Corban stood up. "I don't give a damn about your theory. I don't give a damn if it's true or not. I have to kill it. If you have some advice, now is a great time to open your mouth."

"Now how could I help you?" Masterson gave a small chuckle. "I hardly saw the monsters. I dealt with steel and glass, plastic, ceramic, even wood. And people, unfortunately. People like Harlow. I knew his voice when we got out here, if not his new face. God, I thought they had killed him ages ago."

"How did he get free?"

"When he saw my face, he started ranting and calling me names. I knew who it was just from that whiny voice. It's not the first time he's called me names. I should have known this was all for me."

"You seem to have gotten your old arrogant self back."

"Well, this is really all about me. How is that arrogant? I ruined him by exposing what I knew about his incredibly revolutionary side experiments and who he was selling the data to. The English, of all people. They don't even have a monster program. What a waste. They grabbed Harlow, killed his family, locked him in a dark cell for a year. He played ball after that, but was killed in an accident, or so they said. I retired still thinking he was dead. And now he's come back from the grave to finish me off. It might very well be the most effort any man has expended to enact revenge. I am... truly amazed."

The flashing lights were blocked from the outside. Corban jumped up and put his back against the wall. Masterson didn't react. He sat with a calm smile on his face.

Peeking out a window, Corban saw the monster just outside the building. It was hunched over the pile of

Christmas lights, swaying like a cobra following a playing flute.

"Don't play the hero," Masterson said. "Let it be. Don't give away our position. I have to survive."

"Go to hell, Clark."

Corban walked for the front door.

"Stop," Masterson hissed at him. "This isn't about you. Stop. I'm the important one in this town!"

Corban went out the front, turned the corner at a brisk pace, and walked straight up to the mesmerized monster. He jammed the shotgun into the open maw, noticing the bits of flesh and clothing on the needle teeth. The black tongue squirted out and wrapped about his wrist. It pulled and his hand started to disappear into the maw. But the end of the shotgun barrel struck something unyielding, something deep within the monster's gullet, and that's when Corban pulled the trigger.

His arm was flung away from the maw, the shotgun a ruined projectile that arced into the night. He grabbed his throbbing hand and bent over it. The paw grazed him as the monster spasmed and he ended up on his back, staring at the stars. He turned his head to watch.

The monster was thrashing, drumming the ground with its limbs. It collapsed and wriggled about like a worm on hot pavement. As Corban struggled to sit up, something snapped deep within the monster, an audible breaking sound. Another popping sound proceeded a flying object hissing by Corban's face. He looked over his shoulder, then back to the shuddering monster. Several more popping sounds happened in rapid fire, and a steel plate sagged to the ground, held on now only by stretching muscle tissue.

"Got you," Corban said.

The limbs stopped striking the ground. They seemed to shrink, almost pulled deeper into the monster. A split appeared along the backbone, accompanied by breaking and tearing. A last shiver went through the monster and the steel plates sagged. It lay still.

Corban got slowly to his feet.

The split widened and a burst of pressurized blood flew into the air. Corban shielded his face as he staggered backwards.

Something rose from the split. Something stretched out arms and threw back its head and howled at the sky in absolute defiance.

"You fucking maniac," Corban said.

A man was tearing his way free of the monster's corpse, disengaging ropy nerve bundles and cords of sinew, tearing at the bulky body it was birthing from. It rolled off the carcass and came up gracefully on its two feet and howled at the sky again, this time in triumph.

"Stop," Corban shouted.

The thing turned his head with insectile speed and held there. It had silver eyes with tiny black pupils. It took a step closer, tentative, curious. What had appeared to be blood-slick skin was in fact no skin at all. The muscles and tendons could be seen sliding over each other as it moved. The mere tracings of lips on its mouth moved back and revealed no teeth, but the black ribbon of a tongue lapped at the air. It took another step forward.

Corban drew his pistol and shot it in the chest.

It staggered back, twisting and flailing.

"Fucking die!" Corban shouted, firing wildly as he advanced.

The monster was hit five times rapidly before it leaped high into the air. It landed on the roof of the center. It turned to look down at him. For a moment it appeared unharmed, a demigod on high. It coughed and blood dribbled from its toothless mouth. Corban raised his pistol again, but the monster slipped away.

Corban ran to the other side of the building, keeping his pistol trained on the edge of the roof. He saw nothing. He was scanning the area when he heard the screaming from within. He ran for the front doors. As he laid a hand on the handle, the door was kicked from the other side. It tore off the hinges and knocked Corban flat. The monster ran by him, moving too fast for him to get a shot off.

Pushing hard, he scooted out from under the door. By the time he was free, there was no sign of the monster anywhere. He struck the ground and cursed at the sky.

Jumping up, he rushed into the community center.

Clark Masterson had been eviscerated. He lay on the stage like a sacrifice to evil gods. His belly was hollowed. The organs and intestines were flung against the walls.

"Clark," Corban said as he went to his knees. "Clark! Wake up!"

His eyes flickered. "Damn. I— I—"

"Transports, Clark. You built the transports. What is it? What does it look like?"

"It came through the roof. It's a man, Corban. It's— it's horrible. It tore my stomach open."

"Clark! Where would it run to? I hurt it finally. Would it run for its cage? Would it go back home?"

Bright lights filled the community center as a car pulled up to the front door. Someone shouted, "It's the Captain!"

Corban slapped Clark across the face. "Bastard, pay attention! It's on the run! Where will it go?"

"...truck... I don't know... RV..."

"An RV? An old RV?"

Clark licked his lips. "That was... my... idea... years ago. No one sees the... RV on... the side of the... road. Oh God... can you... finish me?"

"No."

Corban stood and turned. His team was all there. A little more harried and a little bloodier, but all of them stood ready.

"I know where the lair is," Corban said.

"We lost Harlow," Adam said. His eyes were wet and his voice was shaky. "My fault."

"Screw that. I know where Harlow is going, too. Get in the car. We're going to end this now. Right now."

"But—" Titus said. He looked at sticky entrails ripped from Clark Masterson. "Yeah. End this. I'm out of bullets."

"So? You're driving!"

"Where?"

"The damn RV at the old hunting lodge site. It's not an RV. It's the lair. It's a cage disguised as an old RV. We walked right up to it and didn't realize."

Billy pointed toward Masterson, who was holding out one hand toward Corban.

"Let him die alone," Corban said. "He's part of Red Diamond."

Corban rode shotgun as Titus drove. Stories were exchanged in quick order. Corban told about his waking, encountering Chambers and the teenager, Masterson's revelation, and the new human form of the monster. Billy explained how the monster had exploded with rage as the first bullets hit, how people panicked, fired wildly, ran so scared they dropped their guns. The team had tried to lure it away with a strand of lights on the back of a car, but it hadn't followed far before going back to the soccer fields.

"It came back to stare at the bigger lights," Corban said. "But I don't think that will work again. This form seems... different. It didn't attack me right away. It didn't know what to do with me. And it didn't glance at the lights."

"Could it be human?" Titus asked.

"I'm killing it anyway," Billy said. "And that fucker Harlow."

"You don't get them both," Janet said.

Titus turned onto the dirt road toward the old RV and had to slow down to navigate the potholes.

"It is not human," Adam said. "Never was or will be. Just kill it."

"I thought you were always the fan of these things," Billy said.

"I still am. It's a marvel. And it needs to die."

"There's the RV," Titus said as the headlights separated the trees from the long box of the RV. The blue glow of the hexagon wall was visible beyond, a line of mystical power and death.

The rearview mirror disintegrated and left a fist-sized hole in the windshield, glass and plastic splinters spinning about the interior.

"Sniper!" Titus roared. "Sniper!" He flicked off the lights and steered the car off the dirt road.

"Stop!" Corban said.

"We're bugging out to base and waiting for reinforcements, Captain!"

"Stop the God damn car and that's an order!"

Titus immediately hit the brakes and the car bumped to a stop.

The windshield exploded as a second bullet hit them. Titus jerked to the left and slumped over.

"Out! Out! Out!" Corban yelled. He took Titus by the collar and pulled him down. He kicked open the door and dragged Titus from the car. Another bullet punched through the door near his head. He finished pulling Titus out. He rolled them both into the knee-high grass.

A bullet hit the front of the car and steam started boiling out.

"I have a gun now!" screamed Harlow from the RV. "What do you think about that!"

Corban fired twice in the general direction Harlow was firing from. He tugged Titus a few feet away. Adam ran up and half landed on Titus.

"Is he dead?"

"I don't know, Adam! I'm busy!"

A bullet hissed through the grass off to the right, followed by the crack of the rifle from the RV.

Adam pulled a small flashlight to examine Titus. There was blood covering the side of his face. Adam turned aside and took three deep breaths to get steady, but he came back right away, sweaty and determined.

"Where are you guys?" Billy asked from the darkness.

"Stay put," Corban said.

"I've got Janet with me. Do you the other two?"

"Yes."

A bullet sailed overhead.

"How is Titus?" Janet asked.

Adam turned off the light. "Head wound. It grazed him and took off the top of his ear. A lot of blood. I can wrap it up."

"Stay with him here," Corban said. "I don't have time to argue, Adam! The monster is still coming or already here."

"Okay, Captain," Adam said. He turned on the light again. He pulled a T-shirt from his messenger bag and started tearing it into a bandage.

"Billy, Janet, we're going to charge this guy," Corban shouted. "I don't think he's a good shot but stay low and move fast. I'm going straight up the middle."

"I'll go right," Billy called.

"Then I'm left" Janet said. "Don't shoot me, guys."

"Go," Corban said.

He began to crawl through the grass. Billy ran across his path at a sprint, not even trying to get low. "Beat you there," Billy said and laughed.

Corban muttered, "Asshole."

Harlow kept up a steady firing of one wild shot every ten seconds or so. As Corban reached the edge of the grass and was looking into the barren ground and overhanging trees of the hunting lodge, Billy let off a burst of shots that smacked the RV. Janet followed that with a shot of her own that blew out a window. Harlow fired at Janet, missed, and she laughed at him from the darkness. While there had been no flash to give away his location, Corban had seen movement near the side door of the RV.

Corban took off, crossing the open ground and diving behind the RV where he was hidden from Harlow. That's when the stench reached him, the clingy scent of decaying meat. The larder was here. By the glow of the hexagon wall he could see a wide hole had been dug up and filled again with churned up dirt. He could see limbs outlined in the shallow grave. This was the human storeroom of the thing that hunted Pikeburn. Here were his friends and neighbors, reduced to rotting snacks for a thing of terrifying appetites.

Harlow fired again from the opposite side of the RV. Corban ran around the corner and plowed into Harlow, tackling the scientist to the ground and knocking the sniper rifle away.

"Wait!" cried Harlow as he fumbled to get the sniper rifle back.

Corban slammed his pistol across Harlow's wrist and the rifle fell from his stunned fingers.

"Wait, please!"

Corban yanked him up and slammed him against the RV. He jammed his pistol under Harlow's jaw. He pulled the trigger.

Nothing happened.

The men stared at each other.

"Please wait," Harlow said.

Billy and Janet came running up. "Something is out there in the grass," Billy said. "Moving fast right for us."

"Shoot it," Corban said.

"We need more light for that," Janet said. "Find us more light."

"More light," Corban said to Harlow.

"No. Why can't you just give up? Please give up. Please walk away and I won't let it kill you."

Corban holstered his pistol. He wrenched open the outer door of the RV, something that looked a lot like a glass door on any back porch in the world. He forced Harlow's hand across the jam.

"More light."

"I—"

Corban slammed the door with a kick. Harlow screamed and fell to the dirt, all four of his fingers disjointed and broken. The blow had also shattered the glass in the door and long shards cascaded to the ground. Corban picked one up.

"Light," he said. "I'm not fooled by this broke-down RV. It has lights and you'll turn them on or I'll skin you alive."

"A switch! Inside! A switch under a panel to— to the left!"

Corban reached in the door and found a metal toggle. Once turned, lights hidden in the luggage racks on top of the RV blazed to life, lighting up a circle of ground all around them for a hundred feet.

"There!" Billy cried out. He aimed at a tall figure at the edge of the grass that had been watching them without moving. As the M-16 chattered, the monster leaped into the canopy. The branches shook and leaves floated down as it moved from tree to tree. Janet and Billy called out to each other, firing at any shadow or movement, trying to pin down the rapidly moving monster.

Corban lifted the sniper rifle. It was long and heavy, a clumsy weapon, but he fired anyway. He got off five shots before it was empty.

"More bullets," he said to Harlow.

Harlow was gone. There were marks in the dirt where he had crawled under the RV.

The monster dove from the foliage, coiling like a cat in midair, and landed next to Janet. It struck her rifle and the weapon hurtled through the air and smashed against the RV. Janet managed to duck the next blow and scamper away.

Billy put two rounds into it before his clip was dry, two holes in the chest that began bleeding profusely. It sprang at him, driving him backward with a shove that looked like it could have moved a car. Billy tumble like a ragdoll to the edge of the light, his muttered cursing the only sign he was still conscious.

The monster turned its silver eyes on Corban.

A gunshot boomed from the dark and the monster staggered. It went to all fours and coughed black blood and bits of flesh onto the ground. A fist-sized hole had appeared on its back.

Adam emerged from the night with his double barrel shotgun, and Titus was hanging onto the younger man with both arms like he was getting a piggyback ride, looking over his shoulder and grinning.

"Hit him again," Titus said and Adam complied.

The monster twisted wildly and the second slug missed, blasting dirt into the air just beyond it. The monster went into the canopy again with a powerful leap.

Janet crawled to her rifle and started checking it. She looked at Corban. "Harlow! Where is he?"

"On the run."

"Get him!" She winked. "We've got this."

Billy sat up. He flicked open a long-bladed pocket knife. "Can I get a hand standing up?"

Corban had the long chunk of glass again in his hand. He ran around the RV to where Harlow had emerged from under it. The larder had been disturbed here, a dead face staring blindly up from the dirt where it had been covered. Corban skirted the mass grave and entered the tall grass. He went to one knee and searched the night.

His eyes locked on a movement against the blue glow of the wall about one hundred feet away. A figure silhouetted in the night. Corban went after it.

Harlow heard him coming. He turned to the glowing wall that was less than ten feet away with arms up. "Save me! Attics! Save me! Have mercy! I've done nothing wrong!"

Corban tackled him. The scientist fought back with an elbow to Corban eye, and Corban only got angrier.

Harlow beat at Corban with his one hand. "Savage! How dare you! Get off me! Attics! Save me!"

Corban forced Harlow's arms down and pinned them with his knees. He was sitting on Harlow's chest and nothing could dislodge him. He leaned down with the glass dagger in his fist.

"You piece of shit, I am—"

Something heavy landed in front of Corban. A pair of skinned feet were next to Harlow's head. Corban looked up, too stunned to make a quick move. The monster, lit by the unearthly blue hexagon wall, loomed over him. Its silver eyes reflected the wall, appearing dazzling and terrifying. Blood leaked from a dozen bullet holes and its slightly open mouth. It was breathing in jagged little gasps.

It reached for him.

Corban rolled himself over and managed to keep Harlow with him, putting the scientist up as a shield. Harlow fought to get free, succeeding in spinning around to face the monster.

"No!" Harlow shouted. "Not me! Don't hurt me! I made you!"

The monster took Harlow by the arms and lifted him easily up. Corban wrapped his left arm across Harlow's throat and was hoisted up as well. The three of them stood so close they were all breathing the same air.

"Don't hurt me," Harlow said.

The monster raised a hand that had steel talons on the end. It hesitated, though, staring at Harlow. It tilted its head.

"Don't hurt me. Kill him! Kill him! Kill them all!"

Corban tightened his left arm and Harlow started choking.

Again, the monster raised a hand to strike, only to pause. Corban ducked his head behind Harlow as best he could without losing sight of the monster's next action. It held still, arm up in the air, staring at Harlow.

From the RV, the others were calling Corban's name. The silver eyes flickered to the sound, then back to Harlow. It lifted the clawed hand once more. Corban jabbed the glass shard into Harlow's thigh and shoved the scientist to the left. A scream burst out of Harlow as he went down. The monster followed the motion and sound for a second. A single second it stood staring at Harlow on the ground and was not paying attention to anything else.

Corban planted the glass shard through its eye, ramming it with his palm, fueling the blow with all his might and rage. The shard cut his hand to the bone and he cried out in pain as the flesh was peeled away. He staggered back, clutching the bloody appendage to his chest, feeling the warm cascade of blood soaking his shirt.

The monster did not move. It tilted its head at him. Blood was dribbling down its flayed face now. At least five inches of sharp glass was buried in its head.

Corban drew his pistol with his left hand. He took a step to the monster that towered over him. With a great backhand blow, he slammed the pistol butt against the protruding glass. It shattered along the length, breaking into a million cutting blades deep within the skull.

The monster went to its knees. It reached up both hands and began grabbing at the ruined eye. It tore at the flesh trying to dislodge the offending spike. Corban went around behind the monster and kicked it. It flopped gracelessly to the ground. It tried to rise and Corban jumped with both feet on its back, driving it down again. He knelt on its back. With a quick toss, he reversed the pistol so he held it by the barrel like a hammer. He rained blow after blow on the base of the skull, on the curve of the top of its spine, laughing as he felt the muscle and bone giving way under his assault.

Harlow was sobbing, utterly broken in the dirt, sobbing and shaking as if the world had ended.

At some point Corban realized he had stopped swinging. He was just sitting on a monster, staring at the night.

The blue lights were all gone.

The wall was down.

He got to his feet unsteadily. It took him three tries to holster his pistol. By the faint light of the moon and stars, Corban looked at the caved in skull of the monster. He sighed.

"Savage," Harlow whispered into the dirt his face was pushed into.

Corban kicked Harlow in the head as hard as he could as he went by. He staggered for the lights of the RV and the sounds of his name being called. When he entered the light, they rushed to him, helped him sit down.

"I'm tired," Corban said.

"Where is it?"

"Out there. Dead."

"It's over," Adam said. He had the rest of his shredded T-shirt and was binding Corban's damaged hand. "The walls are down. We won."

"We won," Billy said softly. He took off his hat and threw it into the night where the soldiers still kept watch. "Hear that, you fuckers! We won! You sorry ass losers! You pieces of shit!"

"Okay, okay," Janet said as she was laughing with him. "They probably aren't too happy. How about we don't get shot to death."

Billy sat down, grimacing as his left arm swung loose at his side. "My arm might be broken."

"It is," Titus confirmed from the dirt next to him. He held a bloody rag to his injured head.

"And I lost my dad's M-16."

"Loser," Adam said, earning a punch in the arm and a few laughs.

From the direction of the line of soldiers, an engine was approaching. A heavy military transport rumbled up. It parked just outside their circle of light and shut down. The driver door swung open and a booming voice said, "Congratulations, people. May I approach?"

"Who the fuck are you?" Billy challenged. "This is a private party."

"I'm General Attics. I've got a real medic with me, if you need aid."

"My town needs that help more than me," Corban said.

The general came into the light. He was a broad-shouldered black man in a green uniform covered in colored ribbons and brass little stars. "We have over five hundred well trained men and woman going into your town right now. As fast as we can, we want everything put right."

"Put right?"

"Calm down, son. You can't make me feel bad for what happened here. Better men than you have tried. I'm a bone-deep patriot. This is needed for the war effort."

"Get lost," Corban said. "I don't want your help."

"Don't be ungrateful like that. No one expected you to survive. That thing Harlow built should have chewed this town for months. Hell, I've got a trailer full of my personal supplies down the road that I've barely tapped. My wife is going to be in for a surprise when I come home early." He belly-laughed at his joke.

"You don't have a wife," Adam said. "She died of cancer three years ago, General Attics."

The General shrugged. "I did forget you were still here, Adam. You fans sometimes know a little too much for my liking. But I'm not mad at you, son. You're not the first fan to make his way into the event. You're just the first to survive. I tip my hat to you."

"This is bullshit," Billy said. "Come on. Let's walk back to town."

"I really would like to talk to you folks. Won't take long. You know, we aren't really testing monsters here. We've been testing you. My God, Sheriff, it's been a great show! The enemies of our country are going to have nightmares after seeing how well your group fought."

Corban got to his feet with Janet's help. "What happens to Harlow?"

"Nothing. He goes back into his lab and won't see daylight again for a few years. He's too much of an asset to this country to let him go."

"He should be executed," Titus said.

"Don't be so dramatic. The man was doing his job."

"Did you know he was after Masterson?" Janet asked. "All this for petty revenge?"

"Masterson did get his family killed, so I think he had it coming. Of course I knew! Hell, revenge is a great motivator if you can harness it right."

"And what if we had killed him?" Corban asked. "Would you have saved him? Killed us for killing your pet madman?"

The general shrugged his big shoulders. "It was his idea to come in here. I've got no control once the walls are up."

"You cheated this year," Adam said. "I count five major Red Diamond rules broken. Want me to tell you what they are?"

"Five? Gosh, that's a lot." He laughed again. "Son, I cheat every year. You fans and your rulebooks. I've never read those rules. Rules don't mean shit to me."

"So, you do all this for fun," Janet said.

"We have to test the population, young lady. I am very proud of Pikeburn. There was the usual crumbling of civil behavior, naturally, but you people really pulled together like I've never seen before. I am very proud."

"I need away from this maniac," Corban said. They all started walking away. Titus was being helped by Adam. Janet was holding up Corban. Billy was limping and had his left arm tucked into his belt so it wouldn't swing about.

"I'll be in touch," General Attics said. "You can't sell your story until you run it by me. That's the law. After that, you get to be famous! This is your ticket to anywhere you want to go! Survivors always make money!"

No one looked back. After a while as they trudged along the dirt road, they saw the lights spring to life in Pikeburn ahead.

"Oh, that's a thing of beauty," Titus said.

"Sure is," Corban said.

"What do we do now?" Janet asked.

"You know the town is going to try to tear itself apart. Remember that meeting in the courthouse? Us versus the hiders? Even though we won, they aren't going to hand us any medals. Those who stayed are going to hate those who got out before the walls went up. Even if I wanted to, I can't hire the deputies back. Everyone will hate them. They may as well stay gone. They have no place in Pikeburn now. I'm going to need some new deputies. How about it, guys?"

"Count me out," Billy said. "I'm going to Kansas City."

"What?" Corban said.

"Oh, yeah. Been thinking about it for years. They have a good culinary school. I'm going to learn to cook. I'm getting out of this town. Small towns suck. I'm leaving it all behind. And KC is way too big for next year's Red Diamond."

"They wouldn't do it to the same town twice," Titus said. "We're safe."

"Maybe," Billy said with obvious doubt.

Titus shook his head. "Anyway, Captain, I'll be your deputy. My shop doesn't make any money anyway. I got a nice settlement from getting the leg blown off, but it's boring. I could use less boring."

"Me, too," Janet said. "I hate my job. I'm too good for phone surveys and customer service. How do you go back to the phones anyway after something like this?"

"Adam?" Corban asked.

"I— I'm sorry, Captain. I have something important to do." He stopped walking and looked around the night. "I suppose it's all safe now. They don't care what we do after the walls are down. No one is listening for real. Take a look." He opened his messenger bag. Amid the notebooks and clothes and assorted traveler's debris, there was a steel box about the size of a laptop.

"And what is that, genius?" Billy asked. "Is that a—"

"It's a fifth generation, multi-spectral, recording device and transmitter. I've been recording everything. Video and audio and a few other things. I can tell you the monster's core body temperature each time we were within fifty feet from it. And now that the walls have come down, so have the jamming signals. The instant that stopped, I broadcast all the data to six different secret locations. I can throw this bag in a river and get my data from online."

"Holy shit," Janet said. "Are you a reporter?"

"No. I'm going to bring down the Red Diamond. No one ever sees what this is really like, so no one ever stops it. They edit it all to look like some kind of adventure or a patriotic duty. It's awful. It's stupid and terrible and serves no purpose at all. Now," he smiled as a set of tears coursed down his cheeks, "now they will see. Everyone will see how Goddamned horrible it is. Now it will stop for good. Forever."

"They will kill you," Corban said.

"They will have to catch me first."

"They don't stop, Adam."

Adam's smile widened. "I wasn't supposed to be here, or survive the first day, or help kill two monsters. I think I can handle myself. And if I die, I'm okay with that. I'm bringing them down, Captain. They don't know it yet, but this was the last Red Diamond event. That's worth my life."

No one could speak. The idea settled into them and they had no words left. They started walking again toward the glittering lights of Pikeburn.

ABOUT THE AUTHOR

Michales Joy is based in Joplin, Missouri, where he writes fantasy and horror and lives with his wife and two teenagers. Since his first publication in 1995, he has written novels, short stories, screenplays, comics, and background settings for games.

He loves to talk and teach anything to do with writing, so feel free to contact him online. *Red Diamond* is his first full length horror novel, but certainly not his last.

WELCOME TO THE BLACK
MOUNTAIN CAMP FOR BOYS!

Summer,1989. It is a time for splashing in the lake and exploring the wilderness, for nine teenagers to bond together and create friendships that could last the rest of their lives.

But among this group there is a young man with a secret-a secret that, in this time and place, is unthinkable to his peers. When the others discover the truth, it will change each of them forever. They will all have blood on their hands.

ODD MAN OUT is a heart-wrenching tale of bullies and bigotry, a story that explores what happens when good people don't stand up for what's right. It is a tale of how far we have come . . . and how far we still have left to go.

Available in paperback or Kindle on Amazon.com

http://bit.ly/OddMANPB

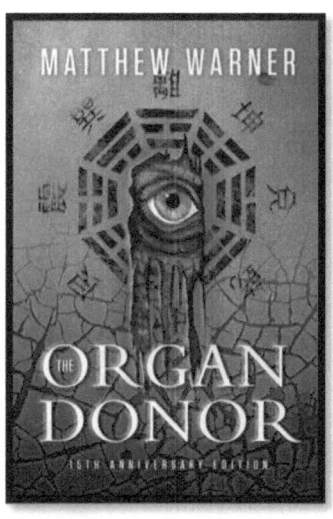

They knew it was wrong to purchase a kidney off the Chinese black market. But what the Taylor brothers didn't realize was that its unwilling donor was an executed prisoner—and an immortal being from Chinese mythology. Pursuing them to Washington, DC, this ancient king will stop at nothing to recover what was once his.

This special 15th anniversary edition of Matthew Warner's acclaimed first horror novel includes nearly 7,000 words of new material, including the author's riveting account of his true-life encounter with China's illegal organ trade.

"A classic of modern horror literature."
— E.C. "Feo Amante" McMullen, Jr.

THE ORGAN DONOR

Available in paperback or Kindle on Amazon.com

http://amzn.to/organ

Psychiatrist Dr. Desmond Carter had always believed that his former patient, author Simon Ryan, was dead.

But, when a bloodstained manuscript penned by Ryan arrives at his office, Desmond begins to doubt everything he thought he had known—not just about the troubled author's past, but his own sanity. Desmond seeks the truth. Instead, he discovers the wellspring of madness.

In Pandemonium, the sequel to his acclaimed 2011 novella The Noctuary, Greg Chapman drags you deeper into the nightmarish reality of the Dark Muses—creatures forged from the very darkness in our own souls.

The words contained within will drive you mad... *and damn you to Hell.*

THE NOCTUARY: PANDEMONIUM

Available in paperback or Kindle on Amazon.com

http://bit.ly/Pandemonium

BLOODSHOT BOOKS

READ UNTIL YOU BLEED

www.ingramcontent.com/pod-product-compliance
Lightning Source LLC
Chambersburg PA
CBHW030649260626
47157CB00007B/2562